MAGIC'S PROMISE

BOOK TWO OF
THE LAST HERALD-MAGE

MERCEDES LACKEY

A ROC BOOK

ROC

Published by the Penguin Group
Penguin Books Ltd, 27 Wrights Lane, London W8 5TZ, England
Penguin Books USA Inc., 375 Hudson Street, New York, New York 10014, USA
Penguin Books Australia Ltd, Ringwood, Victoria, Australia
Penguin Books Canada Ltd, 10 Alcorn Avenue, Toronto, Ontario, Canada M4V 3B2
Penguin Books (NZ) Ltd, 182–190 Wairau Road, Auckland 10, New Zealand

Penguin Books Ltd, Registered Offices: Harmondsworth, Middlesex, England

First published in the USA by Daw Books, Inc., New York, 1990
First published in Great Britain by Roc, 1992
10 9 8 7 6 5 4 3 2 1

RoC Roc is a trademark of Penguin Books Ltd

Printed in England by Clays Ltd, St Ives plc

Dedicated to:
Elizabeth (Betsy) Wollheim
Who said—"Go for it"

One

The blue leather saddlebags and a canvas pack, all bulging with filthy clothing and miscellaneous gear, landed in the corner of Vanyel's room with three dull *thuds*. The lute, still in its padded leather case, slithered over the back of one of the two overstuffed chairs and landed with a softer *pumph*, to rest in the cradle of the worn red seat cushion. Once safely there it sagged, leaning over sideways like a fat, drunken child. The dark leather lute case glowed dully in the mid-morning sun still coming in the single eastward-facing window. Two years of mistreatment had not marred the finish *too* much, although the case was scuffed here and there, and had been torn and remended with tiny, careful stitches along the belly.

Vanyel grimaced at the all-too-visible tear. *Torn? No; no tear would be that even. Say* cut, *or* slashed *and it would be nearer the truth. Pray nobody else notices that.*

Better the lute case than me . . . that came closer than I really want to think about. I hope Savil never gets a good look at it. She'd know what that meant, *and she'd have a cat.*

Herald-Mage Vanyel took the other chair gracelessly, dropping all his weight at once into the embrace of comfortable upholstered arms.

Home at last. Havens, I sound like the pack hitting the corner.

"O-o-oh." Vanyel leaned back, feeling every muscle in his body crying out with long-ignored aches and strains. His thoughts fumbled their way into his conscious mind through a fog of utter exhaustion. He wanted,

7

more than anything, to close his gritty eyes. But he didn't dare, because the moment he did, he'd fall asleep.

Someday I'm going to remember I'm not sixteen anymore, and keep in mind that I can't stay up till all hours, then rise with the dawn, and not pay for it.

A few moments ago his Companion Yfandes *had* fallen asleep, standing up in the stable, while he was grooming her. They'd started out on this last leg of their journey long *before* dawn this morning, and had pushed their limits, eating up the last dregs of their strength just to get to the sanctuary of "home" the sooner.

Gods. If only I would never *have to see the Karsite Border again.*

No chance of that. Lord and Lady, if you love me, just give me enough time to get my wind back. That's all I ask. Time enough to feel like a human again, and not a killing machine.

The room smelled strongly of soap and the beeswax used to polish the furniture and wall paneling. He stretched, listening to his joints crack, then blinked at his surroundings.

Peculiar. Why doesn't this feel *like home?* He pondered for a moment, for it seemed to him that his modest, goldenoak-paneled quarters had the anonymous, overly-neat look of a room without a current occupant. *I suppose that's only logical,* he thought reluctantly. *They haven't been occupied, much. I've been living out of my packs for the last year, and before that I was only here for a couple of weeks at a time at most. Gods.*

It was a comfortable, warm—and quite average—room. Like any one of a dozen he'd tenanted lately, when he'd had the luxury of a guest room in some keep or other. Sparsely furnished with two chairs, a table, a desk and stool, and a wardrobe, a curtained, canopied bed in the corner. That bed was enormous—his one real indulgence: he tended to toss restlessly when—and if—he slept.

He smiled wryly, thinking how more than one person had assumed he'd wanted that particular bed for another reason entirely. *They'd never believe it if I told them Savil gets more erotic exercise than I do. Oh, well. Maybe it's a good thing I don't have a lover; he'd wake up black and blue. Always assuming I didn't strangle him by accident during a nightmare.*

But other than that bed, the room was rather plain. Only one window, and that one without much of a view. It certainly wasn't the suite he could have commanded—

But what good is a suite when I hardly see Haven, much less my own room?

He put his feet up on the low, scarred table between the chairs, in defiance of etiquette. He could have requisitioned a footstool—

But somehow I never think of it until I'm five leagues down the road headed out. There's never enough time for—for anything. Not since Elspeth died, anyway. And gods—please let me be wrong about Randale.

His eyes blurred; he shook his head to clear them. Only then did he see the pile of letters lying beside his feet, and groaned at the all-too-familiar seal on the uppermost one. The seal of Withen, Lord of Forst Reach and Vanyel's father.

Twenty-eight years old, and he still makes me feel fifteen, and in disgrace. Why me? he asked the gods, who did not choose to answer. He sighed again, and eyed the letter sourly. It was dauntingly thick.

Hellfire. It—and every other problem—can damned well wait until after I've had a bath. A bath, and something to eat that doesn't have mold on it, and something to drink besides boiled mud. Now, did I leave anything behind the last *time I was here that was fit to wear?*

He struggled to his feet and rummaged in the wardrobe beside his bed, finally emerging with a shirt and breeches of an old and faded blue that had once been deep sapphire. *Thank the gods.* Not *Whites. and I* won't *be wearing Whites when I get home. It's going to be so nice to wear something that doesn't stain when you look at it.* (Unfair, nagged his conscience—properly treated, the uniform of Heraldic Whites was so resistant to dirt and stains that the non-Heralds suspected magic. He ignored the insistent little mental voice.) *Although I don't know what I'm going to do for uniforms. Dear Father would hardly have known his son, covered in mud, stubbled, ashes in his hair.*

He emptied the canvas pack on the floor and rang for a page to come and take the mishandled uniforms away to be properly dealt with. They were in exceedingly sad shape; stained with grass and mud, and blood—some of it his own—some were cut and torn, and most were nearly worn-out.

He'd have taken one look and figured I'd been possessed. Not that the Karsites didn't try that, too. At least near-possession doesn't leave stains . . . not on uniforms, anyway. What am I going to do for uniforms? Oh, well—worry about that after my bath.

The bathing room was at the other end of the long, wood-paneled, stone-floored hallway; at mid-morning there was no one in the hall, much less competing for the tubs and hot water. Vanyel made the long trudge in a half-daze, thinking only how good the hot water would feel. The last bath he'd had—except for the quick one at the inn last night—had been in a cold stream. A *very* cold stream. And with sand, not soap.

Once there, he shed his clothing and left it in a heap on the floor, filled the largest of the three wooden tubs from the copper boiler, and slid into the hot water with a sigh—

—and woke up with his arms draped over the edges and going numb, his head sagging down on his chest, and the water lukewarm and growing colder.

A hand gently touched his shoulder.

He knew without looking that it had to be a fellow Herald—if it hadn't been, if it had even been someone as innocuous as a *strange* page, Vanyel's tightly-strung nerves and battle-sharpened reflexes would have done the unforgivable. He'd have sent the intruder through the wall before he himself had even crawled out of the depths of sleep. *Probably* by nonmagical means, but—magical or nonmagical, he suddenly realized that he could easily hurt someone if he wasn't careful.

He shivered a little. *I'm hair triggered. And that's not good.*

"Unless you plan on turning into a fish-man," Herald

Tantras said, craning his head around the partition screening the tub from the rest of the bathing room and into Vanyel's view with cautious care, "you'd better get out of that tub. I'm surprised you didn't drown yourself."

"So am I." Vanyel blinked, tried to clear his head of cobwebs, and peered over his shoulder. "Where did *you* pop out of?"

"Heard you got back a couple of candlemarks ago, and I figured you'd head here first." Tantras chuckled. "I know you and your baths. But I must admit I didn't expect to find you turning yourself into a raisin."

The dark-haired, dusky Herald came around the side of the wooden partition with an armload of towels. Vanyel watched him with a half-smile of not-too-purely artistic appreciation; Tantras was as graceful and as handsome as a king stag in his prime. Not *shay'a'chern*, but a good friend, and that was all too rare.

And getting rarer, Vanyel thought soberly. *Though, Havens, I haven't exactly had my fill of romantic companionship either, lately . . . well, celibacy isn't going to kill me. Not by any stretch of the imagination. Gods, I should apply for the priesthood.*

There was concern in the older Herald's deep, soft eyes. "You don't look good, Van. I figured you'd be tired—but from the way you passed out here—it must have been worse out there than I thought."

"It was bad," Vanyel said shortly, reluctant to discuss the past year. Even for the most powerful Herald-Mage in the Circle, holding down the positions of *five* other Herald-Mages while they recovered from magical attack, drainage, and shock was *not* a mission he wanted to think about for a long while, much less repeat. He soaped his hair, then ducked his head under the water to rinse it.

"So I heard. When I saw you playing dead in the tub, I sent a page up to your room with food and wine and sent another one off for some of my spare uniforms, since we're about the same size."

"Name the price, it's yours," Vanyel said gratefully, levering himself out of the tub with a groan and accepting the towel Tantras held out to him. "I have *nothing* worth wearing right now in the way of uniforms."

"Lord and Lady—" the other Herald swore, looking at him with shock. *"What* have you been doing to yourself?"

Vanyel paused in his vigorous toweling, looked down, and was a little surprised *himself* at the evidence of damage. He'd always been lean—but now he was whipcord and bone and nothing else. Then there were the scars—knife and sword scars, a scoring of parallel claw marks on his chest where that demon had tried to remove his heart. Burn marks, too—he was striped from neck to knee with three thin, white lines where mage-lightning had gotten through his shields. And there were a few other scars that were souvenirs of his bout with a master of mage-fire.

"My job. Living on the edge. Trying to convince the Karsites that I was five Herald-Mages. Playing target." He shrugged dismissively. "That's all. Nothing any of you wouldn't have done if you could have."

"Gods, Van," Tantras replied, with a hint of guilt. "You make me feel like a shirker. I hope to hell it was worth what you went through."

Vanyel compressed his lips into a tight line. "I got the bastard that got Mardic and Donni. And you can spread that as official."

Tantras closed his eyes for a moment, and bowed his head. "It *was* worth it," he said faintly.

Vanyel nodded. "Worth every scar. I may have accomplished something else; that particular necromancer had a flock of pet demons and I turned them back on Karse when I killed him." He smiled, or rather, stretched his mouth a little. "I hope it taught the Karsites a lesson. I hope they end up proscribing magic altogether on their side of the Border. If you can believe anything out of Karse, there's rumor that they're doing just that."

Tantras looked up again. "Hard on the Gifted—" he ventured.

Vanyel didn't answer. He was finding it very hard to feel sorry for *anyone* on the Karsite side of the Border at the moment. It was uncharitable, un-Heraldic, but until certain wounds healed—and *not* the physical ones—he was inclined to be uncharitable.

"There's more silver in your hair, too," Tantras observed, head to one side.

Vanyel made a face, just as glad of the change in subject. "Node-magic. Every time I tap into it, more of my roots go white. Moondance k'Treva was pure silver by the time he was my age; I guess I'm more resistant." He smiled, it was faint, but a *real* smile this time. "One nice thing; all those white hairs give me respect I might not otherwise get!"

He finished drying himself and wrapped the towel around his waist. Tantras grimaced again—probably noting the knife wound on his back—and handed him another towel for his hair.

"You already paid that forfeit, by the way" he said, plainly trying to lighten the conversation.

Vanyel stopped toweling off his hair and raised an eyebrow.

"You stood duty for me last Sovvan."

Vanyel clamped down on the sudden ache of loss and shrugged again. *You know you get depressed when you're tired, fool. Don't let it sink you.* "Oh, that. Any time, Tran. You know I don't like Sovvan-night celebrations, I can't handle the memorial services, and I don't like to be alone, either. Standing relay duty was as good as anything else to keep my mind off things."

He was grateful when Tantras didn't press the subject. "Think you can make it to your room all right?" the other asked. "I said you don't look good; I mean it. Falling asleep in the tub like that—it makes me wonder if you're going to pass out in the hall."

Vanyel produced something more like a dry cough than a laugh. "It's nothing about a week's worth of sleep won't cure," he replied. "And I'm sorry I won't be able to stand relay for you this year, but I have the Obligatory Familial Visit to discharge. I haven't been home in—gods, four years. And even then I didn't stay for more than a day or two. They're going to want me to make the long stay I've been promising. There's a letter from my father waiting for me that's probably reminding me of just that fact."

"Parents surely know how to load on the guilt, don't

they? Well, if you're out of reach, Randale won't find
something for you to do—but is that going to be *rest?*''
Tantras looked half-amused and half-worried. "I mean,
Van, that family of yours—''

"They *won't* come after me when I'm sleeping—which
I fully intend to do a lot of." He pulled on his old, clean
clothing, reveling in the feel of clean, soft cloth against
his skin, and started to gather up his things. "And the
way I feel right now, I'd just as soon play hermit in my
rooms when I get there—''

"Leave that stuff," Tantras interrupted. "I'll deal with
it. You go wrap yourself around a decent meal. You don't
look like you've had one in months."

"I haven't. They don't believe in worldly pleasures
down there. Great proponents of mortification of the flesh
for the good of the spirit." Vanyel looked up in time to
catch Tantras' raised eyebrow. He made a tragic face. "I
know what you're thinking. That, too. *Especially* that.
Gods. Do you have *any* idea what it was like, being surrounded by all those *devastatingly* handsome young men
and not daring to so much as *flirt* with one?''

"Were the young ladies just as devastatingly attractive?" Tantras asked, grinning.

"I would say so—given that the subject's fairly abstract
for me."

"Then I think I can imagine it. Remind me to avoid
the Karsite Border at all costs."

Vanyel found himself grinning back—another real
smile, and from the heart. "Tran, gods—I'm glad to see
you. Do you know how long it's been since I've been
able to talk freely to someone? To *joke,* for Lady's sake?
Since I was around people who don't wince away when
I'm minus a few clothes?''

"Are you *on* about that again?" Tantras asked, incredulously. "Do you *really* think that people are nervous
around you because you're shaych?''

"I'm *what?''* Van asked, startled by the unfamiliar
term.

"Shaych. Short for that Hawkbrother word you and
Savil use. Don't know where it came from, just seems
like one day everybody was using it." Tantras leaned

back against the white-tiled wall of the bathing room, folding his arms across his chest in a deceptively lazy pose. "Maybe because you're as prominent as you are. Can't go around calling the most powerful Herald-Mage in the Circle a 'pervert,' after all." He grinned. "He might turn you into a frog."

Vanyel shook his head again. "Gods, I *have* been out of touch to miss *that* little bit of slang. Yes, of course because I'm *shay'a'chern,* why else would people look at me sideways?"

"Because you scare the hell out of them," Tantras replied, his smile fading. "Because you *are* as powerful as you are; because you're so quiet and so solitary, and they never know what you're thinking. Havens, these days half the *Heralds* don't even know you're shaych; it's the Mage-Gift that makes them look at you sideways. Not that anybody around *here* cares about your bedmates a quarter as much as you seem to think. They're a lot more worried that—oh—a bird will crap on you and you'll level the Palace."

"Me?" Vanyel stared at him in disbelief.

"You. You've spent most of the last four or five years in combat zones. *We* know your reflexes are hypersensitive. Hellfire, that's why *I* came in here to wake you up instead of sending a page. We know what you can do. Van, nobody I've *ever* heard of was able to take the place of *five* Herald-Mages by himself! And the very idea of *one* person having that much power at his beck and call scares most people witless!"

Vanyel was caught without a reply; he stared at Tantras with the towel hanging limply from his hands.

"I'm telling you the plain truth, Van. I wish you'd stop wincing away from people with no cause. It's *not* your sexual preferences that scare them, it's *you.* Level the Palace, hell—they know you could level Haven if you wanted to—"

Vanyel came out of his trance of astonishment. "What do they think I am?" he scoffed, picking up his filthy shirt.

"They don't know; they haven't the Mage-Gift and most of them weren't trained around Herald-Mages. They

hear stories, and they think of the Mage Wars—and they
remember that once, before there *was* a Valdemar, there
was a thriving land to the far south of us. Now the Dhorisha Plains are there—a *very* large, circular crater. No
cities, no sign there ever *was* anything, not even two
stones left standing. Nothing but grass and nomads. Van,
leave that stuff; I'll pick up after you.''

"But—'' Vanyel began to object.

"Look, if *you* can spend most of a year substituting
for five of *us*, then *one* of us can pick up after you once
in a while.'' Tantras took the wet towels away from him,
cutting off his objections before he could make them.
"Honestly, Van.''

"If you insist.'' He wanted to touch Tantras' mind to
see if he really *meant* what he said. It seemed a fantas-
tical notion.

But Tran had not invited, and a Herald did not intrude
uninvited into another's mind, not unless there was an
overriding need to do so.

"Is . . . that how *you* feel?'' he asked in a whisper.

"I'm not afraid of you, but let me tell you, I wouldn't
have your powers for *any* reward. I'm *glad* I'm just a
Herald and not a Herald-Mage, and I don't know how
you survive it. So just let me spoil you a little, all right?''

Vanyel managed a weak smile, troubled by several
things—including that "just a Herald.'' business. That
implied a division between Heralds and Herald-Mages
that made him very uneasy. "All right, old friend. Spoil
me. I'm just tired enough to let you.''

The fog of weariness came between him and and the
corridor, and he was finding it all he could do to put one
foot in front of the other. *Lady, bless you for Tantras.
There aren't many even among the Heralds I trained with
that will accept what I am as easily as he does. Whether
it's that I'm a Mage or that I'm fey—although I can't see
why Mage-powers would frighten someone. We've had
Herald-Mages since there was a Valdemar.*

*I wish he was as right about that as he thinks he is; I
still think it's the other thing.*

The stone was so cool and soothing to his feet; it eased
the ache in them that was the legacy of too many hours—

days—weeks—when he had slept fully clothed, ready to defend the Border in the blackest, bleakest hours of the night.

That reminder brought bleaker thoughts. Every time he came back to Haven it was with the knowledge that there would be fewer familiar faces to greet him. *So many friends gone—not that I ever had many to begin with. Lancir, Mardic and Donni, Regen, Dorilyn. Wulgra, Kat, Pretor. All gone. Not many left besides Tran. There's— Jays. Savil. Andy, and he's a Healer. Erdane, Breda, a couple of the other Bards. How can I be anything but solitary? Every year I'm more alone.*

True to Tantras' promise, Vanyel found an overflowing plate waiting for him beside the pile of letters. It held a pair of meat pies, soft white cheese, and apples, and beside the generous plate of food was an equally generous pitcher of wine.

I'd better be careful with that stuff. I'm not used to it anymore, and I bet it'll go straight to my head.

He stifled a groan as he sagged down into the empty chair, poured a goblet of wine, then picked up the topmost letter. He broke the seal on it, gritted his teeth, and started in.

To Herald-Mage Vanyel from Lord Withen Ashkevron of Forst Reach: My dear Son—

Vanyel nearly dropped the letter in surprise, and reread the salutation to be certain that his eyes hadn't played tricks on him.

Great good gods. "My dear Son?" I haven't been "dear," much less "Son" for—years! I wonder what happened—

He took a long breath and continued.

Though you might find it difficult to believe, I am pleased and grateful that you are going to be able to find the time for an extended visit home. Despite our differences, and some hard words between us, I am very proud of my Herald-Mage son. I may not care for some aspects of your life, but I respect your intelligence and good sense. I confess, Vanyel, that your old father has need of

*some of that good sense. I need your help in dealing with
your brother Mekeal.*

Vanyel nodded to himself with cynicism. *Now we come
to it.*

*He has made some excessively poor judgments since I
turned over the management of some of the lands to him,
but this spring he has outdone himself. He's taken the
cattle—good, solid income-producing stock—off Long
Meadow and installed sheep down there instead!*

Vanyel chuckled. Whoever Withen had roped into being his scribe on this letter had reproduced his father's
tones perfectly. He could *feel* the indignation rising from
the page.

*And as for that so-called "Shin'a'in warsteed" he
bought—and a more ill-tempered, ill-favored beast I never
saw—the less said, the better! All these years I spent in
building up the Forst Reach line—and he'll undo it all
with one unmanageable stud! I feel sure he'll listen to
you; you're a Herald—the King himself trusts your judgment. The boy has me ready to throw him down the
blamed well!*

Vanyel shifted a little and reached for a wedge of
cheese. This letter was proving to be a lot more enlight-
ening than he'd had any reason to expect.

*This is no time for Meke to be mucking about; not when
there may be trouble across the Border. Maybe you remember that alliance marriage between Deveran Remoerdis of Lineas and Ylyna Mavelan of Baires? The one
that brought a halt to the Linean-Baires war, and that
brought that minstrel through here that you were so taken
with as a boy? It doesn't seem to be working out. There've
been rumors for years that the oldest child was a bastard—now Deveran seems to have given substance to
those rumors; he's disinherited the boy in favor of the
next in line. In some ways I can't blame him too much;
even if the lad didn't look so much like his uncle—I've
seen both the boy and the man, and the resemblance is
uncanny—the rumors alone would have been enough to
make his inheritance shaky. I wouldn't trust that entire
Mavelan family, frankly. A pack of wizardly snakes, the
lot of them, the only time they stop striking at each other*

is when they take on an outsider. I only thank the gods that they've stayed at each other's throats all this time. But there've been some nasty noises out of them about Tashir's disinheritance and if it gets to be more than noises, we may have trouble across the Border. Your brother is all fired up for a war, by the way. Gods, that is the last thing we need. I just thank the Lady that Randale had the good sense to send a plain Herald into Lineas as envoy, and not a Herald-Mage. A good solid Herald might be able to keep this from growing into another feud like the one the marriage was supposed to stop in the first place. The Lineans will certainly be far more inclined to listen to a plain Herald; they don't trust anything that smacks of wizardry, and given what the Mavelans did to them, who can blame them?

Vanyel bit his lip, the half-eaten scrap of cheese dangling forgotten from his fingers. Withen was showing a great deal more political astuteness than he'd ever given his father credit for. But this business in Lineas—

Please, he sent up a silent prayer. *Not now—*

It's evidently worrisome enough that Randale sent your sister Lissa and her Guard Company to keep a cross-Border eye on the Mavelans. You'd know what that would mean better than your old father, I think. If we're lucky and things stay calm, perhaps she can slip off for a few days' visit herself. I know you'd both like that. By the way—I hope you aren't planning on bringing any of your—friends—home with you, are you? You know it would upset your mother. You wouldn't want to upset your mother. By the hand of Radevel Ashkevron and my seal, Lord Withen Ashkevron.

Vanyel grimaced, dropped the letter back down on the table, and reached for the wine to take the bitter taste of those last words out of his mouth. He held the cool metal of the goblet to his forehead for a moment, an automatic reaction to a pain more emotional than physical.

:He doesn't mean to hurt, Chosen.: Yfandes' mind-voice touched the bitterness, but could not soothe it.

:Awake again, dearling? You should sleep—:

:Too much noise,: she objected. *:Equitation lessons, and I'm too tired to find a quiet corner of the Field. I'll*

just stand here by the stable and let the sun bake my sore muscles and wait for the babies to go away. Your father truly does not mean to hurt you.:

Vanyel sighed, and picked up a meat pie, nibbling the flaky crust listlessly. *:I know that. It doesn't stop it from hurting. If I weren't so tired, it probably wouldn't hurt as much. If I weren't so tired, it might even be funny.:* He swallowed another gulp of wine, painfully aware that even the simple act of chewing was becoming an effort. He put the pie down.

:You have nothing left,: she stated. *:No reserves at all.:*

:That's ridiculous, love. It's just that last push we made. And if I haven't anything left, then neither have you—:

:Not true. I may be spent physically, but you are spent emotionally, magically, mentally. Chosen, beloved, you have not spared yourself since Elspeth Peacemaker died.:

:That's because nobody had a choice,: he reminded her, reaching for a piece of cheese, but holding it up and staring at it, not eating it, seeing other times and places. *:Everybody else has been pushed just as hard. The moment poor Randale took the throne that fragile peace she had made for us fell to pieces. We had no warning it was going to come to that. Mardic and Donni—:*

The cold hand of grief choked his throat. The life-bonded couple who had been such steadfast friends and supporters to him had been two of the first victims of the Karsite attacks. He could feel the echo of his grief in the mourning of Yfandes' mind-voice.

:Poor children. Goddess hold them—:

:'Fandes—at least they died together. I—could wish—: he cut off the thought before he could distress her. He contemplated the white wedge of cheese in his hand as if he had never seen anything like it, and then blinked, and began nibbling at it, trying to force the food around the knot of sorrow blocking his throat. He had to eat. He'd been surviving on handfuls of parched corn, dried fruit, and dried beef for too long. He *had* to get his strength back. It wouldn't be long before Randale would need him again. Well, all he really needed was a couple of weeks of steady meals and sleep. . . .

:You ask too much of yourself.:

:Who, me? Strange thoughts from a Companion. Who was it who used to keep nagging me about duty?: He tried to put a measure of humorous teasing into his own mind-voice, but it felt flat.

:But you cannot be twenty places at once, Chosen. You are no longer thinking clearly.:

The cheese had finally migrated inside him, and most of the lump in his throat was gone. He sighed and reached for the meat pie again. With enough wine to help, he *might* be able to get that down, too.

The trouble was, 'Fandes was right. For the past few months he'd been reduced to a level where he really wasn't thinking much at all—just concentrating on each step as it came, and trying to survive it. It had been like climbing a mountain at the end of a long and grueling race; just worrying about one handhold at a time. Not thinking about the possibility of falling, and not able to think about what he'd do when he got to the top. If he got to the top. If there was a top.

Stupid, Herald. Looking at the bark and never noticing the tree was about to fall on you.

The sun coming in his window had crept down off the chair and onto the floor, making a bright square on the brown braided rug. He chewed and swallowed methodically, not really tasting what he was eating, and stared at the glowing square, his mind going blank and numb.

:Randale uses you beyond your strength, because of the nodes,: Yfandes said accusingly, breaking into his near-trance. *:You should say something. He'd stop if he realized what he was doing to you. If you were like other Heralds, unable to tap them—:*

:If I were like other Heralds, the Karsites would be half-way to Haven now, instead of only holding the disputed lands,: he replied mildly. *:Dearest, there is no choice. I lost my chance at choices a long time ago. Besides, I'm not as badly off as you think. All I need is a bit of rest and I'll be fine. We're damned lucky I can use the nodes— and that I don't need to rest to recharge.:*

:Except that you must use your power to focus and control—:

He shook his head. *:Beloved, I appreciate what you're telling me, but this isn't getting us anywhere. I have to do what I'm doing; I'm a Herald. It's what any of the others would do in my place. It's what 'Lendel—:*

Grief—he fought it, clenching his hand hard on the arm of his chair as he willed his emotions into control. *Control yourself, Herald. This is just because you're tired, it's maudlin, and it doesn't do you or anyone else any good.*

:I could wish you were less alone.:

:Don't encourage me in self-pity, love. It's funny, isn't it?: he replied, his lips twitching involuntarily, though not with amusement. *:Dear Father seems to think I've been seducing every susceptible young man from here to the Border, and I've been damned near celibate. The last was—when?:* The weeks, the months, they all seemed to blur together into one long endurance trial. A brief moment of companionship, then a parting; inevitable, given his duties and Jonne's.

:Three years ago,: Yfandes supplied, immediately. *:That rather sweet Guardsman.:*

Vanyel remembered the person, though not the time.

"Hello. You're The Herald-Mage, aren't you?"

Vanyel looked up from the map he was studying, and smiled. He couldn't help it—the diffident, shy smile the Guardsman wore begged to be answered.

"Yes—are you—"

"Guardsman Jonne. Your guide. I was born not half a league from here." *The guileless expression, the tanned face and thatch of hair, the tiny net of humor lines about the thoughtful hazel eyes, all conspired to make Vanyel like this man immediately.*

"Then you, friend Jonne, are the direct answer to my prayers," *he said.*

Only later, when they were alone, did he learn what other prayers the Guardsman had an answer for—

:Jonne. Odd for such a tough fighter to be so diffident, even gentle. Though why he should have been shy, when he was five years older and had twice my—uh—experience—:

:Your reputation, beloved. A living legend came down off his pedestal and looked to him for company.: Yfandes

sent him an image of a marble saint-statue hopping out of
its niche and wriggling its eyebrows in a come-hither look.
There was enough of a tired giggle in her mind-voice to
get an equally tired chuckle out of him. But he sobered
again almost immediately. :*And that lasted how long? Two
months? Three? Certainly not more.*:

:*You were busy—you had duties—both of you. It was
your duties that parted you.*:

:*I was,*: he replied bitterly, :*a fool. More than duties
would have parted us in time. I know exactly what I'm
trying to do—when I admit it to myself. I'm trying to replace 'Lendel. I can't; I can't ever, so why do I even bother
to try? A love like that happens* once *in a lifetime, and
I'm not doing myself or my would-be partners any favor
by trying to recreate it. I know it, and once the first glow
wears off, they know it. And it isn't fair to them.*:

Silence from Yfandes. There really wasn't much she
could say. He was left to contemplate the inside of his own
thoughts, as faint sounds of distant people and a bit of
birdsong drifted in his window.

*Damn it, I'm feeling sorry for myself again. Heralds are
all lonely; it isn't just me. We're different; made different
by our Gifts, made even more so by the Companions, then
driven even farther away from ordinary people by this fa-
natic devotion to duty of ours. Herald-Mages are one step
lonelier than that.* He couldn't help himself; the next
thought came automatically, despite his resolution not to
fall into a morass of self-pity. *Then there's me. Between
the level of my Gift and my sexual preferences—*

He buried his face in his free hand. *Gods. I am a fool.
I have 'Fandes. She loves me in a way no one else ever
will or ever did, except 'Lendel. That ought to be enough.
It really ought—if I wasn't so damned selfish.*

She interrupted his thoughts. :*Van, you almost need a
friend more than a lover. A different kind of friend than
me; one that can touch you. You need to be touched, you
humans—*: Her mind-voice trailed off, grew dim, in the
way that meant she was losing her battle to fatigue and
had fallen asleep again.

"You humans." That phrase said it all. *That* was the
telling difference, he realized suddenly. The telling lack.

Yfandes was not human—and she never *felt* exactly the way a human would. There was always the touch of the ''other'' about her, and the strange feeling he got, sometimes, that she was hiding something, some secret that she could only share with another Companion. It was not a comfortable feeling. He was just as glad she wasn't awake to pick it up from him.

He dragged himself up out of the depths of his chair to rummage paper and a pen and inkpot out of his desk. He slouched back down into the cushions and chewed thoughtfully on the end of the pen, trying to compose something that wouldn't set Withen off.

To Lord Withen Ashkevron of Forst Reach from Herald-Mage Vanyel Ashkevron.

So far, so good.

Dear Father: I'm sorry I've had to put off spending any length of time at home—but duty must always come before anything else, and my duty as a Herald is to the orders of my King.

He licked his lips, wondering if that was a bit excessively priggish. *Probably not. And I don't think I'll say anything about how visits of less than a day keep Mother from having vapors at me.* He reached for the goblet again, and another swallow of wine, before continuing.

As for Meke, I'll do my best with him, Father. You must remember though, that although I am a Herald I am also his brother—he may be no more inclined to listen to me than he does to you. With regard to your news about Baires and Lineas—may the gods help us—I have seen far too much of conflict of late. I was praying for some peace, and now you tell me we may have a Situation on our very doorstep. Unless Randale asks me to intervene, there isn't much I can do. Let us hope it doesn't come to that. I promise I will try to put some sense into Meke's head about that *as well; perhaps when he has heard some of what I have seen, a war will no longer seem quite so attractive. Perhaps when he sees some of what war has done to me— no, Father, I was not badly hurt, but I picked up an injury or two that left scars. It may be that will impress him.*

He closed his eyes and carefully picked out the least loaded words he could think of for the next sentence. When he thought he had it, he concentrated on setting it carefully down on the paper so that there could be no mistake.

With regard to my—friends; I promised you ten years ago that I would never indulge in anything that you did not approve of or that made you uncomfortable under your roof. Do you still find it so difficult to believe that I would keep my word?

He nobly refrained from adding—"Odd, no one else seems to have that problem." That would *not* serve any purpose, and would only make his father guilty, and then angry.

I do have a request to make of you, and a reminder of a promise you made to me at the same time. You pledged to keep Mother from flinging young women at me—under other conditions I would not feel that I needed to remind you of this promise, but I truly cannot handle that particular situation this time, Father. I'm exhausted; you can't know how exhausted. All I really want is some peace, some quiet time to rest and catch up with the family matters. Please do me this one small favor; I don't think it's too much to ask. Yours, Vanyel.

He folded the letter and sealed it quickly, before he had a chance to add a postscript to that temptingly empty space at the bottom. *All I want from you and Mother is to be left alone. I need that rest. Before I fall on my face.*

He picked up the second letter, and heaved a sigh of relief. *Liss. Oh, bless you, big sister. My antidote to Father.*

To Herald-Mage Vanyel Ashkevron from Guard-Captain Lissa Ashkevron: Dearest Van—if half of what I've been hearing about you is true, I'm tempted to abandon my command and kidnap you and hide you someplace until you've had some rest! Thank the gods somebody saw enough reason to give you a leave! And before you bleat to me about "duty," just you remember that if you kill yourself with overwork you won't be around to do that duty!

Vanyel smiled, biting his lip to keep from chuckling. Good old Liss!

I should tell you what's going on out here, since you may be riding right into another hotbed of trouble. Dev-

eran of Lineas has disinherited his eldest. The boy sup-
posedly has mage-power, which, since his mother does not,
is being read that he is probably a bastard. The Lineans
in any case are not likely to allow anyone with Mage-Gifts
to rule over them—but this Tashir is altogether too like his
Uncle Vedric for comfort. And Vedric is protesting the tacit
slur on his "good name"—not that he has one—and is
being backed by the entire Mavelan Clan. I suppose it is
a bit much to imply that your brother-in-law was fornicat-
ing with his own sister before your marriage to her. Ha-
vens bless—talk about soiled goods!

At any rate, I suspect there's far more to it than that;
what, I don't know, but the Mavelans seldom unite for
anything and they're uniting on this one. I much doubt it's
over concern for Vedric's reputation or tender feelings for
Tashir. My guess is there's another attempt at acquiring
Lineas in the offing—but since they're both clients-by-
alliance to Valdemar, the Mavelans can't just begin fling-
ing mage-fire over there. Randale would definitely take
exception to that.

So here we are, camped on the Border, and watching
for one false note. What really worries me is that it's Ved-
ric who's fronting this; they're all snakes, but he's a viper.
The only reason he's not Lord Mavelan is because his
brother's been very lucky—or smart enough to buy some
really good spies and bodyguards. Vedric is definitely the
most ambitious of the lot; my guess is he's been promised
Lineas if he can get it quietly. Through Tashir, perhaps.

Vanyel found his eyebrows rising with every sentence.
Lissa had come a long way from the naive swordswoman
who had accepted that commission in the Guard. She was
a *lot* more politically astute than Van would have
dreamed—which gave him the second surprise of the day.
First Father, then Liss—no bad thing, either. No one living in the days of King Randale could afford to be politically naive.

I hope to steal away long enough to spend at least a
little time with you, love, but don't count on it. There's
nothing going on overtly, but the whole thing feels very
touchy to me; like the moments before the storm hits. If I

*feel the situation has calmed down enough, I'll come. Be
well. Love, Liss.*

That was by far and away the easiest letter to answer
he'd had in a long time. He scrawled a quick reply of
affection, including the fact that he missed her badly,
sealed the note, and laid it with the other.

There were two or three other letters, all nothing more
than invitations to various entertainments; hunting parties,
mostly, at noble estates, parties meant to last a week or
more. Despite the fact that he *never* attended these things—
wouldn't have even if he'd had the *time*—the invitations
never stopped coming. He wrote brief, polite notes, and
sat back again, staring at the packs in the corner. He knew
he had to sort things out of his traveling kit for his trip
home—and he just couldn't muster the energy. It was *so*
much easier just to sit and let all the kinks in his muscles
respond to the soft—motionless!—chair.

A rap at the door interrupted his lethargy; it was the
page sent by Tantras, with the promised uniforms. And
one more thing; a note—and Vanyel recognized Randale's
handwriting on the outside.

Oh, gods—no, no! For a moment he tensed, fearing another call to duty on the eve of his promised chance to
rest. Then he saw that it wasn't sealed, not even by Randale's personal seal.

He relaxed. No seal meant it wasn't official. He took it
from the wide-eyed page and motioned to the youngster to
stay for a reply.

Vanyel; come by after Court and say good-bye—don't
*come before then; if I'm not being official, I don't have to
find something for you to do. Or rather, I don't have to
assign you to one of the hundred messes that needs dealing
with. I'm sorry you aren't staying, but I understand, and
if you* weren't *planning on leaving, I'd probably tie you to
Yfandes and drive you off before I work you to death. But
do come by; Jisa wants to see her "Uncle Van" before he
vanishes again. Randale.*

*:If you don't make the time to see her, I'll bite you when
you try to saddle me.:*

Vanyel had to smother a laugh. *:Woke up again, did*

you? Why is it anything about Jisa snags your attention like nothing else does?:

:Because she's adorable—as most six-year-old humans are not. *Besides, she's your daughter.:*

:I'm just grateful she doesn't look anything like me,: he replied, sobering. *:If she'd gotten these silver eyes of mine, for instance—or black hair when both Randale and Shavri are light brown. Don't you dare let that slip to anyone!:*

:Not even another Companion,: she reassured him. *:I'm not sure I understand what the problem could be, though. Shavri won't let Randale marry her, so should it matter who Jisa's father is?:*

:It would disturb some folk, because they're lifebonded. Besides, we don't want anyone to know that Randale's sterile. If he has to make an alliance marriage—that could ruin it. And there are damn few people even inside the Heralds who would understand someone wanting a child badly enough to go to bed with someone other than her lifebonded.:

Yfandes' mind-voice was hesitant. *:Truth, Chosen—it seems to bother you.:*

Vanyel leaned farther back into the chair, scrawling replies to the invitations with half his attention. It *did* bother him, and in a way that made him reluctant to even think about Shavri, sometimes. *:It's not that,:* he temporized. *:It's just that I'm worried about them.:*

But the uneasy feeling continued, an uncomfortable unhappiness that he couldn't define. So he continued hastily, *:Poor Shavri; you can't know how much she wanted that child. That was the only reason we did it.:*

:You like her.:

:Of course *I like her!:* he answered—again, just a shade too quickly. *:She and Randale—they're friends; how could I have told them no?:* He shied away from examining his feelings too closely. *:Besides, it was never anything more than a—physical exercise for either of us. No more involved for me, certainly, than dancing. Shavri being a Healer, she could make sure she "caught" the first time. Neither of us were emotionally involved, or ever likely to be.:*

:I suppose that could have been a problem,: she replied.

:Exactly. That's why Shavri and Randale asked me to help in the first place: I was perfect; a Herald, already a friend, physically able, *and not going to get romantically entangled.:*

:Don't you . . . want the child, sometimes?: Yfandes sounded wistful. Vanyel was a bit surprised.

:Frankly, no. I'm not very paternal. It takes more than seed to make a father, love. Great good gods, can you see me *as a parent? I'd be awful. Randale has what I lack in that department.:* His thoughts darkened, as he recalled what had been bothering him since he scanned the palace when they rode in. *:'Fandes, I'm worried about them. When Lancir died—truth, I almost expected Taver to Choose me King's Own. Instead—instead he chose Shavri, and I'm desperately afraid it wasn't because she was Randale's lifebonded. I'm afraid it was because she's a Healer.:*

There was a long silence on Yfandes' part. Then, *:Why haven't you said something before this?:*

:Because—I wasn't sure. I've been wrong about things so many times—and I didn't really want to think about it. Shavri told me once that she was afraid that Randale's sterility was a symptom of something worse. I didn't know what to say, so I told her not to worry about it. But now—you know how sensitive I am; follow my line to Randale—:

Vanyel could "feel" every Herald and Herald-Mage in Haven, all tied to him by a kind of tenuous network of lines of life-energy, with every identity as plain to him as if he could see the faces. Most Herald-Mages could follow the line to anyone who had shared magic with them; Vanyel could follow the line of anyone who had "shared magic" just by virtue of being a Herald. He had the line that led to Randale without even thinking about it, and "felt" Yfandes follow it down with him, Seeing what he Saw.

:There's—something not right,: she said, after a moment's study. *Something out of balance. Physically, not mentally or emotionally. But I can't tell what it is.:*

:Exactly,: he agreed. *:I felt it as soon as we came in; he wasn't like that when we left. I wish I was a Healer—*

Adept like Moondance k'Treva or even little Brightstar. They're much *better at understanding imbalances than I am.:* He rubbed his forehead, his headache starting again.

:I don't think I will ever forget the look on Shavri's face when you told her this wasn't the first time you'd done someone the favor of—uh—stud service.: Yfandes' mind-voice colored yellow with laughter, and *he* was just as pleased to change the subject.

:Moondance and Starwind wanted a child to raise, and neither of them *can function with a female,:* he reminded her, *:and Snowlight was willing to have twins, one for her, one for them.:*

:You certainly produce lovely children.:

:Brightstar is a good lad,: he said, shyly. *:They're rightly proud of him—and that's* their *doing, not mine. But I'm beginning to think I ought to rent myself out. Do you think I could command the same fees as a* Shin'a'in *stud?:*

:Oh, at least,: she giggled, as he reached for pen and paper. *:Double if your Gift and beautiful silver eyes breed true!:*

He smothered a chuckle, and turned all his attention to the reply the page was waiting for. *Dearest friends; of course I'm coming by. Don't you realize that you're my last taste of sanity before I spend the fall with my lunatic family?*

He sealed this last note and handed them all to the page to take away. He stood and hauled the packs over to his bed, resisting the temptation to throw *himself* there instead of his belongings, and began sorting out the items he'd need for his visit home.

There was an awful lot of money in there—money he didn't remember getting, but it all seemed to be in those silly little sealed "stipend" bags, most of them still unopened. At least a half-dozen. Then again—he hadn't had much to spend it on, going from post to post like a madman, never getting regular meals, seldom sleeping in a real bed. He combined all the bags into one, and tossed the empties onto the table for the servants to collect. Then had second thoughts, and added some coins to the pile of empty bags. No harm in leaving a little something for the ones who kept things picked up for him; they did a good job. They *could* have just sealed the room up until he returned, but they kept it open and aired, even though that meant extra work. He'd acquired a much greater appreciation for good servants since he'd become a Herald.

He returned to his packs; there were a lot of small, valuable trinkets he just barely remembered being gifted with in there.

:Why do people insist on giving me all this stuff?: he asked Yfandes, a little irritably. *:It isn't bribery; I'd have sensed that and given it back.:*

:I told you,: she replied. *:They wanted something of the excitement of your life to rub off on them, so they give you things. That's what it means to be Herald Vanyel, second only to King's Own.:*

He made a sound of contempt, as he sorted through the things; jewelry mostly. *:I bet they think I have everything I could want. I suppose on a lot of levels, I do. I'm ungrateful, I guess. I don't know why I'm not happier.:*

:Vanyel Ashkevron, you are being an idiot,: she replied acidly. *:Stop feeling guilty about feeling like you're overworked and unhappy! You're* only *human!:*

:Beloved, I think you know me better than I know myself.: He laughed to keep from wincing; she was cutting a bit too close to the truth. His hand fell on more jewelry, and he changed the subject. *:Ah, now these I remember; I bought them honestly.:* He selected the three trinkets that he had thought would please Randale, Shavri, and Jisa when he'd seen them; a cloak-clasp for Randale in the form of a vine of Heal-All twining around a beryl the green of a Healer's robes—a pendant that matched for Shavri—and a wonderful little articulated carving of a Companion complete with formal panoply for Jisa. The rest went back into the pack; he would need presents for the mob at Forst Reach, and there was surely enough there to make a start. He paused with the last piece, a crystal mage-focus stone (rose-quartz, sadly, and not a stone he cared to work with) still in his hand.

:Think Savil would like this?:

:You know she would. Rose-quartz is her Prime Focus, and you don't often see a crystal that big or that clear.:

:Good.: He put it with the little gifts on his bedside table.

The bed looked better than ever.

:Courtesy calls,: Yfandes reminded him. *:Then you can take a nap. Lazy.:*

He groaned. *:Too true. Oh, well.:* He picked up the crystal and slipped it into his pocket. *:Savil first. She'll put me in a good mood for the others.:*

There was a touch of smile in Yfandes' mind-voice as he slipped out his door and down the hall—still barefoot. *:You don't really need to be* put *in a good mood for Jisa do you?:*

He grinned; although she couldn't see it, she would feel the rise in his spirits. *:No—but if Randi ends up giving me an assignment* anyway, *I won't feel so bad about it!:*

Two

Vanyels room was in the "old Palace," the original building dating back to King Valdemar; in the oldest section still used for Heralds' quarters. Savil's suite was in the new wing added some fourteen years ago. She no longer occupied the suite he'd had when he first was put in her custody by Lord Withen—she didn't teach more than one pupil at a time these days, so having no use whatsoever or a suite with four bedrooms, she'd moved instead to another suite, still on the ground floor, though without an outside door to the gardens; Moving had been something of a relief to both of them; her former quarters held too many sad memories, memories of the painful weeks following Tylendel's suicide.

Vanyel had helped with that move, since it had coincided with their return—him in full Whites—from the Pelagir Hills and the Vale of the *Tayledras* k'Treva. The touchiest part had been moving the magic Work Room: a transfer of energies rather than physical furniture. Savil had left that to *him;* since they'd shared magic so intimately and so often he knew her "resonances," and more importantly, her protections "recognized" him.

The magical transfer had been a kind of graduation exercise for him—not to prove to Savil that he could do it, but to prove his ability—and his training—to the rest of the Herald-Mages. He could still remember Jaysen Kondre's face, when he'd stood in the middle of the new Work Room and "called" the shields and protections—and they'd swarmed up and followed him like bees with a migrating queen, settling into place as solidly as if they'd been cast on the new room from the beginning. Jays had looked as if he'd just swallowed a live fish.

Savil's suite now was of four rooms only; her protege's bedroom, and her bedroom, sitting room and Work Room.

:Van—: Yfandes said sleepily into his mind. *:Ask Jays to get you a Work Room this time. You need a Work Room.:*

:I thought you were asleep. How many times do I have to tell you that I don't need one before you'll believe me?: he replied.

:But—: Even after all these years, Yfandes *still* wasn't used to the idea that Vanyel's methods weren't *quite* the same as the other Herald-Mages'.

:I can use Savil's if I'm working formal magic. When I'm in the field, I don't have time to muck about with formalities.:

:But—:

He shook his head, glad that the only other people about were used to Heralds and the way they seemed to mutter at themselves. When he'd been in the field, he'd frequently gotten knowing looks and averted eyes. *:Go back to sleep, 'Fandes.:*

She gave up. *You ought to know by now that you can't out-stubborn me, sweetling.*

Savil was still his master when it came to magic that required long, painstaking setups. Vanyel's talents lay elsewhere. He had neither master nor even peer when a crisis called for instant decision and instant action. It was that ability to use his powers on a moment's notice that made him second-rank to no one in power, and second only to Shavri in the Heraldic Circle; that, and the ability to use the lines and currents of power, and the nodes where they met, as the Ancients had done and the *Tayledras* could still do, though none of the other Herald-Mages except Savil could.

He squinted against the light as he entered the new wing. The paneling of the new section had not had time to darken with age: the halls here seemed very bright, though they no lon er smelled "new."

This section feels even emptier than the old quarters; I don't think more than half the ground-floor rooms have claimants, there's less than that on the second floor, and none at all on the third. I can't see how we'll ever fill it.

The hall was so quiet he could hear the murmur of voices from one of the farther suites without straining his ears at all. A quick Look gave him identities; Savil and Jays. He paused for a moment and sent the tentative little mind-probe on ahead of him that was the Thought-sensing equivalent of a knock on the door, and got a wave of welcome from both minds before he had taken two steps.

Now sure of his reception—and that he wasn't interrupting anything—he crossed the remaining distance to Savil's door and pushed it open.

Savil, her silver hair braided like a coronet on the top of her head, was enthroned in her favorite chair, a huge, blue monstrosity as comfortable as it was ugly. Tall Jaysen (who always looked bleached, somehow) was half-sprawled on her couch, but he rose at Vanyel's entrance—then did a double take, and staggered back a step, hand theatrically clutched to his chest.

"My heart!" he choked. "Savil, *look* at your nephew! Barefoot, shaggy-headed, and *shabby!* Where in Havens has our peacock gone?"

"He got lost somewhere south of Horn," Vanyel replied. "I last saw him in a tavern singing trios with my mind and my wits. I haven't seen either of *them* in a while, either."

"Well, you surely couldn't tell it from the reports we got back," Jaysen answered, coming quickly forward and clasping his forearms with no sign of the uneasiness he'd once had around the younger Herald. "There's three new songs about you out of your year down south, in case you didn't know. Very accurate, too, amazingly enough."

Vanyel sighed. "Gods. Bards."

Jaysen cocked his graying head to the side. "You should be used to it by now. You keep doing things that make *wonderful* songs, so how can they resist?" He grinned. "Maybe you should stop. Become a bricklayer, for instance."

Vanyel shook his head and groaned. "It's not my fault!"

Jaysen laughed. "I'd best be off before that trio wrecks

my workroom. Did Savil tell you? I've been given the proteges *you'd* have gotten if you hadn't been in a combat zone. Count your blessings—one's a farmgirl who had *much* rather be a fighter than a Herald-Mage, thank you; one's a very bewildered young man who can't for a moment imagine why *he* was Chosen and as a result has no confidence whatsoever; and the third is an *overly* confident sharpster who's actually a convicted lawbreaker!"

"Convicted of what?" Vanyel asked, amused at the woebegone expression on Jaysen's face.

"Chicanery and fraud. The old shell-and-pea game at Midsummer Fair; he was actually Chosen on the way to his sentencing, if you can believe it."

"I can believe it. It's keeping you busy, anyway."

"It is that. It's good to see you, Van." Jaysen hesitated a moment, and then put one hand on his shoulder. "Vanyel—" He locked his pale, near-colorless blue eyes with Vanyel's, and Van saw disturbance there that made *him* uneasy. "Take care of yourself, would you? We *need* you. I don't think you realize how much."

He slipped out the door before Vanyel could respond. Van stared after him with his mouth starting to fall open.

"What in the name of sanity was *that* about?" he asked, perplexed, turning back to his aunt, who had not left the comfortable confines of her chair. She looked up at him measuringly.

"Have you any notion how many Herald-Mages we've lost in the last four years?" she asked, her high-cheekboned face without any readable expression.

"Two dozen?" he hazarded.

Now she looked uneasy. Not much, but enough that he could tell. "Slightly more than half the total we had when you and I came back from k'Treva. We can't replace them fast enough. The Mage-Gift was never that common in the first place, and with a rate of attrition like that—" She grimaced. "I haven't told you about this before, because there was nothing you could do about it, but after the deaths of the last year, you should know the facts. You become more important with each loss, Van. You were the *only* one available to send to replace those five casualties on the Karsite Border. You were the only one who *could* replace all five of them, all by yourself. That's why we couldn't relieve you, lad, or even send you one other Herald-Mage to give you a breather. We simply didn't have anyone to send. Speaking of which—'' She raised one eyebrow as she gave him such a penetrating look that Vanyel felt as if she was seeing past his clothes to count his ribs and mark each of his scars. "—*you* look like hell.''

"Can't *anyone* greet me without saying that?'' he complained. "You, Tran, Jays— Can't you tell me I'm looking seasoned? Or poetic? Or something?''

"Horseturds; you don't look 'seasoned,' you look like hell. You're too damned thin, your eyes are sunken, and if my Othersenses aren't fooling me, you've got no reserves—you're on your last dregs of energy.''

Vanyel sighed, and folded himself up at her feet, resting his back against the front of her chair and his head against her knee. *That* was "home," and always would be—as Savil was more his mother than his birth-mother ever could be. "It's nothing," he replied. "At least nothing a little sleep won't cure. Come on, you know how you feel at the end of a tour of duty. You're still *your* old tactful self, Savil.''

"Tact never was one of my strong traits, lad,'' she replied, and he felt her hand touch, and then begin stroking his hair. He closed his eyes and relaxed; muscles began to unknot that must have been tensed up for the past year. For the first time in months there was no one depending on him, looking to him for safety. It was nice to feel sheltered and protected, instead of *being* the shelter and protection. *There are times when I'd give anything to be a child again, and this is perilous close to one of them.*

"I am mortally tired, Savil,'' he admitted, finally. "I need this leave. It won't take long to rest up—but I do need the rest. You know, I didn't *ask* for this. I didn't *want* to be a Herald-Mage, I wanted to be a Bard. I sure as Havens didn't *ask* to be 'Vanyel Dragonsbreath,' or whatever it is they're calling me.''

"Demonsbane.''

The increasingly shrill tone of his own voice finally penetrated his fog. "Savil, I—am I whining?"

She chuckled throatily. "You're whining, son."

"Hellfire," he said. "I swear, every time I lose a little sleep, I turn fifteen. A *bratty* fifteen, at that. I'm amazed you put up with me."

"Darling boy," she said, her hand somehow stroking his headache away, "You've earned a little whine. You're thinned out in more ways than one." She sighed. "That's the one thing I regret most about the past few years—you never do or say anything anymore without thinking about it. That's good for Herald-Mage Vanyel, but I'm not entirely certain about Vanyel Ashkevron." There was a long silence behind him, then—"There's no joy in you anymore, *ke'chara*. No joy at all. And that bothers me more than the circled eyes and thin cheeks."

"We've all endured too much the last five years to be able to afford to do things without thinking. As for joy—is there joy anywhere, anymore? We've all lost so much—so many friends gone—"

Another long silence. "I don't know."

He cleared his throat, and changed the subject. "I didn't feel a third here. You aren't teaching?"

"Can't; don't have the stamina anymore. Not and be Guardian, too."

He'd half expected that. And he half expected what quarter. "So they made you Guardian? In whose place?"

"Lancir's. Shavri can't; she tried, and she can't. The four Guardians *have* to be Herald-Mages. We'd hoped Healing-Gift was close enough, but she didn't pass the last trial. I think she's relieved. It's a pity; the Guardian of the East has always been King's Own, but—"

"In that case, the present I brought you may be handy." He shifted so that he could get at his pocket, and pulled out the crystal. He closed his hand around it, feeling all the smooth planes and angles pressing into his palm. "Don't you need a Prime Focus stone of your own to set in the Web? I thought you didn't have a good Prime to use for anything but personal stuff."

"You do, and I put a stone there, but it was a Secondary Focus, an amethyst, and not what I'd have—"

He raised the hand holding the crystal above his head, parting his fingers so she could see it, but not opening his eyes or moving his head.

"Sunsinger's Glory!" she breathed. "Where did you find that?"

"Gifted me," he said, as the weight left his hand. "People keep *giving* me things, Savil. An opal or amber I could have used—still—*you* can use it, so do."

"I shall." Her hand began to stroke his hair again, and he heard the little *click* as she set the stone down on the table beside her. "That will make my job a bit easier." She chuckled richly. "I thought I was so lucky when it turned out my resonances worked best with rose-quartz—not like Deedre who was stuck with topaz, or Justen, with ruby. Nice, cheap stone, I thought. Won't have to go bankrupt trying to get a good one. Little did I know how hard it was to find a good, unflawed, *large* crystal!"

"Little did you know you were going to turn out a Guardian," he replied drowsily.

"Hmm, true." Her mind touched softly on his. *:Vanyel, ke'chara, you are* not *well. There's more silver in this lovely black hair.:*

He couldn't lie mind-to-mind, not to her, so he temporized. *:The silver's from working with the nodes; you should know that. As for the rest—I'm just weary, teacher-love. Just weary. Too many hours fighting too many battles, and all of it too much alone.:*

:Heart-wounded?: Her Mindvoice was etched and frosted with concern.

:No, heart-whole. Just lonely. Only that. You know. I haven't time these days to go courting a friend. Not on battle-lines. And I won't *ask for more than friendship—gods, how could I ask anyone to make an emotional commitment to somebody who's out trying daily to get himself killed? I'm better off alone.:*

The hand on his hair trembled a little, and rested.

:I know,: she replied, finally. *:There are times when I wish with all my heart I could take some of that from you.:*

:Now, now, don't encourage me in my self-pity. Hon-

estly, you and 'Fandes—: "If wishes were fishes, we'd
walk on the sea, teacher-love," he said aloud. "I'd rather
you could keep Father and Mother off when I'm home."

"So you're finally making that major visit they've been
plaguing you for?" She took the unspoken cue and
switched to less-intimate vocal speech.

"Randale sent me word just as I was leaving the Border. Several weeks leave of absence at least. And I must
say, that while I'm looking forward to the rest, I'm not
at all sanguine about this little sojourn in the bosom of
my loving family."

"Out of experience I'm forced to tell you: even if they
behave themselves, you're all too likely to find yourself
the court of appeal for every family feud that's been
brewing for the last ten years," she said, and laughed.
"And no one will like your judgments and everyone will
accuse you of favoritism."

He opened his eyes and moved his head around, prop-
ping his chin against the seat cushion. "And Mother will
haul every eligible female for *leagues* about in on 'visits,'
and Father will go cross-eyed trying to see if I'm attempting to seduce *any* of the young men on the estate. And
dear Father Leren will thunder sermons about fornication
and perversity every holy day, and glare. Jervis will snipe
at me, try to get me angry, and glare. And Mother's maid
Melenna will chase me all over the property. And on and
on." He made mournful eyes at her. "If I hadn't promised, I'd be greatly tempted to take my chances with Randale finding another emergency and stay here."

"I thought Lissa was stationed right near Forst Reach.
She always *used* to be able to protect you." Savil gave
him a half smile. "She was a very *good* little protector
when you were a child."

"I don't think she's going to feel she can leave her
assigned post," he said. "It seems *that* Border is heating
up."

"Just what we need. Another Situation."

"Exactly."

"You could have dealt with this earlier, I suppose."

He snorted. "Not likely. That whole monstrous mess
of tangled emotions and misconception is why I never

have spent more than a day at home if I can help it. If it isn't Mother flinging women at me, it's Father watching me out of the corner of his eye.'' He throttled down savagely on the wave of bitterness that crawled up his throat, but some of it emerged despite his good intentions. ''Gods, Savil, I am *so damned tired* of the whole dance. I really need to take a couple of weeks to rest, and where else can I go? *You* know I daren't stay here; if I do, Randale will recruit me. He won't want to, he won't mean to, but something will come up, and he'll have to—and *I* won't be able to say no. If I went to Liss—assuming she *has* someplace to put me!—she'd end up doing the same thing. I'm a tool, and neither of them dares let a tool stand idle, even when it might break.''

''Easy, lad,'' Savil cautioned, her face clouded and troubled.

He grimaced. ''Did it again. Sorry. I won't break. I'm not sure I *can* break. The fact is, I still look all right, and I really *don't* want Randi to guess how drained out I am. If he knows, he'll feel guilty, and there's nothing he can do. He *has* to do what he does to me. So—'' Vanyel shrugged. ''The strain doesn't show; it won't take long to put right. I'm as much to blame for the overload as Randi. I *could* say 'no'—but I never have the heart to.''

''Maybe you should choose somewhere to go besides Forst Reach. Or only stay there for a day or two, then go off visiting friends, or by yourself.''

''I don't want to go off somewhere alone, I'll just brood. And I haven't anyone to go *to;* k'Treva is too far away. You, at least, have had Andy for longer than I've known you.'' He sighed. ''I'm sorry, I'm whining again. I can't seem to help it, which might be a symptom of how on edge I am. *That* is the only thing that really worries me; I'm hair-triggered and dangerous, and I need some peace to get balanced again. All I can hope is that Mother and Father decide that I look as bad as you and Jays think, and leave me alone for a bit. Long enough to get some reserves back, anyway.''

It was the closest he'd come to admitting that he wasn't

really certain how much—or how little—reserves he still had, and he quelled the rest of what he almost said.

"You don't look good, even *they* should see that, *ke'chara.*" She toyed with a bit of his hair, and worried at her lower lip with her teeth. "You know, *I* haven't been back in—ye gods, not since I checked you all for Mage-Gift! *My* Familial Visitation is more than overdue."

"But—you're a Guardian—" Hope rose in him. If only Savil would be there, he'd have *one* kindred soul in the lions' den! He had no doubt she was more than up to the trip; he could feel *her* strength even as he leaned on it.

"Won't take me but a day to set my focus in the Web and then I can Guard from Forst Reach as easily as from here. It's only a matter of Sensing threat and sending the alert, you know. It's not as if I actually had to *fight* anything. And it's only because I need to keep that little corner of my mind tuned to the Web waking and sleeping that I don't have a protege—ten years ago I could have done what Jays is doing; Guard *and* teach three." She nodded. "This is *no* bad notion. Provided you don't mind having me there—"

"Mind?" He seized her hand and kissed it.

"Then expect me in about—oh, two weeks after you arrive. It'll take Kellan a little longer to make the trip than you youngsters."

"Savil, if you only knew how grateful I am—"

"Pish. I'm selfish, is what I am." A smile started to twitch at the corners of her mouth. "We can guard *each other's* backs this way. I'm counting on you to save me from Withen as much as you are counting on me to save you."

He rose and kissed her forehead. "I don't care what you say, it's the most generous, *unselfish* thing anyone's done for me in a year. And you just may save this visit from becoming the legend of how Herald Vanyel went berserk and left his entire family tied to trees with rags stuffed in their mouths! About what time is it? I'm all turned round about from being so far south."

She checked the angle of the sun coming in her window. "I'd guess just after Court."

"Good; I have to catch Randale and Shavri and say

good-bye. *He* promised if I didn't come when he was being 'official' he wouldn't find something for me to do.''

"Then off with you, *ke'chara,* and I'll see you at Forst Reach—and thank you for thinking of me,'' she finished, touching the stone on the table beside her.

"Because you think of me, love.'' He kissed her cheek, then her forehead again, and left her suite.

He stopped first at his room to change back into a set of Tran's Whites and put on the soft, low boots Heralds wore indoors; not as comfortable as going barefoot, but they beat the riding boots hands down. And if he didn't change, he *might* not be let into the King's quarters— every time he came back, it seemed fewer folk knew his face.

That accomplished, and now every inch his usual neat self, he headed down to the oldest part of the Palace, the extensive set of rooms shared by King Randale; his life-bonded and King's Own, Shavri; and their daughter.

He had scarcely crossed the threshold of the sparsely furnished audience chamber—his unfamiliar face giving a moment's apprehension to the two Guards posted at the door—when a six-year-old, curly-headed, miniature whirlwind burst through the farther door and flung herself across the audience chamber at him, evidently blithely certain he would catch her before she fell.

Which he did, and swung her around, up and over his head while she squealed with excitement and delight. "Uncle Van!'' she crowed at the top of her lungs. "UncleVanUncleVanUncleVan!''

He started to put her down, but she demanded a hug and a kiss with the same infectious charm her ''father'' Randale could display whenever he chose. Vanyel hoisted her into a comfortable carrying position and complied without an argument, thinking as he did so that it was a good thing that she was still so tiny.

"Now how did you know I was coming?'' he asked her, as her bright brown eyes looked solemnly down into his.

"Felt you,'' she said, giving him another hug. "Felt you in my head, all blue-glowy and swirly.''

He nearly dropped her in shock. That was surely the most vivid—and accurate—description of his aura he'd ever heard out of anyone but another high-ranking Herald-Mage.

"Or a Healer," said Shavri, coming up beside him as he gaped at the child, and Jisa giggled at the face he was making. "Healers see you that way, too, Van. And no, I wasn't eavesdropping on your thoughts—they were plain enough from that poleaxed look on your face." There was strain and fear under Shavri's light tone, as if she walked a narrow bridge above a bottomless chasm. "Besides, you aren't the only one she's 'felt in her head' during the last three months. Let's start this greeting over; hello, Van, have you a hug for me?"

"Always." He was already bracing himself for trouble; with *that* look on her face there was something seriously wrong. And that meant *he'd* have to be the strong one.

He included Shavri in his arms, while Jisa flung her arms around both their necks and cuddled. "Jisa sweet, can I put you down long enough for presents?"

"Presents?" Jisa was no different from any other six-year-old when *that* word came up. She squirmed a little, and he set her down, then extracted the little Companion-figure from his pouch and handed it to her. She shrieked with delight, and ran outside to show it to the two Guards. Shavri watched her go, her gypsy-dark eyes darker with unconcealed love—and something else. Something secret and profoundly unhappy. His first reaction was to want to hold her, protect her, make that unhappiness go away.

Randi's lifebonded—

"That's quite a little impling you're raising, Shavri," he said, instead. "Incredibly unspoiled, given that I'd lay odds she's the pet of the Circle."

"You say that every time you see her, beast," she replied, flashing an uncertain smile, startlingly bright in her sober, dark face.

"Well, it's true." Vanyel Looked quickly around, ascertained that they were going to be alone for a few moments, and asked quickly, "How is he?"

The smile vanished, and the fear and unhappiness were

plain for anyone who knew her to read. *:Oh, gods—Van, he's sick, I can't make it go away, and I think he's dying. And I don't know why.:*

:What?: He gathered his scant resources to support her—and to hide the fact that *her* fear was making *him* tremble inside.

"He's well enough," she said lightly, but Mindspoke him with a vastly different tone. *:There's something wrong; it isn't affecting him much at the moment other than steady weakness and a dizzy spell now and again— but—it keeps getting worse with each spell. And—oh, Van—I'm so afraid—:*

He tightened his arm around her shoulders. *:Easy, flowerlet—:* "Then it sounds like there's no problem with my taking this leave." *:How long has this been going on?:*

Her unshed tears knotted both their throats. *:Eight months. It's something I can't Heal, the gods know I've tried!:*

He felt chill creep over him. *:Forgive me, Shavri, but I have to ask this. Given worst case—if it is something life-threatening, and it keeps getting worse, how long do you think he has?:*

:If he keeps weakening at the same rate? Fifteen years—maybe less, certainly not more. Gods, Van, he won't even see fifty*—he won't even see his grandchildren! Elspeth was seventy-six when she was Called!:*

There was another thought, unspoken—but Vanyel felt it, since it touched so nearly on his own private loneliness.

I'll have to go on alone—

He held her close to his chest, with her face pressed into his shoulder as she struggled not to cry, and clamped down a tight shield to prevent any stray thought from reaching her and frightening her. *Savil supported you. You support Shavri the same way,* he told himself, below the threshold of her ability to Mindhear. *Let her know she won't be alone. Gods, gods, they're both so young, not even twenty-five . . . and so sheltered all their lives. Oh, Shavri—your pain hurts me—*

"Easy, love," he murmured into her hair. :*Does he know?*:

:*No. Not yet. Healer's Collegium does; they're working on it. We don't want him to know until it's certain. Now you know why I won't marry him. Van, I couldn't, I'm not strong enough, I can't rule! Not alone! And when he dies—and I won't have Jisa forced onto the throne too young, either.*: Her mind-voice strengthened with stubbornness. :*So long as we're unwedded, it can't be forced on me nor on Jisa until all the collateral lines are exhausted. I—*:

He felt the surge of terror and grief, and tried to project strength to her, not allowing her to see how fragile that strength was at the moment. With grim certainty he knew that she would not be able to cope if the worst came—unless someone she trusted was there to help. And the only one she trusted to that extent—the only one Randi trusted—was him. *Gods. They really think I can do anything—and I'm no more ready for this than she is.*

He pushed the thought away, concentrated on trying to ease some of that fear. :*Gently, sweet. Don't borrow trouble. Don't assume anything. You may cure him yet; this may turn out to be something ridiculous—and you both may get run over by a beer-wagon tomorrow!*:

That startled a weak chuckle out of her, and she blinked up at him through tears she was doing her best not to release.

:*Worry about tomorrow when it comes; enjoy* now. *Now, what's all this with Jisa "feeling people in her head?"*:

Footsteps made both of them look up. "Are you seducing my lady, Herald Vanyel?" asked Randale, King of Valdemar, holding out his arms to embrace both of them.

"I'd *rather* seduce you, you charmer," Vanyel replied coyly, batting his eyelashes at the King. But there was an edge of bitterness there in his banter, and despite his best intentions it must have crept into his voice. He saw a hint of startlement, then of worry, creep into both their expressions.

Lighten up, dammit, he told himself angrily. *They've got their own problems—they* don't *need yours.*

He grinned and winked, and both of them relaxed again.

Randale laughed heartily, and hugged him hard, taking Shavri away from Vanyel as he did so. And Vanyel felt a strange twinge; another flash of uneasiness.

Gods, what's wrong with me?

He didn't stop to think about it. The hug wasn't as hard as it had been a year ago—and there was a transparency about Randale that made Vanyel's heart lurch. Randale had grown a neat brown beard—was it to hide the fact that his cheeks were a little hollower? Was that tidy-to-a-fault brown hair a little lackluster? There *were* shadows under his dark eyes; were they there from lack of sleep, or some more sinister reason? Within a few breaths Vanyel had noted a dozen small signs of ''something wrong''—all of them little things, things that someone who saw him day-in, day-out might not have noticed. But *Vanyel* had been away for a year, and the things he saw shook him. *Gods, gods—my King, my friend—Shavri is right. You're ill, at the very least—*

Randale was *not* a Herald-Mage; his Gift was FarSight, and his Mindspeech was not as sure a thing as Vanyel's and Shavri's. For once Vanyel was grateful for that lack. He changed the subject before Randale could note his unease.

''It seems your little shadow is developing precocious Gifts,'' he said. ''At least she said she 'felt me coming in her mind.' '' Jisa ran back in, and attached herself to Vanyel's leg. ''Didn't you, imp?'' He looked down at her, surprised by the surge of love he felt for the child.

She nodded, very well pleased with herself.

''We thought about taking her to Savil, but she's been so busy,'' Randale replied, shrugging. ''I don't suppose *you'd* test her, would you? That's a major spell for anyone else but you and Savil.''

''*Now* I see the reason for all the concern that I stop by!'' Vanyel teased. ''*Not* that you've missed me!''

''*Van—*'' Shavri said indignantly. ''I never—''

Randale chortled, and she hit his shoulder. "You can just *stop* that, you beast."

Jisa giggled, and Vanyel looked down at her. "Hold still for a minute, impling," he said. "I'm about to make your head feel funny, like Mama did when you had the measles."

"All right," Jisa said calmly, and Vanyel had the sudden unsettling feeling that she would permit her totally-trusted "Uncle Van" to chop off her hand if he wanted to.

He rested his palm on the top of her brown curls, and focused *out* and *down*—

—and came out again, blinking. "Well."

"Well, *what?*" Shavri and Randale demanded in the same breath.

"She won't be a Herald-Mage, not unless she gets blasted open the way I did—which I do *not* recommend," he added lightly, trying to catch his breath. Even that little magic had been more of a strain than he had thought it would. "But she's carrying the potential in a double dose; she'll certainly pass it to her children. She *will be* a MindHealer; she *is* an active Empath, and her Mind-speech center is opening early, too. With that combination, Randale, she'll very likely be King's Own after Shavri."

Gods, she is so *like me. Right down to the Mage-potential. Jisa, sweetling, I swear I will do anything to keep you safe—*

Shavri trembled, and Randale's arm tightened around her shoulder. "Is she likely to be Chosen anytime soon?"

Vanyel did not answer immediately. *:'Fandes?:* he called, softly. *:Are you awake?:*

:And following the conversation. Yes, provided it's needful for her to get the training and she stays as sweet as she is. I'd say by age ten. Maybe sooner, two years from now.:

"Yfandes guesses that if she needs the training, between age eight and ten. Remember, for the presumptive King's Own, that won't be a bonded Choosing—she won't bond until—until she gets the office. Then she'll bond with Taver." Vanyel ignored both Shavri's frightened face and Randale's elation. "So, given that—there's a little something she and I ought to do."

He focused himself *down* again, pulling on Yfandes' strength to assist his own, and thanking the gods he could do so, because Jisa should not remain as open as she was now. This time he did not close his eyes, but locked them with the child's, and showed her without words—for she did not yet have sufficient Mindspeech to use words— how to shield herself from unwanted thoughts and emotions, and unshield again at will. He was, he feared, the only person who *could* have taught her at this stage; Empathy not being a normal Heraldic Gift, and most Healers not using it in the way a Herald-Mage could.

He showed her how to find her center—she knew with an instant of studying *him* how to ground. The fundamentals it had taken him so long and so painfully to learn came to her with the ease of breathing, perhaps because learning *was* as easy as breathing at her age, and perhaps because *his* learning had come at the cost of so much loss and pain that had nothing to do with his Gifts.

"—there. That should hold her until she's got enough to be taught formally. Teach her yourself, Shavri. You won't find anyone in the Heralds with Empathy as strong as hers. When she's got it at full power, she'll be able to control a mob in full cry."

Shavri had herself back under control again, and the smile she gave Vanyel was genuine. "Thank you, love."

He shrugged. "No thanks needed. Before I forget it— I brought you two some 'pretties' also."

Shavri took the pendant with an exclamation of genuine delight as he handed the matching cloak-brooch to Randale. "Van, you shouldn't have—" she began.

"Of course I should have," he said. "Who else have I got to bring things to?" It came out bleaker than he intended.

"Oh, Van—" Her eyes softened, and Randale cleared his throat and blinked. They reached out in the same moment and each took one of his hands. He closed his eyes, and for an instant allowed himself to feel a part of their closeness.

But it was *their* closeness, not his.

And I have no right.

"Mama, I have lessons," said a small voice, still at Vanyel's knee.

"Bright Havens, so you do!" Shavri exclaimed. "Van—"

"Go," he said, wrinkling his nose at her. "I'll be back in a few weeks, and maybe this tyrant of a King will let me stick around for a while this time."

She shooed Jisa out and followed her with the light step of a young girl. Randale's gaze followed both of them.

"You sire wonderful children, Van," he said softly.

"*You* raise better ones," Vanyel replied, uneasily. "*You* are Jisa's papa, don't you ever forget it. I was nothing more than the convenient means to a rather attractive little end."

The King relaxed visibly. "I keep thinking you're going to want her back—especially now that she's showing Gifts. She's more like you than you know."

Vanyel laughed. "Whatever would I *do* with her? Great good gods, what kind of a parent would *I* make? I can't even train the palace cats to stay off my pillow! No, Randi, she's all yours, in everything that counts. *I* would rather be Uncle Van, who gets to spoil her."

Randale reached out without looking and snagged a chair with one hand. He swung it around and put it in front of Vanyel. "She'd make a good Queen."

"She'd make a very bad Queen," Vanyel replied, draping himself over it as Randale took another. "The things that make a *good* Monarch's Own are weakness in the Monarch."

"Like?"

"Empathy. She'd be vulnerable to everyone with a petition and the passion to back it. She'd be tempted to use projective Empathy on her Council to make them vote *her* way. MindHealers are *drawn* to the unbalanced; but a Monarch can't waste time dealing with every Herald in trauma she encounters." Vanyel shook his head. "No. Absolutely not. Jisa is going to be a lovely young woman and a good Monarch's Own; be satisfied with that."

Randale gave him a wry look. "You sound very sure of yourself."

"Shouldn't I be?" Vanyel folded his arms over the back of the chair and rested his chin on them. "Forgive me if I sound arrogant, but other than Savil, I *am* the expert in these things. Ask my aunt when I'm not around and I'll bet money she'll tell you the same thing."

Randale shrugged, and scratched the back of his head. "I guess you're right. I was hoping you'd back me, though—"

"Why?" Vanyel interrupted. "So you can have something else to pressure Shavri into marrying you?"

Randale winced at his bluntness, and protested weakly, "But that's—I mean—dammit, Van, I *need* her!"

Gods, so young . . . so uncertain of himself, of her. So afraid that without bonds *he won't hold her.* "You think she doesn't need you? Randi, she's your *lifebonded,* do you really *need* any further hold on her than that? She'd rather die than lose you!"

Randale studied the back of his hand. "It's just . . . I want something a little more—"

"Ordinary?" Vanyel finished wryly. "Randi, Heralds are *never* ordinary. If you wanted 'ordinary,' you should have become a blacksmith."

Randale shook his head.

Vanyel gritted his teeth and prepared to say to Randale what no one else could—or *would.* "Now you *listen* to me. You're making her miserable with the pressure you've been putting on her. She's doing exactly what she should; she's putting Valdemar and Valdemar's King ahead of her own wishes."

Mostly.

"She knows the situation we have just as well as you do, but *she's* willing to face it. Things went to pieces when your grandmother Elspeth died, and they've been getting worse since—steadily."

"I'm not *blind,* Van," Randale interrupted. "I—"

"Quiet, Randi. I'm making a speech, and I don't, often. I want you to *think.* There's a very real probability that you'll have to buy us peace on one of our Borders with an alliance marriage—*exactly* how your grandmother bought us peace with Iftel. And why do you think she never married Bard Kyran after your grandfather died, hmm? She knew her duty, and so should you. You *have* to stay free for that.''

Randale was flushing; Vanyel didn't need Empathy to know he was getting angry. "So what business is it of yours?" he burst out. "I thought you were a friend—"

"I am. But I'm a Herald first. And my first duty is to Valdemar, not to you." Vanyel sat straight up and let his face grow very cold; knowing what he was doing and hating himself for it. Randi *wanted* his friend, and at some levels, *needed* his friend. He was going to *get* Herald-Mage Vanyel Ashkevron. "You, Herald-King Randale, cannot permit your personal feelings to interfere with the well-being of this kingdom. You are as much Herald as I. If you cannot reconcile yourself to that— give up the Crown."

Randale slumped, defeated. No one knew better than he that there was no Heir or even Heir-presumptive yet. The Crown was his, like it or not. "I . . . I wish I . . . there's no one else, Van. No one old enough."

"Then you can't resign your Crown, can you." Vanyel made it a statement rather than a question.

"No. *Damn.* Van—you know I never wanted this—"

Memory.

Balmy spring breezes played over the lawn. Randi laughing at something, some joke he had just made— Shavri playing with the baby in a patch of sun. Bucolic, pastoral scene—

Shattered by the arrival on a lathered horse of a Queen's Messenger. In black.

Randi jumped to his feet, his face going white. The man handed Randale a sealed package wrapped in silk, but Randi didn't open it.

"Herald Randale—your grandmother the Queen sends me to tell you that your father—"

The package fell from Randale's fingers. The blue silk wrappings unwound from the contents.

The silver coronet of the Heir.

An accident. A stupid accident—a misstep on a slippery staircase in full view of everyone—and the Heir,

Herald-Mage Darvi, was dead of a broken neck. And Randale was Heir.

Vanyel's heart ached for him. And he dared not show it. Pity would be wrong at this moment, but he softened his voice and his expression.

"I *told* you Jisa would make a bad Queen. I meant every word. Shavri knows all this, too, you can bet on it. And I'm telling you you're tearing her in pieces, putting her between love for you, and what she knows is her duty." Randale looked at him as if he wanted to interrupt. "No, hear me out—you've sympathized often enough with me and my matchmaking mother. How in Havens do you think Shavri feels with you putting that same kind of pressure on her?"

"Not good," Randale admitted, after a long moment.

"Then stop it, before you put her under more pressure than she can take. Leave her alone. Let it lie for another ten years; if things haven't come to a conclusion one way or another, *then* bring it up. All right?"

"No," Randale said slowly. "It's not all right. But you're absolutely correct about there being no choice. Not for any of us."

Vanyel rose, and swung the chair he'd been slouched over out of the way. Randale did the same.

"Don't spoil what you have with what you only *think* you want, Randale," he said softly, taking his friend and King's arm. "This is experience talking; the one thing about the brief time *I* shared with my love that I have *never* regretted is that I never consciously did anything to make him unhappy. Had our time been longer, maybe I would have; I can't ever know. But at least I have no memories of quarrels or hard words to shadow the good memories."

Randale took his hand. "You're right; I'm wrong. I'll stop plaguing her."

"Good man."

Randi—oh, Randi— Close; Randale was coming too close. It was beginning to hurt—

Then Randale's servant entered behind him, the King's formal uniform draped over one arm, the royal circlet in the other hand, and a harried expression on his face.

Vanyel forced a laugh, and took the welcome opportunity to escape. "Now unless I haul myself out of here, I'm going to make your man there very unhappy."

"What?" Randale turned, startled. "Oh. Oh, hellfire. I *have* got that damned formal audience before dinner, don't I?"

"Yes, sire," the servant replied, as expressionless as a stone.

"Then I'd better get changed. Vanyel—"

Vanyel put his arm around the younger man's shoulders and gave him an affectionate embrace. "Just go do *your* duty, and make her happy. That's what counts. I'm off; I'll see you by Midwinter, certainly."

"Right. Van, be well." Randale looked at him—really *looked* at him, for the first time. He started to reach for Vanyel's arm with an expression of concern; Vanyel ducked his head to conceal the signs of weariness.

"I'm never ill. Go, go, go—before your man kills me with a look!"

Randale managed a grin, and followed the servant back into the private rooms of the suite. Vanyel spent a moment with his eyes closed in unvoiced prayer for him, then took himself back to his own room and his longed-for reunion with his bed.

Three

Morning. Vanyel woke slowly, surrounded by unfamiliar warmth and softness, and put bits of memory together as they drifted within reach.

He vaguely remembered getting to his room, surrounded by fatigue that increasingly fogged everything; recalled noting a brief message from Tran, and getting partially undressed. He did not remember lying down at all; he didn't even remember sitting on the bed.

By the amount of light leaking around the bedcurtains it was probably midmorning, and what had wakened him was hunger.

His soft bed—*clean* sheets, a *real* featherbed, and those wonderful dark curtains to block out the light—felt so *good.* Good enough to ignore the demands of his stomach and give preference to the demands of his weary body. He'd had a fair amount of practice in shutting off inconvenient things like hunger and thirst; there'd been plenty of times lately when he'd had no other choice.

He almost did just exactly that, almost went back to sleep, but his conscience told him that if he didn't get up, he'd probably sleep for another day. And he couldn't afford that.

Clothing, clothing, good gods, what am I going to do about clothing?

There was no way his uniforms would be cleaned and mended, and he was going to need to *take* a few with him even if he didn't plan to wear them. And he had to have uniforms to travel in, anyway; technically a Herald traveling was on duty.

Wait a moment; wasn't there something in that note from Tran about uniforms?

He pushed off the blankets with a pang of regret, pulled the bed curtains aside, winced away from the daylight flooding his room, and sat on the edge of the bed, waiting for leftovers from half-recollected dreams to clear out of his brain. His shoulders hurt.

Have to do something about that muscle strain before I start favoring that arm . . . remember to put liniment on it, and do some of those exercises.

Birds chirped news at each other right outside his window. It had been a very long time since he'd paid any attention to birdcalls—except as signals of the presence or absence of danger.

The musical chatter was quite wonderful, precisely because it was so sanely ordinary. *Ordinary. Peaceful. Gods, I am so tempted just to fall back onto the mattress and to hell with starting for Forst Reach today.*

But a promise was a promise. And if he delayed going one day, it would be easy to rationalize another delay, and another, all of which would only lead to Randale's recruiting him. Which was what the trip was supposed to *prevent.*

He pulled himself up out of bed with the aid of the bedpost and reached for one of Tantras' uniforms. *Clean, Lord and Lady, clean and smelling of nothing worse than soap and fresh air.* Once he managed to get himself started, habit took over.

He reached with one hand for one of yesterday's leftover apples in their bowl on the table, and Tantras' note with the other.

Go ahead and take my stuff with you. I don't need these; they're spares that were made before I put on all that muscle across the shoulders. A bit tight on me, they should be just a little big on you. Tell me what you want done and get out of here; I don't mind taking care of some of your paperwork for you. I'll see that your new uniforms are ready by the time you get back; Supply told me there's no chance of salvaging your old ones. Tran.

More than a little *big,* Vanyel thought wryly, standing up and surveying himself in the rather expensive glass mirror (a present from Savil) on the back of the door. He'd had to tie the breeches with an improvised drawstring just so they'd stay up, and the tunic bagged untidily over his belt. He looked—except for the silver in his hair—rather like an adolescent given clothing "to grow into." *They'd have been all right a year ago, but—oh, well. Nobody's going to see me except the family. I certainly don't have anyone to impress!*

But Tran's volunteering gave him a notion about some other things he needed. He rummaged out the pen and paper he'd used yesterday; by now he reckoned those notes were well on the way to the Border and Forst Reach.

Another reason to hail out of here. If I don't arrive soon after the letter, they'll worry. His letters should beat him to the holding by a few days, at least.

He wrote swiftly, but neatly; "neat as a clerk," Tran was wont to tease. *Order me new cloaks, would you? And new boots. I need them badly; I'd be ashamed to stand duty the way they are now.*

And since you're being so kind as to keep track of this, ask Supply to work me up a set of spare uniforms to leave here, and have them keep a set here at all times. Next time there might not be anyone my size with extras for me to borrow! Thanks, Van.

He packed quickly, without having to think about what he was doing, now that he'd finally gotten his momentum. After the last four years, he could pack fatigue-drunk, pain-fogged, drugged to his eyebrows, or asleep—and he *had,* at one time or another.

He swung his cloak—it was more gray than white, and a little shabby, but there was nothing to be done about *that*—over his shoulder, picked up his packs, plucked his lute off the chair, and headed out. In the dark and echoing hall on his way to Companion's Field and the stable, he intercepted a page, gave the child the note for Tantras, and asked for some kind of breakfast to be brought to him while he saddled Yfandes.

She was already waiting calmly for him at the entrance to the tackshed. *:They've cleaned all my tack,:* she told him, *:but the saddle needs mending and the rest isn't what it should be. I wouldn't trust the chestband to take any strain at all, frankly.:*

:Swordcuts and burns aren't fixed with saddlesoap,: he

reminded her. :*We'll just have to—wait a moment—what about your formal gear? That's next thing to brand new. Gods know we've used it what—once? Twice?*:

Her ears went up—her sapphire eyes fixed on him—

And he had that curious and disorienting doubled image of her that he'd gotten sometimes in the past, the image of a dark, wise-eyed woman, weary, but smiling with newly-kindled anticipation, flickering in and out with the graceful white horse.

Gods, if I needed a sign of how dragged-out I am, that's it. Hallucinating again. Dreaming awake. Got to be because I never really think of her as a "horse" even when I'm riding her.

He blinked his eyes and forced himself to focus properly as she replied, as excited as a girl being told she could wear her holiday best—:*Chosen, could we use it? Please?*:

He chuckled. :*You like being dressed up and belled like a gypsy, don't you?*:

She tossed her head, and arched her neck. :*Don't you? I've heard you preening at yourself in the mirror of a morning, especially when there was someone to impress!*:

"You fight dirty," he said aloud; and went in search of her formal tack, grinning.

One of the kitchen wenches, a bright-eyed little brunette, barely adolescent, brought him hot bread and butter, cider, and more apples about the time he managed to find where Yfandes' formal panoply had been stored. The saddle was considerably lighter than the field saddle, and fancier; it was tooled and worked with silver and dyed a deep blue. The chest and rump bands had silver bells on them, as did the reins of what was essentially an elaborate hackamore. The reins were there more for *his* benefit than his Companion's, and more for show than either. There was light barding that went along with the outfit, but after regarding it wistfully for a moment, Yfandes agreed that the barding would be far more trouble than it was worth and Vanyel bundled it away.

He paused a moment and bit into the bread; it was

dripping with melted butter, and he closed his eyes at the unexpected pleasure the flavor gave him.

Oh, gods—fresh bread!

The taste was better than the manna that the priests said gods ate. "Bread" for the past year had meant rock-hard journey-bread at best, moldy crusts at worst, and anything in between—and it was *never* fresh, much less hot from the oven. There *had* been butter—sometimes—rancid in summer, as rock-hard as the journey-bread in winter.

It's the little things we miss the most—I swear it is! Ordinary things, things that spell "peace" and "prosperity." He thought briefly of the sword-comrades he'd left on the Border, and sent up a brief prayer. *Brightest gods, grant both, but especially peace. Soon, before more blood is shed.*

After that he alternated between bites of food and adjusting of harness. The kitchen wench lingered to watch him saddle Yfandes, draped over the open half-door of the stable, squinting into the sunlight. There was something between hero-worship and starry-eyed romance in her gaze; finally Vanyel couldn't stand it any longer and gently shooed her back to her duties.

He noted out of the corner of his eye—with more than a little alarm—that she was clutching the mug he'd drunk from to her budding bosom as though it had been transformed into a holy chalice.

:Looks like you've got another one, Chosen,: Yfandes commented sardonically as he fastened his packs behind her saddle.

:Thank you for that startling information. That's just what I needed to hear.:

:It's not my fault you have a face that breaks hearts.:

:But why—oh, never mind.: He gave the girth a last tug and swung up into the saddle. *:Let's get out of here before someone else decides she's fallen in love with me.:*

They got through the city as quickly as they could, and out onto the open road where it was possible to breathe without choking on the thick cloud of dust and other odors of the crowded city. It was a little strange to ride with the soft chime of the bells marking every pace Yfandes took; it made him nervous for the first few leagues, until he managed to convince his gut that they were in *friendly* territory, and in no danger of alerting enemy scouts with the sound. After that, the sound began to soothe him. Like muted, rhythmic windchimes—

I've always adored windchimes. And I never get to meditate to them anymore.

He slowly began to relax. Yfandes was in no great hurry, although her "traveling" pace would have run a real horse into the ground after half a day. This had been a gentle summer, turning into a warm and even gentler fall, just enough frost to ensure that the harvests ripened, not enough yet to turn the leaves. Once out of Haven, Exile's Road wound lazily through rustling, golden grain-fields, and fields of sweetly ripening hay. The morning air was slightly cool, but the sun was warm enough that Vanyel soon rolled his cloak and bundled it behind his saddle.

It was very hard to stay awake, in fact. His muscles relaxed into the familiar configurations of riding.

Memory flicker—the k'Treva Vale. Savil, schooling him on Yfandes. *"You think you're a rider now, lad. When I'm done with you, you'll be able to do* anything *ahorse that you can do on the ground."*

Himself, slyly. "Anything?"

She threw a saddlebag at him.

From here to the Border the land was the next thing to flat; long, rolling hills covered with cultivated fields, interrupted by fragrant oak groves that occasionally amounted to small forests.

:You really could *sleep, you know,:* Yfandes chided him. *:I'm not going to let you fall off. It won't be the first time you've taken a nap that way.:*

"I'm hardly going to be company for you like that."

She shook her head, and the bells on her halter laughed for her. *:Your presence is company enough, Chosen. I ran lone for ten years before you bonded to me. Just having you with me, whole and healthy, is pleasure; you needn't think I need entertaining when we aren't working.:*

With a brief flash of pain and pleasure he remembered

how *he* had never needed anything but Tylendel's presence either. . . .

:Yes,: she agreed, following the thought. *:Exactly.:*

So he hooked his leg around the saddle pommel, crossed his arms and tucked the ends of his fingers into his belt, then sagged into a comfortable slouch; chin on chest. It didn't take long.

He came awake all at once, his hand reaching automatically for the sword he wasn't wearing. There was an instant of panic before he remembered where he was going, and why he was going there.

"Why did you stop?" he asked Yfandes, who had come to an unmoving halt—which was what had waked him—in the middle of the completely deserted road. There was nothing but open meadow on either side of him, dotted with sheep, though there was no sign of the shepherd. Crows cawed overhead, and the sheep bleated in their pastures; otherwise silence prevailed. The sun was low enough ahead of them to force him to squint. *It must be late afternoon, early evening.*

:There's an inn just beyond the next curve, sleepy one,: Yfandes said, a hint of amusement tingeing her thought. *:It's later than lunch and earlier than dinner, but I'm tired and I'd really like to stop before I go any farther.:*

"Havens, love, you should have—"

:No, I shouldn't have. This is the first time you've really relaxed in I don't know how long. Have you thought about the way we resonate?:

He saw instantly what she meant. "So—you were relaxing with me."

:In very deed, and reveling in it. First journey I've been able to enjoy in a while. But I would like to stop now.:

"Then so would I." He unwrapped his leg from the pommel and stretched it; she waited until his foot was back in the stirrup, then resumed her easy amble, not quite a walk, not quite a canter. "Is this a temporary halt, or are we stopping for the night?"

:The night?: she asked, wistfully. There was a hint of something more there than she was sending.

"You're not telling me everything," he accused. "Why *this* inn?"

:Well—you won't be the only Herald there. Herald-Courier Sofya is there—:

"Chosen by?" He had a shrewd hunch where this was leading.

She curved her neck coquettishly, and looked up and sideways at him out of one huge blue eye. *:Gavis.:*

He shook his head at her. "Ah, yes—the one that has been setting all the courier-records lately. Why this penchant for over-muscled courier-types, all legs and no brains—"

:He is not *over-muscled,:* she replied indignantly, breaking into a teeth-rattling trot to punish him.

"But brainless?" he taunted, feeling unusually mischievous.

:He just doesn't speak up unless he has something to say. Unlike certain Herald-Mages I know.: She kicked once, jarring every vertebra in his spine, before settling, all four feet braced in the dust of the road, and plainly going nowhere.

He reached forward before she could stop him, and tweaked her ear. "Well, since you want to arrange a little assignation, don't you think you'd better get the cooperation of *your* Chosen?"

:I can't imagine why,: she replied.

"We *could* move out of the center of the road, and I *could* groom you so that you looked your usual lovely self when we rode into that inn yard, instead of being all covered with road dust. I *could* even braid your tail up with some of the blue and silver cord that was with the barding. *If* I felt like it."

:I—Vanyel—I—: she floundered.

"And I *do* feel like it, you ridiculously vain creature," he said, leaning down and putting both arms around her neck, resting his cheek on her crest. "And to think that they call *me* a peacock! Has it been so long since I teased you that you've forgotten what it sounds like?"

:Oh, Vanyel—it has *been a long time.:*

"Then we'll have to remedy that." He dismounted, still a bit stiff from his long doze, and opened the pack

with the currycomb in it. Something else occurred to him
as he wormed his hand down inside the pack. "Just—do
me a very big favor, sweetling—"

:*Hmm?:* She turned her head and blinked back at him.

He fished out the comb and the cords. "Please, *please*
remember to shield me out of your trysting, all right?
You forgot to, the last time. Here, let's get out of the
road." He stifled a sigh, as they moved under the shade
of tree beside the roadway. "I don't grudge you any pleasure at all, but it's been a very long time since I did any
number of things—and teasing you is only one of them."

Yfandes twitched, the closest to blushing a Companion
could come.

Vanyel allowed no hand to tend Yfandes but his own,
no more than he would have permitted a stranger to see
to the comfort of his sister, the cloistered priestess.
'Fandes frequently protested this wasn't necessary, but
this afternoon she wasn't complaining. Especially not
when young Gavis pranced up to the fence of the inn's
open wagon-field with a proud curve to his neck and a
certain light of anticipation in his eye. Vanyel kept his
amused thoughts to himself as Yfandes flirted coyly with
the handsome Companion, and wished her nothing more
risque than a "pleasant evening" when he opened the
gate into the meadow for her.

She gave him a long look over her shoulder. :*Vanyel,
you aren't made of stone. I wish you would find a—com-
rade. You would be much happier.*:

He winced away from the idea. :*I've been over this
with Savil. And you. Until I can* stop *trying to replace
'Lendel, I'm not going to cheat myself* and *my would-be
partner.*:

:*I don't see that. If you're friends, it wouldn't be cheating . . . never mind.*:

:*Go, and enjoy yourself.*:

:*Oh, I think I can manage that,*: she said with deliberate innocence, gave him a slow wink, then frisked off
with Gavis in close attendance.

The tack he *did* entrust to the stableboy, though the
lad's wide-eyed awe in his presence left him feeling just

a bit uneasy. "Awe" was not something he wanted aimed in his direction. It felt too close to "fear."

He stepped into the open door of the inn's common room with his packs over one shoulder, and stood blinking in the sawdust-scented gloom, waiting for his eyes to adjust. The lean and nervous innkeeper was at his elbow in a breath, long before Vanyel could see anything other than shadows, more shadows, and a dim white form in one corner that was probably Herald Sofya. It seemed as if he and the other Herald were the only guests this early in the afternoon, but this *was* harvest-season. The locals were undoubtedly making the maximum use of every moment of daylight.

"Milord Herald, an honor, a pleasure. How may this humble inn serve you, milord?"

"Please—" Vanyel flushed at his effusiveness. "Just dinner, a room if you've one to spare, use of your bathhouse, food for my Companion—I took the liberty of turning her loose with Companion Gavis." Now his eyes had adjusted enough that he could see what he was doing; he fumbled in his belt-pouch and pressed coins into the innkeeper's hand. "Here; I'm on leave, not on duty. This should cover everything." Actually it was too much, and he knew it—but what else did he have to spend it on? The man gaped at the money, and began babbling about the room: "Royalty slept there, indeed they did, King Randale himself before his coronation—" Vanyel bore with it as patiently as he could, and when the man finally wound down, thanked him in a diffident voice and entrusted everything but the lute to the hands of one of the servants to be carried away to the rented room.

Now he could make out Herald Sofya in the corner; a dark, pretty woman, quite young, *quite* lean, and not anyone he recognized. She was paying studious, courteous attention to her jack of ale; Vanyel drifted over to her table when the innkeeper finally fled to the kitchen vowing to bring forth a dinner instantly, which—from the description—would have satisfied both the worst gourmand and the fussiest gourmet in the Kingdom.

"Herald Sofya?" he said quietly, and she looked at him in startlement. He surmised the cause, and smiled.

In all probability her Companion had been so taken up with Yfandes that he'd neglected to tell *his* Chosen Vanyel's identity. Or else she wasn't much of a Mindspeaker, which meant Gavis wouldn't be able to give her more than images. She had probably assumed the same was true for him. "Your Gavis Mindspoke my Yfandes on the road, and she told me both your names before we arrived. Might I join you?"

"Certainly," she replied, after swallowing quickly.

He sat on the side of the table opposite her, and saw the very faint frown as she took in the state of his Whites. "I apologize for my appearance." He smiled, feeling a little shy. "I know it won't do much for the Heraldic reputation. But I only *just* got leave, and I didn't want to wait for replacement uniforms. I was afraid that if I did, they'd find some reason to cancel my leave!"

Sofya laughed heartily, showing a fine set of strong, white teeth. "I know what you mean!" she replied. "It seems like all we've done is wear out saddle-leather for the past three months. There're four of us on this route, and the farmers are beginning to count on us like a calendar; one every three days, out to the Border and back."

"To Captain Lissa Ashkevron?"

"The same. And let us hope the Linean Border doesn't heat up the way the Karsite Border did."

Vanyel closed his eyes, as a chill crawled up his backbone and shivered itself along all of his limbs. "Gods spare us *that*," he said, finally.

When he opened his eyes again, she was staring at him very oddly, but he was saved from having to say anything by the appearance of the innkeeper with his dinner.

Vanyel started in on the smoked-pork pie with an appetite he didn't realize he'd had until the savory aroma of the gravy hit him. Sofya leaned back against the wall and continued to nurse her drink, giving him an odd and unreadable glance from time to time.

He'd been too numb from the long, grueling ride to appreciate his meal yesterday. He'd stowed it away without tasting it, as if it had been the iron rations or makedo of the combat zone. But this morning—and now—the home fare seemed finer than anything likely to be set before Randale.

"I hope you don't mind my staring," Sofya said at last, as he literally cleaned the plate of the last drop of gravy, "but you're going after that pie as if you hadn't seen food in a week, and you're rather starved-looking, and that seems very odd in a Herald—unless you've been standing duty somewhere extraordinary."

He noticed then the "blank" spot in the back of his mind that meant 'Fandes was keeping her promise and shielding him out. He grinned a little to himself; that probably meant that Gavis was doing the same, so Sofya's curiosity about him must be eating her alive.

"I've seen nearly no food for a week," he replied quietly, and paused for a moment when the serving girl took the plate away and replenished his mug of cider. "I don't know if you'd call my duty extraordinary, but it was harder than I expected. I've been on the Karsite Border for the last year. Meals weren't exactly regular, and the food was pretty awful. There were times I shared 'Fandes' oats because I couldn't even attempt eating what they gave me; half-rotten meat and moldy bread aren't precisely to my taste. All too often there wasn't much to go around. And, to tell you the truth, sometimes I just forgot to eat. You know how it is, things start happening, and the next thing you know, it's two days later. That's why—" he gestured at his too-large uniform, and grinned wryly. "The situation was harder on clothing than on stomachs."

Her sable eyes widened, and softened. "You were on the Karsite duty? I don't blame you for running off," she replied, with a hint of a chuckle. "I think I would, too, Herald—you never did give me your name."

"Vanyel," he said. "Vanyel Ashkevron. Lissa's brother. I know, we don't look at all alike—"

But her reaction was not at all what he had expected. Her eyes widened even farther, and she sat straight up. "Herald-Mage *Vanyel?*" she exclaimed, loud enough that the farmers and traders who'd begun trickling in while Vanyel was eating stopped talking and turned to look with their mouths dropping open. "You're *Vanyel?*" Her voice carried embarrassingly well, and rose with every word. "Vanyel Demonsbane? The Shadow Stalker? The Hero of—"

"Please—" Vanyel cut her off, pleadingly. "Please, it—yes, I'm Vanyel. But—honestly, it wasn't like you think." He groped for the words that would make the near-worship he saw on her face go back to ordinary friendliness. "It wasn't like that, it really wasn't—just— things had to get done, and I was the only one to do them, so I did. I'm not a hero, or—I'm just—I'm just— another Herald," he finished lamely.

He looked around the common room, and to his dismay saw the same worship in the expressions of the farmfolk around him. And something more.

Fear.

An echo of that fear was in Sofya's eyes as well, before she looked down at her ale.

He closed his eyes, settling his face into a calm and expressionless mask, that belied the ache that their fear called up in him. He'd wanted—acceptance, only that.

Tran, Tran, you were right, I was wrong. "Be careful what you ask for, you may get it." Gods, I asked for signs that Tran was right. And now I have them. Don't I?

He opened his eyes again, but the reverence and adulation hadn't vanished. There was a palpably clear space around him where the "common folk" had moved a little away, as if afraid to intrude too closely on him.

Even Sofya.

And the room had taken on the silence of a chapel.

I'm about to ruin their evening as well as mine. Unfair, unfair—there must be something I can do to salvage this situation, at least for them.

"You know," he said, with forced lightness, "if there was one thing I missed more than anything, it was a chance for a little music—"

He reached blindly down beside him for the lute he'd left leaning against the wall, stripped the case off it and tuned it with frantic speed. "—and I hate to sing alone. I'll bet you all know 'The Crafty Maid,' don't you?"

Without waiting for an answer, he launched into the

song. He sang alone on the first verse—but gradually other voices joined his on the chorus; Sofya first, with a kind of too-hearty determination, then a burly peddler, then three stout farmers. The local folk sang timidly to begin with, but the song was an old and lively one, and the chorus was infectious. By his third song the whole room was echoing, and they were no longer paying much more attention to him than they would have to a common minstrel.

Except between songs.

And except for Sofya, who worshiped him with eyes that sent a lump of cold to live in the bottom of his throat. She waited on him herself, as if he was some kind of angel, to be adored, but not touched.

He slipped out of the room early, when she was getting something; another musician had joined the crowd, a local, and he used the lad's talent as a screen to get out during a particularly rowdy song. He thought he'd gotten away without anyone noticing, but the innkeeper intercepted him in the hallway.

"Milord—Vanyel—" The tallow candles lighting the hall smoked and flickered and made the shadows move like the Shadows he'd once hunted. The memory knotted his stomach. He concentrated on the innkeeper, but the man gulped and would not meet his eyes. A breath of cooked onions drifted up the hall from the common room. "Milord, if I'd known who it was I was serving, I'd have made you special fare, and I'd not have accepted your coin."

"Please," Vanyel interrupted, trying to conceal his hurt. The innkeeper jumped back a pace. "Please," he said; softly, this time. "I told you, I'm not on duty, I'm on leave. I'm just another traveler. You fed me the best meal I've had in months, truly you did. You've earned every copper I paid you, and honestly."

"But milord Vanyel, it was nothing, it was common plowman's pie—surely you'd have preferred wine to cider; venison or a stuffed pheasant—and you paid me far too much—"

Vanyel felt a headache coming on. "Actually, no, innkeeper. The truth is I've been on iron-rations for so long anything rich would likely have made me ill. And venison—if I *never* have to see another half-raw deer—Your good, solid fare was feast enough for me. I'll tell you what—" He decided on the lie quickly. "I've been too long within walls. I have a fancy for trees and sky tomorrow; if you'll have your *excellent* cook make me up a packet for breakfast and lunch, I'll consider us more than even. Will that serve your honor, good sir?"

The innkeeper stared, chewing his mustache ends nervously, as if he thought Vanyel might be testing him for some reason, and then nodded agreement.

"Now I—I'm just a little more tired than I thought. If I could use the bathhouse, and get some sleep, do you think?"

To the man's credit, he supplied Vanyel with soap and towels and left him alone. In the steamy quiet of the bathhouse Vanyel managed to relax again. But the cheer of this morning was gone.

He sought release in sleep, finally, in what must have been the finest room in the inn—a huge bed wide enough for an entire family, two featherbeds and a down comforter, and sheets so fresh they almost crackled, all of it scented with orris and lavender. Far below he could still hear the laughter and singing as he climbed into the enormous bed. He blew out the candle then, feeling as lonely as he had ever been in his life, and prayed that sleep would come quickly.

For once his prayers were answered.

"I wish I dared Gate," he mused aloud, carefully examining, then peeling a hard-boiled egg. Yfandes had not said anything about his early-morning departure from the inn, or the fact that he had not waited for breakfast. It was chilly enough that he needed his cloak, and there was a delicate furring of frost on some of the tall weeds beside the roadway. "Gating would shorten this trip considerably."

:*You try and I'll kick you from here to Haven,*: Yfandes replied sharply, the first time she'd spoken to him this morning. :*That is absolutely the stupidest thing you've said in months!*:

He bit into the egg and looked at her backward-pointing ears with interest. "Havens, ladylove—didn't your tryst go well?"

:My "tryst" went just fine, thank you,: she replied, her mind-voice softening. *:I just get sick every time I think about what happened the last time.:*

"Oh, 'Fandes, it wasn't that bad."

:Not that bad? When you were unconscious before you crossed the threshold? And hurting so badly I nearly screamed?:

"All right, it was bad," he admitted, popping the rest of the egg into his mouth and reaching into the "breakfast packet." "And I'm not stupid enough to Gate without *urgent* need." He studied a roll, weighing it in his hand. It seemed *awfully* heavy. As good as the food had been so far, it didn't seem likely that it was underbaked, but he was *not* in the mood to choke down raw dough. He nibbled it dubiously, then bit into it with a great deal more enthusiasm when it proved to have sausage baked into the middle of it. "It would just be very convenient to not have to stop at inns."

:Don't tell them your real name,: she interrupted.

"What?"

:If reactions like last night bother you, you don't have to tell them your real name. Tell them you're Tantras. Tran won't mind.:

" 'Fandes, that's not the point—never mind." He finished the last of his breakfast and dusted his hands off. A skein of geese flew overhead, honking. The farmers already out in the fields beside the road, scything down the grain and making it into sheaves, paused a moment and pointed at the "v" of birds. "Tran was right, and I'm going to have to get used to it, I guess. And I can't do that hiding behind someone else's name." He managed a wan smile. "It could be worse. They could be treating me like a leper because I'm *shay'a'chern,* instead of treating me like a godlet because I'm Herald-Mage Vanyel Demonsbane." He grimaced. "Gods, that sounds pretentious."

She slowed her pace a trifle. *:It isn't that important—is it?:*

"It's that important. I'm a very fallible mortal, not an Avatar. Magic is a force—a force I control, no more wonderful than a Mindspeaker's ability, or a Healer's. But *they* don't see it that way. To them it's something beyond anything they understand, and they're not sure it *can* be controlled." He sighed. "Or worse, they think magic can solve every problem."

:You thought that, once.:

"I know I did. When I was younger. Magic seemed to offer solutions to everything when I was nineteen." He shook his head, and stared out at the horizon. "For a while—for a little while—I thought I held the world. Even Jays respected me, came to be a friend. But magic couldn't force my father to tell me I'd done well in his eyes—or rather, it *could* force him, when I *wanted* the words to come freely from him. It couldn't make being *shay'a'chern* any easier. It couldn't bring back my Tylendel. It was just power. It's dividing me from ordinary people. Worse than that—it seems to be doing the same between me and other Heralds—and 'Fandes, *that* scares the hell out of me."

:You won't be getting any of the godlet treatment from your kin, I can promise you that.:

"I suppose not."

It was getting warmer by the moment. He bundled his cloak, and wondered if he should get out his hat. *Gods! Change the subject—before you brood yourself into depression again.* "Do *you* think Father will be able to keep Mother off my back?"

:Not to put too fine a point upon it, no.:

"I didn't think so." His shoulders were beginning to hurt again. He clasped his arms behind him and arched his back, looking up at the blue, cloudless sky. "Which means she'll keep trying to cure me by throwing every female above the age of consent within *leagues* at me. I could almost feel sorrier for the girls than I do for myself."

:You ought to, Van.:

He looked down at Yfandes' ears in surprise.

:Did it ever occur to you that you could well have broken a fair number of susceptible young hearts?:

He raised an eyebrow, skeptically. "Aren't you exaggerating?"

:Think! What about the way you charmed that poor little kitchen girl back at the Palace?:

He winced a little, recalling the romance in her eyes, but then irritation set in. " 'Fandes, I've never done anything other than be polite to any of them."

She snorted. *:Exactly. Think about it. You're polite to them. Gallant. Occasionally even attentive. Think about the difference in your station and that kitchen maid's. What in Havens do you think she was expecting when you were polite to her? What does any young man of rank want when he notices a servant or a farmer's daughter?:*

Now he was something more than irritated. "I don't *suppose* it's occurred to you that it *might* just be the simple fact that I'm a Herald, a safe sort of romance object? Great good gods, 'Fandes, I doubt she had any notion of my rank!"

:Well what about all those young women your mother parades before you—telling them they're prospective brides? What do they think that gallantry is?:

"I would imagine that *Mother* tells them plenty," he replied with heat, beginning to flush, and *very* glad there was no one about to overhear this conversation.

:Well, you imagine wrong. Talking to servants is beneath her. As for the others, all she ever tells them is that you—and I quote—"lost your first love tragically." Now what in the Lady's name do you think that makes them want to do?:

"Gods, 'Fandes, is that somehow *my* fault? Was I supposed to interrogate them while they were chasing me?"

:You,: she said, ice dripping from every word, *:never asked. Or bothered to ask. Or wanted to ask. It never occurred to you that Withen might not want it spread about the neighborhood that his first-born son prefers men?:*

" 'Fandes," he replied, after a long, bitter moment of silence. "I don't see where it's any of your business. It has nothing to do with my duties as a Herald."

Silence on her part. Then, *:You're right. I'm sorry. I*

. . . overstepped myself. I—I just wanted you to think about what was going on.:

"Is that what I've been doing?" he asked quietly.

:Well—yes.:

"Then I *should* apologize. I can't afford to react automatically to things—not even in my personal life. And—gods. Not when I'm *hurting* people."

A wash of relief. Then a tinge of sarcasm. *:You're thinking. And about time, too. Now are you going to enjoy a long wallow in self-accusation?:*

Something about the tone of her mind-voice—and the exact wording she'd used—made him pause for a moment. "Wait a minute—let me look at this from another angle." He made a mental checklist of all the young women Lady Treesa had pushed off on him, and what they'd done when he'd failed to succumb to their various charms. And the more he thought about it—

"You *are* exaggerating, aren't you?" he accused.

:Well—yes. But the situation exists. What are you going to do about it?:

"Be careful, I suppose. But I'll have to watch what I say."

:Good. You're still thinking.:

"The ones Mother keeps flinging at me are the hardest. If I tell them the truth, I'll hurt Father. I'll shame him, at the least. Even if I pledge them to silence, it'll get out."

:So?:

"I don't know. But I'll think about it."

:Now that is the Vanyel I Chose.: Her mind-voice was warm with approval. *:You're not "just" reacting anymore.:*

"Havens, I've been going numb between the ears for the past year, haven't I?"

:Well—yes. You had reason but—.:

He nodded, slowly. "This last year—I've gotten into a lot of habits."

:Exactly. You can't let your heart or your habits control you. Not when you're who you are, and wield the power you do. Think about reacting emotionally in a bat-

tle situation. Think about even reacting reflexively, in-stead of tactically.:

He did, and shuddered.

He always stopped at Halfway Inn—the name, he'd learned since, was a conscious pun—the hostelry that sat in the middle of the forest that cut Forst Reach off from the rest of the Kingdom.

In a way, what he had become had started here. The Inn had certainly marked his passage into a different world, though young Vanyel Ashkevron, more than half a prisoner of his escort, had not gotten the attention that Herald-Mage Vanyel got now.

It was an enormous place, and in the normal run of things very few travelers even saw the Innkeeper. A Herald was an exception. The Innkeeper himself saw to Vanyel's every whim—not that there were very many of those. The Inn was quite comfortable even for those who were less noteworthy than Vanyel.

There was less of the hero-worship here than there had been in other inns along the road. Vanyel was "local"; everyone attached to the inn and most of those staying there knew his family, his holding. They seemed to regard him with proprietary pride rather than awe, as if the things he had done were somehow reflections on *them;* as if his fame brought *them* fame. And as if *they* had something to do with what he had become.

In a way, perhaps they had. If events that occurred here had not made him feel so utterly alienated from the rest of the world he might not have responded as strongly as he had to Tylendel.

He left Halfway Inn just after dawn, hoping to reach Forst Reach by early afternoon at the very latest. He had always made excellent time on this last leg of his journey every other time he'd made his trips home—though he always *left* much faster than he arrived. . . .

But he stopped Yfandes before they had traveled more than a candlemark, while fog still wreathed the under-growth and it was dark beneath the silent trees. The air was damp-smelling, with the tang of rotting leaves, and a hint of muskiness. No birds sang, and nothing rustled the fallen leaves underfoot or the branches overhead. This forest was *always* quiet, but this morning it was *too* quiet.

"Something's wrong," he said, straightening in his saddle, and pulling his cloak a little tighter around his shoulders.

:*I can feel it, too,*: Yfandes agreed, :*but it's very subtle.*:

This forest—unnamed, so far as he knew—had frightened him to the point of near-hysteria the first time he'd traveled this road. *Now* he knew why; there was magic here, old magic of the kind that the *Tayledras* used, that they frequently drained off in order to weaken it, and open the lands to more "normal" human settlements. The kind of magic that made the Pelagir Hills the changeling-haunted places they were. Anyone with so much as the potential for the Mage-Gift could feel enough to make them unhappy and uncomfortable.

But this magic had been dormant for a very long time.

"I'm going to probe," he said, and closed his eyes, going *in,* then opening *out*—

The magic was still there, but it lay even deeper below the fabric of the forest than it had the last time he had passed this way. Now that his Gift was fully trained, he could even see the traces that told him it *had* been drained by the *Tayledras* at least twice, which meant it should be "safe." The Hawkbrothers never left wild magic behind when they abandoned an area.

But that draining and abandonment had been long ago—very long ago.

Yes, the magic still slept, deeper than the taproots of the trees and harder to reach—but it slept uneasily. All magic was akin, and all magic touched all other magic—an affinity that made the Gate-spell possible. But close proximity meant stronger ties to magics that neighbored one another; disturbance to one site frequently disturbed another.

Vanyel could feel that disturbance in the magics here. A resonance with another pole of power at a distance—probably across the Border, and *most* probably in Baires, given that the ruling family was composed of mages.

Something somewhere was powerfully warping kindred magic fields, and this field housed in the forest was resonating to that disturbance, like a lute string resonating to a touch on the one beside it.

But it was too far away, and the resonances too tenuous, for Vanyel to determine *who* was causing it, or *where* it originated, or even *what* was being done. Although—

Vanyel brought himself up out of his scanning-trance, and bit his lip in thought.

" 'Fandes, did you get anything?"

:No more than you,: she replied uneasily, resuming her pace without his prompting. *:Except—the root of all this is evil.:*

"And I know better than to ask you to probe anything I can't reach. But I don't like it either. I like it even less now, with the Border uneasy. It makes me wonder if someone is forcing an issue—and if so, what, and to what end?"

:Tell Lissa. That's all you can do for now.:

He glanced uneasily to either side of him. "I'm afraid you're right, ladylove," he agreed. "I am afraid you're only too right."

Four

Despite everything he'd told himself, despite being adult and with experiences behind him Withen could not even imagine, Vanyel felt his shoulders beginning to knot with anxiety the moment he crossed the gate marking the edge of the Forst Reach lands. By the time he rode through the gate in the wall that surrounded the Great House of the estate, he was fighting to keep himself from hunching down in the saddle like a sullen, frightened child.

It never changes. Outside these walls I may be a Herald-Mage who can admonish the King himself; inside—I'm Vanyel, prodigal son, with habits we don't talk about, and tastes best politely ignored. Gods, when are they ever going to accept me for who I am?

:Perhaps never. Perhaps when you accept yourself, Chosen.:

The unsolicited reply nettled him a little.

:Perhaps,: she continued, *:when you* know *who you are, and know it well enough that you can't be reduced to an adolescent just by riding through the gates.:*

He glanced down at Yfandes' ears, and then ahead, down the road to the destination that was causing him such discomfort. *:Are you saying I don't know who I am?:*

She didn't reply, but picked her pace up to a trot—the easy kind—and rounded the final curve and hill that brought them within sight of Forst Reach itself, bulking heavy and gray against the brilliant autumn sky.

The building had once been a defensive keep, and still had something of that blocky, no-nonsense look about it. It had long since been renovated and converted into a dwelling far more comfortable, though even at this distance Vanyel could see the faint outline of the moat under the lush grass surrounding it. Surrounded as it was by newer, smaller outbuildings of whitewashed stucco, it resembled a vast and rather ill-natured gray granite hen squatting among a flock of paler chicks.

Someone had been watching for him. Vanyel saw a small, fairly androgynous figure leave a position on a little rise beside the road and run toward the main building. It vanished somewhere in the vicinity of one of the old postern gates, which were now doors, and Vanyel assumed he (or she, though it was probably a page) had gone to tell the rest of the household that he had arrived. Heralds were distinctive enough to be spotted at any distance, and few enough that it would be safe to assume that any Herald coming to Forst Reach was going to be Vanyel.

Sure enough, people began emerging from doors all over the building, and by the time Vanyel and Yfandes reached the main doors—impressive black oaken monstrosities that had been set into a frame in what had once been the gateway to the center court—there was a sizable group waiting for him.

There was the usual babble of greetings—Treesa wept all over him, Withen gingerly clapped him on the shoulder, his brothers all followed Withen's example. There was the usual little dance when Withen told a page to "take Vanyel's horse" and Van—*again*—had to explain that Yfandes *wasn't* a horse, she was a Companion and his partner and that *he* would see to her. And as usual, Withen looked puzzled and skeptical, as if he was wondering if his son wasn't a bit daft.

But Vanyel was firm—as usual—and got his way. Because if he hadn't insisted (and the first visit home, he hadn't) Yfandes would be stripped of tack and given a good rubdown, then locked into a stall like the "valuable animal" she seemed to Withen to be. Van hadn't known what had happened that time until she wistfully Mindspoke him at dinner, asking if he'd come let her out, since she couldn't reach the lock on the door of the stall. That night he had gone immediately down to the stable leaving his dinner half-eaten, and with profligate use of magic, created a new split door to the outside in one of the big loose boxes Withen used for mares in foal. Whenever he came home now, *that* stall was Yfandes', no matter if he had to move a mare out and scour it down to the wooden floor with his own two hands first. And no matter what sort of contrivance Withen had installed on the new door to keep it locked, Vanyel magicked it so that Yfandes could come and go as she pleased. Maybe Withen wondered why the box never had to be cleaned; certainly the stablehands did. But Withen never seemed to grasp that Yfandes was *exactly* what his son said she was; a brilliant, thinking, creative lady, with all of a great lady's manners and daintiness, who just happened to be living in a horse's body.

Yfandes was still moderately amused. But Vanyel frequently thought that it was a good thing he'd never mentioned Withen's proposition on that first visit to breed her to the best of his palfrey-studs, or he'd have been using his magic to repair the gaping holes in the stable, instead of adding a door.

This time, at least, Withen had learned enough through repetition that the loose box had been vacated, scoured and bleached, and then filled with straw. But he *still* had left the outer door latched and double-locked.

Vanyel just sighed, magicked the locks in the *open* position, and pulled the top half of the door wide. He moved the latchstring for the lower half back through the hole to where Yfandes could get at it, then rummaged through his own packs for a longer bit of string so that she could pull it closed if she chose. Needless to say, the strap he'd attached there last time was gone.

"How hungry are you?" he asked her, stripping her tack and hanging it over the edge of the stall for the stablehands to clean, then beginning to rub her down. Straw dust tickled his nose and made him want to sneeze.

:Very,: she replied, testing the depth of the straw with a forehoof and nodding approval. :*Just take the sweat off and get the knots out of my tail; I'm going to roll when I get out, and maybe swim in the pond.*:

He heard Withen's footsteps on the path to the stable, and switched to Mindspeech. *:Fine, love, just have your swim when nobody's watching or they'll send half the stablehands to pull you out. Now watch; I will bet you money that Father says, "Are you sure you should leave her that much food so soon after a long ride? She might founder.":* He finished currying her, took the bucket off its hook, and went after grain for her.

"Are you sure you should leave her that much food so soon after a long ride?" Withen said dubiously from the stable-door proper, his square bulk blocking nearly all the light. "She might founder."

"Father, she isn't a horse; she knows better than to stuff herself silly. She told me she's very hungry. It's been a hard tour of duty for both of us, and both of us need to get back a little weight." Vanyel hung the bucket of mixed grains where Yfandes could get at it easily. *:Now he'll say, "I suppose you know best, son, but—":*

"I suppose you know best, son, but—" Withen moved cautiously up to the loose box as Vanyel forked in hay.

"Father, would *you* stuff yourself sick after a long day at the harvest?" At harvest-time Withen made it a point of spending one day with each of his tenants and several days with his own fieldhands, working beside them. It was one of the many things he did that endeared him to his people.

"Well—" Withen's heavy brows creased, and for once he looked uncertain. "—no."

"So, neither will she." He rinsed her water-bucket until it squeaked, filled it with absolutely clear, cold water, and hung it beside the grain bucket. Withen stepped forward as if he couldn't help himself.

"Son, she'll foul the water."

"Would Mother drop food into the wine in her goblet?" Vanyel sighed.

"Well—no."

"So, Yfandes wouldn't." *Since she has better manners than Mother.*

He Mindtouched Yfandes gently. *:All set, ladylove?:*

:Quite, beloved.: Yfandes' mind-voice was yellow and

effervescent with amusement. *:Does he do that to you every time we come?:*

Vanyel rubbed her forehead between her eyes and she closed them with pleasure. *:Just about. Normally he doesn't follow me into the stable, but I get it when he hears from the stablehands what I did with you. Watch out for that so-called "Shin'a'in stallion;" I think he's sometimes allowed to run loose in this field. He might try and bully you; he might decide you're one of his mares and give you a little excitement.:*

She bared her front teeth delicately. *:I'd rather like to see him try anything on me. I could use a good fight.:*

He nearly choked. *:Now, love, you'll scare him impotent, and how will I explain that to Meke?:*

:Cleverly, of course. Go on with you; I'm fine and your father is fretting.:

"All right, Father, she says she's comfortable," he said aloud, forcing himself *not* to grin. "Let's go."

"Are you sure she should be left like that? What if she gets out?"

"Father," Vanyel sighed, sending the gods a silent plea for patience, "I *want* her to be able to come and go as she pleases."

"But—"

Vanyel wondered if his father ever really heard anything he said. "She's *not*," he repeated for the hundredth time, "a *horse.*"

Vanyel was in time for dinner, a pleasure he would just as soon have done without. But once bathed, settled into the best guest room, and dressed in clean clothing—*not* a uniform, he wasn't on duty now, not even technically— his good sense prevailed over his reluctance. When the summons for dinner came, he followed the page and took his place at the high table. Withen *tried* to put him at his right, between himself and Vanyel's mother. Vanyel managed to convince him to let him take the usual seat guests took, on the end, displacing Radevel, who didn't look at all unhappy to be sitting down at the low table.

Sitting at the end he was spared having to make conversation with two people at once. His seat-mate proved to be Mekeal's thin, little red-haired wife Roshya, who took *all* the burden of conversation from him. She chattered nonstop, sparrowlike, without ever seeming to pause for breath. All *he* had to do was nod and make vague noises of agreement or disagreement from time to time, and he actually didn't mind; Roshya's gossip was cheerful and never malicious—if she had a fault it was that she seemed to assume he *must* know every highborn and family member for leagues around. After all, *she* did.

The dark, high-ceilinged hall seemed far more cramped than Vanyel remembered—until he counted heads, and realized that there were twice the number of folk dining than there had been when he was fifteen. He blinked, but the number didn't change. The low table had been lengthened, and a second table set at right angles to it at the other end, making an "H" shape with the high table.

And the high table had been lengthened, too; when Van had been sent to Haven and his aunt Savil, only Withen, Treesa, Jervis, Father Leren, and any guests they might have had been seated there—which had then included Vanyel's Aunt Serina and her Healer. Now, besides the original four, the table included the unmarried children, all three married sons, and their wives.

Great good gods, this isn't a family, it's a tribe!

The only one missing since his last visit seemed to be his youngest sister Charis; it looked like the only ones still home were the boys. After a moment of thought it seemed to him that he recalled getting word of Charis' wedding to somebody-or-other just after Elspeth's death. *Did I send a present? I must've, or I'd have heard about it five breaths after being greeted. That's right—I remember now—I sent that hideously pious tapestry of the Lady of Fertility. Aunt Savil took care of Meke and Roshya for me, and I sent Deleran those awful silver-and-crystal candlesticks. . . .*

But gods, did I do anything about Kaster and whatever-her-name-is? That was just seven or eight months ago, I was so tangled up in the Border-fight—I don't remember—

He continued to fret about that until Roshya's dropped

comment about the "delightful bedcurtains, Kaster and Ria were *so* pleased," told him that if *he* hadn't, *Savil* must have sent something in his name. At that point he relaxed a little. From Roshya's chatter, Vanyel learned that she and Mekeal had *six* children thus far; Deleran and *his* wife had two, and Kaster's rather plump new bride—

Looks ready to spawn at any moment. Lord and Lady, they certainly didn't waste any time.

It made his head swim to think about it. Forst Reach was hardly a small holding, but it must be near to bursting at the seams.

He must have looked as if he were marginally interested in the new bride. Roshya waved her beringed hands in an artful imitation of Treesa, and launched into a dissertation on Lady Ria that was partly fact and mostly fancy—Vanyel was in a position to know. She'd been one of the young women his mother had thrown into his path the last time he'd been home. She looked content enough now with Kaster, which was something of a relief to his conscience.

He looked back down at the low table in one of Roshya's infrequent pauses for breath.

No wonder she's thin. She never stops talking to eat.

Radevel was the only face he recognized down there, although a good half the youngsters had the Ashkevron build and look. Radevel was stolidly munching his way through a heaping plateful of bread and roast when he caught Vanyel looking at him, and gave the Herald a shrug of the shoulders aimed at the mob of children, then a slow and quite deliberate wink.

Vanyel stifled a laugh. *So Father is still fostering dozens of cousins, and Radevel is still stuck here. Poor Rad; what is he, fifth son? Nowhere else to go, I guess. I bet Father's put him in charge of the younglings. Good choice. He'll keep them moderately in line. Better him than Jervis.*

He looked back up in time to catch crag-faced Jervis, the Forst Reach armsmaster, giving him an ugly glare. He met the glare impassively, but with an inward feeling of foreboding. *He's going to try something, I feel it in my bones. Great, that means I'll get to play cat-and-mouse with him through the whole visit.* He looked away when the armsmaster's eyes fell, only to find that saturnine Father Leren was giving him a look of ice and calculation, too, from beneath hooded lids. *Delightful, so I have* both *of them to deal with. Just what I needed. What a wonderful friendly visit this is going to be.*

He continued to make the appropriate noises at Roshya, and ignored the further stares of Jervis and Leren.

Mekeal had become so like Withen that Vanyel had to blink, seeing them together. Broad shoulders, brown beards trimmed identically, brown hair held back in identical tails with identical silver rings, dark brown eyes as open and readable as a dog's—dissimilar clothing was about all that differentiated them. That, and a few wrinkles in Withen's face, a few gray streaks in his hair and beard. Meke was perhaps a touch less muscular; not surprising since Withen's muscles had been built up in actual fighting during his career as a guard officer, and Meke had never seen any fighting outside of an occasional skirmish with bandits. But otherwise—Withen did *not* look his age; with all the silver in *his* hair and the stress-lines around his eyes, *Vanyel* could be taken for older than his father.

Treesa, on the other hand, had not aged gracefully. She was still affecting the light, diaphanous gowns and pale colors appropriate to a young girl. Even if he had not been aware of the various cosmetic artifices employed by the ladies of Randale's Court, Vanyel would have known the coloring of her hair and cheeks to be false.

She's holding onto youth with teeth and nails, and it's still getting away from her, he thought sadly. *Poor Mother. All she ever had to make her feel like she had some worth was being pretty and me, and she's losing both. Every year I become more of a stranger to her; every year her looks fade a little more.* He glanced over at Roshya, who seemed to be doing her best to imitate Lady Treesa, and was relieved to see a gleam of lively good humor in her green eyes, and to hear a little of that sense of humor reflected in what she was saying. Treesa would likely become a bitter, unpleasant old woman on her own—but not with Roshya around.

The rest of Vanyel's brothers had become thinner, more reckless copies of Meke. They ate heavily and drank copiously and roared jokes at each other across the length of table, emphasizing points with a brandished fork. *They're probably terrors on the hunt—and I bet they hunt every other day. And probably fighting when they aren't hunting. They need something to keep them occupied, can't Father see that?*

The more Vanyel saw, the uneasier he became. There was a restlessness in Withen's offspring that demanded an outlet, but there wasn't any. *No wonder Meke is hoping for a Border-war,* he realized as the meal drew to a close. *This place is like a geyser just about to blow. And when it does, if there isn't any place for that energy to go, someone is going to get hurt. Or worse.*

Servants began clearing the tables, and the adults rose and began to drift out on errands of their own. By Forst Reach tradition, the Great Hall belonged to the youngsters after dinner. Vanyel lingered until most of the others had gone out the double doors to the hallway; he was not in the mood to argue with anyone right now, or truly, even in the mood to make polite conversation. What he wanted was a quiet room, a little time to read, and more sleep.

It didn't seem as if the gods were paying much attention to *his* wants, lately.

Withen was waiting for him just beyond the doors.

"Son, about that horse—"

"Father, I keep telling you, Yfandes is *not—*"

Withen shook his head, an expression of marked impatience on his square face. "Not your Companion—*Mekeal's* horse. That damned stud he bought."

"Oh." Vanyel smiled sheepishly. "Sorry. Lately my mind stays in the same path unless you jerk its leash sideways. Tired, I guess."

For the first time Withen actually *looked* at him, and his thick eyebrows rose in alarm. "Son, you look like *hell.*"

"I know," Vanyel replied. "I've been told."

"Bad?" Withen gave him the same kind of sober attention he gave to his own contemporaries. Vanyel was obscurely flattered.

"Take all the horror stories coming north from the Karsite Border and double them. *That's* what it's been like."

For once Withen's martial background was a blessing. He *knew* what Border-fighting was like, and his expression darkened for a moment. "Gods, son—that is *not* good to hear. So you'll be *needing* your rest. Well, I won't keep you too long, then—listen, let's take this out to the walk."

The "walk" Withen referred to was a stone porch, rather like a low balcony and equipped with a balustrade, that ran the length of the north side of the building. Why Grandfather Joserlin had put it there, no one knew. It overlooked the gardens, but not usefully, most of the view being screened off by the row of cypresses he'd had planted just beneath the railing. It could be accessed by one door, through the linen storeroom. Not many people used it, unless they wanted to be alone.

Which actually made it a fine choice for a private discussion.

Blue, hazy dusk, scented with woodsmoke, was all that met them there. Vanyel went over to the balustrade and sat on the top of it, and Withen began again.

"About that horse—have you seen it?"

"I'm afraid so," Vanyel replied. His window overlooked the meadows where the horses were turned loose to graze, and he'd seen the *"Shin'a'in* stud" kicking up his heels and attempting to impress Yfandes who was in the next field over. *She* had been ignoring him. "I hate to say this, Father, but Meke was robbed. I've *seen* a *Shin'a'in* warsteed; they're ugly, but not like that beast. They're smaller than that stud; they're not made to carry men in armor, they're bred to carry nomad horse-archers. They have *very* strong hindquarters, but their forequarters are just as strong, and they're a little short in the spine. 'Bunchy,' I guess you'd say. And their heads are large all out of proportion to the rest of them. The only thing a *Shin'a'in* warsteed has in common with Meke's nag is color. And besides, the only way an outsider could *get* a warsteed would be to steal a *young*, untrained one— and then kill the entire Clan he stole it from—and then kill the other Clans that came after him. No chance. Maybe somewhere there's *Shin'a'in* blood in that one, but it's cull blood if so.''

Withen nodded. ''I thought it might be something like that. *I've* seen their riding-beasts, the ones they *will* sell us. Beautiful creatures—so I knew that stud wasn't one of those, either. The animal is stupid, even for a horse, and that's going some. It's vicious, too—even with other horses; cut up the one mare Meke put it to before they could stop it. It's never been broken to ride, and I'm not sure it can be—and you know how I feel about that.''

Vanyel half-smiled; one thing that Withen knew was his horses, and it was an iron-clad rule with him that *all* studs had to be broken for riding, the same as his geld-ings, and exercised regularly under saddle. No stud in *his* stable was allowed to laze about; when they weren't standing, they were working. It made them that much easier to handle at breeding-time. Most of Withen's own favorite mounts were his studs.

A mocker-bird shrilled in one of the cypresses, and Vanyel jumped at the unexpected sound. As he willed his heart to stop racing, Withen continued. ''It hasn't taken a piece out of any of the stablehands yet, but I wonder if that isn't just lack of opportunity. And *this* is what Meke wants to breed half the hunter-mares to!''

Vanyel shook his head. *Damn! I hope this jumping-at-shadows starts fading out. If I can't calm myself down, I'm going to hurt someone.*

''I don't know what to tell you, Father. *I'd* have that beast gelded and put in front of a plow, frankly; I think that's likely all he's good for. Either that, or use the damned thing to train your more experienced young rid-ers how to handle an unmanageable horse. But I'm a Her-ald, not a landholder; I have no experience with horsebreeding, and Meke is likely to point that out as soon as I open my mouth.''

"But you *have* seen a real *Shin'a'in* warsteed," Withen persisted.

"Once. With a real *Shin'a'in* on its—her—back. The nomad in question told me they don't allow the studs anywhere near the edge of the Dhorisha Plains. Only the mares 'go into the world' as he put it." Even in the near dark and without using any Gift, Vanyel could tell his father was alive with curiosity. Valdemar saw the fabled *Shin'a'in* riding horses once in perhaps a generation and very few citizens of Valdemar had even seen the *Shin'a'in* themselves. Probably no one from Valdemar had ever seen a nomad on his warsteed until *he* had.

"Bodyguard, Father," he said, answering the unspoken question. "The nomad was a bodyguard for one of their shamans, and I met them both in the k'Treva Vale. I doubt the shaman would have needed one, except that he must have been nearly eighty. I tell you, he was the *toughest* eighty-year-old I'd ever seen. He'd come to ask help from the *Tayledras* to get rid of some monster that had decided the Plains looked good and the horses tasty, and moved in."

Withen shivered a little; talk of magic bothered him, and the fact that his son had actually been taught by the ghostly, legendary Hawkbrothers made him almost as uneasy as Vanyel's sexual inclinations.

The mocker-bird shrieked again, but this time Vanyel was able to keep from leaping out of his skin. "At any rate, I don't promise anything more except to try. But I want to warn you, I'm going to go at this the same way I'd handle a delicate negotiation. You won't see results at once, assuming I get any. Meke is as stubborn as that stud of his, and it's going to take some careful handling and a lot of carrots to get him to come around."

Withen nodded. "Well, that's all I can ask. I certainly haven't gotten anywhere with him. And that's *why* I asked you to stick your nose into this. I'm no diplomat."

Vanyel got up off the railing and headed for the door. "The fact is, Father, you and Meke are too damned much alike."

Withen actually chuckled. "The fact is, son, you're too damned right."

* * *

Vanyel slept until noon. The guest room was at the front of the building, well away from all the activity of the stables and yards. The bed curtains were as thick and dark as he could have wished. And someone had evidently given the servants orders to stay out of his room until he called for them. Which was just as well, since Van was trusting his reflexes not at all.

So he slept in peace, and rose in peace, and stood at the window overlooking the narrow road to the keep feeling as if he *might* actually succeed in putting himself back together if he could get a few more nights like the last one. A mere breath of breeze came in the window, and mocker-birds were singing—pleasantly, this time—all along the guttering above his head.

He could easily believe it to be still summer. He couldn't recall a gentler, warmer autumn.

He sent out a testing thought-tendril. *:'Fandes?:*

:Bright the day, sleepy one,: she responded, the Hawk-brother greeting.

He laughed silently, and took a deep breath of air that tasted only faintly of falling leaves and leafsmoke. *:And wind to thy wings, sweeting. Would you rather laze about or go somewhere today?:*

:Need you ask? Laze about, frankly. I think I'm going to spend the rest of the day the way I did this morning—napping in the sun, doing slow stretches. That pulled tendon needs favoring yet.:

He nodded, turning away from the window. *:I don't doubt. Makes me glad I was running lighter than normal after you pulled it.:*

She laughed, and moved farther out into her field so that he could see her from the window. *:I won't say it didn't help. Well, go play gallant to your mother and get it over with. With any luck, she hasn't had a chance to bring in one of the local fillies.:*

He grimaced, rang for a servant. One appeared with a promptness that suggested he'd been waiting right outside the door. Vanyel felt a pang of conscience, wondering how long he'd been out there.

"I'd like something to eat," he said, "And wash water, please. And—listen, there is no reason to expect me to wake before midmorning, and noon is likelier. I surely won't want anyone or anything before noon. So pass that on, would you? No use in having one of you cool his heels for hours!''

The swarthy manservant looked surprised, then grinned and nodded before hurrying off after Vanyel's requests. Vanyel hunted up his clothing, deciding on an almost-new dark blue outfit about the time the wash water arrived. It felt rather *strange* not to be wearing Whites, but at the same time he was reveling in the feel of silk and velvet against his skin. The Field uniforms were strictly utilitarian, leather and raime, wool and linen. And he hadn't had many occasions to wear formal, richer Whites. *No wonder they call me a peacock. Sensualist that I am— I like soft clothing. Well, why not?*

The manservant showed up with food as Vanyel finished lacing up his tunic. He considered his reflection in the polished steel mirror, and ended up belting the tunic; it had fit perfectly when he'd last worn it, but now—it looked ridiculously baggy without a belt.

He sighed, and applied himself to his breakfast. It was *always* far easier to gain weight than to lose it, anyway, that was one consolation!

After that he felt ready to face his mother. And whatever lady-traps she had baited and ready.

She always asked him to play whenever he stayed long enough, so he stripped the case from his lute and tuned it, then slung it on his back, and headed for her bower. Maybe he could distract her with music.

''Hello, Mother,'' Vanyel said, leaning down to kiss Treesa's gracefully extended, perfumed fingertips. ''You look younger every time I see you.''

The other ladies giggled, pretended to sew, fluttered fans. Treesa colored prettily at the compliment, and her silver eyes sparkled. For that moment the compliment wasn't a polite lie. ''Vanyel, you have been away *far* too long!'' She let her hand linger in his for a moment, and he gently squeezed it. She fluttered her eyelashes happily. Flirtation was Treesa's favorite game; courtly love her choice of pastime. It didn't matter that the courtier was her son; she had no intention of taking the game past the graceful and empty movements of the dance of words and gesture, and he knew it, and she knew he knew it, so everyone was happy. She was never so alive as when there was someone with her willing to play her game.

He fell in with the pretense, quite pleased that she hadn't immediately introduced anyone to him; that might mean she didn't have any girls she planned to fling at him. And she hadn't pouted at him either; so he was still in her good graces. He had *much* rather play courtier than have her rain tears and reproaches on his head for not spending more time with his family.

In the gauze-bedecked bower, full of fluttering femininity in pale colors and lace, he was quite aware that he looked all the more striking in his midnight blue. He *hoped* it would give him enough distinction—and draw enough attention to the silver in his hair—so that Treesa would remember he wasn't fifteen anymore. "Alas, first lady of my heart," he said with a quirk of one eyebrow, "I fear I had very little choice in the matter. A Herald's duty lies at the King's behest."

She dimpled, and patted the rose-velvet cushion of the stool placed beside her chair. "We've been hearing so many *stories* about you, Vanyel. This spring there was a minstrel here who sang *songs* about you!" She fussed with the folds of her saffron gown as he took his seat at her side. Her maids (those few who weren't at work at the three looms placed against the wall) and her fosterlings all gathered up their sewing and spinning at this unspoken signal and gathered closer. The sun-bright room glowed with the muted rainbow colors of their gowns, and Vanyel had to work to keep himself from smiling, as faces—young, and not-so-young, pretty and plain—turned toward him like so many flowers toward the sun. He'd not gotten *this* kind of attention even when he was the petted favorite of this very bower.

But then, when he'd been the bower pet, he'd only been a handsome fifteen-year-old, with a bit of talent at playing and singing. *Now* he was Herald-Mage Vanyel, the *hero* of songs.

:And all too likely to have his foot stepped on if he comes near me *with a swelled head,:* said Yfandes.

He bent his head over the lute and pretended to tune it until he could keep his face straight, then turned back to his mother.

"I know better songs than those, and far more suited to a lovely lady than tales of war and darkness."

There was disappointment in some faces, but Treesa's eyes glowed. *"Would* you play a love song, Van?" she asked coquettishly. "Would you play 'My Lady's Eyes' for me?"

Probably the most inane piece of drivel ever written, he thought. *But it has a lovely tune. Why not?*

He bowed his head slightly. "My lady's wish is ever my decree," he replied, and began the intricate introduction at once.

He couldn't help noticing Melenna sitting just behind a knot of three adolescents, her hands still, her eyes as dreamy as theirs. *She* was actually prettier now than she had been as a girl.

Poor Melenna. She never gives up. Almost fourteen years, and she's still *yearning after me. Gods. What a mess she's made out of her life.* He wondered somewhere at the back of his mind what had become of the bastard child she'd had by Mekeal, when pique at his refusing her had led her to Meke's bed. Was it a boy or girl? Was it one of the girls pressed closely around him now? Or had she lost it? Loose ends like that worried him. Loose ends had a habit of tripping you up when you least expected it, particularly when the loose ends were human.

He got the answer to his question a lot sooner than he'd guessed he would.

"Oh, Van, that was *lovely,"* Treesa sighed, then dimpled again. "You know, we haven't been *entirely* without Art and Music while you've been gone. I've managed to find myself another handsome little minstrel, haven't I, 'Lenna?"

Melenna glowed nearly the same faded-rose as her gown—one of Treesa's, remade; Vanyel definitely recollected it. "He's hardly as good as *Vanyel* was, milady," she replied softly.

"Oh, I don't know," Treesa retorted, with just a hint of maliciousness. "Medren, why don't you come out and let Vanyel judge for himself?"

A tall boy of about twelve with an old, battered lute of his own rose slowly from where he'd been sitting, hidden by Melenna, and came hesitantly to the center of the group. There was no doubt who his father was—he had Meke's lankiness, hair, and square chin, though he was smaller than Mekeal had been at that age, and his shoulders weren't as broad. There was no doubt either who his mother was—Melenna's wide hazel eyes stared at Vanyel from two faces.

The boy bobbed at Treesa. "I can't come close to those fingerings, milord, milady," he said, with an honesty that *felt* painful to Vanyel.

"Some of that's the fact that I've had near twenty years of practice, Medren," Vanyel replied, acutely aware that both Treesa and Melenna were eyeing him peculiarly. He was not entirely certain what was going on. "But there's some of it that's the instrument. This one has a very easy action—why don't you borrow it?"

They exchanged instruments; the boy's hands trembled as he took Vanyel's finely crafted lute. He touched the strings lightly, and swallowed hard. "What—" his voice cracked, and he tried again. "What would you like to hear, milord?"

Vanyel thought quickly; it had to be something that wouldn't be so easy as to be an insult, but *certainly* wouldn't involve the intricate fingerings he'd used on "My Lady's Eyes."

"Do you know 'Windrider Unchained'?" he asked, finally.

The boy nodded, made one false start, then got the instrumental introduction through, and began singing the verse.

And Vanyel nearly dropped the boy's lute as the sheer *power* of Medren's singing washed over him.

His voice wasn't *quite* true on one or two notes; that didn't matter, time, maturity, and practice would take care of those little faults. His fingerings were sometimes uncertain; that didn't matter either. What mattered was that, while Medren sang, Vanyel *lived* the song.

The boy was Bardic Gifted, with a Gift of unusual power. And he was singing to a bowerful of empty-headed sweetly-scented marriage-bait, wasting a Gift that Vanyel, at fifteen, would willingly have sacrificed a leg to gain. *Both* legs. And counted the cost a small one.

It was several moments after the boy finished before Vanyel could bring himself to speak—and he really only managed to do so because he could see the hope in Medren's eyes slowly fading to disappointment.

In fact, the boy had handed him back his instrument and started to turn away before he got control of himself. "Medren—*Medren!*" he said insistently enough to make the boy turn back. "You are *better* than I was, even at fifteen. In a few years you are going to be *better* than I could ever hope to be if I practiced every hour of my life. You have the Bardic-Gift, lad, and that's something no amount of training will give."

He would have said more—he *wanted* to say more—but Treesa interrupted with a demand that *he* sing again, and by the time he untangled himself from the concentration the song required, the boy was gone.

The boy was on his mind all through dinner. He finally asked Roshya about him, and Roshya, delighted at having actually gotten a question out of him, burbled on until the last course was removed. And the more Vanyel heard, the more he worried.

The boy was being given—at Treesa's insistence—the same education as the legitimate offspring. Which meant, in essence, that he was being educated for exactly *nothing*. Except—perhaps—one day becoming the squire of one of his legitimate cousins. Meanwhile his *real* talent was being neglected.

The problem gnawed at the back of Vanyel's thoughts all through dinner, and accompanied him back to his room. He lit a candle and placed it on the small writing desk, still pondering. It might have kept him sleepless all night, except that soon after he flung himself down in a chair, still feeling somewhat stunned by the boy and his Gift, there came a knock on his door.

"Come—" he said absently, assuming it was a servant.

The door opened. "Milord Herald?" said a tentative voice out of the darkness beyond his candle. "Could— you spare a little time?"

Vanyel sat bolt upright. "Medren? Is that you?"

The boy shuffled into the candlelight, shutting the door behind him. He had the neck of his lute clutched in both hands. "I—" His voice cracked again. "Milord, you said I was good. I taught myself, milord. They—when they opened up the back of the library, they found where you used to hide things. Nobody wanted the music and instruments but me. I'd been watching minstrels, and I figured out how to play them. Then Lady Treesa heard me, she got me this lute. . . ."

The boy shuffled forward a few more steps, then stood uncertainly beside the table. Vanyel was trying to get his mind and mouth to work. That the boy was this good was amazing, but that he was entirely self-taught was miraculous. "Medren," he said at last, "to say that you astonish me would be an understatement. What can *I* do for you? If it's in my power, it's yours."

Medren flushed, but looked directly into Vanyel's eyes. "Milord Herald—"

"Medren," Vanyel interrupted gently, "I am *not* 'Milord Herald,' not to you. You're my nephew; call me by my given name."

Medren colored even more. "I—V-Vanyel, if you could—if you would—teach me? Please? I'll—" he coughed, and lowered his eyes, now turning a red so bright it was painful to look at. "I'll do anything you like. Just teach me."

Vanyel had no doubt whatsoever what the boy thought he was offering in return for music lessons. The painful— and very potently sexual—embarrassment was all too plain to his Empathy. *Gods, the poor child*— Medren wasn't even a temptation. *I may be shaych, but—not children. The thought's revolting.*

"Medren," he said very softly, "they warned you to stay away from me, didn't they? And they told you why."

The boy shrugged. "They said you were shaych. Made all kinds of noises. But hell, you're a Herald, Heralds don't *hurt* people."

"I'm shaych, yes," Vanyel replied steadily. "But you— you aren't."

"No," the boy said. "But hell, like I said, I wasn't worried. What you could teach me—that's worth anything. And I haven't got much else to repay you with." He finally looked back up into Vanyel's eyes. "Besides, there isn't anything you could do to me that'd be worse than Jervis beating on me once a day. And they all seem to think *that's* all right."

Vanyel started. "Jervis? What—what do you mean, Jervis beating on you? Sit, Medren, please."

"What I said," the boy replied, gingerly pulling a straight-backed chair to him and taking a seat. "I get treated just like the rest of them. Same lessons. Only there's this little problem; I'm *not* true-born." His tone became bitter. "With eight *true-born* heirs and more on the way, where does that leave me? Nowhere, that's where. And there's no use in currying favor with *me,* or being a little easy on *me,* 'cause I don't have a thing to offer anybody. So when time comes for an example, who gets picked? Medren. When we want a live set of pells to prove a point, who gets beat on? Medren. And what the hell do I have to expect at the end of it, when I'm of age? Squire to one of the *true-born* boys if I'm lucky, the door if I'm not. Unless I can somehow get good enough to be a minstrel."

Vanyel's insides hurt as badly as if Medren had punched him there. *Gods*— His thoughts roiled with incoherent emotions. *Gods, he's like I was—he's* just *like I was—only* he *doesn't have those thin little protections of rank and birth that I had. He doesn't have a Lissa watching out for him. And* he *has the Gift, the precious Gift. My gods*—

" 'Course, my mother figures there's another way out," Medren continued, cynically. "Lady Treesa, she figures you've turned down so many girls, she figures she's got about one chance left to cure you. So she told my mother you were all hers, she could do whatever it took to get you. And if my mother could get you so far as to marry her, Lady Treesa swore she'd get Lord Withen to allow it. So my mother figures on getting into your breeches, then getting you to marry her—then to adopt me. She says she figures the last part is the easiest, 'cause she watched you watching me, and she knows how you feel about music and Bards and all. So she wanted me to help.''

Poor Melenna. She just can't seem to realize what she's laying herself open for. "So why are you telling me this?'' Vanyel found his own voice sounding incredibly calm considering the pain of past memories, and the ache for this unchildlike child.

"I don't like traps,'' Medren said defiantly. "I don't like seeing them being laid, I don't like seeing things in them, and I don't much like being part of the bait. And besides all that, you're—special. I don't want anything out of you that you've been tricked into giving.''

Vanyel rose, and held out his hand. Medren looked at it for a moment, and went a little pale despite his brave words. He looked up at Vanyel with his eyes wide. "You—you want to see my side of the bargain?'' he asked tremulously.

Vanyel smiled. "No, little nephew,'' he replied. "I'm going to take you to my father, and we're going to discuss your future.''

Withen had a room he called his "study,'' though it was bare of anything like a book; a small, stone-walled room, windowless, furnished with comfortable, worn-out old chairs Treesa wouldn't allow in the rest of the keep. It was where he brought old cronies to sit beside the fire, drink, and trade tall tales; it was where he went after dinner to stare at the flames and nurse a last mug of ale. That's where Vanyel had expected to find him; and when Vanyel ushered Medren into the stuffy little room, he could tell by his father's stricken expression that Withen was assuming the absolute worst.

"Father,'' he said, before Withen could even open his mouth, "do you know who this boy is?''

Candlelight flickered in his father's eyes as Withen

looked at him as if he'd gone insane, but he answered the question. "That's—uh—Medren. Melenna's boy."

"Melenna *and Mekeal's,* Father," Vanyel said forcibly. "He's Ashkevron blood, and by that blood, we owe him. Now just how are we paying him? What future does he have?" Withen started to answer, but Vanyel cut him off. "I'll tell you, Father. None. There are *how* many wedlock-born heirs here? And *how* much property? Forst Reach is big, but it isn't *that* big! Where does that leave the little tagalong bastard when there may not be enough places for the legitimate offspring? What's he going to do? Eke out the rest of his life as somebody's squire? What if he falls in love and wants to marry? What if he doesn't *want* to be somebody's squire all his life? You've given him the same education and *the same wants* as the rest of the boys, Father. The same expectations; *the same needs.* How do you plan on making him content to take a servant's place after being raised like one of the heirs?"

"I—uh—"

"Now I'll tell you something else," Vanyel continued without giving him a chance to answer. "This young man is Bardic-Gifted. That Gift is as rare—and as valued in Valdemar—as the one that makes me a Herald. And we Ashkevrons are letting that rare and precious Gift *rot* here. Now what are we going to do about it?"

Withen just stared at him. Vanyel waited for him to assimilate what he'd been told. The fire crackled and popped beside him as Withen blinked with surprise. *"Bardic-Gifted? Rare?* I knew the boy played around with music, but—are you telling me the boy can make a future out of *that?"*

"I'll tell you more than that, Father. Medren *will be* a first-class Bard *if* he gets the training, and gets it *now.* A Full Bard, Father. Royalty will pour treasure at his feet to get him to sing for them. He could earn a noble rank, higher than yours. But only if he gets what he needs now. And I mean *right* now."

"What?" Withen's brow wrinkled in puzzlement.

Vanyel could see that he was having a hard time connecting "music" with "earning a noble rank."

"You mean—send him to Haven? To Bardic Collegium?"

"That's exactly what I mean, Father," Vanyel said, watching Medren out of the corner of his eye. The boy was in serious danger of losing his jaw, or popping his eyes right out of their sockets. "And I think we should send him as soon as we can spare him an escort—when the harvest is over at the very latest. I will be *happy* to write a letter of sponsorship to Bard Chadran; if Forst Reach won't cover it, I'm sure my stipend will stretch enough to take care of his expenses."

That last was a wicked blow, shrewdly designed to awake his father's sense of duty and shame.

"That won't be necessary, son," Withen said hastily. "Great good gods, it's the least we can do! If—if that's what *you* want, Medren."

"What I want?" the boy replied, tears coming to his eyes. "Milord—I—oh, Milord—it's—" He threw himself, kneeling, at Withen's feet.

"Never mind," Withen said hastily, profoundly embarrassed. "I can see it is. Consider it a fact; we'll send you off to Haven with the Harvest-Tax." The boy made as if to grab Withen's hand and kiss it. Withen waved him off. "No, now, go on with you, boy. Get up, get up! Don't grovel like that, dammit, you're Ashkevron! And don't thank me, I'm just the old fool that was too blind to see what was going on under my nose. Save your thanks for Vanyel."

Medren got to his feet, clumsy in his adolescent awkwardness, made clumsier by dazed joy. Before the boy could repeat the gesture, Vanyel took him by the shoulders and steered him toward the door.

"Why don't you go tell your mother about your good news, Medren?" He winked at the boy, and managed to get a tremulous grin out of him. "I'm certain she'll be *very* surprised."

That sentence made the grin widen, and take on a certain conspiratorial gleam. Medren nodded, and Vanyel pushed him out the door, shutting it tightly behind him.

He turned back to face Withen, and there was *no* humor in his face or his heart now.

"Father—we have to talk."

Five

"What?" Withen asked, his brow wrinkling in perplexity.

"I said, we have to talk. Now." Vanyel walked slowly and carefully toward his father, exerting every bit of control he possessed to keep his face impassive. "About you. About me. And about some assumptions about me that you keep making."

He stood just out of arm's length of Withen's chair, struggling to maintain his composure. "When I brought Medren in here, I *knew* what you were thinking, just looking at your expression."

The fire flared up, lighting Withen's face perfectly.

And you're still *thinking it—*

Vanyel came as close as he ever had in his life to exploding, and kept his voice down only by dint of much self-control. It took several moments before he could speak.

"Dammit, Father, *I'm not like that!* I don't *do* things like that! I'm a Herald—and dammit, I'm a decent man—I *don't* molest little boys! Gods, the idea makes me want to vomit, and that *you* automatically assumed I *had—*"

He was trembling, half in anger, half in an anguished frustration that had been held in check for nearly ten years.

Withen squirmed, acutely uncomfortable with this confrontation. "Son, I—"

Vanyel cut him off with an abrupt shake of his head, then held both his hands outstretched toward Withen in entreaty. "Why, Father, *why? Why* can't you believe what I tell you? What have I *ever* done to make you think I have no sense of honor? When have I ever been anything other than honest with you?"

Withen stared at the floor.

"Look," Vanyel said, grasping at anything to get his point across, "let's turn this around. I know damned good and well you've had other bedpartners than Mother, but do I assume *you* would try to—to seduce that little-girl chambermaid of hers? Have I looked sideways at *you* whenever you've been around one of her ladies? So why should *you* constantly accuse me in your mind—*assuming* that I would *obviously* be trying to seduce every susceptible young man and vulnerable little boy in sight?"

Withen coughed, and flushed crimson.

He'd probably be angry, Vanyel thought, in a part of his mind somewhere beyond his anguish, *except that this frontal assault isn't giving him time to be anything other than embarrassed.*

"You—could use your reputation. As a—the kind of person they write those songs about." Withen flushed even redder. "A hero-worshiping lad would find it hard to—deny you. Might even think it your due and his duty."

"Yes, Father, that's only too true. Yes, I *could* use my reputation. Don't think I'm not acutely aware of that. But I *won't*—would *never!* Can't you understand that? I'm a Herald. I have a moral obligation that I've pledged myself to by accepting that position."

By the blankness of Withen's expression, Vanyel guessed he had gone beyond Withen's comprehension of what a "Herald" was. He tried again. "There're more reasons than that; I'm a *Thought-senser,* Father, did you ever think what *that* means? The constraints it puts on me? The things I'm open to? It's a harder school of honor than *ever* Jervis taught. There are no compromises, mind-to-mind. There are no falsehoods; there can't be. A relationship for me has to be one of absolute equals; freely giving, freely sharing—or nothing." Still no flicker of understanding. He used blunter language. "No rape, Father. No unwilling seduction. No lies, no deception. No harm. No one who doesn't already know what he is. No one who hasn't made peace with what he is, and accepted it. No innocents, who haven't learned what they are. *No children.*"

Withen looked away, fidgeting a little in his chair. Vanyel moved swiftly to kneel between him and the fire, where Withen couldn't avoid looking at him. "Father—dammit, Father, I *care* about you. I don't want to make you unhappy, but I can't help what I am."

"Why, Van?" Withen's voice sounded half-strangled. "Why? What in hell did I do wrong?"

"Nothing! Everything! *I* don't know!" Vanyel cried out, his words trembling in the air, a tragic song tortured from the strings of a broken lute. "Why am I Gifted? Why am I *anything*? Maybe it's something I was born with. Maybe the gods willed it. Maybe it's nothing more than the fact that the only person I'll *ever* love happened to be born into the same sex body that I was!" Grief knotted his throat and twisted his voice further. "All I know is that I *am* this way, and nothing is going to change that. And I care for my father, and nothing is going to change *that*. And if you can't believe in me, in *my* sense of honor—oh, *gods,* Father—"

He got to his feet somehow, and held out his open hands toward Withen in a desperate plea for understanding. "Please, Father—I'm not asking for much. I'm not asking you to *do* anything. Only to believe that I am a decent human being. Believe in Herald Vanyel if you won't believe in your son. Only— *believe;* believe that no one will ever come to harm at my hands. And *try* to understand. Please."

But there still was no understanding in Withen's eyes. Only uncertainty, and acute discomfort. Vanyel let his hands fall and turned away, defeated. The last dregs of his energy had been burned out, probably for nothing.

"I—I'm sorry, son—"

"Never mind," Vanyel said dully, bleakly, walking slowly toward the door. "Never mind. I've lived with it this long, I should be used to it. Listen; I'm going to make you a pledge, since you won't believe me without one. Medren is safe from my advances, Father. Your grandsons are safe. *Every damned thing on this holding down to the sheep is safe*. All right? You have my damned oath as a damned Herald on it. Will that be enough for you?''

He didn't wait to hear the answer, but opened the door quickly and shut it behind him.

He leaned against it, feeling bitterness and hurt knotting his gut, making his chest ache and his head throb. And eleven years' experience as a Herald was all that enabled him to cram that hurt back down into a little corner and slap a lid on it, to fiercely tell the lump in his throat that it was *not* tears and it *would* go away. Maybe he would deal with all this later—not now. Not when he was drained dry, and not when he was alone.

''Heyla, Van!'' The voice out of the dark corridor beside him startled him, and he whirled in reaction, his hands reaching for weapons automatically.

He forced himself to relax and made out who it was.

Gods—just what I needed.

''Evening, Meke,'' he replied; tired, and not bothering to hide it. ''What brings you out tonight?''

Lady Bright, that sounds feeble even to me.

''Oh,'' Mekeal replied vaguely, moving into the range of the lantern beside the study door, ''Things. Just— things. Where were you off to?''

''Bed.'' Vanyel knew his reply was brusque, even rude, but it was either that or let Meke watch him fall to pieces. ''I'm damned tired, Meke; I've got a lot of rest to catch up on.''

Mekeal nodded, his expression softening a little with honest concern. ''You look like hell, Van, if you don't mind my saying so.''

Gods. Not again.

''The last year hasn't been a good one. Especially not on the Borders.''

''That's exactly what I wanted to talk to you about,'' Mekeal interrupted eagerly, coming so close that Vanyel could see the lantern flames reflected in his eyes. ''Listen, can you spare me a little time before you go off to bed? Say a candlemark or so?''

Vanyel stifled a sigh of exasperation. *All right, stupid, you gave him the opening, you have only yourself to blame that he took it.* ''I suppose so.''

"Great! Come on." Mekeal took Vanyel's elbow and hauled him down the ill-lit corridor, practically running in his eagerness. "You've seen that stud I bought?"

"From a distance," Vanyel replied cautiously.

"Well I want you to come have a good look at him, and he really doesn't settle down until well after dark."

I can believe that.

They walked rapidly down the hollow-sounding corridor, Mekeal chattering on about his acquisition. Vanyel made a few appropriately conversational sounds, but was far more interested in reestablishing his "professional" calm than in anything Meke was saying. Meke was obviously heading for the corridor that led to one of the doors to the stable yard, so Vanyel pulled his arm free and picked up his own pace a little. *Might as well get this over with now, while I'm still capable of standing.*

Mekeal obviously had this planned, for when they emerged into the cool darkness and a sky full of stars, Vanyel saw the dim glow of a lantern in the stable across the yard. They crossed the yard at something less than a run, but not for lack of Mekeal's trying to hurry his steps.

The famous stud had pride of place, first stall by the entrance, by the lantern. Vanyel stared at it; if anything it was worse up close than at a distance.

Ugly is not the word for this beast.

It glared over its shoulder at him as if it had heard his thought, and bared huge yellow teeth at him.

I've never seen a nastier piece of work in my life. You couldn't pay me enough to try and saddle-break this *nag!*

"Well?" Meke said, bursting with pride. "What do you think?"

Vanyel debated breaking the bad news easily, then remembered what his little brother was like. He not only did not take hints well, he never even knew there was such a thing as a subtle hint. Vanyel braced himself, and told the truth. "Meke—there's no way to say this tactfully. That monster is no more *Shin'a'in* than I am. You were robbed."

Mekeal's face fell.

"I've *seen* a *Shin'a'in* warsteed," Vanyel said, pressing his advantage. "She was under a *Shin'a'in*. The nomad told me then that they don't ever sell the warbeasts, and that they literally would not permit one to be in the hands of an outsider. And they never, *never* let the studs off the Dhorisha Plains. I'll give you a full description. The mare I saw was three hands shorter than this stud of yours, bred to carry a *small* horse-archer, not anyone in heavy plate; she was short-backed, deep-chested, and her hindquarters were a little higher than her forequarters. She had a *big* head in proportion to the rest of her: and if anything, this stud's head is small. Besides being large, her skull had an incredibly broad forehead. *Lots* of room for brains. Need I say more? About the only things she had in common with your stud are color and muscles.'' He sighed. ''I'm sorry, Meke, but—''

''A half-breed? Couldn't he be a cross?'' Mekeal asked desperately.

''*If* a common stud caught the mare in season and *if* she didn't kill him first and *if* the mare's owner decided— against all tradition—to sell the foal instead of destroying it or sending it back to the Plains. Maybe. Not bloody likely, but a very bare possibility. It is also a *very* bare possibility that this stud has *Shin'a'in* cull blood some-where *very* far back in his line.'' Vanyel rubbed his nose and sneezed in the dust rising as the stud fidgeted in his stall. The precious stud laid his ears back, squealed, and cow-kicked the door to the box as hard as he could. More dust rose, there was a clatter of hooves all through the stable, and startled whinnies as the rest of the horses reacted to the stud's display of ill-temper. ''Meke, *why* did you buy this monster? Forst Reach has the best line of hunters from here to Haven.''

''Hunters won't do us a hell of a lot of good when there's an army marching toward us,'' Mekeal said, turn-ing to look at him soberly. ''And even if this lad isn't *Shin'a'in,* crossed into our hunters he'll sire foals with the muscle to carry men in armor. I just hope to hell we have them *before* we need them.''

Incredulous at *those* words coming from *this* sibling, Vanyel looked across his shoulder at his younger brother. ''*That's* what this is about?''

Meke nodded, the flickering lantern making him look

cadaverous—and *much* older. "There's trouble coming up on the West. Even if it *doesn't* come from Baires and Lineas, one or both, it'll come from the changeling lands beyond them. It's been building since Elspeth died. Every year we get more weird things crossing over into Valdemar. Plenty of them here. Check the trophy room some time while you're visiting; you'll get an eyeful. Liss thinks they're either being driven here by something worse, or they're being sent to test our defenses; neither notion makes me real comfortable. Hunters are all very well, but they *can't* carry a fighter in full armor. And the tourney-horses I've been seeing lately don't have the stamina for war. One thing this lad *does* have is staying power."

Gods. Oh, gods. If the problems are so evident even Meke is seeing them— Vanyel's spine went to ice.

"Do you want my advice with this beast?" he asked bluntly.

Mekeal nodded.

"Given what you've told me, he might be useful after all. Breed him to the best-tempered and largest of the hunter-mares. *And* see what comes of breeding him to plowhorse mares. Maybe make a second-generation three-way cross—if you have time."

Meke nodded again, smoothing his close-cropped beard. "I hadn't thought about plowbeasts; that's a good notion. He *is* vicious. I like the willingness to fight, but I can do without viciousness. So, you agree with me?"

Vanyel turned slowly, a new respect for his brother coloring his thoughts. "Meke, even if this Border stays quiet, there's Karse, there's Hardorn, there's Iftel—Rethwellan *seems* quiet, but *their* king is old and that could change when he dies. There's even the north, if those barbarians ever find a leader to weld them into a single fighting force. May the gods help us—you'll have a ready market all too soon if you can breed the kind of horses you're talking about." Vanyel pondered the worn, scrubbed wooden floor of the stable. "What have *you* heard? About here, I mean."

"The Mavelans want Lineas. Badly enough to chance a war with us, I don't know. The Lineans don't much like either Baires or Valdemar, but they figure Valdemar is marginally better, so they'll put up with us enforcing the peace as third-party. It all comes down to what's going to happen with this mess with Tashir being disinherited.''

Lady Bright, more words of political wisdom where I never expected to find them. His view may be short-sighted—he may not see the larger picture—but where his neighbors are concerned, my little brother seems to have them well weighed and measured.

"I heard Lord Vedric is behind the protests," Vanyel ventured. Mekeal looked skeptical.

"One thing I've learned watching them, anything the Mavelans do openly has about fifty motives and is hiding a dozen other moves. The protest might be a covering move for something else. Vedric might have the backing of the family. Vedric might be operating under orders. Vedric might be acting on his own. Vedric might have nothing to do with it. And Vedric might really be Tashir's father—and might actually be trying to do something for the boy. The gods know he hasn't any true-born offspring and it's not that he hasn't tried.''

Vanyel nodded and stowed that tidbit away. "I'll tell you what, Meke, I'll do what I can to get Father to see why you want to breed this stud—and persuade him that since you *aren't* breeding hunters, he ought to leave you alone to see what you can come up with. But those sheep—''

Mekeal coughed and blushed. "Those sheep were a damnfool thing to do. There's no market, not with Whitefell just south of us, with furlongs of meadow good for nothing *but* sheep. But dammit, the old man goes *on* and *on* about it until I'm about ready to bash him with a damned candlestick! I am *not* going to give in to him! We aren't *losing* money, we just aren't making as much. And if I give in to him on the sheep, he'll expect me to give in to him on the stud.''

Vanyel groaned. "Lady bless! The two of you are stubborn enough to make an angel swear! Look—if I manage to get him to agree on the stud, will you *please* agree to clear out the damned sheep? Bright Havens, can't *one* of you show a little sense in the interests of peace and compromise?''

Mekeal glowered, and Mekeal grumbled, but in the end, on the way back to the keep, Mekeal grudgingly agreed.

The silken voice stopped Vanyel halfway between the keep and the stables, dimming the bright autumn sunlight and casting a pall on the sweetness of the late-morning sky.

"Good—morning, Herald Vanyel." The slight hesitation before the second word called pointed attention to the fact that it lacked little more than a candlemark till noon. The cool tone made it clear that Father Leren did not approve of Vanyel's implied sloth.

Vanyel paused on the graveled path, turned, and inclined his head very slightly in the priest's direction. "Good afternoon, Father Leren," he replied, without so much as an eyebrow twitching.

The priest emerged from the deeply recessed doorway of the keep's miniature temple, a faithful gray-granite replica of the Great Temple at Haven. Leren had persuaded Withen to build it shortly after his arrival as Ashkevron priest, on the grounds that the chapel, deep within the keep itself, couldn't possibly hold the family and all of the relatives on holy days. It had been a reasonable request, although the old priest had managed by holding services in shifts, the way meals were served in the Great Hall. Vanyel alone had resented it; the little gray temple had always seemed far too confining, stifling, for all that it was five times the size of the chapel. The homely wood-paneled chapel made the gods seem—closer, somehow. Forgiving rather than forbidding. He had hated the temple from the moment he'd first stepped into it at the age of five—and from that moment on, had refused to enter it again. In fact, Vanyel wasn't entirely certain that Leren had ever even set foot in the *old* chapel—which was why, as a boy, he had accomplished his own worship *there*.

"I have seen very little of you, my son," came the cool words. The priest's lean, dusky face beneath his slate-gray cowl was as expressionless as Vanyel's own.

Vanyel shrugged, shifted his weight to one foot, and folded his arms across his chest. *If he wants to play word-games—* "I'm not surprised, sir," he replied with detached civility. "I have spent very little time outside of my room. I've been using this time alone to catch up on a year's worth of lost sleep."

Leren allowed one black eyebrow to rise sardonically. "Indeed? Alone?" His expression was not quite a sneer.

Oh, what the hell. In for a sheep— Vanyel went into a full-scale imitation of the most languid fop at Haven.

The man in question *wasn't* inclined to *shay'a'chern*, as it happened: rumor had it he played the effeminate to irritate . . . not Vanyel—but certain of his colleagues— and he *also* happened to be one of the finest swordsmen outside of the Circle or the Guard.

Following that sterling example, Vanyel set out to be *very* irritating.

"*Quite* alone, sad to say," he pouted. "But then again, I *am* here for a *rest*. And company would *hardly* be *restful*."

The priest retreated a step, surprise flashing across his face before he shuttered his expression. "Indeed. And yet—I am told young Medren spends an inordinate amount of time in your rooms." His tone insinuated what he did not—quite—dare say.

I won't take that from Father, you snake. I'm damned if I'll take that from you. Vanyel transformed the snarl he wanted to sport into an even more petulant pout. "Oh, *Medren*. I'm teaching him music. He is a sweet child, don't you think? But still, a child. *Not* company. I prefer my companions to be—somewhat older." He took a single slow step toward the priest, and twitched his hip *ever* so slightly. "Adult, and able to hold an adult conversation, to have adult—interests." He took another step, and the priest fell back, a vague alarm in his eyes. "More— masterly. Commanding." He tilted his head to one side and regarded the priest thoughtfully for a moment. The alarm was turning to shock and panic. "Now, someone like *you*, dear Leren—"

The priest squawked something inarticulate about vessels needing consecrating, and groped behind him for the handle of the open temple door. Within a heartbeat he was through it, and had the gray-painted door shut— tightly—behind him.

Vanyel grinned, tucked his head down to hide his expression, and continued on toward the stables and Yfandes.

"Meke, is there going to be a Harvest Fair this year?" he asked, brushing Yfandes with vigor, as she leaned into the brush strokes and all but purred.

Mekeal did not look up from wrapping the ankles of one of his personal hunters. "Uh-huh," he grunted. "Should be near twice as big as the ones you knew. Got merchants already down at Fair Field."

"Already?" This was more than he'd dared hope. "Why?"

"Liss an' her company, dolt." Meke finished wrapping the off hind ankle and straightened with another grunt, this time of satisfaction. "Got soldiers out here with pay burnin' their pockets off, and nothin' to spend it on. There're only two ladies down at Forst Reach village that peddle their assets, and three over to Greenbriars, and it's too far to walk except on leave-days anyway. So they sit in camp and drink issue-beer and gripe. Can you see a merchant allowin' a situation like *that* to go unrelieved? There's a *good* girl," he said to the mare, patting her ample rump. "We'll be off in a bit."

:Keep brushing. You can talk and brush at the same time.:

Vanyel resumed the steady strokes of the brush, working his way down Yfandes' flank. "Would there be any instrument makers, do you think?" Forst Reach collected a peddling fee from every merchant setting his wagon up at the two Fairs, Spring and Harvest. Withen found that particular task rather tedious—and Vanyel hoped now he'd entrusted it to Mekeal.

Meke sucked on his lip, his hand still on the mare's shoulder. "Now that I think of it, there's one down there already. Don't think we'll likely get more than one. Why?"

"Something I have in mind," he replied vaguely. And, to Yfandes, *:Lady-my-love, do you think I can interest you in a little trip?:*

She sighed. *:So long as it's a* little *trip.:*

:This soft life is spoiling you.:

:Mmh,: she agreed, blinking lazily at him. *:I like being spoiled. I could get used to it very quickly.:*

He chuckled, and went to get her gear.

Before Vanyel even found someone who knew which end of Fair Field the luthier was parked in, he had picked up half a dozen trifles for Shavri and Jisa.

He paused in the act of paying for a jumping jack, struck by the fact that they were so uppermost in his mind.

What has gotten into me? he wondered. *I haven't thought about them for a year, and now—*

Well, I haven't seen them for a year. That's all. And if I can give Shavri a moment of respite from her worry—

He pocketed the toy and headed for the grove of trees at the northern end of the field.

He spotted the faded red wagon at once; there was an old man seated on the back steps of it, bent over something in his hands.

Shavri, bent over a broken doll some child in the House of Healing had brought to her. Looking up at me with a face wet with tears. Me, standing there like an idiot, then finally getting the wits to ask her what was wrong. "I can't bear it, Van, I can't—Van, I want a baby—"

He shoved the memory away, hastily.

"Excuse me," Vanyel said, after waiting for the carver perched on the back steps of his scarlet traveling-wagon (part workshop, part display, and part home) to finish the wild rose he was carving from a bit of goldenoak. He still hesitated to break the old man's concentration in the middle of such a delicate piece of work, but there wasn't much left of the afternoon. If he *was* going to find the purported luthier—

But the snow-pated craftsman's concentration had evidently weathered worse than Vanyel's gentle interruption.

"Aye?" he replied, knobby fingers continuing to shape the delicate, gold-sheened petals.

"I'm looking for Master Dawson."

"You're looking at him, laddybuck." Now the oldster put down his knife, brushed the shavings from his leather apron, and looked up at Vanyel. His expression was friendly in a shortsighted, preoccupied way, his face round, with cloudy gray-green eyes.

"I understand you have musical instruments for sale?"

The carver's interest sharpened, and his eyes grew less vague. "Aye," he said, standing, and pulling his apron over his head. There were a few shavings sticking to the linen of his buff shirt and breeches, and he picked at them absently. "But—in good conscience I can't offer 'em before Fair-time, milord. Not without Ashkevron permission, any rate."

Vanyel smiled, feeling as shy as a child, and tilted his head to one side. "Well, I'm an Ashkevron. Would it be permissible if I made it right with my father?"

The old man looked him over very carefully. "Aye," he said, after so long a time Vanyel felt as if he was being given some kind of test. "Aye, I think 'twould. Come in the wagon, eh?"

Half a candlemark later, with the afternoon sun shining into the crowded wagon and making every varnished surface glow, Vanyel sighed with disappointment. "I'm sorry, Master Dawson, none of these lutes will do." He picked one at random off the rack along the wall of the wagon interior, and plucked a string, gently. It resonated—but not enough. He put it back, and locked the clamp that held it in place in the rack. "Please, don't mistake my meaning, they're beautiful instruments and the carving is fine, but—they're—they're student's lutes. They're all alike, they have no voice of their own. I was hoping for something a little less ordinary." He shrugged, hoping the man wouldn't become angered.

Strangely enough, Dawson didn't. He looked thoughtful instead, his face crossed by a fine net of wrinkles when he knitted his brows. "Huh. Well, you surprise me, young milord—what did you say your name was?"

Vanyel blushed at his own poor manners. "I didn't, I'm sorry. Vanyel."

"Vanyel—that—Vanyel Ashkevron—my Holy Stars! The *Herald?*" the luthier exclaimed, his eyes going dark and round. "Herald Vanyel? The Shadow—"

"Stalker, Demonsbane, the Hero of Stony Tor, yes," Vanyel said wearily, sagging against the man's bunk that was on the wall opposite the rack of instruments. The instrument maker's reaction started a headache right behind his eyes. He dropped his head, and rubbed his forehead with one hand. "Please. I really—get tired of that."

He felt a hard, callused hand patting his shoulder, and he looked up in surprise into a pair of very sympathetic and kindly eyes. "I 'magine you do, lad," the old man said with gruff understanding. "Sorry to go all goose-girl on you. Just—person don't meet somebody folks sing about every day, an' he sure don't expect to have a hero come strollin' up to him at a Border Harvest Fair. Now—you be Vanyel, I be Rolf. And you'll have a bit of my beer before I send you on your way—hey?"

Vanyel found himself smiling. "Gladly, Rolf." He started to pick his way across the wagon to the door at the rear, but the man stopped him with a wave of his hand.

"Not just yet, laddybuck. As I was startin' to tell you, I got a few pieces I don't put out. Keep 'em for Bards. And I got a few more I don't even show to just any Bard—but bein' as you are who you are—an' since they say you got a right fine hand with an instrument—" He opened up a hatch in the floor of the crowded wagon, and began pulling out instruments packed in beautifully wrought padded leather traveling bags. Two lutes, a harp—and three instruments vaguely gittern-shaped, but—much larger.

Rolf began stripping the cases from his treasures with swift and practiced hands, and Vanyel knew that he had found what he was looking for. The lutes—which were the first cases he opened—bore the same relationship to the instruments on the wall as a printed broadside page bears to an elegant and masterfully calligraphed and ornamented proclamation.

He took the first, of a dark wood that glowed deep red where the light from the open door struck it, tightened a string, and sounded a note, listening to the resonances.

"For you, or for someone else?"

"Someone else," he said, listening to the note gently die away in the heart of the lute.

"High voice or low?"

"High now, but I think he may turn out to be a baritone when his voice changes. He's my nephew; he's Gifted, and he is going to be a *fine* Bard one day."

"Try the other. That one is fine for a voice that don't need any help, it's loud, as lutes go—and all the harmonics are low. The other's better for a young voice, got harmonics up and down, and a nice, easy action. That one he'd have to grow into. The other'll grow with him."

Vanyel looked up in surprise at the old man.

Rolf gave him a half-smile. "A good craftsman knows how his work fits in the world," he said. "I got no voice, but I got the ear. Truth is, the ear is harder to find than the voice. Though I doubt you'd find a Bard who'd agree."

Vanyel nodded, and picked up the second lute, this one of wood the gold of raival leaves in autumn. He tightened a string and sounded it; the note throbbed through the wagon, achingly true. He tried the action on the neck; easy, but not mushy.

"You were right," he said, holding the chosen instrument out to the luthier. "I'll take it. No haggling." He looked wistfully over at the other. "And if I didn't already have a lute I love like an old friend. . . ."

Rolf waggled his bushy eyebrows, and grinned, as he took the golden lute from Vanyel and began carefully replacing it in its bag. "Care to try a friend of a new breed?" He nodded at the gittern-shaped objects.

"Well . . . what *are* those things?"

"Something new. Been trying gitterns with metal strings, 'stead of gut; you tell *me* how it came out." He laid the chosen lute carefully down on his bunk, and stripped the case from the first of the gitterns. "I keep 'em tuned; *this* one is a fair bitch to demonstrate if I don't. Hoping to get to Haven one day, show 'em to the Collegium Bards.''

"Great good gods." Vanyel's jaw dropped. *"Twelve* strings? I should say"

"Fingers like a gittern. That one's like it; the other has six. Use metal harpstrings.''

Vanyel took it carefully, and struck a chord—

It rang like a bell, sang like an angel in flight, and hung in the air forever, pulsing to the beat of his heart.

He closed his eyes as it died away, lost in the sound; and when he opened them, he saw Rolf grinning at him like a fiend.

"You," he said, sternly, "are a *terrible* man, Rolf Dawson.''

"Oh, I know," the old man chortled. "It don't hurt that the inside of this wagon's tuned, too. That's one reason why them student lutes sound as good as they do. But *that* lady'll sound good in a privy.''

"Well, I hope you're prepared to work your fingers to the bone," Vanyel replied, snatching up the leather case and carefully encasing *his* gittern. "Because when I take her back to Haven and Bard Breda hears her, *she* will send packs of dogs out to find you and bring you there!''

Rolf chuckled even harder. "Why d'you think I pulled her out and had you try her? You're going to do half my work for me, Herald Vanyel. With you t'speak for me, an' that lady, I won't spend three, four fortnights coolin' my heels with the other luthiers, waitin' my turn to see a Collegium Bard''

Vanyel had to chuckle himself. "You are a *very* terrible man. Now—you might as well tell me the worst.''

"Which is?''

He felt a twinge for his once-full purse. Well, what else did he have to spend money on? "How much I owe you.''

Vanyel shut the door to his room behind him, and set his back against it, breathing the first easy breath he'd taken since he left his chamber this morning. "Gods!" he gasped. "Sanctuary at last! Hello, Medren. Oh, you brought wine—thank you, I need it badly.''

The boy looked up from tuning the new strings on his new lute. Giving it to him had given Vanyel one of the few moments of unsullied joy he'd had lately, a reaction worth ten times what Vanyel had paid.

Medren grinned. "Mother?"

"That was this morning," Vanyel replied, pushing away from the door, heading for the table beside the window seat and the cool flask of wine Medren had brought. "I swear, she chased me all over the keep, with stars in her eyes and the hunt in her blood."

Poor Melenna. Gods. She's driving me insane, but I can't bring myself to hurt her. I've been the cause of so much hurt, I can't bear any more.

"And lust in her—"

"Medren!" Vanyel interrupted. "That's your mother you're slandering!"

"—heart," the boy finished smoothly. "What did you do?"

"I took a bath," Vanyel replied puckishly. "I took a very *long* bath. When I finally came out, she'd given up."

"So who was chasing you this time, if it wasn't Mother?"

"Lord Withen. On the Great Sheep Debate. Meke wants to keep the sheep on Long Meadow until spring shearing; Father wants yearling cattle back there *immediately,* if not sooner." Vanyel groaned, and held both hands to his head. "If it wasn't for the fact that once this door is shut they leave me alone—gods, the *Border* was more peaceful!"

Water droplets beaded the side of the flask and ran down the sides as Vanyel picked it up. "Whoever gets you as protege will bless you for your thoughtfulness, lad." He poured himself a goblet of wine, and took it with him to sip while he stood over Medren at the window seat. No breath of air stirred without or within, and even the birds seemed to have gone into sun-warmed naps. "That instrument still as much to your liking?"

Medren nodded emphatically, if with a somewhat preoccupied expression. He was tuning the last string, a frown of concentration making his young face look adult.

Vanyel warmed inside, as he picked up his own lute.

It takes so little to make the child so happy—and gods, the talent.

"Well, then," he said, laying a hand on the boy's shoulder, "Ready for your les—"

The boy winced away from the light touch on his shoulder. Not in emotional reaction—but in physical pain.

Vanyel snatched his hand away as if it had been a red-hot iron he'd inadvertently set on the bare skin of the boy's back. "Medren! What did I—"

"It's all right," the boy said, and shrugged—which called up another grimace of pain. "Just—old Jervis reckoned we all ought to see how you could trick somebody into dropping his shield and then come in overhand. Guess who got to be the victim." His tone was so bitter Vanyel could taste it in the back of his own mouth. "Like always."

The blur of the blade coming for him, always coming for him; the weight of the shield on his arm getting heavier by the moment. The shock of each blow that he couldn't dodge; shock first and then pain. Breath burning in lungs, side aching with bruises; cramps knotting his calves. Stumbling backward, head reeling, vision clouding.

"Van?"

Cold sweat down his back and the taste of blood in his mouth. Bitter, absolute humiliation. Metallic taste of hate and fear.

"Hey, Vanyel—are you all right?"

Vanyel shook his head to clear it, and locked down his own agitation as best he could, but the memories were crowding in on him so vividly he was almost reliving that moment so many years ago when Jervis finally got him in a corner he couldn't escape.

"I'm all right." His left arm began to ache, and he massaged the arm and wrist, reflexively. *It still aches, after all these years. I still have numb fingers. Oh, gods, not Medren.*

"We could skip the lesson," he began, with carefully suppressed emotion.

"No!" Medren exclaimed, clutching the lute to his

chest and jumping to his feet. "No, it's nothing! Really! I'm fine!"

"If you're sure," Vanyel said, wondering how much of that was bravado on the boy's part.

"I'm sure. I got some horse-liniment, I'd have rubbed it on right after, but I didn't want to stink up your room." The boy grinned half-heartedly and sat down again, his eyes anxious.

"I've got something better than that—if you aren't afraid I'll seduce you!"

The boy made an impudent face at him. "You *had* your chance, Vanyel. What's this stuff you got? I don't mind telling you my shoulder hurts like blazes."

"Willow and wormwood in ointment, with mint to make it smell reasonable. I *always* have some." He put his lute down and leaned over to rummage in the chest at the foot of his bed. "I'm one of those people who bruise just thinking about it. Get your shirt off, would you?"

When he turned around with the little jar in his hand, the boy had stripped to the waist, revealing a nasty bruise the size of his hand spreading all over the left shoulder. It was an ugly thing; purple the next thing to black in the center, blue-gray and red mottled through it.

Crack like lightning striking as the shield split. Sudden darkness, dizziness. Waking to Lissa's anxious face, and a pain in his left arm that sent the blackness to take him again.

"Good gods!"

Medren shrugged with one shoulder. "I bruise that way. Looks worse than it is, I guess. Young Mekeal took one just as hard and you can't hardly see a mark on him." He looked longingly at the pot of salve. "Vanyel, you going to stand there and stare all day, or use that stuff?"

"I'm sorry, Medren." He shook off his shock; got several fingersful of the ointment, and began to massage it as gently as possible into the bruised area, working his way from the edges inward. The boy hissed with pain at first, then gradually relaxed.

Vanyel, on the other hand, was profoundly disturbed, and growing tenser by the moment, his own shoulder muscles knotting up like snarled harpstrings. *Gods, what can I do? Damned if I'll let Jervis ruin Medren the way he ruined me—but how? If I force a confrontation, he'll only take it out on Medren. If I take him on myself—gods, I do* not *trust my temper, not with that old bastard. Not with the hair-trigger I've got right now. He'd make one wrong move, or say something at the wrong time—and I'd kill him before I could stop myself. What can I do? What can I do?*

"Lady Bright," the boy sighed. "I feel like I got a shoulder again, instead of a piece of pounded meat."

"Medren, is there *any* way you can avoid practices until you're safely out of here?" Vanyel asked.

Medren considered a moment. "Now and again," he said, slowly. "Not on a regular basis."

"Are you *sure?*" Vanyel pursued, urgently. "Isn't there any place you can hide?"

"Not since they opened up the back of the library. Anyplace I go, they'll find me, eventually. Isn't there anything *you* can do?"

Vanyel shook his head with bitter regret. "I wish there were. I can't think of anything at the moment. I'll work on it; if there's a way out for you, I'll find it. Look, avoid him as much as you can. Try and stay out of his line-of-sight when you can't avoid the practices. If he doesn't actually *see* you in front of him, sometimes you can manage to keep from becoming his target for the day."

Medren sighed, and shrugged his shirt back on. "All right. If that's all I can do, that's all I can do." He twisted his head around and gave Vanyel a slightly pained grin. "At least you believe me. You even sound like you know what I'm going through."

Vanyel stared at the wall, but what he was seeing was not wood panels, but a thin, undersized boy being used as an object upon which a surly ex-mercenary could vent his spleen. "I do, Medren," he replied slowly, a cold lump settling just under his heart. "Believe me, I do."

Vanyel was more than happy to see his Aunt Savil's serene, beaky face again. And was glad he'd decided to ride out and meet her. It was a lot easier to tell her what had been going on without wondering who was going to overhear.

". . . so that's the state of things," Vanyel concluded, Yfandes matching her pace to Savil's taller Companion. "The only real problems—other than the fact that Lineas and Baires could go for each other's throats any day—is Medren. Melenna I can avoid. The Great Sheep Debate is going to go on until the sheep are gone from Long Meadow. Father seems to have accepted Meke's breeding program, although he's got *his* agent out looking for an alternative to that awful stud Meke bought. But Medren—Savil, I *know* what you're thinking, you're thinking I'm overreacting to seeing another lad in the same position I was in. You didn't see that monster bruise he showed up with. He's not getting love-pats. That bruise was the size of my spread hand, finger-tip to thumb-tip, easily."

"Huh," Savil replied, frowning in thought.

"And to make it worse, Meke told me Jervis wants to—I quote—'go a few rounds with me.' To spar." Vanyel snorted. " 'Spar' indeed. It'll be a cold day—"

She nodded. "Probably a damned good idea to avoid him. He'll push you, Van; he'll push you all he can."

"And I've just spent the last year on the Border."

"Exactly. If he pushed you too far—well, you know that better than me. Kellan, can you and 'Fandes kindly wait until you're loose for the chatter and gossip? We're trying to have a serious briefing here."

Vanyel chuckled. *:Trading stories about the muscular, young courier-types?:*

:Shut up and ride.:

Vanyel caught Savil's eye, and they exchanged a look full of irony. "I can see," she said aloud, "that this is going to be a very—lively—visit."

Six

The argument had been in full flower since Vanyel had arrived at the stable, and from all that he could tell it had evidently begun (well fertilized with invective) long before then. The stable was a good fifty paces from the keep itself, but the voices reached with unmistakable clarity well beyond the stable. The stablehands were doing their best to pretend they weren't listening, but Vanyel could all but see their ears stretching to catch the next interchange.

Havens, Savil has a strong set of lungs!

"Now *listen,* you stubborn old goat—"

"Stubborn!" The indignation in Withen's voice was thick enough to plow. "You're calling *me* stubborn? Savil, that's pot calling kettle if I ever—"

"—and provincial, hidebound, and muddle-headed to boot!"

Vanyel smothered a grin and kept the movement of the brush steady along Yfandes' glossy flank. She sighed with contentment and leaned into each stroke.

:Feel good?:

:Wonderful. All Companions should choose musicians; you have such talented hands. Speaking of which—: She flicked an ear at the open window through which Savil and Withen's argument was coming so very clearly.

:Music to my *ears. If he's yelling at Aunt Savil, he can't be yelling at me. You're looking better. Those hollows behind your withers are gone. And your coat is much healthier.:* He paused for a moment to admire the shine.

:I'm recovering faster than you are.: She swung her head around to fix him with a critical blue eye. *:Are you getting enough sleep?:*

121

:If I slept any longer, I'd wake up with headaches.: He turned his mental focus up toward that open window, avoiding any more of Yfandes' questions.

The fact was, he didn't *know* why he was still sleeping so long, and tiring so easily. He always felt hollow, somehow, as if there were an enormous empty place inside him that he couldn't fill. But he *had* recovered enough that all the problems, major and minor, were starting to make him feel restless because he couldn't *do* anything about them.

Other problems were starting to eat at him, too.

Shavri; I like her—too much? Gods. I must think about her and Jisa every night. I loved 'Lendel. I know I loved him. But have I let Shavri get into me deeper than I'd thought? Gods, she's Randi's lifebonded. He must be my best friend in the world next to Savil. She's one of my best friends. How can I even be thinking this? Gods, gods. Am I really even shaych? Or am I something else?

The question ate at him, more than he cared to admit.

Am I avoiding Melenna because I'm shaych, or because I hate to be hunted?

He shied away from the uncomfortable thoughts, and sent out a thin, questing thought-tendril toward Savil.

:What can I do for you, demon-child?: came her prompt reply.

:Just wondering if you needed rescuing.:

The answer came back laughter-tinged. *:Havens, no! I'm enjoying this one! I'm opening your father's eyes to politics and policies under Randale. Elspeth was always conservative, and got more so as she grew older. Randale is her opposite. This is coming as quite a shock to Withen.:*

Vanyel fought down another grin. *:What's he up in arms about now?:*

:The mandatory education law Randale and the Council just passed.:

:Remind me; I'm behind.:

:Every child in Valdemar is to be taught simple reading, writing, and arithmetic in the temples from now on; every child, not just the highborn, or the few the priests single out as having vocations or being exceptional.

Morning classes in the winter from harvest-end to first planting. And it's the duty of the Lord Holders to see that they get it.

Vanyel blinked. *:Oh, my. I can see where he wouldn't be pleased. I know where Randale's coming from on this one, though; he talked it over with me often enough. I just didn't know he'd managed to get it past the Council intact.:*

:Enlighten me, I need ammunition.:

:He believes that an informed *populace is more apt to trust its leaders than an ignorant populace, assuming that they feel the leaders are worthy of trust.:*

:That isn't much of a problem in Valdemar,: Savil replied.

:Thanks be to the gods. Well. The only way to have an informed populace is to educate them, so they don't have to rely on rumors, so they're willing to wait for the official written word. *It was the near-panic when Elspeth died that decided him.:*

:I didn't know that; good points, ke'chara. Young as he is, our Randale can be brilliant at times. As soon as your father pauses for breath—:

"Now see here, you old boneheaded windbag! Do you *want* those farmers of yours to be the prey of every scoundrel with a likely rumor under his hat?" Savil had the bit in her teeth and she was off again. Vanyel gave up trying to control himself, and leaned all his weight against Yfandes, laughing silently until his eyes teared.

This is ridiculous, Vanyel thought irritably, pausing for a moment on the narrow staircase. *Absolutely ridiculous. Why should I have to act as though I was sneaking through enemy-held territory just to get to my own bed every night?*

He took the last flight of back stairs to the fourth floor, poorly lit as they were, with not so much as the betraying squeak of a stair tread. He flattened himself against the wall at the top, and probed cautiously ahead.

No Melenna.

So far, so good.

His right eye stung and watered, and he rubbed at it

with one knuckle; his eyelids were sore and felt puffy. *I should have gotten to bed candlemarks ago, except every time I tried, Melenna was lurking around a corner to waylay me. I hope she's given up by now.*

He peered down the dark corridor one more time before venturing out into it. This was the servants' floor, and if she were still awake and hoping to ambush him, Melenna wouldn't think to look for him up here.

He counted the doors—the fifth on the right opened, not into a room, but into a tiny spiral staircase that only went as far as the third floor. He probed again, delicately. Nothing in the staircase, or at the foot of it.

The stair was of cast iron, and in none too good repair. He clung to the railing, gritted his teeth, and moved a fingerlength at a time to keep it from rattling. The journey through the stuffy darkness seemed to take all night.

Then his foot encountered wood instead of metal, and he slipped off the staircase and groped for the door. He put one hand flat against the wooden panel and concentrated on what lay beyond it. This stair let out only two doors from his own room, and if Melenna were waiting, she'd be in the corridor.

Politeness—and Heraldic constraints—forebade Mindsearching for her, even if he had the energy to spare. Which he didn't, he had been chagrined to discover.

And anyway, the non-Gifted were always harder to locate by Mindsearch than the Gifted.

I'm getting very tired of this. I don't want to set Mother off, and I don't really want to hurt Melenna, but if this cat-and-mouse game keeps on much longer, I may have to do just that. I tell her "no," politely, and she doesn't believe it. I avoid her, and she just gets more persistent. I almost killed her two days ago when she popped out of hiding at me. He leaned his forehead against the door for a moment, and closed his aching eyes. *I'm about at my wits' end with that woman. Damn it all, she's old enough to know better! I* don't *want to hurt her; I don't even want to embarrass her.*

Well, there was no sign of her in the corridor. He relaxed a little and stepped out onto the highly polished wood of the hall of the guest rooms, where the brighter lighting made his smarting eyes blink and water for a moment.

He opened the door to his own room—

And froze; hand still on the icy metal of the doorhandle.

Candles burned in the sconces built into the headboard. Melenna smiled coyly at him from the middle of his bed. She allowed the sheet to slide from her shoulders as she sat up, proving that she hadn't so much as a single thread to grace her body.

Vanyel counted to ten, then ten again. Melenna's smile faltered and faded. She tossed her hair over one shoulder and began to pout.

Vanyel snatched his cloak from the peg beside the door, turned on his heel without a single word, and left, slamming the door behind him hard enough to send echoes bouncing up and down the corridor.

:'Fandes, beloved,: he Mindsent, so angry he was having trouble staying coherent. *:I hope you don't mind sharing sleeping-space.:*

Straw was not the most comfortable of beds, although he'd had worse. And he'd spent nights with his head pillowed on Yfandes' shoulder before this. But "day" for the occupants of the stable began long before *he'd* been getting up. The stablehands had no reason to be quiet— and neither did the horses. Meke's famous stud was the worst offender; he began cow-kicking the side of his stall monotonously from the moment color touched the east.

:Stupid brute thinks that if he keeps kicking, somebody will come to let him out,: came Yfandes' sleepy thought. *:I usually move out under a tree about now.:*

Vanyel raised his head and yawned. He'd gotten some sleep, but not nearly as much as he would have liked. *:You move. I think I'll go back to my room. If Melenna hasn't taken herself off to her own room by now, I swear I'll throw her out. Maybe a dose of humiliation will convince her to leave me alone.:*

:Sounds as good a plan as any.: Yfandes waited for him to move out of the way, then got herself to her feet and nudged open the outside door. Vanyel stood up,

shoulders aching from the strange position he'd slept in, and brushed bits of straw off his clothing. He ignored the startled glances of the stablehands, picked up his cloak and shook it out as Yfandes ambled out into her meadow.

:Go get some more sleep, dearheart,: she Mindsent back toward him.

:I'll try,: he replied, smoldering. *:Maybe I'll bring my sleeping roll down here. Maybe when word gets around that I'm sleeping with horses she'll stop this nonsense.:*

:And if she's stupid enough to try and waylay you down here, I'll chase her around the meadow a few times to teach her better manners,: Yfandes sent, irritation of her own coloring her thoughts a sullen red. *:This is getting exasperating. I don't care if she thinks she's in love with you, that doesn't excuse imbecilic behavior.:*

Vanyel didn't reply; he was too close to temper that could do the woman serious damage. He folded his cloak tidily over his arm, pretending he didn't notice the whispers of the stablehands as he let himself out of the stall and shut the door behind him.

"There was a problem with my bed last night," he told Tam, the chief stableman and Withen's most trusted trainer.

Tam was no fool, and he'd been quietly on Vanyel's side since Van was old enough to ride. He was one of the few at Forst Reach who hadn't changed his behavior toward Vanyel when the nature of Vanyel's relationship with Tylendel became known at the holding. Since his wife was one of the cooks, he was quite conversant with "house" gossip. He smiled slowly, showing the gap where he'd had three teeth kicked out. "Aye, milord Van. I ken. There's some invites a body wish t' give hisself."

Van winced inwardly a little, knowing that this was going to do Melenna's reputation no good at all once this tale got around the keep.

The stablehands went back to their chores, and he wound his way past them, out into the yard between the outbuildings and the keep. He blinked at the sunlight, seeing just one other person, a vague, unidentifiable shadow in the door of the armory.

"Vanyel," called a raspy, far-too-familiar voice. "A word with you."

Jervis. The armsmaster moved out past the door of the armory to stand directly in his path and Vanyel felt his stomach start to churn. In no way could he successfully avoid a confrontation this time. Jervis was between him and the keep.

"Yes, armsmaster?" he said.

"I left you messages, Meke told me he'd passed them on." Jervis moved closer, a frown making his seamed and craggy face more forbidding than usual.

Vanyel kept his own feelings behind an expressionless mask. "That you wanted to spar, yes I know. He did tell me. I'd rather not, thank you."

"Why not?"

"Frankly, because I don't feel up to it," Vanyel replied with cool neutrality, though his back was clammy with nervous sweat. *Because I know damned well it won't stay polite exercise for long. Because I know you're going to push me just as far as you can, armsmaster. I'm going to have to* hurt *you. And dammit, I·don't want to let you do that to me.*

"What's that supposed to mean?" Jervis growled, his face darkening. "You think this old man isn't good enough for you?"

"I'm *worn out,* for one thing. I just spent the night in the stable because there was an unwelcome visitor in my room; that's *not* my bed of choice, and Meke's damned stud makes more noise than a herd of mules. For another—Jervis, I've been on a battle-line for the last year. *You* were a mercenary, what does that tell you?"

I don't want to inflict more pain when I don't have to. And I'm on a hair-trigger; gods, think about this, you old bastard! Remember what it was like, how some things became reflex, no matter how hard you tried to control them.

Jervis narrowed his eyes. "You look in good enough shape to me. There's nothing you can do, young Vanyel, that *I* can't handle. Unless you're really no better than, say, young Medren, no matter what all those songs say about you."

The reminder of the treatment Medren was receiving at Jervis' hands was the spark to the tinder. Vanyel's temper finally snapped. "On your head be it," he growled. "I take *no* responsibility. You want to spar so badly, all right, let's get it over with."

He stalked off toward the armory, a sturdy wooden building between the stables and the keep, with Jervis at his heels. He had a set of practice gear here, made up soon after he returned from k'Treva, gear put together at Withen's insistence and unused until now. It was gear unlike any other set at Forst Reach: light, padded leather gambeson; arm, thigh, and shin guards; main-gauche and heavy rapier; and a very light helm, all suited to his light frame and strike-and-run style.

The armory was not dark; there were clerestory windows glazed with bubbly, thick third-rate glass; stuff that wouldn't admit a view, just light. Vanyel found the storage chest with his name on it. He pulled his gear out and stripped off yesterday's tunic, pulling on the soft, thick linen practice tunic, strapping on the gambeson and guards, and gathering up his helm and weighted wooden practice blades.

This armory was new; built since Vanyel had left home. There was enough room for sparring inside; most of the interior had been set up as a salle. Vanyel was just as pleased to see that. The older building had been so small that all practices had to be held outside. So far as Vanyel was concerned, the fewer eyes there were to witness the confrontation, the better he'd like it.

He was shaking and sick inside; he was going to give Jervis a lesson the old man would never forget, and the very idea made his gut knot. He was *not* proud of what he was going to do.

But the old man asked *for it. He wouldn't take "no," and he wouldn't back down. Dammit, it's going to be* his *fault, not mine!*

Van dwelled on that while he armed up; a sullen anger making him feel justified, and burning the knots out of his gut with self-righteousness and a growing elation that he was *finally* going to pay Jervis back for every bruise and broken bone.

Until he realized where *that* train of thought was leading him.

I'm rationalizing the fact that I want to beat him bloody. That I want revenge on him. Oh, gods.

The realization made him sick again.

He went to the center of the practice area, crossing the unvarnished wooden floor with no more noise than a cat. Jervis looked around after donning his own gear—*much* heavier than Vanyel's—as if he had actually expected Van to have slipped out while he was arming. He seemed surprised to see Vanyel standing on the challenger's side, waiting for him.

I'll let him make the first move, Van thought, keeping himself under tight control. *He's probably going to give me a full rush, and I wouldn't be surprised if he tried to hurt me. Damned bully. But I will not lose my temper. I can't stop my reflexes, but I can keep my temper. I will not let him do that to me.*

But Jervis astonished him by simply walking up to his side of the line, giving a curt salute that Vanyel returned, and waiting in a deceptively lazy guard position.

Dust tickled Vanyel's nose, and somewhere in the building a cricket was chirping. *Well do something, damn you!* he thought in frustration, as the moments continued to pass and Jervis did nothing but stand in the guard position. Finally the waiting was too much for his nerves. *He* rushed Jervis, but he pulled up short at the last second, so that the armsmaster was tricked into overextending. There was a brief flurry of blows, and with a neat twist of his wrists, Vanyel bound Jervis's blade and sent it flying out of his hands to land with a noisy clatter on the floor to Vanyel's left.

Now it comes. Vanyel braced himself for an explosion of temper.

But it didn't. No growl of rage, no snatching off of helm and spitting of curses. Jervis just *stood,* shield balanced easily on left arm, glaring. Vanyel could feel his eyes scorching him from within the dark slit of his helm for several heartbeats, while Vanyel's uneasiness grew and his blood pounded in his ears with the effort of holding himself in check. Finally the armsmaster moved—

only to fetch the blade, return to his former position, and wait for Vanyel to make another attack.

Vanyel circled to Jervis' right, bouncing a little on his toes, waiting for a moment when he could get past that shield, or around it. Sweat began running down his back and sides, and only the scarf around his head under his helm kept it out of his eyes. He licked his lips, and tasted salt. His concentration narrowed until all he was aware of was the sound of his own breathing, and the opponent in front of him.

Jervis returned his feints, his blows, sometimes successfully, sometimes not. Vanyel scored on him *far* more often than vice versa. But every time he made a successful pass, Jervis would back out of reach for a moment. It was maddening and inexplicable; he'd just fall completely out of fighting stance, shuffle and glare, and mutter to himself, before returning to the line and mixing in again.

This little series of performances began to wear on Vanyel's nerves. It was far too like the stalking he used to get when Jervis wanted to beat him to a pulp and didn't quite dare—and at the same time, it was totally unlike anything in the old man's usual pattern.

What's he doing? What's he waiting for? Those aren't any love-taps he's been giving me, but it isn't what I know he's capable of, either.

Finally, when he was completely unnerved, Jervis made the move he'd been expecting all along—an all-out rush, at full-strength and full-force, the kind that had bowled him over time after time as a youngster—the kind that had ended with his broken arm.

Blade a blur beside Jervis' shield and the shield itself coming at him with the speed of a charging bull, the horrible crack as his shield split—the pain as the arm beneath it snapped like a green branch.

But he *wasn't* an adolescent, he was a battle-seasoned veteran.

His boot-soles scuffed on the sanded wood as he bounced himself out of range and back in again; he engaged and used the speed of Jervis' second rush to spin himself out of the way, and delivered a good hard stab to

Jervis' side with the main-gauche as the man passed
him—

—or meant to deliver it. For all his bulk, Jervis could
move as quickly as a striking snake. He somehow got his
shield around in time to deflect the blow and then continued into a strike with the shield-edge at Vanyel's face.

Vanyel spun out of the way, and let the movement carry
him out of sword range. But now his temper was gone,
completely shattered.

"*Damn* you, you bullying bastard! Preach about honor
and then turn a shield-bash on me, will you!" His voice
cracked with nerves. "Come on! Try again! *Try* and take
me! I'm not a child, *armsmaster* Jervis. I'm not as *easy*
to knock down and beat up anymore! You can't make a
fool and a target of me the way you do with Medren! I
know what I'm doing, damn you, and my style is a match
for yours on any damned field!"

Jervis pulled off his battered helm with his shield hand,
and sweat-darkened tendrils of gray-blond hair fell into
his eyes. "That's enough," he said. "I've seen what I
wanted t' see. Seems those songs got a grain of truth in
'em."

Vanyel choked his temper down. "I trust you won't
require any more *sparring sessions,* armsmaster?"

Jervis gave him another long, measuring look. "I didn't
say that. I'll be wantin' t' practice with you again, master
Vanyel."

And he turned on his heel and left Vanyel standing in
the middle of the salle, entirely uncertain of who had won
what.

*Have we got a truce? Have we? Or is this another kind
of war?*

"*My Shadow-Lover, bear me into light,*" Vanyel sang
softly, as the odd, minor chords blended one into another, each leaving a ghost of itself hanging in the air for
the next to build from. This new gittern did things to this
particular song that carried it beyond the poignant into
the unearthly. He paused a moment, brushed the last
chording in a slow arpeggio, and finally opened his eyes.

Medren sat on the edge of the bed, his mouth open in a soundless "O."

Vanyel shook off the melancholy of the song with an effort. "How long have you been there?" he asked, racking the gittern on its stand, and uncoiling from his window seat.

"Most of the song," Medren shivered. "That's the *weirdest* love song I ever heard! How come I never heard it before?"

"Because Treesa doesn't like it," Vanyel replied wryly, stretching his fingers carefully. "It reminds her that she's mortal." He saw the incomprehension on Medren's face, and elaborated. "The lover in the song is Death, Medren."

"Death? As—" the boy gulped. "—a lover?"

The stricken look on the boy's face recalled him to the present, and he chuckled. "Oh, don't look that way, lad. I'm in no danger of throwing myself off a cliff. I have too much to do to go courting the Shadow-Lover."

The boy's face aged thirty years for a moment. "But if He came courting you—"

I'd take His kiss of peace only too readily, Vanyel thought. *Sometimes I'm so damned tired.* He *thought* that—but smiled and said, "He courts me every day I'm a Herald, nephew, but He hasn't won me yet. What brings you here?"

"Oh," Medren looked down at his hands. "Jervis. Some of the other kids—they told me he's got something special going today. For me."

Vanyel thought of the "sparring session" and went cold. And a seed of an idea finally sprouted and flowered. He stood, and walked slowly to the bed, to put his hand lightly on Medren's shoulder. "Medren, would you rather deal with Jervis, or be sick?"

"What?" The boy looked up at him with the same incomprehension in his eyes he'd shown when Vanyel had spoken of the Shadow-Lover.

"I have just enough of the Healing-Gift that I can *make* you sick." That wasn't exactly what he would do, but it was close enough. "Then I can *keep* you sick; too sick to go to practice, anyway." There was measles in the nursery; that would keep the boy down for a good long time.

"Will I lose my voice?" The boy looked up at him with the same complete trust Jisa had, and that shook him.

He grinned, to cover it. "No, you'll just come out in spots, like Brendan. In fact, I want you to sneak into the nursery and spend a candlemark with Brendan when I'm done with you." *As much as I'm going to depress his body, if he isn't fevered by nightfall I'll eat my lute.* "Make sure nobody sees you, and go straight to your mother after and tell her you have a headache."

"As long as I won't lose my voice," Medren said, grinning, "I think I can take spots and itching."

"It won't be fun."

"It's better than being beat on."

"All right." Vanyel put his hand on Medren's shoulders, and focused *down* and *out*—

"Funny about Medren," Radevel said, "coming down with spots so sudden-like. I would've sworn he had 'em once already."

Vanyel just shrugged. He was in Radevel's room following another "sparring session"—this time one in which *he* sparred with Rad under Jervis' eye. It had been easier to deal with than the *last* one, but Jervis was still acting out of character. *We have a truce of sorts. I don't know why, but I won't take the chance that it will extend to cover Medren. I daren't.*

Radevel had invited him here afterward in a burst of hearty comradeship, and Vanyel had decided to take him up on it. Over the past hour he'd come to discover he *liked* this good-natured cousin more than he'd ever dreamed.

" 'Nother funny thing I can't figure," Radevel continued, feet propped up on a battered old table, mug of watered wine in hand. "Old Leren. Saw him watching you an' Jervis an' me at practice this afternoon, an' if looks were arrows, you'd be a damned pincushion. What in hell did you ever do to him?"

Vanyel shrugged, took a long drink of the cool wine,

and turned his attention back to repairing his torn leather gambeson with needle and fine, waxed thread in a neat, precise row of carefully placed stitches. The past four years had seen him out more often than not beyond the reach of the Haven-bred comforts and the servants that saw to the needs of Heralds. He'd gotten into the habit of repairing things himself, and around Radevel, that habit (which Radevel shared) made itself evident at the smallest excuse. "Don't know," he said shortly. "Never did. I would almost be willing to pledge to you that he's hated me from the moment he came here. Mother swears it's because I asked too many questions, but I thought priests were supposed to *encourage* questions. Our old priest did. I may have been only four when he died, but I remember *that.*"

Radevel nodded agreement. "Aye, I remember that, too. Jervis always said that Osen was a good man. Made you feel like taking things to him, somehow. 'The gods gave you a brain, boy,' he'd say. 'If you want to honor them, *use* it.' Never made you feel like you were beneath him." He brooded over his mug, his plain face quiet with thought. "This Leren, now—huh. I dunno, Van. You know, I stopped going to holydays *here* a long time ago— hike down into the village with Jervis when we feel like we need a dose of priest-talk. Tell you something else— young Father Heward down in the village don't care much for Leren either. He did his best not to let on, but he was downright gleeful to see us come marching down to the village temple, an' I *know* he don't care much for fighters, being a peace-preacher. Figure *that.*"

"I can't," Vanyel replied.

He "felt" Savil's distinct "presence" coming up to the door of Radevel's room, so he didn't jump when she spoke. "Is this a 'roosters only' discussion, or can an old hen join?"

Vanyel did not bother to turn around. Radevel grinned past Vanyel's shoulder at Savil, and reached—without needing to look—into the cupboard over his head for another mug. "I dunno," he mused. "Old hens, welcome, but old bats—?"

"*Give* me that, you shameless reprobate," she mock-snarled, snatching the clean mug out of his hand and pouring herself wine from the jug. She tasted it and made a face. "Gods! What's that made of, old socks?"

"Standard merc ration, milady Herald ma'am, an' watered down, too. Grows on you, though. Got into liking it 'cause of Jervis."

"Huh. Grows on you like foot-rot."

Vanyel stuck the needle under a line of stitches and moved over to make room for her. She sat down beside him, careful to avoid unbalancing the bench. She sipped again. "You're right. Second taste has merit—unless it's just that the first swallow ate the skin off my tongue. What was all this about Leren?"

"Radevel said he was watching me and Rad spar with Jervis this afternoon," Vanyel supplied, frowning at his work. The leather was scraped thin here, and likely to tear again if he wasn't careful where he placed his stitches.

"To be precise, he was watching Herald Van, here. Like he was hoping me or Jervis would slip-up like and break his neck for him," Radevel said. "I'll tell you again, I *do* not like that man, priest or no priest. Makes my skin fair crawl with some of those looks he gives."

"I've noticed," Savil said soberly. "*I* don't like him either, and damned if I know why."

Radevel held up one hand in a gesture of helplessness. "I spent more time around him than either of you, and I just can't put a finger on it. Treesa doesn't like him either; only reason she goes to holyday services is 'cause she reckons herself right pious, and facing him's better'n not going. But if she had her druthers, he'd be away and gone. It's about the one thing I agree with that featherhead on. Pardon, Van."

"Mother *is* a featherhead; I won't argue there. But—Savil, did you realize that she's very slightly sensitive? Not Thought-sensing, not Empathy, but like to it—something else, some kind of sensitivity we haven't identified yet. The gods only know what it is; *I* haven't got it nor have you. But it's a sensitivity she shares with Yfandes."

"Treesa? Sensitive like a *Companion?*" Savil gave him

a look of complete incredulity. "Be damned! I never thought to test *her.*"

He nodded. "The channel's in 'Fandes, wide open. The same channel Treesa has, only hers is to 'Fandes the way a melting icicle is to a waterfall. *I* don't know what it is, but I'd say we shouldn't discount feelings of unease just because Treesa shares them. She could *very* truly be feeling something."

"Huh," Radevel said, after a moment. Then he grinned. "I got a homely plain man's notion. That mare of yours ever dropped a foal?"

"Why, yes, now that you mention it. Two, a colt and a filly—both before she Chose me. Dancer and Megwyn. Why?"

"Just that about every mother *I* ever saw, human to hound, knew damned well when somebody had bad feelings toward her children, no matter how much that somebody tried to make out like it wasn't true. Even Milady Treesa." He grinned as Vanyel's jaw fell, and Savil's expression mirrored his. "Now Savil, you never had children, and it'd take a miracle from the Twain themselves to make Van a momma. So, no—what you call—channel. Make sense?"

"Damned good sense, cousin," Vanyel managed to get out around his astonishment. "For somebody who has no magic of his own, you have an uncanny grasp of principles."

Savil nodded. "You know, this enmity could also be partially that the man was pushed into the priesthood by his family and hates it. A priest with no vocation is worse than no priest at all."

"Could be," Radevel replied. "One thing for sure, it wasn't this bad 'fore Van came home. It's like something about Van brings out the worst in the old crow. Thought I'd say something." He shrugged. "I don't like him, Jervis don't like him. Jervis's got a feel for things like enemies sneakin' up on your back. You might want to keep an eye on Leren."

Oh, yes, cousin, Vanyel thought quietly. *If you are seeing the hint of trouble, stolid as you are, I will surely keep an eye on him.*

* * *

:Things in your bed again?: Yfandes asked sweetly.

Vanyel snarled, hung the lantern he was carrying on a hook, climbed up on the railings of the box, and hauled his bedroll down from the rafters above her stall. "This is *not* my idea of a good time," he replied. "I didn't come home with the intention of sleeping in the stable!" The bedroll landed on the floor, and he jumped down off the top rail to land beside it. "Here I thought I'd get past her by getting dinner with the babies and sneaking up to my room at sunset, and there she is waiting for me, bold as a bad penny. Not nude this time, but *in my bed*. 'Fandes, this is the *third* night in a row! Has the woman *no* shame? And I locked the damned door!"

:Why didn't you just put her out the door?:

He glared at her, and heaved the bedding into the stall. "I do not," he said between clenched teeth, "feel like engaging in a wrestling match with the woman. Dammit, there's going to be frost on the ground in the morning. It's getting *chilly* at night."

:Poor abused baby. I know somebody who'll gladly keep you warm.:

He glared at her again, poised halfway over the railings of the box-stall, one foot on either side. " 'Fandes, you're pushing my patience."

:Me.:

"Oh, 'Fandes. . . ." His tone cooled a little, and he swung his leg over the top rail of the stall, and hopped down beside her to hug her neck. "I'm sorry. I shouldn't take the fact that I'm ready to kill *her* out on *you*."

She rubbed her cheek against his, her smooth coat softer than any satin, and nibbled at his hair. Her breath puffed warm against his ear, sweet, and hay-scented. Farther down in the stable, beyond the light of Vanyel's lantern, one of the horses whickered sleepily, and another stamped.

:I'm rather selfishly glad to have you with me,: she said, watching him heap up straw and spread his sleeping roll on it. *:I like having you here with no danger to keep us wakeful, a quiet night, nothing to really disturb us.*

Remember how you used to spend nights out in the Vale with me, watching the stars?:

"And waiting for Starwind to take a header out of his treehouse!" Vanyel laughed, with her rich chuckle bubbling in his mind. "You're right; that *was* a good time, even if I *did* spend the first few months of it in various states of hurting. Gods of Light, 'Fandes, I miss them. It's been far too long since I last saw them. Brightstar must be—what—nearly ten? I wish we had time to go back there."

They don't shake me to my shoes the way Shavri and Randi do. Is it only because I don't see them too often, or—

Yfandes' interrupted his thought.

:You'd have to Gate, or else spend months on the road.: she replied sadly. *:We daren't take the time, and I won't let you Gate yet, not unless it's an emergency. You're still drained.:*

Her tone cheered him a little. "Yes, little mother," Vanyel chuckled, climbing into his crude bed, good humor fully restored. And to prove that he wasn't *quite* so drained as Yfandes seemed to think, he snuffed the lamp with a thought.

:Show-off,: she teased, settling down carefully next to him so that he could curl up beside her, for all the world like a strange sort of gangly foal. He wriggled himself and blankets in against her warm, silken side, and slipped one hand out to rest on her foreleg.

He yawned. With his anger gone, his energy seemed to be gone too. " 'Night, dearheart," he mumbled, suddenly unable to keep his eyes open.

She nuzzled his cheek. *:Goodnight, beloved.:*

They howled around him, trying to crawl inside his mind. Horrible, vile, they made him retch to look at them, but he couldn't look away from their distorted faces and maimed bodies. They drove fear before them and raised terror about them, making a whirlwind with himself in the center; they had knives for teeth and scythes for claws, red eyes full of madness and an insatiable hunger he could feel beating at his frail shell of protection in waves

*of heat. They were shadows, deadly, killing shadows,
and they couldn't get at* him, *but they* could *and* would
*find other prey. They howled off and away on the wind,
and he screamed (or tried to) and hid his head and made
himself as small as he could while the killing and dying
began. And he wept with terror and shrieked—*

Vanyel shook off the grip of the nightmare and came
up out of it with a rush, choking against the black bile
of fear in his throat. He clawed his way out of his blankets, and lay panting and unthinking against Yfandes'
side in the aftermath of all-consuming horror, while his
heart pounded in his ears.

The night about him was quiet, peaceful, undisturbed.

On the surface. But—

Beneath the surface?

Automatically he reached *out* with his Othersenses, to
touch the energy currents that lay beneath the material
night.

No, it hadn't been a nightmare; his Othersenses showed
him the new, churning eddies in the currents of power
all about him. *Something* had happened tonight. Somewhere out there *something* had used Power, used it freely,
and to a terrible end. His nightmare had only been the
far-off echo of something much, much worse. There was
evil on the Otherwinds—and the world beneath shivered
to feel it.

If I'd been in my room, I'd never have felt this, he
realized, coming fully awake. *My room is shielded and
so is Savil's. But I never shield when I'm with Yfandes.
That means Savil hasn't felt this. I'm the only one who
knows there's something wrong.*

" 'Fandes?'' He reached out for her shoulder; the
muscles were bunched with tension, and her head was
up, sniffing the crisp breeze.

:Hush. Listen.:

Faint, and far off—a mind-cry for help? Or just a mind
crying in despair? It wavered maddeningly in and out of
his sensing-range.

*:That's because he's bonded. It's a Companion, a
young one. He's Chosen, and his Chosen is emperiled. I
can hardly hear him.:* She stretched her neck out, as if

simply trying harder could make what she sensed clearer. *:That's—he's caught in his Chosen's fear, and he's nearly hysterical.:*

"Which, Companion or Chosen?" Vanyel scrambled completely out of his bedroll, and flared the lamp to life with a blink of thought. *We'd better deal with this. We may be the only ones close enough to hear them.*

:Both—the Companion, at least.: She lurched to her feet, her eyes black with distress. Moonlight poured in through the open upper half of the door to the paddock, silvering her. *:Vanyel, please—we* must *go to them!:*

"What's it look like I'm doing?" he demanded, throwing her blanket over her, then pulling down the saddle itself. "I'll have you saddled in half a moment. Where is this?"

:Lineas. Highjorune.:

"The Linean throne-seat." He made a quick check of his mental maps. "That's relatively near our Border. Can we be there by dawn?"

:Before.: All her attention was back on the West.

"Good, because I have the feeling what we're about to do isn't legal, at least by Linean standards, and I'd rather not break laws while people are awake to catch me. Kellan!"

A stamp and a whicker told him that Savil's Companion had heard him.

"Get Savil awake and tell her what we know and where we're going. And why."

Snort of agreement.

" 'Fandes, wait a minute, I'd better change." He began stripping his clothing off, cursing the laces that wouldn't come undone, and snapping them when he realized how much time this was taking.

She swung her head around to stare at him frantically. *:We can't afford the time!:*

"We can't afford *not* to take the time," he said reasonably. "Think about it, love. I had damn well *better* be in uniform. Even the Lineans will think twice about stopping a Valdemar Herald, but a man on a white horse won't rate that second thought. I am something less than fond of being a target, even a moving one." He rummaged in the saddlebags, coming up with a slightly crumpled set of Whites. "Thought I left those here. Thank the gods for battle-line habits." He shrugged on the breeches and tunic and belted them tight; pulled on the boots he'd pulled off when he'd wormed into his blankets. "Good thing I've only got the one pair of boots. Damn, I wish I'd thought to leave a sword here."

:Meke left one in the tack bin by the stud.:

"Bless you—"

He vaulted the railings to fetch it; it was not a good blade, but it was serviceable. He strapped it and his long dagger on, inserted the short ones into their pockets in his boots.

His cloak—he looked for it quickly; he'd need it out there. There it was, half tangled with the blankets. He pulled it out of the tangle, shook it out, flung it over his shoulders, fastened the throat-latch, and returned to the task of harnessing Yfandes. He swung the saddle onto her back, gave a quick pull of the cinch, got chest- and rump-bands buckled and snugged in—she was ready.

He snatched her hackamore off its peg and tossed it over her head; he mounted while she shook it into place as the bells on it jangled madly. She booted the bottom of the door into the paddock open with her nose while he grabbed for the reins and brought them over her neck, and then with a leap a wild deer would envy she was off into the darkness.

Seven

Gods, it's like another Border-alert. Though Yfandes was frantic with the call in her mind, Vanyel kept his wits about him and reached out with a finger of power to snuff the lantern as they cleared the stable-door.

Yfandes raced across the black-velvet of the paddock, hooves pounding dully on the turf, uncannily surefooted in all the moon-cast, dancing shadows. He'd forgotten for a moment that their path out was going to be blocked. He glanced ahead barely in time to see the fence at the far end coming at them and set himself instinctively when he felt her gather under him. They flew over the bars and landed with a jar that drove his teeth together and threw him against the pommel of the saddle. He fought himself back into balance and felt her begin to hesitate in midstride.

:Van?:

He clenched his teeth and wrenched himself into place. *:Just go—I'm fine.:*

She stretched out flat to the ground and ran with all the heart that was in her. Vanyel pulled himself down as close to the level of her outstretched neck as he could, kept his silhouette low and clean, and balanced his weight just behind her shoulders where she could carry it easiest. And fed her with his power.

No one except another Herald could know how exhausting "just riding" could be, especially on a ride like this. He was constantly moving, altering his balance to help her without thinking about it. It was *work,* and involved tiny muscle adjustments to complement her exertions.

He kept his cloak tucked in all around, but it didn't

142

help much; the wind cut right through it, and chilled him terribly. His hands and face were like ice before a candlemark had passed. The wind whipped his hair into snarls and numbed his ears, and there was *nothing* he could do except endure it all, and keep his Othersenses alert for trouble.

I'll have to do something about the Border Guards when we get there. Something that isn't intrusive.

The Border—friendly in name only, neutral in truth— was guarded by sentries and watchtowers. They reached it at just about midnight, and Vanyel blinked in amazement when the first of those towers loomed up above the trees on the horizon, a black column against moon-whitened clouds. He'd had no way to judge Yfandes' speed in the dark; only the wind in his face and the thin, steady pull of power from him, power that he in turn drew from the nodes and power-streams they passed as they came into sensing range. Her speed wasn't natural, and required magic to sustain over any distance.

:The watchtowers—: That was the first time she'd Mindspoken him since they'd leapt the paddock fence, and her mind-voice, though preoccupied, was dark with apprehension. *:The Border Guards—:*

:I've got it figured,: he told her; got a wash of relief, and then felt her turn her attention back to the race and her footing, secure in the belief that he would handle the rest.

He closed his eyes against distractions, and Looked out ahead. He found and identified each mind that could *possibly* see them passing—those who were awake and those who were not—he left nothing to chance anymore. Not after he'd once been detected on a crawl through the enemy camp by a cook who happened to head for the privy-trench at *just* the wrong time. So, calling on more of that node-energy he'd garnered on the run, he built a *Seeming* that touched all those minds.

There is nothing on the road, his mind whispered to theirs. *Only shadows under the moon, the drumming of a partridge, the hooves of startled deer. You see nothing, you hear only sounds you have heard before. There is nothing on the road.*

There were plenty of circumstances that could break this *Seeming*. It was too delicate to hold against a counterspell and it would certainly break if they had the misfortune to run into someone physically. But anyone touched by the spell would see only shadows, hear only sounds that could easily be explained away.

More importantly, they would feel a subtle aversion to investigating those sounds, a bored lassitude that would keep them in the shelter of their posts.

They passed the Border-guard station, vaulting the twin gates that barred the road, Valdemar and Lineas sides, as lightly as leaves on the wind. The Linean Guard was actually leaning on the gatepost, lounging beneath a lantern, his face a startlingly pale blur above his dark uniform. He looked directly at them, and Vanyel felt him yawn as they leaped the gate. Then he was lost in the dark behind as they raced on. Vanyel did not look back, but set the spell to break the moment they were out of sight. He would cloak his own passing; he would not leave the Border to spell-mazed guardians.

He spent no more magical energies in such spells; he didn't particularly care if the common folk of Lineas saw them. They were familiar enough with the uniform of the Heralds. If any Lineans saw him, they would assume, reasonably enough, that he'd been properly dealt with at the Border and belonged here.

Yfandes raced on, through pocket-sized villages in tiny, sheltered river-hollows, even through a larger town or two. All were as dark as places long abandoned. Finally, in the dead hours of the night, the time when death and birth lie closest, they came to Highjorune.

Most of the city was as dead and dark as the villages, but not all; no city slept the night through. More and stronger magic would be required to get them to their goal—whatever it was—without being stopped. Vanyel reached, seeking node-energy to use to pass the city gates as they had the Border, and recoiled a little in surprise.

For a place so adamantly against mages and their Gifts, Highjorune was *crawling* with mage-energy. It lay on the intersection of three—five—*seven* lines of force, none of them trivial, all flowing to meet at a node beneath it, liquid rainbows humming the random songs of power, strong enough for even new-made Adepts to use, provided they had the sensitivity to detect them—though the node where they met would be too wild, too strong for any but an experienced Adept.

:Yfandes, stop a bit.:

Yfandes obeyed. He raised his hands, preparing to spin out a true spell of illusion and sound-dampening; taking the power directly from the closest stream, bracing himself for the shock as his mind met the flow of energy.

The city gate was too well-guarded and well-lit, and the city itself too crowded with people to chance the kind of spell he'd worked on the Border Guards. He wanted to hurry the spell, but knew he didn't dare. *Careful*— he told himself. *This is Savil's area of expertise, not yours. Rush it, and you could lose it.*

Yfandes fidgeted, her bridle-bells chiming, her hooves making a deeper ringing on the hard paving of the road. *:Hurry,:* she urged, her own Mindvoice dense with fear. *:Please. He'll die, they'll die—there's another Companion, she's nearly gone mad, she can't speak—:*

:'Fandes, don't interrupt. I'm working as fast as I can, but if I don't pull power now, I won't have anything when we need it.: The raw power was beginning to fill him, fill all the echoing *emptiness*. Natural, slow recovery had not been able to do *this!* He was going to have to wait until the achingly empty reservoirs of power within him were full again before he could spin a shield this complicated, though at this rate it wasn't going to take long. Besides, he was all too likely to *need* power. If everything went to hell and he had to Gate out of here—

Gods. It's like—eating sunlight, breathing rainbows, drinking wind— Force poured into him, wild and untamed, and for the first time in months he felt complete and revived. There was *nothing* this strong anywhere near Forst Reach.

No mystery now why the Mavelans wanted Lineas, not with this *kind of power running through Highjorune going untapped and unused.* He could almost pity the magelords. It must be like living next to people who mined up precious gems with their copper, and threw the gems out with the tailings, but wouldn't let *you* in to glean them. *Got to hurry this. We're running out of time.*

Cautiously he *pulled* at the power, until it responded, flowing faster into him.

That's it. Now I make it mine.

He tapped into the wild power he'd taken; learned it, tamed it to his hand.

He was sweating now; both with effort and impatience. *Gods, this takes too much time, but I can't afford any surprises.*

Slowly, carefully, he began to spin the energy out into threads, visible only to his Othersight, making a cocoon of the threads that would absorb sound within it, and send the eyes that lit upon it to looking elsewhere. Layer on layer, thread on delicate thread, this was a spell that required absolute concentration and attention, for the slightest defect would mean a place where the eye could catch and hold, where sound could leak out. Yfandes stood like a statue of ice in the moonlight, no longer fidgeting.

Finally, with a sigh of relief, he completed the web. He replaced what he had spent, then cut off his connection to the mother-stream.

His arms hurt, but he had the feeling that more was going to hurt than his arms before this was over.

:Go!: he told Yfandes, who leaped off into the dark, heading for the open city gates ahead of them.

He grabbed for the reins and pommel as she shot forward, a white arrow speeding toward a target only she knew.

:'Fandes! Where are we going?:
:The palace!:

The streets wound crazily round about, with no sense and no pattern; some were illuminated by torches and lanterns, some only by the moon. They sped from dark to light to dark again, Yfandes' hooves sliding on the slippery cobbles. They splashed through puddles of water and less pleasant liquids. He could hear her hooves, oddly muffled, beneath him; and both intriguing scents and

noisome, foul stenches that met his nose only to be
snatched away before he could recognize them. There
were people about; street cleaners, beggars, whores,
drunks, others he couldn't identify. The spell held; the
eyes of the townsfolk they passed slid past the two of
them with no interest whatsoever.

*:The first Companion, the young one—I can't even
reach him now, he's too crazed, Van, he's so frightened!:*
Yfandes was not particularly coherent herself; stress was
distorting her mind-voice into a wash of emotion through
which it was hard to pick up words. *:The second one—
she's—her Chosen—she can't bear what he's doing, she's
shutting everything out.:*

Vanyel clung to the pommel and balanced out sideways
a bit as Yfandes rounded a corner, hindquarters skewing
as her hooves slipped a little. This "second one"—she
was probably the Companion with Randale's envoy. But
what could a *Herald* be doing that would stress his Companion to the point of breakdown?

Vanyel didn't have long to wait to discover the answer;
they entered a zone of wider streets and enormous resi-
dences; homes of the noble and rich. The streets were
near daylight-bright with cressets and lanterns of scent-
less oils. *The palace can't be far,* he thought, and just as
he finished the thought, they pounded around a corner
and into a huge square, then down a broad avenue. At
the end of that processional avenue was a huge structure,
half fortress, half fantasy, looming above the city, a black
eagle mantling above her nest against the setting moon.
And at the eagle's feet, an egg of light—the main courtyard, brightly lit. Vanyel banished the spell of *unsight* as
they thundered in the gilded gates.

The dark-charcoal palace walls cupped the courtyard
on three sides, the wall they'd just passed beneath forming the fourth. There must have been a hundred lanterns
burning.

He only got a glimpse of confusion; to his right, half
a dozen armed and armored men, and a Companion down
and moaning on the black cobbles. To his left—a younger
Companion, blood streaked shockingly red on his white

coat, teeth bared and screaming with rage and battle-fury; a blond boy clinging dazedly to his back, and—

It was like something out of his worst nightmares. A *Herald,* with a heavy carter's whip, *beating* the stallion until his skin came away in strips and blood striped bright on the snowy hide, trying to separate him from the boy.

Yfandes literally rode the Herald down, swerving at the last moment to shoulder him aside instead of trampling him. Vanyel leaped from her saddle as he had so many times before in Border-fights; hit the cobbles and tumbled to kill his momentum, and sprang to his feet with sword drawn.

He didn't give the other Herald a breath to react. Whatever insanity was going on here had to be *stopped*. Without thinking, Van reversed the grip on the sword in his hand.

And lashed up to catch the stranger squarely on the chin with a handful of metal.

The other Herald went flying backward, and landed in an untidy heap.

Damn, he's still moving.

Vanyel put himself in fighting stance between the young stallion and his abuser. He touched the young ones' minds just long enough to try and get some sense out of either the boy or the stallion—but from the first picked up only shock, and from the second, fear that drowned everything else out.

Vanyel pulled on the power within him, feeling it leap, wild and undisciplined, as the other Herald staggered to his feet, bleeding from a split lip, and prepared to lash out with the whip again. Flinging out his left hand, Van sent a lash of his own, a lash of lightning from his outstretched finger to the whipstock. The spark arced across the space between them with a crackle and the pungent smell of burning leather, and the dark, sallow-faced Herald dropped the whip with an exclamation of pain. Behind him, Yfandes was holding off the armsmen with squeals, lashing hooves and bared teeth; faced with her anger, they were not inclined to come to the Herald's rescue.

"What in *hell* do you think you're doing?" Vanyel

thundered, letting the other feel his outrage, a wave of red anger. The older man backed up an involuntary pace. "What in the name of the gods themselves is going on here?"

Vanyel sheathed his sword then. The other Herald drew himself up, nursing his injured hand against his chest, rubbing the blood off his bruised chin with the other. "Who are *you* to interfere—" he began, his face a caricature of thwarted authority.

Vanyel tried to Mindspeak, but the other's channel was weak, and he was blocking it besides. And the personality was not one for much hope of compromise. Stolid and methodical—and affronted by the stranger's intervention in *his* jurisdiction. The *young* stranger, too young, surely, to have any authority.

Gods bless—I'm going to have to pull rank on this thickheaded idiot. And he's never going to forgive me for that.

And the only reason I didn't put him out is because *he's so damn thick-headed!*

"Herald-Mage Vanyel Ashkevron," Vanyel cut him off. "Called Demonsbane, called Shadowstalker, First Herald-Mage in Valdemar. I outrank you, Herald, and your damn fool actions tonight called me out of my bed and across the Border. You've exceeded your authority, and I'm ordering you to *let this boy be.* Who in hell are *you?*"

Vanyel could feel the older man's resentment and smoldering anger, heavy and hot, a ponderous weight of molten emotional metal. "Herald Lores," he said sullenly, rubbing his hand. "King Randale's envoy to the court of Lineas."

Over his shoulder, Vanyel watched Yfandes backing away from the armsmen. She cautiously nudged the downed Companion's shoulder—still keeping one eye on them. After a couple of false tries, the other mare managed to get back to her feet, but stood with her head down and her legs splayed and shaking.

:'*Fandes?*:

:*She's Hearing again, and Speaking, a little; when you got her Chosen to stop, it resolved the conflict inside her—*

but she is not well. She is still in turmoil, and her heart bleeds.:

:*Take care of her.*: He turned his attention back to Lores. ''Tell me—slowly—just *what* you thought you were doing, taking a *whip* to a Companion, trying to drive him away from his Chosen.''

Lores snarled. ''That *boy* is a bloody-handed murderer, and that *thing* you call a Companion is his demon shape-changed! He called it up and was trying to escape on it.''

''What?'' Vanyel backed up a step, inadvertently bumping into the young stallion, who snorted in alarm but stood rock-steady, ready to protect his Chosen against *anything*, be it man, beast, or creature of magic. Vanyel reached out, still keeping his eyes on Lores, and laid his hand along the stallion's neck. If *anyone* in the wide world would know what a demon ''felt'' like, *he* did, after having them close enough to score his chest with their claws, and after turning them back against Karse! He extended his mind toward the young stallion's, and touched again, gently. No demonic aura met his mind, only the pure, bright, blue-white pulsing that was the signature of a Companion, an aura that *only* a Companion, of all the creatures he had ever Mindtouched, possessed.

Anger rose in him, as his hand came away bloody, and the young stallion shivered in fear and pain. He clenched his fist and stared at the older Herald. ''You—'' he groped for words. ''If I didn't *know* Randale, and *know* that neither he nor Shavri would send anyone at all unbalanced out here as an envoy, I'd say you were insane.'' The man gaped at him, taken completely aback. ''As it is, I'm forced to say I've never encountered anyone so incredibly *stupid* in my life!'' He relaxed his clenched fist and patted the stallion's neck without looking around, then advanced on Lores with such anger filling him that he was having trouble keeping his voice controlled. ''What in *hell* makes you think this youngster is a demon?''

''You could be fooled, spell-touched—''

''Not bloody likely! And a demon could *never* fool my Companion, *nor* yours. Gods, man, if *they* wouldn't know

a real Companion, who would? Look, you fool—*look!*"
He reached Lores—withstood the desire to strangle the
older man—and spun him around so that he could see his
own Companion, legs bowed and shivering from nose to
tail with shock, head nearly touching the cobbles. His
right hand left a bloody smudge on Lores' shoulder.
"Look what you've *done* to her! Didn't you *feel* it? You
came *quite* close to driving her catatonic. She couldn't
obey you, and she couldn't stop you! *Look at her!*"

Lores took one step toward her—two—and the third
step became a stumbling run that ended with him on his
knees beside her, stroking her neck, whispering in her
ear. Her trembling stopped; she began to relax. He got
to his feet, and urged her a little more upright, until she
finally stood naturally, with her head pressed against the
front of his tunic.

She was so anguished that Vanyel nearly wept. He finally had to block her out of his mind, or he knew he
would lose control of his own small Gift of Empathy.

:*'Fandes,*: he Mindsent softly, :*what about the other?
Can you calm him now?*:

:*Yes.*: She picked her way across the cobbles, hooves
chiming on the hard black stone, until she was behind
him and presumably dealing with the young stallion.
Vanyel took a few steps closer to Lores. The armsmen
began edging toward the gate and slipping out of the
courtyard, and Vanyel was not inclined to stop them.

Lores looked up, his face twisted and tear-streaked.
"I—didn't know. I couldn't—I don't feel anything from
Jenna, not really, I—my Gift—it's Fetching. I don't
Mindspeak even with her, much—I—told her what to do,
but she didn't do it, I thought the demon must have—"
His eyes fell upon the boy, and his face hardened. "It
doesn't matter. That boy is *still* a murderer."

Vanyel lost his hold on his temper. "*Dammit* man,
Companions *don't* Choose murderers!"

"Oh, no?" Lores spat back. "*Gala* did!"

Lightning and rain; madness and grief.

Present rage replaced past grief.

"That," he said angrily, "was *after* she Chose. And
she repudiated him, cast him off. As *you* should know.

After she Chose, and after—her Chosen—was pressed past all sanity. It has *no* bearing on what happened here. *You* would not listen to your *own Companion* try to tell you the truth.''

He took a step toward the other, bloody finger pointed in accusation. ''You blocked her out with *your* anger and *your* fear. You allowed *your* emotions to interfere with your ability to see the truth. You blocked her so you couldn't hear what you didn't *want* to hear.''

Lores' resentment smoldered in his eyes, but he could not deny Vanyel's accusations.

:Van—the boy—:

Vanyel spun, just in time to see the young man losing his death grip on his Companion's mane, sliding to the ground. He sprinted to the boy's side, startling the young stallion so that he threw up his head and rolled his eyes, and caught the boy in mid-collapse, draping the boy's arm over his own neck and shoulder, supporting him, and looked around for an open door—*any* door—

:Your left,: Yfandes prompted: one of the double doors into the main entranceway was cracked open. He half-carried, half-dragged the boy there, with Lores following sullenly behind, and kicked the door open enough to squeeze through.

It was pitchy dark in the palace—which was *damned* odd for the throne-seat, even at a few hours till dawn. Even odder, all that commotion in the main courtyard had brought *no one* out to see what the ruckus was about. Van couldn't see a thing past the little light coming in the doorway. The building might just as well have been deserted.

First things first; they needed light. So— *Be damned to local prejudice,* he thought, and set a globe of blue mage-light to spinning above his head. Behind him, he heard a stifled gasp as Lores watched it appear out of nowhere.

They were in a bare entryway; that was all he had time to notice in his brief glance. *Someplace to put this boy—* A seat was what he was looking for, and he spotted one: a highly-polished wooden bench, bare of cushions and bolted to the floor, over against the wall just clear of the door. Presumably it was for the use of low-rank servants waiting for something or someone at the main entrance. Whatever, it was a seat. He supported the boy over to it, and got him seated, shoved his head down between his legs, and worked the little Healing he knew to clear the shock out and get him conscious again.

The boy was aware enough to interpret that as some kind of coercion or confinement; he tried to fight, and raised his head into the light.

And Vanyel saw his face for the first time.

It was Tylendel's face, dazed with shock and vacant-eyed, that looked up at him in confusion beneath the blue mage-light.

Vanyel choked, and the floor seemed to heave beneath him. Only one hand on the wall saved him. For a moment he thought that his heart had stopped, or that his mind had snapped.

His eyes cleared again, and he took a closer look, reached out to tip the boy's face into the light, and *almost* Mindtouched—

But he stopped himself, as he began to see the little differences. The boy couldn't be more than sixteen, and looked it; 'Lendel had always looked *older* than he really was. The boy's nose was snubbed, or more than 'Lendel's had been; the eyes were farther apart and larger, the chin rounded and not squared, the hair wavy, not curly, and darker than the golden-brown of Tylendel's. Subtle differences, but enough to let him shake off his ghosts, enough to tell him that this *was not* Tylendel.

Whatever the boy in turn saw or sensed in *his* eyes, it reassured him enough that he stopped fighting, and obeyed Vanyel's half-audible order to keep his head down.

Not now, he told himself. *Deal with your ghosts later, not now.*

For the first time since entering the gilded door, he looked around to see if there was *finally* anyone coming. He looked past the barren entryway and froze at the sight of the wreckage in the mage-light.

He'd seen less destruction after the sacking of a keep.

No wonder no one came, he thought, dumbly. *Nobody human could have survived this.*

Vanyel stood at the edge of the staircase and stared. This entry was hardly more than twenty feet long, and made of the same black stone as the exterior, but polished to a reflective shine; it led to a short stone stair that in turn led down into the wood-paneled Great Hall. This Hall had been a reception area—lit by chandeliers and wall sconces, hung with tapestries, lined with dark wood tables and chairs polished to mirror-brightness. It was demolished.

The chandeliers had been torn from the beams, tapestries ripped from the walls. The walls, the floor, the ceiling beams themselves were scored and gouged as though with the marks of terrible claws. The tapestries had been shredded, the furniture reduced to splinters, the wreckage scattered across the floor as though a whirlwind had played here.

Vanyel remembered his dream, and felt his hair rise and a chill creep up his backbone.

"What—" His voice cracked, and he tried again. "What *happened?*"

Lores' lip lifted a little, but he answered civilly enough. "That boy—that's Tashir. You know who he is?"

Vanyel nodded. "Tashir Remoerdis. Deveran of Lineas' oldest child."

"You know Deveran figured him for a bastard, the worst kind, fathered on Ylyna by her own brother, so they say."

"Is that really germane?" Van looked back at the wreckage.

"Damn right it's *germane.*" Lores lifted his lip scornfully. "It's why the brat *did* all this."

"Lores, you'd better tell me everything you know." Vanyel requested simply, still trying to take in the implications of the wrecked palace.

Lores snorted and rambled on. "Ylyna was no virgin, though in honesty the Mavelans never claimed she was. Still, fourteen's a bit young to have been as—let's say—*experienced* as she was. Tashir was born eight months after the wedding. That's suspicious enough. Boy looks like his uncle Vedric and *nothing* like Ylyna or Deveran did. That's the second reason; another is that he's known to have Gifts; Fetching, for one—things have been flying around when he got upset ever since he was thirteen. No Gifts manifested in Ylyna, and there's *never* been any in Deveran's line. The locals called it wizardry and pressured Deveran to disinherit Tashir.''

''I'd heard about the Gift,'' Vanyel said, looking back at the boy to see if he'd overheard them. They were only twenty paces away, and Lores was making no effort to keep his voice down. Tashir was still sitting where they'd left him, head and hands dangling between his knees. ''How did the boy take being disinherited?''

''The boy?'' For a moment Lores seemed puzzled. ''That was the odd part; boy seemed relieved. It was Vedric Mavelan that made all the fuss. But tonight— something happened at dinner, and I'm not sure exactly what.'' Lores wrapped his arms around his chest, and his expression turned introspective, and a little fearful.

''Were you there?'' Vanyel asked.

Lores nodded. ''Always, as the Valdemar envoy. To-night . . .'' He looked into the distance, frowning. ''I remember I was chatting with Deveran's armsmaster and the boy came up to the high table to say something to Deveran. Next thing I knew, they're at it hammer and tongs, screaming at each other, the boy going white and Deveran going red. Then Deveran backhanded the boy, knocked him to the floor.''

Vanyel chewed his lip. ''Was that unusual?''

Lores shrugged. ''Well, it had never happened in public before. Deveran asked us all to leave in the kind of voice that makes an order out of a request. We left—don't look at me like that, what else could we do?''

''I don't know,'' Vanyel replied soberly. ''I wasn't there. But I don't think I would have left a situation that volatile.''

''Well *I* left; it's not Valdemar and it wasn't my business. I went out to the stable and Jenna, was outside with her for a while.'' He shook his head. ''They'd moved the fight up to Deveran's study, toward the back of the palace; I could hear 'em both shouting at each other through the window. Then it got real quiet for a bit—and then all hell broke loose.'' He gestured at the wreckage in the Great Hall, and his expression became strained. "You can figure what *that* sounded like; enough screaming for a war. Nobody wanted to break in on that, and anyway we found out that the doors were all like they were welded shut.''

His voice was casual, but he was trembling and sweating, and his skin was dead white.

"It didn't last long. Then it was quiet again, sudden, like everything had been cut off. Me, the outside servants, and Deveran's armsmen from the palace, and the town guard and a couple of the town council with some courage in them, we all broke the doors open.''

"And you found?''

"That's what we found. The boy knocked out under that bench, and when we went to look for bodies—gods. Everyone inside these walls . . . was dead. The boy's sibs, the servants, everybody. Torn to pieces, just like . . . that stuff. *Nothing* bigger than palm-sized pieces of everybody else.'' He was shaking now, his teeth chattering, and his pupils dilated. *"Nothing,''* he repeated.

"You're not saying *Tashir* did all that?'' Vanyel said incredulously. "That's impossible—it's insane!'' The mage-light flared a little, setting shadows shrinking and growing again, flickering as he whirled to look at the boy, and his attention wavered.

Lores turned away from the wreckage, clutching his arms against his chest, and gradually stopped trembling. His eyes fell on Tashir again; just the sight of the boy seemed to reawaken his anger. "What's insane about it?'' he demanded. "Fetching can wreck, or even kill. I should know that better than *you,* it's *my* Gift.''

"It's one of my Gifts, too, you damned fool!'' Vanyel growled. "And at one point I *almost* got out of control, but my Gift was blasted open and I was in pain enough to drive a strong man mad. Nothing like that happened here! This boy *never* showed a hint of anything on *this* scale! And he was *untrained?* Not bloody likely!''

"How do we know he was untrained?'' Lores demanded, his eyes reflecting blue glints from the mage-light over Vanyel's head. "He was the *only* one left alive! He *had* to have done it!"

Vanyel had a dozen retorts on the tip of his tongue, but none of them seemed wise.

So how did you come to be such an expert on Gifts and magic, you idiot? And did you search to find someone who might have hidden himself—or herself—until you'd found and dealt with Tashir? Or did you identify everyone, or at least count all the bodies and come up with the same number as those known to be in the palace?

He kept his teeth shut on all those questions. It was obvious that this had been bungled from the start, and dressing down this fool wasn't going to undo the bungling.

"We couldn't really believe it, not at first," Lores admitted reluctantly. "We thought it must have been—oh, something out of the Pelagir wilderlands, or even something cooked up by the Mavelans. We really didn't know what it could have been, especially not the Lineans, but there wasn't anyone or anything else, and when we tried to question Tashir, the boy wouldn't answer. At first he was—dazed-like. Then he just refused to speak except to say he didn't remember." Lores shook his head. "Not *remember?* How could he not remember something that did *that?* Unless he was lying, or he'd done it in anger and had blanked it out of his mind." Lores clasped his folded arms still tighter against his chest, as if he was trying to protect himself. "What could we do? The guards were spooked, nobody wanted something like *that* on their hands. In the end, we just threw him in the guardhouse at the front gate there, since the townsfolk didn't want him in *their* jail and nobody wanted to have to go down to the cells under the palace. We sent off a messenger for Vedric, since he was the one making all the fuss about the boy in the first place. He may be a Mavelan, but he's not going to be able to talk the boy out of *this* mess. He'll have to deal with him, and he *is* a mage. We reckoned it was better for one mage to deal with another. *Especially* a murderer."

"That's not proved."

Lores glared at him. Vanyel repeated his words stubbornly. "That's *not* proved. *Nothing* is proved. And furthermore, I'd like to know how the hell a *Herald* could come to attack a Companion."

Lores began pacing, four steps away from Vanyel, four steps back. "We shoved him in there, picked up the bodies—what was left of them. Things quieted down. Then, less than a candlemark ago, that *demon* showed up."

"*Companion.*"

Lores wheeled to glare again, but the look in Vanyel's eyes cowed him. "That *Companion* showed up; he began breaking down the door. The guard got me, I sent for reinforcements—*I* thought it was a demon—more men showed up about the time the de—Companion got the door smashed in and started to run off with the boy. That whip was in the guardhouse and I grabbed it—figuring demon or not, it was horse-shaped." He shrugged. "You know the rest."

"Didn't you even try the boy under Truth Spell?" Vanyel snarled, out of patience with the lack of *thought,* the complete bullheaded stupidity of the man.

Lores looked baffled. " 'Truth Spell'? Why? What's that got to do with me?"

"Goddess Incarnate! *Any* Herald can work first-stage Truth Spell! Didn't your mentor ever—" Vanyel paused at the dumbfounded look on Lores' face. "Your mentor never told you?"

Lores shook his head.

"*Gods,*" Vanyel strode over to the adolescent, who was still slumped over his own knees. "Tashir?" he said, gently, kneeling beside him. He braced himself when the young man looked up, it still made his heart lurch to see those eyes, that face—and that dazed, lost, and pleading expression. "Tashir, do you remember anything that happened tonight? Anything at all?"

Tashir's eyes were still not focusing well; he shook his head dumbly.

Vanyel shook him gently. "Think. Dinner. Do you remember your father calling you up at dinner?"

"I . . ." The boy's voice was quite low, almost a match

for Vanyel's baritone. "I think so. Yes. He . . . wanted me to go somewhere."

"Where, Tashir?" Vanyel prompted.

"I . . . don't remember."

"Do you remember arguing with him?"

A hesitant nod. There were shadows under Tashir's eyes that had nothing to do with the way the light was falling on him. "I didn't want to go. He wanted to send me somewhere. I don't remember where, I just remember that I didn't want to go. I told him I wouldn't. He hit me."

"Did he hit you very often?"

The eyes cleared for a moment, bright with fear. "Often enough," the boy confessed cautiously. "When I was around too much. I tried not to get in his way. Sometimes he'd get mad about something, and take it out on me. But not in front of people, not before tonight."

"So he hit you. Then he sent everyone else away. What then?"

"He . . . came around the table. He grabbed me before I could get away, twisted my arm up behind my back, and made me go with him to his study. And . . ."

The eyes clouded again.

"And?"

"I don't remember!" Tashir wailed softly. "Please, I *don't remember!*"

Vanyel set in motion the spell that called the *vrondi,* the mindless air elemental that could not abide the emotional emanations associated with falsehood. In *his* hands, because he could give it energy beyond its own, the *vrondi* would be able to settle within the youngster's mind: he would be incapable of lying so long as it was there. Vanyel watched the *vrondi* settle into place, a glowing blue mist like a visible aura about Tashir's head and shoulders. *He* would not see it, but Vanyel and Lores certainly could. He glanced over at Lores, and saw the older man's lips compress, his face grow speculative.

"Are you sure, Tashir?" he urged. "Think. Your father took you up to his study; what happened in the study?"

"*I don't remember!*" Tashir whimpered. "I *don't!*"

Vanyel sighed, and dismissed the *vrondi* with a word.
The mist dissolved, faded away, but slowly, not all at
once as it would have if it had met with a lie. There was
only one other thing he could try. He reached out tentatively with a Mindtouch.

Tashir should not have been able to detect it. But suddenly he jerked away, his eyes wild and unreasoning, and
a shield snapped up so quickly Vanyel barely had time to
pull back his Touch.

"Look out!" Lores cried, diving for the floor, as half
a vase rose from the wreckage, flung itself across the
room and smashed against the door. More fragments followed it, all rising from the wreckage to smash against
the door, creating a rain of flying shards that pelted them
both like fine hail.

Vanyel didn't move so much as a hair. He clenched his
jaw, and reached out with his own power to damp Tashir's
Gift with an external shield.

Sudden silence.

"Tashir," he reached out for the youngster, with his
hand this time, not his mind. "Tashir, I want to help
you. I *believe* you. I *will not* allow anyone to harm you,
or to imprison you for something you didn't do."

The adolescent's eyes slowly calmed; grew saner. He
stared at Vanyel for a long moment, then buried his face
in his hands and began sobbing, trembling on the jagged
edge of hysteria.

"I—don't—remember—" he choked. "Oh, *please*, I
don't, I really don't."

Before he could do anything to comfort or calm the
youngster, Vanyel heard a noise in the distance, muffled
by the door, that made his hair stand on end.

The sullen, angry roaring of a mob—

Lores' head snapped up, and a look of grim satisfaction spread over his face. "The armsmen," he said
smugly. "They must have spread the word. That's the
people of Highjorune out there, *Milord Herald-Mage.* You
don't rank *them,* and they aren't likely to listen to you.
What's your plan *now?* They're going to want the boy. I
think you should let them have him."

Tashir gave a kind of choking gasp, and looked straight

into Vanyel's eyes, his whole body pleading for rescue. His eyes were swollen, tears smeared across his face, and hair tumbled into one eye, his expression was tragic and hopeless.

Vanyel could no more have resisted a boy who looked like *that* than he could have given up Yfandes.

"I still outrank *you,* Lores," he said coldly. "You are still under *my* orders. Get out there and do what you can to keep them off."

"Keep them off? You're madder than *he* is!"

"Move!" Vanyel snapped, rising to his feet, as the flickering of torches lit the gap in the open door

Lores made no further protest; he snorted, and stalked across the entryway to the door, his backbone stiff with unspoken resentment.

Vanyel followed him as far as the door, and once he had barely cleared it, slammed it shut practically on his heels. He heard a muffled exclamation, and the muttering of the mob grew louder and nearer. Vanyel threw the bolt into place across the door; it was metal, but it was *not* going to hold up against a concerted attack.

"That . . . isn't going to hold them for long," Tashir said fearfully, brushing the hair out of his eyes with the back of one hand.

"It won't have to," Vanyel answered absently, moving his Othersenses *out* and *down* and hoping that it was no coincidence.

There was that node, the most powerful node he'd ever encountered outside *Tayledras* lands. Given that Highjo-rune was situated *on top* of the convergence of those energy-streams, given that the node *had* to be around here somewhere. . . .

Had the palace been built where *he'd* have put it?

It was no coincidence. The palace was situated *directly* over the node; a node so strong it roared in Vanyel's mind.

"Now that pompous peabrain is going to find out *why* I outrank him," he growled to himself, and *reached*—

The current-power had been wild; it was nothing to this. He had compared channels in his mother and Yfandes to a dripping icicle and a waterfall. *This* was to those streams what a raging Firestorm was to a campfire. But Vanyel knew its secrets and how to control it, and it raged to *his* will.

He set his mind in the spell-cycle; he murmured a few words, gathered his will, and cupped his hands, unconsciously mirroring the *shape* he wanted to create.

Then he snapped his hands open, crying out a single word of *command.*

A flash of light made his closed eyelids burn red for a moment. Tashir cried out fearfully.

Absolute and complete silence descended on them like sudden deafness.

He opened his eyes; a steady, yellow glow on the outer walls was just barely visible to his Othersight.

He had erected a mage-barrier about the palace that would keep out anything *he* didn't want in, including such intangibles as thought—or other magic. *He* could pass through: so could anything he brought with him. No one and nothing else.

With effort his thoughts passed it.

:Yfandes? How are you and the stranger?:

:They are ignoring us,: she said. *:You have frightened the Young One, and angered Lores. The mob has not made up its mind.:*

:Even if they do, it won't get them anywhere. Give me a moment to make up my *mind.:*

Vanyel severed the connection between himself and the node. He could control it, yes, but at a price. He'd just earned himself another scattering of silver hairs. Among other things.

He opened his eyes and saw Tashir huddled up against the wall, shaking so hard his teeth rattled. He walked stiffly to the bench, and touched the young man's shoulder. He got no response. He turned Tashir's face into the light, and saw his eyes glazed over in withdrawal.

"Damn." Vanyel sat down heavily beside him. "Now what?"

He thought hard for a moment; made up his mind quickly, and *reached* for the node again.

The shock as he touched it the second time was a little less. When he could catch his breath again, he used the

node-energy to boost his own Mindspeech far beyond
what he could have reached alone, sending his mind out
questing for a Mindpresence so dear and familiar it could
almost have drawn him on its own.

Touch.

Startlement. *:Who?:*

:Savil?:

Recognition and relief. *:Gods!* Ke'chara, *what has been
bloody going* on? *Where are you?:*

He told her everything that had happened, from the
time he'd been awakened by the nightmare. He compressed as much of it as he could, warned her in advance
before he Mindsent her an image of Tashir, and even so,
the close resemblance to Tylendel came as a shock to her
that mirrored his own. He had been Tylendel's lover—
but Savil had been mentor, friend, confidant, and near-
mother to Tylendel, the role she filled now for Vanyel.

:So,: she sent, after she regained her mental balance.
:Plans?:

*:I'm taking him into protective custody, and getting him
out of here.:*

:How, with a mob—oh, gods.: Realization and fear.
Flatly *:You're going to Gate.:*

:Do you see any other choice?: he asked. *:Even if the
mob weren't there—I tried to remember what little I've
heard about investigative procedures.* Preserve the evidence. *If I break the shield-spell to get out, anybody can
get in, and I don't have the power to set a second spell,
not this solid, not from the outside. From the inside I can
tap the node, but the interference I'd create with the shield
would keep me effectively* out *of the node. You know that.
Shields are permeable to the creator, but they still resist
penetration. We have to find out what happened here,
and we won't if anyone can get in and muddle things up.:*

Her mind-voice was gritty and gray with grim concern.
:Far too logical to make me happy, love. But you rank
me *these days, and there's reasons enough for that for
me to follow* your *lead. Where are you coming in?:*

He'd thought about that very carefully. *:The door to
the old chapel. It's on sanctified ground, it's one of the
few doors inside Forst Reach big enough to use as a Gate-*

*terminus, but it's not under constant use, and I know it
as well as I will ever know any place. So be ready for
me, because I'm not going to be worth much when I come
through.:*

:As if I didn't know. Be careful—please.:

:I'll try.:

He cut the connection to the node, which dropped him
out of the link with Savil, and turned his mind to one
nearer at hand.

:Brightlove—:

:Chosen—:

*:I'm Gating myself and Tashir out of here. You and the
Young One make a run for it. If that damned fool calling
himself a Herald can't take the hint, it's not my fault;
I've got too many balls in the air as it is.:*

She trembled with concern. *:I will warn Jenna; if she
can get him to mount, she can carry him off whether he
likes it or not. I won't tell you not to use that means of
escape, only—take care!:*

He touched her with a mental caress. *:I shall.:*

He opened his eyes, and considered the possibilities,
finally deciding on the open archway onto the stairs as
his best bet. Putting a Gate-terminus on the outer door
where the shield was would be risking more magically
than he cared to. At full powers, maybe. Not now.

But first—

He shoved outward a little, chuckling nastily as the
expanding shield shoved Lores down the stairs and into
the courtyard. *There. That should keep them quiet for a
bit.*

He walked to the center of the hallway, raised his
hands, and *began.*

He spun bits of himself, his stored powers, into the
structure. He could not tap the node for this; the only
possible way to use external mage-energy for a Gate
would be—at least as far as he had learned—if two mages
were lifebonded, for at some deep level, two lifebonded
were *one.* And, as always, as soon as he had formed the
Portal around the edge of the archway, his uniquely sensitized channels began to burn painfully as he resonated

to Gate-energy. When the Gate was complete, he'd be in torment.

But that was something he had learned to accept and work around.

The Weaving—

He spun *himself*, his own substance, out into threads that quested for the unique *place* he sought, the place where he would build the other end of the Gate. At some point he was no longer having to *send* those searching filaments; they were *pulling* on him, and it was all he could do to keep them from spinning away from him and taking everything that *was* him with them. Then, finally, one of them *found* the chapel door—another—a third—

There was a flare of light, not so bright as the one when he'd built the shield, and his knees gave.

Oh, hell— he thought dazedly. *I wasn't as ready as I thought I was.*

He crouched on the filthy, shard-covered floor, panting in pain, for a long, long moment before he had the strength to look up. But when he did, he saw, not the wreckage of the Highjorune Great Hall, but the welcoming, familiar corridor that led to the old Forst Reach chapel. And thrice-blessed Savil, tunic on backward, waiting.

The pain—

I . . . think I'm in trouble. I've never . . . been this drained . . . before, he thought, somewhere under the red wash of burning. *Oh, gods—if I'd known it was going to be like this, I'd never have had the courage. . . .*

He got to his feet, somehow; he staggered like a mortally-wounded drunk trying to get to Tashir. He was so dizzy he could hardly see, and only concentrating on each step, one at a time, enabled him to cross the hallway to the young man.

"Ta—shir," he croaked, and prayed for a little intelligence in those eyes. His prayers were answered *this* time; the young man stared at him with a kind of foggy awareness, though he still trembled in every limb. "Go . . . get up . . ." His feeble tugs on Tashir's arm were answered, the young man stumbled to his feet. "Go . . .

there . . .'' He pushed Tashir toward the Gate, every step bought with black-red waves of pain.

Maddeningly, Tashir *stopped*, right on the edge.

Vanyel screamed in frustration and torment, and *shoved*, sending the young man stumbling through, and unable to keep his balance, fell right through after him.

Fell from torment into agony; strength gone, control gone, sight, sound, all senses. There was only the pain—

And then there was nothing.

Eight

"**Y**ou look like hell," said a rough voice just above his head.

What an amazing coincidence, Savil, Vanyel thought without opening his eyes. *I feel like hell.*

"I seem," his aunt continued dryly, "to spend an inordinate amount of time at your bedside. And don't try to pretend you're not awake."

"I wouldn't think of it," he whispered, cracking his right eye open. Savil was lounging in the chair she'd pulled up next to his bed, feet *on* his bed. "Mother will have a cat," he observed, prying his left eye open as well. "You *know* how she feels about boots on the bedcovers."

"Your mother isn't here at the moment. How are you feeling?"

He took a quick inventory. "Other than some assorted joint-aches, about the same as when I got back to Haven. Which is to say, as you pointed out, like hell. What's been going on? How long was I out this time?"

"Your outside matches your inside, we're not in a war with Lineas *quite* yet, and three days." She quirked one corner of her mouth as he groaned, and continued. "I took the liberty of deep-scanning you while you were wit-wandering, and I got in touch with a couple of merchant-contacts in Highjorune. Useful birds, pigeons. Particularly when one can *tell* their little heads *exactly* where you want them to go. You want your briefing in sequence, or by specifics?"

He had been inching into a sitting position while she was talking. She poured a goblet of cider from a pitcher next to her, and handed it to him when he was secure.

"In sequence," he said, after a sip to help moisten his throat. "And you'd better start with how Father is taking the new houseguest."

"Your father doesn't know about him, thank the gods." The other corner of her mouth twitched up to make a real smile. "Your old aunt is no fool, *ke'chara;* he was due to make his Harvest-tide inspection round of the freeholders the same morning you Gated back and fell on your nose. I simply installed Tashir in the guest room next to yours and didn't bother to tell anyone until after Withen was gone." She hesitated a moment before continuing. "I have to tell you, having that boy around is unnerving. He *acts* like a ghost, whisking out of sight when he sees me coming; he's given me chills more than once. He's too like our lost one. . . . Well. He is *not* well-wrapped, even I can tell that, and I'm no MindHealer."

Vanyel nodded thoughtfully. "I've got too many questions, and nowhere near enough answers. So Tashir is here, and Father doesn't know about it. A not insignificant blessing. Keep going."

"Yfandes and the new Companion got back about noon. By nightfall I'd gotten a pigeon or two back with news. Lores is going back to Haven to protest your actions to Randale, and he's carrying a demand from what's left of Deveran's Council that Tashir be turned over to them. Vedric finally stuck his nose in; he showed up the next day. *He* seems to be on the side of the Lineans, but he wants Tashir turned over to the Mavelans for trial and sentencing." She paused for breath. "That's the bad news. The good news is that since that fathead Lores— yes, dear, I know him, he's a fathead and always has been one—*isn't* a Herald-Mage, he can't Gate back to Haven. It's going to take him a good long while to get there, especially since the Companions are in on our little conspiracy."

"The—how?"

"Jenna is going to be an invalid all the way home. If he makes the same time he'd make on a spavined horse, he'll be lucky."

He coughed on a swallow of cider. Savil patted his back, a gleam of amusement in her eye. "I got that from

'Fandes through Kellan. Jenna is *not* happy with her Chosen, and intends to make him pay for it. So, Lores is going to be delayed. So far as I know, nobody knows where you and the lad are; *Lores* assumed you'd gone to Haven. That's more good news. So you're safe for a bit, maybe long enough to find out what *really* happened.''

''Even when people do find out where we are,'' Vanyel pointed out, ''I can't be countermanded by anyone other than Randale. Randi is going to stall, I *know* him. He knows that if there weren't something damned odd going on, I'd have Gated to Haven with Tashir. So—what about our guest?''

''Well, I told you, he's been acting like a ghost. He's been hovering over *you* whenever there wasn't someone in here, but he seems to know when someone is coming, and slips back into his own room just before they get here. Fortunately I scanned you *before* I tried to read his mind. *Someone* or *something* certainly made him sensitive to *that*. I judged we didn't need any broken vases.''

''Exactly.'' Vanyel sat up a little straighter, feeling better by the moment. ''I *wish* I dared Mindtouch him long enough to figure out what his Gifts are. Fetching for certain probably Mindspeech; that would account for knowing when someone was coming. Has anybody been seeing that he's fed?''

''Oh, he comes to meals, but not with the family. He slips down to the kitchen at First Call for the servants and the armsmen; gets himself something portable, and pelts back up here. I *guess* he returns whatever dishes he takes after the kitchen shuts down for the night; nobody's complained to me about missing plates. Your mother is alive with curiosity about him, and he won't get any nearer to her than he will to me.''

''*Why* is he so—I don't know what to call it; battle-shy, maybe?'' Vanyel chewed at a fingernail. ''I never heard that Deveran was all that bad a man.''

''Rumor and the truth are sometimes fairly different things, *ke'chara*,'' Savil reminded him. ''And Deveran was a man well-beset by problems, saddled with a wife he didn't care for, an enemy on one of his Borders which forced him to make his little kingdom into a client-state

of Valdemar, his eldest was a problematical bastard, and
he was unsteady enough on his throne that his people
could pressure him into disinheriting the boy.'' She
shrugged eloquently. ''This doesn't make for happy times
in Lineas. Men under pressure have been known to take
their unhappiness out on the defenseless.''

''Tashir.'' Vanyel sighed. ''So we have a new presumptive Herald with major Problems. Not good, Savil.
What do we tell Father when he gets back?''

''Good question. No more than that you've retrieved
Tashir newly-Chosen and—damaged. The less he knows
of this mess, the better. I can't remember if he's ever
seen Vedric or Tashir; if he hasn't, it might be best not
to—''

:*FearfearfearTRAPPED. Away! Get away! DON'T
TOUCH ME! FEAR!*:

''What in hell!'' Savil exclaimed.

''Tashir,'' Vanyel croaked, throwing himself out of
bed, staggering across the room.

''Van!''

He ignored Savil, and pulled open the door to his room.
''He's in the bower. Treesa must have cornered him
somehow, and frightened him.''

He stumbled down the hall at an unsteady run, bare
feet slapping on the wooden floor, weaving a little from
side to side, but not slowing. He was halfway down the
hallway before Savil caught up with him and threw a robe
over him.

''Treesa would *not* appreciate a naked man breaking
into her solar,'' she rasped at him, as he wrestled it on,
then outraced his aunt again.

It was a damned good thing that Treesa's bower wasn't
far from the guest quarters, because he was winded when
he got there, and holding his aching side.

Feminine shrieks met him halfway there. The pain—
that was Tashir's and *that* was all emotional. So whatever
was happening, it *wasn't* a repetition of the slaughter at
Highjorune.

He yanked open the door on chaos. Heavy furniture
was dancing all over the room; lighter things like em-
broidery frames and stools circled the ceiling like de-

mented bats, now and again pausing to throw themselves at the wall before circling again. Piles of shards showed where a few fragile ornaments had performed the same maneuvers to a more fatal end. Tashir was cowering in the corner nearest the doorframe, head buried in his arms; the women were cowering against the far wall, screaming at the tops of their lungs.

Vanyel and Savil acted in concert. *He* clamped down on Tashir; the furniture froze in mid-dance, and the flying pieces began gently lowering themselves to the floor. Savil took the women, collectively paralyzing their throats so they couldn't scream.

It was a fragile solution, at best; Vanyel sensed that the moment he or Savil loosed control, the young man would continue to panic.

The clatter of boots on the staircase heralded the unlikely answer to his prayers; Withen and Jervis stormed into the mess with drawn swords, probably expecting looting and rapine from all the screams. They stopped cold on the threshold. Vanyel would remember the looks on their faces for a long time.

Then Tashir looked up at the intruders; Vanyel got ready to tighten down on the youngster if another surge of fear broke him out of control. But instead, he felt the first flickers of hope and something very like trust when Tashir focused on Jervis.

Jervis? Lady have mercy—but I am not *looking sideways at a gift horse!*

The women clearly saw Withen and Jervis as deliverers; they relaxed immediately, and Savil let them go, one at a time. "Sorry about this, Withen. We've got a presumptive Herald here with a problem," Savil said, slowly and carefully. "Van rescued him, he's very jumpy—his Gift is Fetching, ladies, and he was just trying to get you to leave him alone. He panicked when you started screaming. It's all right, Withen, nobody's hurt, and it looks like the only damage is a couple of ornaments."

Treesa, white and shaking, actually managed a tremulous smile. "Th-they were those horrible ch-cherubs Thorinna insisted on g-g-giving me," she stammered. "I shan't m-m-miss them."

Vanyel, meanwhile, managed to snag Jervis' elbow and draw him away from Withen. "I've got a *very* frightened lad here, Jervis," he whispered. "I'll tell you everything I can later. For now, he seems to see you as somebody he can depend on. Do you think you can handle him, get him calmed down?"

Jervis didn't waste any time with questions or arguments. He took one look at Tashir's strained, white face, sheathed his sword, and nodded.

Vanyel, with Jervis at his elbow, moved toward Tashir as quietly and unthreateningly as he could. The youngster looked up at them with a measure of both hope and fear. "I'm going to take the shields off you, Tashir," Vanyel said, as if none of this had happened, projecting calm with all his power. Empathy was not one of his strong Gifts, but he *did* have it, and he used it to the limit. "I want you to go back to your room with Jervis. Jervis, this is Tashir. Lad, Jervis is our armsmaster."

Again that flash of hope, and trust—stronger this time— in response to the identification of Jervis.

"I want you to get yourself calmed down. I know you can. Once you do, all these strange things will stop happening. What you have is something we call a Gift, and it's no more unnatural than being able to paint well or fight well. And the proof of *that* is that you're going to feel exhausted in a minute, *just* like you'd been fighting. You *have*—only with your mind. We'll help you figure out how to keep it under control so that things like this won't happen again. No one is angry at you—you heard Lady Treesa—and no one is going to punish you for any of this. These things happen to some people, and we understand that here in Valdemar; we *look* for people like you, Tashir, and we train them to *use* what they have. This little mess wasn't your fault, and I won't allow anyone to blame you for it."

"Vanyel's all right," Jervis said gruffly, clapping Vanyel on the shoulder and making him stagger a little. "If he says you're going to be fine, you will be. He won't lie, and he keeps his promises."

Without daring to Mindtouch, Vanyel couldn't tell what the youngster was thinking; he was forced to rely on what

Tashir was projecting that *he* was picking up Empathically. There was doubt there—but a trust in Jervis that was increasing by the moment. Clearly, Tashir would trust Jervis where he wouldn't trust anyone else.

There was a glimmering, a hint of something else for a moment, then it was gone, slithering away before Vanyel could read it. *That* was frustrating in the extreme, but he certainly didn't want to set Tashir off again. So he slowly let his control over the youngster fade, little by little, until it was gone. Tashir slumped against the wall in total exhaustion, closing his eyes.

"Here, lad," Jervis stepped forward and took him by the elbow; the boy transferred his weight from the wall to Jervis; a sign Vanyel read with relief. "Come on, let's get you back to your room, hey? If what young Van here says is true, you're probably feeling like you've just gone through a round-robin tourney in weighted armor."

Tashir nodded, and let Jervis lead him out, stumbling a little with fatigue.

With Tashir gone, the tension left the solar, and everyone in it reacted to the relief differently. Treesa and her ladies were twittering in their corner like a flock of flustered sparrows. Vanyel found a chair and sat in it before his knees gave out on him. Withen suddenly seemed to remember the sword in his hand, and sheathed it.

"Fine, we've got Tashir taken care of, now can *any* of you tell us what happened?" Vanyel asked wearily.

The women started, and stared at him—with fear. Even his mother. Everyone except Melenna.

Their fear hit him like a blow to the heart, making him feel sick. That fear— *Gods. They never saw me work magic before. The stories were just—stories. Now I've conjured myself from Highjorune in a night, brought a wizardling with me—dispelled his magic with a look. Now I'm Vanyel Demonsbane. I'm not anyone they know anymore. I'm not anyone they could know. I'm someone with powers they don't understand, someone to fear.*

He could deal with this now—or let the situation worsen. He chose for the Heralds; chose to withdraw *himself*, Vanyel, inside a kind of mental shell and let Herald-Mage Vanyel come to the fore.

"Ladies, please," the Herald-Mage said, gently, and with a winning smile, exerting all the charm he had. "This is important to all of you if I'm to understand what set the lad off. The idea *is* to keep him from doing it again, after all."

One or two tittered nervously, the rest looked at him with wide, frightened eyes. Then after a moment during which his smile remained steady, they relaxed a little.

His heart sank when Melenna worked her way to the front of the group. He wasn't hoping for much coherency out of *her.*

But she was surprisingly calm. "Lady Treesa found the young man with Medren," she said quietly, her eyes downcast. "She's been *terribly* curious about him—well, we *all* were, really—so she ordered him to come with her to the solar and present himself properly right then. He didn't want to—well, that's what Medren said—but she ordered him, so he followed her. He was *very* polite, but even I could see that he was very unhappy, and the more Treesa asked about his family—because he told us who he was right off—the unhappier he got. As soon as Treesa noticed it, that was when she did—like she does with you, milord Van. You know, she gets sort-of flirty, but at the same time she starts getting very *mothering.* She got up and started to go to him, to put him at ease—and he sort of jumped back, and one of the couches jumped right between him and Treesa. It just—jumped, like a trained dog, or something. Lady Treesa nearly had heart failure, and she screamed, she was so surprised—that was when Tashir went absolutely white and everything in the room began flying around."

She paused, then looked up, very shyly, with none of her usual coquettishness. "We were terribly frightened, milord Van. I mean, I know you and milady Savil are magicians, and I'm sure it all seems very tame to you, but—we've never seen magic like that. Furniture—just shouldn't *do* that. I'm going to feel funny sitting on a chair for the next *week,* wondering if it's going to take it into its head to fly."

Vanyel almost felt himself liking her, for the first time

in years. "I can't say I blame you; I keep forgetting most of you have never even seen me do—oh, *this*."

He made a tiny mage-light in the center of the palm of his outstretched hand. It was about all he had the energy for, and it impressed the ladies out of all proportion to its size. They ooh'd and ah'd, but they did not come any nearer.

"Milord Van," Melenna said, recapturing his attention, "there's something you really need to know. *Nothing hit anyone*. Nothing even came close. Even when those horrid cherubs hit the wall and shattered, no one was cut, no one was hurt. And do you know, that almost made the whole thing scarier."

Vanyel nodded; this incident only confirmed his feeling that the youngster *couldn't* have been guilty of that wholesale slaughter in Lineas. If he didn't remember what had happened, it could have been sheer terror that made his mind hide the memory.

But he found himself seeing the other possibilities.

That works both ways. He could *have done it, just as Lores pointed out. And because he's basically a* good *lad, the sheer horror of what he did made his mind hide the memory so deeply there was no sign of it.*

He shivered, in a preoccupied way, and drifted out of the bower, ignoring the following gazes of Treesa, her ladies, and Melenna.

He dressed and ate, all in a fog comprised of weariness and preoccupation. It was hours later when he finally faced the obvious—that he'd put a very vulnerable young man in the hands of someone who had abused *him*.

He wouldn't. Would he? Oh, gods.

He went looking for Jervis in a state of increasing alarm, and found him in the salle, working out against the pells. And by the time he found the armsmaster, he was ready to kill the man himself if Jervis had even *thought* of bullying the boy.

Bluff him. He doesn't know how worn out I am. If I go on the offensive right away, he won't have time to think.

Planting both feet firmly on the sanded wooden floor, he took an aggressive stance, arms crossed over his chest.

"Jervis," he called, loudly enough to be heard over the racket of practice blade against pells.

The armsmaster pivoted and pulled off his helm. He must have been at the exercise for some time; sweat beaded his brow, and dripped off the ends of his hair. "Aye?"

Vanyel did not move. "One word for you. I don't know what this game you've been playing with me means, and at this point I don't dare take any chances. I'm warning you now; harm Medren—harm Tashir—you'll be dealing with me. *Not* Herald Vanyel—plain Vanyel Ashkevron. And you know now I can take you; any time, any place; with magic, *or* without. And I *won't* hesitate to use any weapon I've got."

Jervis flushed; looked dumbfounded. "*Harm* 'em? *Me?* What d'you take me for?"

"The man who broke my arm, Jervis. The man who's been trying to intimidate me on this very floor for the past week. The man that was too damned inflexible to suit the style to the boy—so he tried to break the boy."

Jervis flung his helm down, going scarlet with anger. The helm dented the floor and rolled off. "*Dammit,* you fool! Don't you see that was what I was tryin' t'do? I was *tryin'* t'learn *your* damned style—and *for* Medren! Hellfire! A fool could see that poor little sprout Medren was no more suited t' my way then puttin' armor on a palfrey!"

Vanyel felt as if someone had just dropped him into a vat of cold water. He blinked, relaxed his stance, and blinked again. *Feeling poleaxed is getting to become a regular occurrence,* he thought, trying to get his jaw hinged again. His knees were trembling so much with reaction that he wasn't certain they'd hold him.

Jervis saved him the trouble. He threw his gear over into his chest at the side of the practice area, stalked over to Vanyel's side, and took his elbow. "Look," he said, gruffly, "I'm tired, and we've got a lot between us that needs talking about. Let's go get a damned drink and settle it."

* * *

I shouldn't be drinking unwatered wine this tired, Vanyel thought, regarding the plain clay mug Jervis was filling with unease.

It seemed Jervis had already thought of that. "Here," he said, taking a loaf of coarse bread, a round of cheese, and a knife out of the same cupboard that had held the mugs and wine bottle, and shoving them across the trestle table at Vanyel. "Eat something first, or you'll be sorry. Not a good idea t' be guzzling this stuff if you ain't used t' it, but there's some pain between us, boy, and *I* need the wine t' get it out, even if you don't."

They were still in the armory, in a little back room that was part office, part repair-shop, and part infirmary. Vanyel was sitting on a cot with his back braced against the wall; Jervis was on the room's only chair, with the table between and a little to one side of them, a table he'd cleaned of bits of harness and an arm-brace and tools by the simple expedient of sweeping it all into a box and shoving the box under the table with his foot.

The armsmaster followed his own advice by hacking off a chunk of bread and cheese and bolting it, before taking a long swallow of his wine. Vanyel did the same, a little more slowly. Jervis sat hunched over for a long moment, his elbows on his knees, contemplating the contents of the mug held between his callused hands.

"Do you begin," Van asked awkwardly, "or should I?"

"Me. Your father—" Jervis began, and coughed. "You know I owe him, owe him for takin' me on permanent: Oh, he owed me some, a little matter of watchin' his back once, but not what I figured would put me here as armsmaster. So I figure that put me on the debit side of the ledger, eh? Well, that was all right for a while, though it weren't no easy thing, makin' fighters out of a bunch of plowboys an' second an' third sons what couldn't find the right end of a spear with both hands an' a map. Your granther—he reckoned it best t'hire what he needed. Your father—he figured best t' train his own, an' that was why he kept me. Gods. Plowboys, kids, it was a damn mess. No, it weren't easy. But I did it, I did it—an' then along comes you, first-born, an' Withen calls in the *real* debt."

The former mercenary sighed, and wiped his forehead with the back of his hand. He gave Vanyel a measuring look before taking another drink and continuing. "I 'spect by now it ain't gonna come as a surprise t' hear your old man figured you for—what're they sayin' now, *shaych?*— yeah, figured you for that from the time you came outa the nursery. Times were you looked more girl than boy— gah, that stuck in his craw for sure. Hangin' about with Liss, fightin' shy of th' foster-boys—then you took up with music, an' gods, he was sure of it. Figured he could cure you if he made sure you never knew there was such a thing, and he got somebody t' beat you into shape. That somebody was s'pposed t' be me."

He stabbed a gnarled thumb toward his chest and snorted. "Me! Kernos' Horns! 'Make the boy a man,' he says. 'I don't care what you have to do, just make 'im a man!' An' every day, just about, askin' me how you was shapin' up. I been under pressure before, but *damn,* this was enough t' make an angel sweat. I *owed* that man, an' what the hell was I supposed t' do? Tell him I never saw no beatin's turn no kids from fey if that was how they was bent? Tell him there were no few of the mercs his father'd hired was shieldmates, an' looked about as fey as me an' fought like hell's own demons?"

"You could have *tried*—"

Jervis snarled a little. "*And lose my place?* You think there's jobs for old mercs 'round any corner? I was flat *desperate,* boy! What in hell was I supposed to do?"

Vanyel bit back his resentment. "I didn't know," he said finally. "I didn't guess."

Jervis grimaced. "You weren't supposed to, boy. Well, hell, my style suited you, you poor little scrap, 'bout as well as teats on a bull. 'Bout the same as Medren."

"If you knew that—" Vanyel bit back his protest.

"Yeah, I knew it. I just couldn't face it. Then *you* went all stubborn on me, you damned well wouldn't even *try,* an' I didn't know what the hell t' do! I was 'bout ready t' bust out, you made me so damned mad, an' your old da *on* me every time I turned around—an' if that weren't enough, gods, I useta get nightmares 'bout you."

"Nightmares?" Vanyel asked. He knew he sounded skeptical, mostly because he *was*.

"Yeah, *nightmares*," Jervis said defensively. "Shit, you can't live on the damn Border without seein' fightin' sooner or later. An' you likely t' get shoved out there with no more sense of what t' do t' keep yourself alive than a butterfly. Look, smart boy—you was *firstborn;* you *bet* I figured you for bein' right in th' front line some day, an' I figured you for dead when that happened. An' I *don't* send childer outa my damned hands t' get killed, dammit!"

His face twisted and his shoulders shook for a moment, and he finished off the wine in his mug at a single gulp. Vanyel could sense more pain than he'd ever dreamed the old man could feel behind that carved-granite face. Somewhere, some time, Jervis *had* sent ill-prepared "childer" out of his hands to fight—and die—and the wounds were with him still. His own anger began to fade.

"Well, that's what you were headin' *straight* for, boy, an' I just plain didn't know how t' keep it from happening. *You* made me so damned mad, an' then your old man just gave me too much leash. Told me I had a free hand with you. An' I—lost it. I went an' took the whole mess out of your hide."

He shook his head, staring at the floor, and his hands trembled a little where he was clutching the empty mug. "I lost my damned temper, boy. I'm not proud of that. I'm not proud of myself. Should have known better, but every time you whined, it just made me madder. An' I was *wrong*, dead wrong, in what I was trying t' force into you; I knew it, an' that made me mad too. Then you pulled that last little stunt—that was it. You ever thought about what you did?"

"I never stopped thinking about it," Vanyel replied, after first swallowing nearly half the contents of his own mug. The wine could not numb the memories, recollections that were more acid on the back of his tongue than the cheap red wine.

He looked fiercely into Jervis's eyes. "I hated you," he admitted angrily. "If I'd had a real knife in my hands that day, I think I'd have gone for your throat.'' All the bitterness he'd felt, then and after, rose in his gullet, tasting of bile. He struggled against his closing throat to ask the question that had never been answered and had plagued him for more than a decade. ''Why, Jervis, *why?*'' he got past his clenched jaw. ''If you *knew* what I was doing, why did you *lie* and tell Father I was cheating?''

Silence; Jervis stared at him with anger mixed with shame, but it was the shame that won out. ''Because I couldn't admit I was wrong,'' Jervis replied, subdued and flushing a dark red. ''Because I couldn't admit it to myself or anybody else. Couldn't believe a kid had come up with the answer I couldn't find. So I told Withen you'd cheated. Half believed it myself; couldn't see how you'd've touched me, otherwise. But I—I've had a lot of time t' think about it. Years, since you left. An' you turnin' out the way you did, a Herald an' all—shit, anybody turned out like that wouldn't cheat. Came to me after a while I never caught you in a lie, neither. Came to me that the only lies bein' told were the ones *I* was tellin'. Then when I started t' tell myself the truth, began t' figure out how close I came t' breakin' more'n your arm.''

He hung his head, and he wouldn't look at Vanyel. And Vanyel found his anger and bitterness flowing away from him like water from melting ice.

''Boy, I was wrong, and I am sorry for it,'' he said quietly. ''I told Withen the truth a while back, when they sent you out on the Karsite Border; told him everything I just told you. *He* didn't know what they was sendin' you to, but *I* did. Damn, I—if anythin' had happened, an' I hadn't told him—''

He shuddered. ''I told him more things, best I could. Told him that he's got a damned fine son, an' that there've been plenty of shieldmated fighters I'd'a been glad t' have at m'back, an' I'd've trusted with m' last coin and first-born kid—an' just as many lads whose tastes ran t' wenchin' that I'd've just as soon set up against a tree an' shot. Told him if he let *that* stand between him an' you, he was a bigger fool than me. Did m' best for you, boy.

Gonna keep on with it, too. Figure if I tell him enough, he might start believin' me. An' Van—I'm damned sorry it took me so long t' figure out how wrong I was.''

There was profound silence then, while Vanyel waited for his thoughts and emotions to settle into coherency. Jervis was as silent as a man of rock, eyes fixed on the floor. The cricket in the salle broke off its singing, and Vanyel could hear the thud of hooves and sharp commands, faint and muffled, as Tam took one of the young stallions around on the lunge just outside.

Finally, everything within him crystallized into a new pattern—

Vanyel took Jervis' mug from limp fingers and refilled it. But instead of giving it back, he offered the armsmaster his own outstretched hand.

The former mercenary looked up at him in surprise, one of the first times Vanyel had ever seen the man register surprise, and began to smile; tentatively at first, then with real feeling.

He took Vanyel's hand in both of his, and swallowed hard. "Thank you, boy," he said hoarsely. "I wasn't sure you'd—you're a better *man* than—oh, hell—"

Vanyel shrugged, and handed him his refilled mug. "Let's call it truce. *I* was a brat. And if you hadn't done what you did, I wouldn't be a Herald." *And I wouldn't have had 'Lendel.*

"Listen," Jervis said, after first clearing his throat. "About Medren—that boy has no future here, a blind man could see that. What with all the right-born boys—an' I couldn't see *that* one bein' happy as anybody's dogsbody squire, you know? Figured the only chance for him was the way I came up; merc armsman. Lord Kernos knows he's got all the brains t' make officer right quick. So that's what I was tryin' to work him to.''

"There *was* music.''

"Yeah, his other shot was *maybe* music. I'd heard him, boy sounded all right, but what the hell do I know about music? Not a damn thing. But I figured, I figured I could make a damned fine armsman out of him, what with his reactions an' his brains an' speed an' all, if I could just figure out what they'd taught you over to Haven. Been tryin'—*damn* if I haven't been tryin'. *Could* not seem t'get it worked out, an'—shit, Van, hate t' use th' boy like a set of pells, but it seemed like th' only way t' work it out was to work it out usin' *him*. But,'' Jervis held up a knotted finger, ''just on th' chance th' boy *was* good at the plunkin' I been *damned* careful of his hands. *Damned* careful.''

Vanyel's arm began to ache, and he put his mug down to rub it. ''I never did get all the feeling back,'' he said, still resentful, still feeling the last burn of the anger he'd nursed all these years. ''If things hadn't turned out the way they did—even being *careful* you could have hurt him, and *ruined* his chance at music.''

Jervis visibly stifled an angry retort, but in the face of Vanyel's own anger, winced and looked away. ''Can't undo what I did, boy,'' he said, after an uncomfortable silence. ''Nobody can. But the least I can do is keep from makin' the same mistake twice. An' I *was* tryin'. I swear it.''

Vanyel sat on his anger.

Jervis gulped his wine. ''Truth now, between you an' me. Were you any good? Did I—''

''No,'' Vanyel said honestly. ''I didn't have the Gift. And it's taken a while, but I learned how to make up for the lost feeling. You didn't take anything away from me, not really.''

Jervis' shoulders sagged a little. ''How about the bastard? Medren, I mean.''

''I'm sponsoring him into the Bardic Collegium. He's better than I was at fifteen, and he's got the Bardic Gift.'' Vanyel nodded at Jervis' swift intake of breath. ''Exactly; he'll make a full Bard.''

The memory suddenly sprang up, unprompted, of Medren and his succession of bruises—just bruises. Nasty ones, some of them, but not broken bones, not even sprains. No worse than Vanyel had seen his brothers and cousins sport, back in the long ago. And Vanyel began to look a little closer at those memories, while Jervis stared at him askance. Finally he began to smile.

''It just occurred to me—Medren. With a full Gift. He has been *manipulating* me, the little demon, using that Gift of his. Doing it just fine, too, and with no Bardic training. Given that, I'd say he's going to be outstanding, and I think I'd better have a little word with him on the subject of ethics!''

Jervis chuckled. ''I don't think it's a-purpose; at least, I don't think he knows he shouldn't. He's another one that's good at bottom. An' let me tell you, even *without* havin' a decent style, he's no slouch with a blade!''

Vanyel cut them both more bread and cheese, and reached for the wine to refill both mugs. He leaned back against the wall, with a feeling that something that had been festering for a long time had begun to heal. He didn't *like* Jervis, quite. Not yet, anyway. But he was beginning to see why Jervis had done what he'd done, and beginning to respect the courage that made the arms-master admit—if belatedly—that he was wrong.

''You know,'' Vanyel said slowly, ''he'll be taught blade right along with music; Bards end up finding themselves in some fairly unpleasant places from time to time. *They're* in Valdemar's service no less than Heralds are, so being handy with a sword surely can't hurt. Hellfire, you should have seen Bard Chadran in his prime; he'd have been a match for *both* of us together!''

Jervis looked up with interest. ''Chadran—that the one that was s'pposed t' have got picked up by bandits, got 'em t' trust 'im, then fought himself an' a handful of prisoners loose?''

''That's the one, only he went in on Elspeth's request.''

When he finished that story, Jervis managed to coax the Shadow Stalker tale out of him, after half the bottle was gone. Most people never heard the real story. It took half a bottle before he was ready to face those memories.

Before *that* tale was over and the bottle was empty, Vanyel had decided he had an ally he could count on. He was certain of it after Jervis' final words when Vanyel got up to leave.

''Never understood Heralds before,'' the armsmaster admitted. ''Never could figure out what all the fuss and feathers was about. Didn't *really* have any notion of what you people did, until them stories about you started up. Never paid much attention t' who the hero was before, then I started noticin' that in the Valdemar songs most of the heroes turn out t' be Heralds. Somethin' else I started noticin'—most of the Heralds ended up comin' down with a serious case of dead in them stories. *You* come pretty close to it, a time or two, eh?''

Vanyel nodded ruefully, stretching sore muscles. "Stupidity, mostly."

Jervis snorted. "My ass. Wasn't stupidity so much's puttin' yourself in harm's way. Right, so tell me this—a merc like me, he puts himself on the line for money. Knows what he bought himself into, knows what he'll get out of it if he lives. An' he only gives so much; what he was paid for, but not past it. But—you—you Heralds? What's in it for you? I mean, look at you right now— you've about wore yourself down to a thread, somethin' *no* merc would do. And you showed up *here* in th' same state. What for?''

Vanyel shook his head. "It's hard to tell you; it's a feeling, more than anything. Something like a priestly vocation, *I* would guess.'' He looked inside himself for the answer, an answer he hadn't really looked for since he first realized what it was that had made Tylendel *need* to be a Herald. "I do it because I have to. Because I'm needed. There isn't anybody—I'm not boasting, Jervis, you can ask Savil—there isn't *anybody* else in the whole Kingdom that can do what I can do. I can't give up, I can't just shrug things off and tell myself somebody else will take up the slack, because there *isn't* anybody else. There are too many people out there who need my protection; *because* I'm this powerful, I have an obligation to use that power. I'm the lone Guard at the Gate—I daren't give up, because there's nobody behind me to take up what I lay down.''

Jervis' face went absolutely still. Vanyel wished he knew what the old man was thinking. "Nobody?" he asked.

Vanyel shook his hair out of his eyes. "Nobody," he echoed, staring into space. "I have no choice; it's that, or know *my* inaction dooms others. Sometimes lots of others. Too many times, others I know and care for.''

Jervis's eyes grew deep and thoughtful, and Vanyel

could feel them on his back as he left, headed for the bathhouse.

There was a light tap at Vanyel's door that woke him from the nap he was trying to take—in part to make up for the sleep he had been losing to Melenna. It hadn't been a very successful attempt. He was still too on edge; his mind was too active. He yawned, and then grinned, identifying Medren by a stray thought-wisp. *So we've recovered from the measles, hmm? And about to have a little moment of truth with Uncle Vanyel. Or rather, though he doesn't know it, Herald Vanyel.*

"Come," he said, sitting up and stretching, then swinging his legs off the bed.

"Vanyel?" Medren plodded into the room and sagged down into the window seat. "Can I hide up here? I just found out from young Meke that old Jervis is gonna have some 'special demonstration' this afternoon, and you *know* what that means." The boy shuddered. "Good old Medren for pells."

"Actually, no, not this time," Vanyel grinned. "It means 'good old Radevel for pells.' I've been teaching Rad my style, and the pells plan on giving Jervis as good as he gets. Then you and Radevel will have at each other while I coach so Jervis can watch. He says he wants to know my style 'because sooner or later he's going to get another puny 'un.' And some time this week, my young friend, you will have another sparring partner; once I recover, you and *I* are going to pair off. And *I'll* run you around the field for a while. And *meanwhile* we'll find out what Tashir is good for."

The boy's mouth dropped open, and Vanyel continued mercilessly.

"This is for your benefit. Bardic Collegium includes bladework for Bards right along with the music lessons, and I wanted you to have as much of a head start as possible. A Bard's duty has been known to carry him into some dangerous places, and the Bardic Circle can't spare Guards to tag along behind you to keep you out of trouble."

The boy's mouth worked, but for a long moment, no sound emerged.

"Oh—" he said weakly. "I—ah—"

"Medren, I have a very serious question to ask you." Vanyel let the smile drop from his mouth and eyes, and moved to stand over the boy. "When you were fishing for my sympathy, what else were you doing? And don't tell me that you weren't doing anything. We both know better than that."

"I . . ." the boy gulped, and dropped his eyes. "I was trying to make you feel sorry for me. That's why I was kind of . . . playing while I was talking to you; singing but not singing, you know? Putting music behind what I was doing. I . . . it feels sort of like when I really get taken up by a song. Like I'm pushing something. Only with the inside of my head."

"Did you ever think about whether that was a good idea?" Vanyel asked, with no inflection in his voice.

"No. Not really." A long pause, then Medren hung his head. "It isn't, is it?" he asked, in a very small, and *very* subdued voice. "I was doing something I shouldn't have. I . . . I guess it's something like being a bully because you're bigger than somebody, isn't it?"

Vanyel nodded, relief relaxing his shoulders. *Good. He knows, now. He saw it for himself. He'll be all right.* But he spoke sternly. "It is. And if you do it at Bardic, they'll have the Heralds block your Gift, and they'll turn you out. That *is* your Gift; this ability to make people feel what you want them to feel through music. And there are only three times it's permissible for you to use that Gift; when you're performing, when you're helping someone who *needs* help, and at the King's orders."

"Yessir," Medren whispered, head sunk between his shoulders, where he'd pulled it when Vanyel spoke of having his Gift blocked and being turned out of the Collegium. "Nossir. I'll remember."

"You'd better. On this, you get *one* chance. Now, come on, lad," Vanyel said with a renewal of cheerfulness, urging Medren up out of his chair and propelling him out the door with a hand behind his shoulders. "Time for you to show those plowhorse cousins of yours how a *real* fighter does things."

Nine

They returned to his room after practice; Vanyel had *thought* to give Medren another music lesson, but even though *he* hadn't done any fighting, he realized as he directed Medren's movements that he was drained—and that was long before the practice was over.

Medren was no fool; he could see how exhausted Vanyel was. *He* suggested that the lesson be put off; he even offered to have servants bring Vanyel's dinner to his room.

Vanyel accepted both offers; he bolted the food as soon as the servant brought it, and threw himself facedown on his bed again with a groan. The bed had somehow been made up in his absence, *despite* all the hurly-burly in Treesa's bower. *Baby Heralds wrecking rooms, adult Heralds making magic Gates and then falling through them half-dead, a possible war on the Border, and still somehow the beds get made. What a world.*

He tried to think of what he would have done if Tashir hadn't run berserk, and realized he hadn't *yet* spoken with Yfandes. She probably knew what was going on, of course; since the moment he had first accepted the notion of becoming a Herald she had made a habit—which he encouraged—of eavesdropping on just about everything as a kind of silent observer in the back of his mind. He didn't in the least mind her using his eyes and ears; it saved a lot of explaining, and if there was something he *didn't* want her "present" for, he'd tell her. But it was very rude of him not to have *said* something, at least in greeting, before this. He rolled over on his back and closed his eyes.

:*'Fandes?*: he called, tentatively. :*I'm sorry—I got tan-*

gled—and then I fell on my nose for a while—and then I had a visit to make—and then I had a visitor myself.:

She chuckled. *:So I saw. You're forgiven.:*

:Have you got anything for me? I'm sorry I made you run all the way home instead of taking the shortcut.:

:You're forgiven. And oddly enough,: she replied promptly, *:I have got something for you. Brightest gods, let me tell you, it hasn't been the easiest information to obtain. And I am not sorry I was apart from you for a bit; I am very glad you were far away by the time you completed the Gate. I felt your pain quite enough as it was.:* The love in her mind-voice softened her words. *:The Young One—I have taken to calling him "Ghost," for he has been haunting this place like the veriest spirit, never coming near enough to touch and only rarely to be seen, and frightening the farmers no end. He is quite closely locked into his Chosen's mind. I can speak with him, but only distantly; most of his attention and his concentration are with Tashir. But I can Mindtouch with him as you cannot his Chosen; Mindtouch does not frighten him. And so, because of the close bond between him and the youngling, I can sometimes pick up things as if I was in Mindtouch with Tashir.:* Overtones of deep uneasiness. *:The youngling is something less than steady; his mind is fragile and unbalanced. There are terrible things which haunt him, and which he fears to tell, and which he even blocks from his thoughts. Still. Ghost may yet balance him, if he can regain balance; the stallion is something of a MindHealer.:*

Vanyel sat bolt upright. *:A MindHealer? A* Companion? *But—:*

:It happens from time to time,: she interrupted, the overtones of her mind-voice telling him clearly that she was very reluctant to speak of it. *:It happens when it is needed. . . . Listen, I was in Mindtouch when the boy was making such a ruin of Treesa's bower, and I remained in touch. I saw what you only glimpsed. Here.:*

It was a feeling she Sent, as well as an image. A feeling of profound trust, and the image of an older man, much like Jervis, in practice armor.

:Looks like Jervis may be our key,: Vanyel mused, ly-

ing back down again, and putting his hands behind his head. *:Could that man have been Deveran's arms-master?:*

:I cannot tell you; that is all I could obtain,: she replied. *:Tashir is much too traumatized for any questioning, I would say. He—:* she slipped out of the link for a moment, then slipped back in again. *:—he is better, steadier, and Jervis is with him again. They are taking supper in the Great Hall, though with the servants, not the family. But I would not disturb him.:*

He winced at the thought. *:Even if I wanted to, I'm not up to dealing with him, beloved,:* he confessed, feeling every joint in his body ache. *:I'm not entirely certain I could contain him again. I am about down to my last dregs. This is getting to be a habit I'd rather not have.:*

:Then rest. This won't be solved in a day.:

He grimaced silently. *:I know. I told Savil that I have more questions than answers. Like—why are Highjorune and that palace built where they are? I can't believe that it's accident. Why are the people of Lineas so against magic—and yet have no laws forbidding its use? Where did Deveran want to send Tashir, and why did the prospect frighten him enough to defy his father in public? And why is the boy so afraid of women that a bowerful could send him skirting the edges of hysteria?:* He made a mental shrug. *:I know some of those questions seem trivial, yet it all ties together, somehow, but how—:*

:Rest,: Yfandes repeated. Then, mischievously, *:There is at least one thing you will not need to beware of.:*

:Which is?:

:Visitors in your bed. I do believe you have frightened Melenna enough that she is thinking about things you might choose to do with her.:

:Such as?:

:Flying her out the window in the nude.:

He laughed aloud, and decided to stay in his room. Right now what he wanted was some quiet and solitude. . . .

Three days of unconsciousness seems to make for insomnia, he thought, after trying to fall asleep for what seemed like half the night. He gave up, finally, and moved to the window seat. He lit the candle beside it the ordinary way—from the coals in the fireplace—and found a book. It was a volume of history he would have found perfectly fascinating under normal circumstances, but he found himself rereading pages two and three times and *still* not getting the sense of them.

He abandoned it in favor of the new gittern, letting his fingers wander across the strings as he tried to relax. It was earlier than he'd thought. This evening was very much like the one three nights ago; cool and crisp, with a light breeze. The moon was waning now into her last quarter, so there was less light, but the same kind of clouds raced across her face.

Gods, how life can change in one night.

This afternoon had been hard. Hard on emotions. Dealing with Jervis—purging that old hate. And before that, Tashir. Seeing Tashir in daylight, looking *so* much like Tylendel, only a younger, more vulnerable Tylendel, had reawakened all the old hurt and loss. He was trying to deal with the young man *as himself,* but it was not easy, not with his insides in knots every time Tashir turned those eloquent eyes on him . . . all he wanted to do was take the young man in his arms and . . . never mind.

And is that because he looks like 'Lendel? Or is it because of me? He picked out the refrain of "Shadow-Lover," as he tried to sort himself out. *I don't know what I am anymore. Shavri and Randi, they're more to me than friends. And Shavri more than Randi. A lot more. I don't know what that means. I just* don't. *Now Tashir—hellfire. But the reason—is it because he's attractive, or because he reminds me of 'Lendel?* He tried to think if he'd ever been the *least* bit attracted to any other women but Shavri, and couldn't think of any. *But how much of* that *is because they kept throwing themselves at me? Gods, I hate being pursued. I especially hate being pursued in public. And the idea of going to bed with somebody I don't care for—* His stomach knotted. *Gods, gods, where does friendship end and love start? How much of my being*

*shaych was being shaych, and how much was just be-
cause of 'Lendel?*

His unhappy thoughts were interrupted by a knock on
the door, and he started. He'd already dealt with Medren.
Melenna was *not* likely to show up, according to Yfandes.
He wasn't expecting anyone; not even Savil.

He turned away from the window with the gittern cra-
dled against his chest, and racked the instrument carefully. He walked soundlessly across the room and
answered the door just as the would-be visitor made a
second, more tentative knock.

It was Tashir; pale as bleached linen, with the eyes of
a lost soul. As Vanyel stood there stupidly, the young
man slipped inside and closed the door behind him, putting his back to it, and facing Vanyel with a fear-filled
and haunted expression, a strange expression Vanyel
could not interpret.

And in the dim light the young man looked even more
like Tylendel. Vanyel's heart seemed to be squeezed up
into an area just below his throat, and his chest hurt. "I
heard you playing," the youngster said, hoarsely. "I
wouldn't have troubled you if you hadn't been awake.
Can I—bother you?"

"Please, sit," Vanyel managed, finding it very hard to
get his breath. "Certainly, you're welcome here, and it
isn't 'bothering me.' How can I help you?"

The young man walked hesitantly toward the table, and
paused, with his hands on the back of one of the chairs.
He looked back over his shoulder at Vanyel. His face—
thank the gods!—was in shadow. Vanyel succeeded in
getting two full breaths in a row.

"Jervis says you're . . . shaych," Tashir whispered.
"Are you?"

Vanyel moved over to the other chair and motioned him
to sit; he did so, but on the very edge of the chair. Vanyel
had a flash of image, a young stag at the edge of a bright
meadow in the midst of hunting season. Which was also
mating season. Wanting, needing, looking for something, not knowing *what* he needed, and full of fear and
less definable emotions. "It's no secret," Vanyel replied

cautiously, unable to predict what was coming. "Yes. Yes, I am."

"Would you be my lover?" Tashir blurted desperately.

Vanyel found he *needed* to sit down. He did, just before his legs refused to hold him. He stared at Tashir, quite unable to speak for a moment.

Do you have any idea what you're doing to me, lad? No, you can't. Poor boy. Poor, confused child—

He gathered his emotions and put a tight rein on them. The youngster did *not* have the feel of *shay'a'chern*, not in any way. This was the last question Vanyel would ever have expected from him. And his initial reaction was to tell him "no."

And yet—and yet—he looked *so* like Tylendel. *And I've enough experience I could be certain he'd enjoy it—* was the unbidden thought. *I could convince him he was. It would be so easy. And I'm so lonely. Oh, gods. Oh, gods. The temptation—*

Instead of answering, he stood slowly and moved to stand before the boy, gently reaching out and placing the fingers of his right hand just beneath the line of Tashir's jaw. Ostensibly, this was to make the youngster look up into his eyes—but Vanyel wanted to *know* something of what was going on in the young man's mind, and if he could not Mindtouch, well, physical contact made his Empathy *much* sharper. As the dark eyes met his silver, he could feel the youngster's pulse racing beneath the tip of his middle finger. And the *feel* he received was of fear and unhappiness, *not* attraction. Not in the slightest. *That* was both relief and disappointment.

"Why?" Vanyel asked, much more calmly than he felt, striving with all his might for impartiality. "Why do you want me as a lover?"

Tashir flushed, and his fear deepened. And there was something new: shame. "It—this afternoon—" he stammered. "Lady Treesa—I was so—I—I—she—Vanyel, she—" his voice dropped to a humiliated whisper. "She scares me, ladies scare me—I—"

"Oh." Vanyel made the one word speak volumes, not of contempt, but understanding and compassion. "*Now* I think I see what the problem is; and why you're here.

My mother frightened you, and women in general frighten you, so you think you *must* be *shay'a'chern,* right?''

Tashir nodded a little, and paled again.

Vanyel sternly told his insides to leave him alone. They didn't listen. They ached. He ignored them, grateful that training had made it possible for him to control his voice and his face, if not his emotions. "Well, let's really analyze this before we go making assumptions, shall we? Do you know my aunt, Herald Savil? Have you met her formally yet?''

"The o—the lady who was with you?'' Now Vanyel picked up only respect, mixed with the good-natured contempt of the young for the old.

"Does *she* frighten you?'' He half-smiled, stiffly. "She should, you know, she's a *terrible* tyrant!''

Tashir shook his head.

"How about Kylla? She's the baby who's always getting out of the nursery, usually without a stitch on. I expect she's done it at least once while I was sleeping. Does *she* bother you?''

Bewilderment. "She's kind of cute. Why should I be afraid of *her?*''

Vanyel worked his way up and down the age scale of all the women at Forst Reach that he thought the youngster might have seen. Only when he neared women between twenty and Treesa's age did he get any negative responses, and when he mentioned a particularly pretty fourteen-year-old niece, there was *definite* interest—and real attraction.

From time to time Vanyel dropped in questions about his feelings toward *men;* not just himself, but Jervis, Medren, some of the servants the youngster had encountered. And at no time, even as he began to relax, did Tashir evidence any attraction to men in general or Vanyel in particular—except, perhaps as a protector. Certainly not as a potential lover. Whenever that topic came up, the fear came back.

Finally Vanyel sighed, and took his hand away. It ached, ached as badly as the injured left did when it rained. He rubbed it, wishing he could massage away the ache in his own heart. "Tashir—let me say that I'm very flattered, but—no. I will *not* oblige you. Because you've come to me for all the wrong reasons. You aren't here because you *know* you're *shay'a'chern;* you aren't even here because you're attracted to me. You're here because women of a certain age frighten you. That's not enough to base a relationship on, not the kind you're asking me for. You don't *know* what you want; you only know what you don't want."

"But—" the youngster said, his eyes all pupil, "but you—when you were *younger* than me—Jervis said—"

Vanyel *had* to look away; he couldn't bear that gaze any more. "When I was younger than you I *knew* what I was, and I *knew* what I wanted, and who I wanted it with. You're looking for—for someone to like you, for someone to be close to. You're just grasping at something that looks like a solution, and you're hoping I'll make up your mind for you. And I *could* do that, you know. Even without using magic, I could probably convince you that you *were shay'a'chern,* at least for a little while. I could . . . do things, say things to you, that would make you very infatuated with me." He paused, and forced a breath into his tight chest, looking back down at Tashir's bewildered eyes. "But that wouldn't solve your problems, it would only let you postpone finding a solution for a while. And I truly don't think that would help you in the least. Any answers you find, Tashir, are going to have to be answers you decide on for yourself. Here—" He offered the youngster his hand. Tashir looked at it in surprise, then tentatively put his own hand in Vanyel's.

He looked even more surprised when Vanyel hauled him to his feet, put his palm between his shoulderblades, and shoved him gently toward and out the door. "Go to bed, Tashir," Vanyel said, trying to make his tones as kindly as he could. "You go have another chat with Jervis. Go riding with Nerya. Try making some friends around the Reach. We'll talk about this later."

And he shut the door on him, softly, but firmly.

He began to shake, then, and clung to the doorframe to keep himself standing erect. He leaned his forehead against the doorpanel for a long time before he stopped trembling. When he thought he could walk without stumbling, he turned and went back to his chair, and sat down in it heavily.

He hurt. Oh, gods, he hurt. He felt so empty—and twice as alone as before. He stared at the candleflame while it burned down at least half an inch, trying to thaw the adamantine lump of frozen misery in his stomach, and having a resounding lack of success.

:You did the right thing, Chosen.: The bright voice in his mind was shaded with sympathy and approval both.

:I know I did,: he replied, around the ache. *:What else could I do? Just—tell me, beloved—why can't I feel happy about it? Why does doing the right thing have to* hurt *so damned much?:*

She had no answer for him, but then, he hadn't really expected one.

If I were just a little less ethical—and how much of that is because he looks like 'Lendel? Gods. It isn't just my heart that hurts. And I'm so damned *lonely.*

Eventually he slept.

It took a week before he felt anything like normal. Challenging Jervis when he had been straight out of his bed had been pure bluff. He wouldn't have been able to stand against the armsmaster for more than a few breaths at most. He wondered if Jervis had guessed that.

Arms practice was interesting. He and Jervis circled around each other, equally careful with words *and* blows. There was so much between them that was only half-healed, at best, that it was taking all his skill at diplomacy to keep the wounds from reopening. And no little of that was because it sometimes seemed that Jervis might be regretting his little confession.

But they were civil to each other, and working with each other, which was a *damn* sight more comfortable than being at war with each other.

"That boy's got more'n a few problems, Van," Jervis said, leaning on his sword, and watching Tashir work out with Medren. The young man was being painstakingly careful with the younger boy, and he was wearing the first untroubled expression Vanyel had seen on his face.

And for once, there was no fear in him. For once, he was just another young man; a little more considerate of the smaller, younger boy than most, but still just another young man.

"I know," Vanyel replied, shifting his weight from his right foot to his left. "And I know you aren't talking about fighting style." He chewed his lip a little, and decided to ask the one question that would decide whether or not he was going to be able to carry out the plan he'd made in the sleepless hours of the last several nights. "Tell me, do you feel up to handling him by yourself for a bit? You'll have Savil in case he does anything magical again, though I don't think he will, but I don't think he'll open up to Savil the way he will to you."

Jervis gave him a long look out of the corner of his eye. "And just where are *you* going to be?"

Vanyel looked straight ahead, but spoke in a low voice that was just loud enough for Jervis to hear him. The fewer who knew about this, the better. "Across the Border. All the answers to our questions are over *there*, including the biggest question of all—if Tashir didn't rip a castle full of people to palm-sized pieces, who did? And why?"

And away from him, maybe I can get my thinking straight.

Jervis considered his words, as the clack and *thwack* of wooden practice blades echoed up and down the salle. "How long do you think you'll be out over there? You're not going as *yourself*, I hope?"

"No." He smiled wanly. A Herald was not going to be a popular person in Highjorune right now. "I've got a disguise that's been very useful in the past; Herald Vanycl is still going to be resting in the bosom of his family. The gentleman who's going to cross the Border is a rather scruffy minstrel named Valdir. Nobody notices a minstrel asking questions; they're *supposed* to. And since the only person who saw my face *clearly* is now on his way to Haven with a rock in his craw, I should be safe. I expect to take a fortnight at most."

"*Get that guard up, Medren!* Huh. Sounds good to

me. Gods know we aren't getting any answers out of the
boy at the moment. What's Savil say?''

Vanyel winced as Medren got in a particularly good
score on Tashir. ''That she never could stand clandestine
work, so she's not about to venture an opinion. Father's
not to know. Savil is going to tell him I'm visiting with
Liss. Yfandes is in favor, since she's going to be with me
most of the time, and within reach when she's not actually *with* me.''

Jervis' shoulders relaxed a trifle. ''That had me worried, a bit. But if you're taking the White Lady, I got no
objections. If *she* can't get you out of a mess, nobody
can. I got a lot of respect for that pretty little thing.''

:Tell him thank you, Chosen.:

Vanyel grinned. Jervis, unlike Withen, had no problem
remembering that Yfandes was not a horse. He'd always
offered her respect; since he and Vanyel had made their
uneasy peace, he'd offered her the same kind of treatment
she'd have gotten from another Herald. Yfandes was a
person to Jervis; a little oddly shaped, but a person. Jervis actually got along with her better than he did with
Vanyel. ''She says to tell you, 'thank you.' I think she
likes you.''

''She's a lovely lady, and I like her right back.'' Jervis
grinned at him. ''There's been a couple of times I've
wished I could talk to her straight out; I kind of wanted
her to know I'm real pleased that she's on *my* side these
days. *Tashir! The boy won't break! Put some back in that
swing! He's* supposed *to learn how to get out of the way,
dammit!*'' Jervis stalked onto the floor of the salle, and
Vanyel took the opportunity to get back to his room and
pack up.

There was one other person who needed to know where
Vanyel was going to be: Medren. This was in part because Vanyel needed to borrow his old lute. Disreputable
minstrel Valdir could never afford Herald Vanyel's lute or
the twelve-stringed gittern. And going in clandestine like
this, Vanyel knew he'd better have *no* discrepancies in his
persona. Vanyel *had* a battered old instrument he'd picked

up in a pawn shop that he carried as Valdir, but he'd left it at Haven, not thinking he'd need it.

But there was a further reason; Tashir was relaxed and open with the boy in a way he was not with either Jervis or Vanyel. Vanyel had come to the conclusion that his nephew was older than his years in a great many ways, and Vanyel had confidence in his inherent good sense.

And, last of all, the boy had the Bardic Gift. That could be very useful in dealing with an unbalanced youngster that no one dared to Mindtouch.

In a kind of bizarre coincidence, they'd given Medren Vanyel's old room, up and under the eaves and across from the library. Vanyel stared out the window, and wondered if he was still up to the climb across the face of the keep to get to that little casement that let into the library.

"How long do you reckon you'll be over there?" Medren asked, sitting on his bed and detuning his old instrument carefully.

"Not long; about a fortnight altogether. Anything I can't find out in that time is going to be too deep to learn as a vagabond minstrel, anyway." Vanyel turned away from the window.

"You aren't planning on going into that palace are you?"

"No. Why?"

Medren shook his head. "I dunno. I just got a bad feeling about it. Like, you shouldn't go in there alone. As long as I think of you going in *with* somebody, the bad feeling goes away. That sound dumb?"

"No, that sounds eminently sensible." Vanyel sat down beside him on the bed. Medren picked up the patched and worn canvas lute case and slid the instrument into it. "I want you to keep an eye on Tashir for me; a *Bardic* eye, if you will."

The boy contemplated that statement for a moment, whistling between his teeth a little. "You mean keep him calmed down? He's as jumpy as a deer hearing dogs. I been trying to do a little of that. I—" He blushed. "I remembered what you told me, about misusing the Gift. I thought this might be what you meant about using it right. He likes music well enough, so I just—sort of make it soothing.''

Vanyel ruffled his hair approvingly, and Medren gave him an urchinlike grin. ''Good lad, that is *exactly* what I meant about using it properly. When you aren't enhancing a performance, *proper* use is to the benefit of your audience, or to the King's orders. And poor Tashir could certainly benefit by a little soothing. So keep him soothed, hmm? There's one other thing, and this is a bit more delicate. He may tell you things, things about himself. I hesitate to ask you to betray confidences, but we just don't know anything about him.''

Medren thought that over. ''Seems to me that the awfuller the thing he'd tell me, and the less he'd want it known, the more *you'd* want to know it.'' He chewed his lip. ''That's a hard one. That's awful close to telling secrets I've been asked to keep. And if I've been making him feel like he could trust me, it doesn't seem fair.''

''I know. But I remind you that he's been accused of murdering fifty or sixty people. What he tells you might be a clue to whether or not he actually did it.'' Vanyel forestalled Medren's protests with an uplifted hand. ''I know what you're going to say, and *if* he did it, I *don't* believe he did it on purpose. But if—say—you found out where it was that his father wanted to send him, and why it frightened him so, we could have mitigating circumstances. I doubt the Lineans would totally accept it, but *we* would, and he could make a very pleasant home here with the Valdemar Heralds, even if he could never return to Lineas. That's not exactly a handicap.''

Medren nodded so vigorously that his forelock fell into his eyes. ''Makes sense. Fine, then if he tells me stuff, I'll tell it to you.''

The boy stuffed a handful of the little coils of sparc lute strings into a pocket on the back of the case and handed the whole to Vanyel. Vanyel stood, and pulled the carry strap over his shoulder. ''Do I look the proper scruffy minstrel?'' he asked, grinning.

Medren snorted. ''You're *never* going to look scruffy, Van. You *do* look underfed, which is good. And if you didn't shave for a couple of days, that would be better.

Then, again—'' He contemplated Vanyel with his head tilted to one side. ''If you didn't shave you'd look like a bandit, and people don't tell things to bandits. Better just stick to looking clean, starving, and pathetic. That way women'll feed you and tell you everything while they're feeding you. Hey, don't worry about that lute—if you gotta leave it, leave it. If you feel bad about leaving it, replace it.''

Vanyel placed his right hand over his heart and bowed slightly. ''I defer to your judgment. Clean and starving it is, and if speed requires I leave the instrument, I shall. And I *shall* replace it. It's a good thing to have one old instrument that you needn't worry about, you never know when you'll want to take one—oh, on a picnic or something. Thank you, Medren. For everything.'' He glanced out the window. ''I want to get to Highjorune by nightfall, so we'd better get on it. Remember, I'm supposed to be on a side trip to see Liss. I sent her a message by one of Savil's birds, so Liss knows to cover for me.''

Medren nodded. ''Right. And I'll keep a tight eye on Tashir for you, best I can.''

''That's all I can ask of anyone.''

Sunset was a thing of subdued colors, muted under a pall of gray clouds. Vanyel slipped off Yfandes' back, and uncinched the strap holding the folded blanket he'd used as a makeshift riding pad. Bareback for most of a day would not have been comfortable for either of them, but he had no place to hide her harness. No problem; they'd solved *this* little quandary the first time he became minstrel Valdir. She wore no halter at all, and only the blanket that *he* would use if he had to sleep in stables or on the floor of some inn. Nothing to hide, and nothing to explain. Yfandes would keep herself fed by filching from farms and free-grazing. If she got *too* hungry, he'd buy or steal some grain and toss it out over the wall to her at night.

:*Be careful,*: she said, nuzzling his cheek. :*I love you. I'll be staying with you as much as I can, but this is awfully settled land. I may have to pull off quite a ways to keep from getting caught.*:

:*I have all that current-energy to pull on if I have to call you,*: he reminded her. :*It's not the node, but it wouldn't surprise me to find out I could boost most of the way back to Forst Reach with it. I'm planning on recharging while I'm here, anyway.*:

:*If Vedric is still here, that could be dangerous.*:

:*Only if he detects it.*: He cupped his hand under her chin and gazed into those bottomless blue eyes. :*I'll be careful, I promise. This isn't Karse, but I'm going to behave as if it was. Enemy territory, and full drill.*:

:*Then I'm satisfied.*: She tossed her head, flicking her forelock out of her eyes. :*Call me if you need me.*:

:*I will.*: He watched her fade into the underbrush of the woodlot beside him with a feeling of wonderment. How something that big and that *white* could just—vanish like that—it never ceased to amaze him.

He rolled the cinch-belt, folded the blanket, and stuffed both into the straps of his pack. With a sigh for his poor feet, he hitched the lute strap a little higher on his shoulder, and headed toward the city gates of Highjorune.

The road was dusty, and before he reached the gates he looked as if he'd been afoot all day. He joined the slow, shuffling line of travelers and workers returning from the farms, warehouses, and some of the dirtier manufactories that lay outside the city walls. Farmworkers, mostly; most folk owning farms within easy walking distance of Highjorune lived within the city walls, as did their hirelings, a cautious holdover from the days when Mavelan attacks out of Baires penetrated as far as the throne city. The eyes of the guard at the gate flickered over him; noted the lute, the threadbare, starveling aspect, and the lack of weaponry, and dismissed him, all in a breath. Minstrel Valdir was not worth noting, which made minstrel Valdir very happy indeed.

Well, the first thing a hungry minstrel looks for is work, and Valdir was no exception to that rule. He found himself a sheltered corner out of the traffic, and began to assess his surroundings.

The good corners were all taken, by a couple of beggars, a juggler, and a man with a dancing dog. He shook his head, as if to himself. Nothing for him here, so close to the gates. He was going to need a native guide.

He loitered about the gate, waiting patiently for the guard to change. He put his hat out, got the lute in tune, and played a little, but he really didn't expect much patronage in this out-of-the-way nook. He actually drew a few loiterers, much to his own amazement. To his further amazement, said loiterers had money. By the time the relief-guard arrived with torches to install in the holders on either side of the gate, he'd actually collected enough coppers for a meager supper.

He had something more than a turnip and stale bread-crust on his mind, however. It was getting chilly; his nose was cold, and his patched cloak was doing very little to keep out the bite in the air. He chose one of the guards to follow, a man who looked as if he ate and drank well, and had money in his pocket; he slung the lute back over his shoulder, and sauntered along after him at a discreet distance.

It *was* possible, of course, that the man was married— but he was unranked, and young, and that made it unlikely. There was an old saying to the effect that, while higher-ranked officers *had* to be married, anyone beneath the rank of sergeant was asking for trouble if *he* chose matrimonial bonds. "Privates *can't* marry, sergeants *may* marry, captains *must* marry." Valdir had noticed that, no matter the place or the structure of the armed force, that old saying tended to hold true.

So, that being the case, an unranked man was likely to find himself a nice little inn or taphouse to haunt. And establishments of the sort he would frequent would tend to cater to his kind. They would have other entertainments as well—and they were frequently run by women. Valdir had traded off his looks to get himself a corner in more than one such establishment.

The man he was following turned a corner ahead of him, and when Valdir turned the same corner, he knew he'd come to the right street. Every third building seemed to be an alehouse of one sort or another; it was brightly lit, and women of problematical age and negotiable virtue had set up shop—as it were—beneath each and every one of the brightly burning torches and lanterns. Valdir grinned, and proceeded to see what he could do about giving those coppers in his purse some company.

The first inn he stuck his nose into was *not* what he was looking for. It was all too clearly a place that catered to appetites other than hunger and thirst. The second was perfect—but it had a musician of its own, an older man who glared at him over the neck of his gittern in such a way as left no doubt in Valdir' mind that he intended to *keep* his cozy little berth. The third had dancers, and plainly had no need of him, not given the abandon with which the young ladies were shedding the scarves that were their principle items of clothing. The fourth and fifth were run by men; Valdir approached them anyway, but the owner of the fourth was a minstrel himself, and the owner of the fifth preferred his customers with cash to spare to spend it in the dice and card games in the back room. The sixth was—regrettable. The smell drove him out faster than he'd gone in. But the seventh—the seventh had possibilities.

The *Inn of the Green Man* it was called; it was shabby, but relatively clean. The common stew in a pot over the fire smelled edible *and* as if it had more than a passing acquaintance with meat, though it was probably best not to ask what species. It was populated, but not over-crowded, and brightly lit with tallow dips and oil lamps, which would discourage pickpockets and cutpurses. The serving wenches—whose other properties were also, evidently, for sale—were also relatively clean. They weren't fabulous beauties, and most of them weren't in the first bloom of youth, but they *were* clean.

There was a good crowd, though the place wasn't exactly full. And Valdir spotted his guide here as well, which was a good omen.

Valdir stuck a little more than his nose in the door, and managed to get the attention of one of the serving wenches. "Might I have a word with the owner?" he asked, diffidently.

"Kitchen," said the hard-faced girl, and gave him a second look. He contrived to appear starving and helpless, and she softened, just a little. "Back door," she ordered. "Best warn you, Bel don't much like your kind. Last songbird we had, run off with her best girl."

"Thank you, lady," Valdir said humbly. She snorted, and went back to table-tending.

Valdir had to make his way halfway down the block before he could find an accessway to the alley. He caught a couple of young toughs eyeing him with speculation, but his threadbare state evidently convinced them that he didn't have much to steal—

That, and the insidious little voice in their heads that said *Not worth bothering with*. He *doesn't have anything worth the scuffle*.

The alley reeked, and not just of garbage, and he was just as glad that he hadn't eaten since morning. He risked a mage-light, so that he could avoid stepping in anything—and when it became evident that there were places he couldn't do that, he risked a little more magic to give him a clean spot or two to use as stepping stones.

Kind of funny, he thought, stretching carefully over a puddle of stale urine. *It was because I couldn't face situations like* this *that I never ran away to become a minstrel. And now, here I am—enacting one of my own nightmares. Funny.*

He finally found the back door of The Green Man and pushed it open. The kitchen, also, was relatively clean, but he didn't get to see much of it, because a giantess blocked his view almost immediately.

If she was less than six feet tall, Valdir would have been surprised. The sleeves of her sweat-stained linen shirt were rolled up almost to the shoulder, leaving bare arms of corded muscle Jervis would have envied. She wore breeches rather than skirts, which may have been a practical consideration, since enough materials to make *her* a skirt would have made a considerable dent in a lean clothing budget. Her graying brown hair was cut shorter than Valdir's. And no one would ever notice her face— not when confronted with the scar that ran from left temple to right jawbone.

"An' what d'*you* want?" she asked, her voice a dangerous-sounding growl.

"The—the usual," faltered Valdir. "A place, milady . . . a place for a poor songster. . . ."

"A place. Food and drink and a place to sleep in return for some share of whatever paltry coppers ye manage to garner," the woman rumbled disgustedly. "Aye, and a chance t' run off with one o' me girls when me back's turned. *Not* likely, boy. And ye'd better find yerself somewhere else t' caterwaul; there ain't an inn on th' Row that needs a rhymester."

Valdir made his eyes large and sad, and plucked at the woman's sleeve as she turned away. "My lady, please—" he begged shamelessly. "I'm new-come, with scarce enough coppers to buy a crust. I pledge you, lady, I would treat your other ladies as sisters."

She rounded on him. "Oh, ye would, would you? Gull someone else! If ye're new-come, then get ye new-gone!"

"Lady," he whimpered, ducking her threatened blow. "Lady, I swear—lady—I'm—" he let his voice sink to a low, half-shamed whisper. "—lady, your maids are safe with me! More than safe—I'm—shaych. There are few places open for such as I—"

She stared, she gaped, and then she grinned. " 'Struth! Ye could be at that, that pretty face an' all! Shaych! I *like* that!" She propelled him into the kitchen with a hand like a slab of bacon. "*All* right, I give ye a chance! Two meals an' a place on th' floor for half yer takin's."

He knew he had to put up at least the appearance of bargaining—but not much, or he'd cast doubt on his disguise. "Three meals," he said, desperately, "and a quarter."

She glared at him. "Ye try me," she said warningly. "Ye try me temper, pretty boy. Three an' half."

"Three and half," he agreed, timidly.

"Done. An' don't think t' cheat me; me girls be checkin' ye right regular. Now—list. I got armsmen here, mostly. I want lively stuff; things as put 'em in mind that me girls serve more'n ale. None of yer long-winded ballads, nor sticky love songs, nor yet nothin' melancholy. Not less'n they *asks* for it. An' if it be melancholy, ye make 'em *cry*, ye hear? Make 'em *cry* so's me girls an' me drink can give 'em a bit 'o comfort. Got that?"

"Aye, lady," he whispered.

"Don't ye go lookin' fer a bedmate 'mongst them lads, neither. They wants that, there's the Page, an' that's where they go. We got us agreements on the Row. I don' sell boys, an' I don' let in streetboys; the Page don' sell girls."

"Aye, lady."

"Ye start yer plunkin' at sundown when I open, an' ye finish when I close. Rest of th' time's yer own. Get yer meals in th' kitchen, sleep in th' common room after closin'."

"Aye, lady."

"Now—stick yer pack over in that corner, so's I know ye ain't gonna run off, an' get out there."

He shed pack and cloak under her critical eye, and tucked both away in the chimney corner. He took with him only his lute and his hat, and hurried off into the common room, with her eyes burning holes in his back.

She was in a slightly better mood when she closed up near dawn. Certainly she was mollified by the nice stack of copper coins she'd earned from his efforts. That it was roughly twice the value of the meals she'd be feeding him probably contributed to that good humor. That no less than three of the prettiest of her "girls" had propositioned him and been turned down probably didn't hurt.

She was pleased enough that she had a thin straw pallet brought down out of the attic so that he wouldn't be sleeping on the floor. He would be sharing the common room with an ancient gaffer who served as the potboy, and the two utterly silent kitchen helpers of indeterminate age and sex. Her order to all four of them to strip and wash at the kitchen pump relieved him a bit; he wasn't looking for comfort, but he had hoped to avoid fleas and lice. When the washing was over, he was fairly certain that the kitchen helpers were girls, but their ages were still a mystery.

When Bel left, she took the light with her, leaving them to arrange themselves in the dark. Valdir curled up on his lumpy pallet, wrapped in his cloak and the blanket that still smelled faintly of Yfandes, and sighed.

:Beloved?: He sent his thought-tendril questing out into the gray light of early dawn after her.

:Here. Are you established?:

:Fairly well. Valdir's seen worse. At least I won't be poisoned by the food. What about you?:

:I have shelter.:

:Good.: He yawned. *:This is strictly an after-dark establishment; if I go roaming in the late morning and early afternoon, I should find out a few things.:*

:I wish that I could help.: she replied wistfully.

:So do I. Good night, dearheart. I can't keep awake anymore.:

:Sleep well.:

One thing more, though, before he slept. A subtle, and *very* well camouflaged tap into the nearest current of mage-power. He *needed* it; the tiny trickle he would take would likely not be noticed by anyone unless they were checking the streams inch by inch. It wouldn't replenish his reserves immediately, but over a few days it would. It was a pity he could only do this while meditating or sleeping. It was an even greater pity that he couldn't just tap straight in as he had the night he'd rescued Tashir; he'd be at full power in moments if he could do that.

But *that* would tell Lord Vedric Mavelan that there was another mage here.

And if it comes to that, I'd rather surprise him.

He'd intended to try and think out some of his other problems, but it had been a full day since he'd last slept, and the walking he'd done had tired him out more than he realized. He started to try and pick over his automatic reactions to Bel's "girls"; had he led them on, without intending to? Had he been *flirting* with them, knowing deep down that he was going to turn them down and enjoying the hold his good looks gave over them? It was getting so that *nothing* was simple anymore.

But before he could do more than worry around the edges of things, his exhaustion caught up with him.

He slept.

Ten

"**B**oy?"

The harsh whisper in the dark startled him out of unrestful sleep; it jerked him into full awareness, dry-mouthed, heart pounding.

"Boy, be ye awake?"

"Yes," Valdir replied. *I am now, anyway.*

Hot, onion-laden breath near his elbow. "Lissen boy, ye needs warnin'. The reason this place don' prosper. Bel drinks up th' profit."

Valdir calmed his heart, nodded to himself. That explained a lot. "I'd wondered," he whispered back.

"She be at the keg in 'er room right now. Come mornin' she'll be up wi' a temper like a spring bear. She won't go hittin' on th' girls, not them as makes her profit—but me an' Tay an' Ri be fair game. An' now you. Ye take my meanin'?"

"I think so."

"Don' doubt me. An' don' go thinkin' ye got any-where's else. Ev'ry inn on th' Row's got its singster or dancer. Bel's the only one did wi'out. That be 'cause she don't care for ye singsters, an' no dancin' girl'l stay where the profits be so lean. How long ye plan on stayin'?"

Valdir was profoundly grateful that he was *not* locked into this life. "I hadn't thought I'd be here long. I really sort of thought I'd look for a place at the Great Houses or the Palace," he began timidly. "I—used to be with a House. They mostly keep at least one minstrel, and I figure the Palace must use—"

The old man choked with laughter, and then broke into a fit of terrible coughing. Valdir acted as would be expected. "I'm not that bad!" he sputtered indignantly. "I'm just—out of luck, lately."

The old man convulsed again. "Outa more'n luck. *First* off, there ain't no Great Houses in the city. They all be outside the walls. Second, the Remoerdis Family's dead. Ain't nobody in th' Palace but ghosts."

Valdir gasped, and let the old gaffer tell the tale as he pleased. It was amazingly consistent with what Lores had told him, save only that the Herald who'd carried off Tashir had been seven feet tall, cut down a dozen guards, and rode away on a fanged white demon. "—an' third thing—" the rheumy voice continued, "—they wouldn't have anyone next or nigh the palace as *wasn't* blood kin; even the servants be blood kin on the backside. So even if they'd been alive an' ye'd been t' see, they'd not 'ave took ye."

"Why?" Valdir asked, bewildered. "That doesn't make any sense! What does being blood relation have to do with serving—or talent?"

The old man coughed again. "Damn if I know. Been that way f'rever. Anyway, I'm tellin' ye, if ye wanta keep that purty face purty, save yer coppers an' get outa here soon as ye can; afore the snow flies be best. Otherwise ol' Bel likely to start seein' how far she can push ye. I've warned ye, now I'm goin' t' sleep." And not another word could Valdir get out of him.

He found out how right the warning was the next day, when Bel stumbled down the stairs, red-eyed and touchy, smelling like a brewery. She started in on the two kitchen girls, looking for excuses to punish one of them. She found plenty; the girls sported a black eye each before she was through with them.

Valdir managed to stay out of her way long enough to get his pack and bed stowed safely and his lute placed beside the door. But then—then he got an unexpected and altogether unpleasant shock. Bel tried—him. First flirting, then, when that brought no result, threatening.

She disgusted and frightened him, and he knew he dared not retaliate in *any* way. Instead he had to stand and take her pawing, while his skin crawled and his stomach churned, trying *not* to show anything except his very real and growing fear of her. She finally convinced herself that she wasn't going to get any pleasure out of him in *that* way, so she chose another.

In the end he escaped with no worse than a darkening bruise on his cheekbone where she'd backhanded him into a wall—without his promised breakfast or lunch, and not willing to endure either more of her clumsy caresses *or* her brutality to get it. He flew out the door as soon as she unlocked it, resolving not to return until nightfall and the time appointed for him to perform. He paused long enough in his flight to snatch up his lute; he would not leave the means of his livelihood unguarded, and anyway, there might be the chance of making a few coins on the street as he had last night. Enough, maybe, to feed him.

Herald Vanyel would not have tolerated that treatment, but Herald Vanyel was far, far away. There was only poor, timid Valdir, fallen indeed on bad luck, scrawny, fearful, and no little desperate.

Gods help her people. If I was what I'm pretending to be, I think I'd go hunting a sharp knife, and I'm not sure if I'd use it on her first, or myself. . . .

"Thought you might end up here," drawled a strange, well-trained voice, as he bolted out the door and into the street. He turned, blinking in the bright sunlight. Lounging against a wall across the street was the grizzled minstrel who'd been playing the gittern in one of the other taverns the night before. He was dressed in dull colors that blended with the wall; he'd taken up a post right opposite The Green Man. He looked bored and lazy; as Valdir watched him suspiciously, he pushed away from the wall and walked slowly toward him across the cobblestones. In the light of day he was clearly much older than Valdir; hair thinning and mostly gray, square face beginning to wrinkle and line. But as he approached Valdir, it was also plain that he had kept his body in relatively good shape; beneath the loose, homespun shirt, leather tunic and breeches, he had only the tiniest sign of a paunch, and the rest of him looked wiry and strong enough to survive just about any tavern brawl.

To someone like Valdir, this stranger meant danger of

another sort. The man could be looking to eliminate a
rival, or intending to bully him—or worse.

*Talk about luck being out. Have I leaped out of the pan
into the fire?*

Valdir backed up a pace, letting his uncertainty show
on his face.

A tired horse pulled a slops-wagon down the center of
the street, and the stranger stepped deliberately toward
him once it had passed.

"Ah, ease up, boy, I'm not about to pummel you,"
the minstrel said, a faint hint of disgust twisting his lips.
Valdir continued to step back, until the minstrel had him
trapped in a corner where a fence met the inn wall. Valdir
froze, his hands pressed against the unsanded wood behind him, and the minstrel reached for his face, grabbing
his chin in a hand rough with chording-calluses. He
turned Valdir's cheek into the light, and examined the
slowly purpling bruise.

"Got you a good one, did she?" He touched the edge
of the bruise without hurting his captive. "Huhn. Not as
bad as it could be."

The minstrel let him go and backed up a few steps.
Valdir huddled where he was, watching him fearfully.
The stranger scratched his chin thoughtfully. "Heard you
last night when I went on break. You aren't bad."

"Thank you," Valdir replied timidly.

"You're also going to get your hands broken if you stay
with Bel for very long," the other continued. "That's
what she did to the one before the one that ran off with
her girl."

Valdir did not reply.

"Well? Aren't you going to say anything?"

"Why are you telling me all this?" Valdir asked, letting his suspicion show. He stood up a little straighter,
and rubbed his sweaty palms on his patched and faded
linen tunic in a conscious echoing of an unconscious gesture of nervousness.

"Because the one before the one that ran off with her
girl was a good lad," the older man said, impatience
getting the better of him. "He was pretty, like you, and
he was fey, like I bet you are, and I don't want it hap-

pening to another one. All right?'' He turned on his heel and started to walk away.

Don't turn away a possible ally!

''Wait!'' Valdir cried after him. ''Please, I—I didn't mean—''

A bit of breeze blew dry leaves up the street. The minstrel halted, turned slowly. Valdir walked toward him, holding out his hand. ''I'm Valdir,'' he said shyly. ''I've been—north. Baires.'' The other showed his surprise with a hissing intake of breath. ''I made a bit of a mistake, and I had to make a run for it.'' He looked down at his feet, then back up again. ''It hasn't been easy; not while I was there, and not getting across the border to here. They got me out of the habit of looking for friends up there, and into the habit of looking for enemies.''

''Renfry,'' said the older minstrel, clasping his hand, with a slow smile that showed a good set of even, white teeth. ''Not many real musicians on the Row. I s'ppose I should be treating you as a rival—but—hell, a man gets tired of hearing and singing the same damn things over and over. Bel had Jonny for a long while before she ruined him, and he trained here.''

''What happened to him? After, I mean.''

''We clubbed together and sent him off to a Healer the very next day, ended up having to send him across the Border. Uppity palace Healer didn't want to 'waste his time on tavern scum.' Never heard anything after that.'' He shrugged. ''If the poor lad ended up not being able to play again, I don't imagine he'd want anyone to know.''

Valdir shuddered; genuinely.

''Ol' Bel don't believe in letting the help sample the goods. She got drunk and thought Jonny had his eye on one of the girls.'' He snorted in contempt. ''Not bloody likely.''

''She must have slipped up once—'' Valdir ventured. ''I mean—the one that romanced her girl, like you said.''

Renfry laughed, and started up the dusty, near-empty street with Valdir following. The thin autumn sunlight stretched their shadows out ahead of them. ''She did, because she was bedding the fellow herself. She never figured him for having the stamina to be double-dipping!

Truth to tell, I hope he was good in bed, because he surely had a voice like a crow in mating season, and maybe four whole chords to his name.''

Valdir thought about the way Bel had tried to come on to *him,* and could actually feel a shred of sympathy for the unknown minstrel. ''Were you waiting out here for *me?''* Valdir asked, as they approached the closed door of The Pig and Stick, the tavern Renfry had been playing in last night.

Renfry nodded, holding the door to ''his'' inn open. ''Why?''

''To warn you, like I said. Let you know you'd better make tracks.''

Valdir shook his head, and his hair fell over one eye. ''I can't. I—I haven't got a choice,'' he confessed sadly. ''I haven't anywhere else to go.''

Renfry paused in surprise, half in, half out of the doorway. *''That* lean in the pocket?'' he asked. ''Lad, you aren't *that* bad. You're a good enough musician, for true. Unless you *really* made more than just a mistake.''

Valdir nodded unhappily. ''Made a bad enemy. Sang the wrong song at the wrong time. Used to be with a House. Now I've got the clothes on my back, my lute, and that's mostly it.''

''Save your coppers and head over the Border into Valdemar,'' the other advised. ''Tell you what, I'll stand you a drink and a little better breakfast than you'd get from old Bel, then I'll steer you over to a decent corner. Not the best, but with the palace a wreck, there's a lot of guards standing about with nothing to do but make sure our High and Mighty Lord Visitor doesn't get himself in the way of a stray knife round about the Town Elder's house. You ought to collect a bit there, hmm?'' He grinned. ''Besides, I got an underhanded motive. You're about as good as me, and you know some stuff new to our folk. I'm going to bribe you with food to learn it, and then I'm going to get you out of town so you aren't competition anymore.''

Valdir smiled back hesitantly, at least as far as his sore cheek permitted. ''Now *that* I understand!''

* * *

By nightfall Bel was sober, and when Valdir crept in at the open door she waved him to his place on the hearth with nothing more threatening than a scowl. He sat down on the raised brick hearth with his bruised cheek to the fire, and began tuning the lute. There were one or two customers; nothing much. Valdir was just as glad; it gave him a chance to think over what he'd picked up.

It had been a very profitable day. The Town Elder's servants were entertainment-starved and loose-tongued; once Valdir had gotten them started they generally ran on quite informatively and at some length before demanding something in return.

Ylyna had been a child-bride; that made Tashir's arrival eight-and-a-half months after the wedding so much more surprising. Several of the Mavelan girls had been offered as prospective treaty-spouse, but of them all, only Ylyna had lacked mage-powers, so only Ylyna had been acceptable to Deveran Remoerdis *or* his people. It was generally agreed that she was "odd, even for a Mavelan." And strangely enough, it was also generally agreed that up until the night of the massacre Tashir had been a fairly decent, if slightly peculiar, young man. "A bit like you, lad," one of the guards had said. "Jumpin' at shadows, like. Nervy." If it had not been for his mage-powers there likely would have been no objection to his eventual inheritance of the throne of Lineas. But once those powers manifested, it became out of the question. No Linean would stand by and see a mage take the seat of power.

"We seen what comes o' that, yonder," an aged porter had told him a bit angrily, pointing with his chin at the north. "Put a mage in power, next thing ye know, he's usin' magic t' get any damn thing 'e want out 'o ye. No. No mages here."

So as soon as it had become evident that several of Tashir's younger brothers—all of whom markedly resembled Deveran—were going to live into adulthood, the Council demanded that Deveran disinherit the boy. They didn't have to pressure him, according to the Lord Elder's first chambermaid; he gave in at once, so quickly that the ink wasn't even dry on the copies of the proclamation when his heralds cried the news.

And strangely enough, Tashir didn't seem the least un-happy about it. "Didn' 'xactly jump for joy, but didn' seem t' care, neither," a fruitseller had observed.

Lord Vedric—that was who Valdir assumed was the "Lord Visitor," though he was never referred to as any-thing but "that Mavelan Lord"—had come as something of a surprise to the folk of Highjorune. They'd expected him to attempt to defend Tashir; instead he'd listened to the witnesses with calm and sympathy, and had expressed his horrified opinion that the boy *had* gone rogue. He'd kept displays of magery to a minimum, and had made himself available to the Council as a kind of advisor until someone figured out how to get Tashir back to be pun-ished, and until they determined who the new ruler of Lineas would be.

As for the startling resemblance between Lord Vedric and Tashir—

" 'E said th' boy could be 'is, 'e didn't know," one of the chambermaids—a pretty one that Valdir suspected of getting gossip fodder via pillow talk—had whispered, sniggering, to Valdir. " 'E said th' girl couldn' keep 'er skirts down, an' that she'd bribed 'er way inta lots o' beds, takin' the place o' th' girls as was s'pposed t' be there. Said 'e'd found 'er in 'is bed more'n once, an' that 'e didn't know it were 'is own 'alf-sister an' not the wench 'e'd called fer till mornin'. That was why 'e were tryin' t' keep th' boy heir, so 'e says; tryin' t' do right by 'im, like, just in case." She sniggered again. "*I* 'eard 'nough fr'm m' cousin 'bout 'Er 'Ighness an' 'er light-skirt ways *I* believe 'im."

And the cousin, it seemed, had been one of Ylyna's per-sonal maids. More importantly, she had been *out* of the palace the night everyone else had been killed. The cham-bermaid had promised an introduction in a day or two.

"You gonna sit there all night diddlin' that thing, or you gonna play?" Bel growled, breaking into his thoughts. With a start and a cowed look, he began play-ing.

The young girl scampered back to her duties, leaving Valdir alone with the last surviving member of the palace staff, her cousin. The woman pondered him for a moment, then, a trifle reluctantly, invited him into her tiny parlor. The cousin was old; that surprised Valdir. And the odd look she gave him as he took the seat she indicated surprised him more.

"Why are ye askin', lad?" she queried, as she settled into her own chair. "If it's just morbid curiosity . . ."

He rubbed the bruise Bel had gifted him with this morning—it matched the first—and tried to get her measure. She was a bit younger than Savil, and small, but proudly erect. There was something very dignified about her, and out of keeping with her purported position; she didn't hold herself with the air of a servant. She was plainly clothed, in dark wool dress and white linen undertunic, but the wool was fine lambswool, tightly woven, and costly, and the linen as fine as he had ever seen on his mother. She watched him from under half-closed lids. Her eyes seemed full of secrets.

She had been out of the palace that fatal evening, the girl had told him, because she had been here, in the home of her aged mother, who had fallen and could not be left alone at night. There was a great deal about her that prompted Valdir to trust in her honesty; enough that he decided to tell her a certain measure of the truth.

"I want to find out what really happened," he said, as sincerely as he could manage. "The stories I've heard so far don't make a lot of sense. If there's something that needs to be told, perhaps I'm the one to tell it. A minstrel can tell an unpleasant truth with more success, sometimes, than anyone else. I'm a stranger, with no interests to protect. It might be I'd be believed more readily than a Linean."

She looked away from him, and her face was troubled. "I don't know," she said, finally. "This . . ." She looked down at her hands, and her attention seemed to be caught by a ring she wore.

It was an unusual ring in the fact that it was so very plain; burnished, unornamented silver, centered with a dull white stone. The stone was nothing Valdir recognized; it looked like an ordinary, water-worn quartz pebble.

Then her attention was more than caught—

The stone flared with an internal, white flame for a moment, and it seemed that she could not look away from it.

The woman's face took on a blankness of expression he'd only seen in the spell-bound.

Valdir felt the back of his neck chill. There was a Power moving somewhere, one he didn't recognize. He longed to be able to unshield and probe, and maddeningly knew he dared not. This felt *almost* like someone was working a Truth Spell, only the feel of this was old—old—

"Lady Ylyna—" she said, in a strangely abstracted voice. "At the bottom of this, it all comes down to Lady Ylyna."

"Tashir's mother?" Valdir asked, biting his lip in vexation when it occurred to him that his words might break whatever spell it was that held her. But her expression remained rapt, and he ventured more. "But—how—"

"She was hardly more than a child when she came here," the woman said, still gazing into the stone of her ring, "but I've never seen a more terrified girl in my life. She'd been the ignored one, until Deveran refused to take any girl to wife that had mage-powers. *Then* she was valuable, and you can believe her family *kept* the strings on her. She was terrified of them. She was so happy when she was first pregnant—Deveran made a great deal of her, you see. But then Tashir came early—there was no telling him that it was just accident the boy looked like his uncle. So he only came to her to get her pregnant, and once pregnant, he ignored her until the children were born."

"But—"

She didn't seem to hear him. "He ignored the boy, too. *She* was scarcely old enough to have left off with dolls, she hadn't a clue what to do with a child. Then the letters started coming—letters from Baires, with the royal seal on them, from *The* Mavelan. She never let us see them, but they terrified her. And she took it all out on the boy. The other children, the ones that took after Deveran, *they* had nursemaids, and careful watching, but not Tashir. *He* was left to *her.* Poor child. Half the time she petted and cosseted him like a lapdog—*that* was when her letters seemed to be good. The other half of the time she'd take a riding crop to him till the poor boy was bruised all over. That was when the letters frightened her. Then the boy started showing wizard-power, and it got worse. I watched her watching him one day—I've never seen such jealousy in my life on a human face.''

''Why would she be *jealous* of him?'' Valdir wondered aloud.

The old woman shook herself, and gave him a sharp look. ''I've said more than I intended,'' she told him, almost accusingly.

He tried to look innocent and trustworthy. ''But what you've said is important.''

She rose and walked slowly across the tiny sitting room to the door, and opened it. ''Come back in two days,'' she said, in tones that brooked no argument. ''I may decide to tell you more then.''

Nearly ready to burst with frustration, Valdir left, doing his best to show none of it.

She shut the door behind him, and he wandered back down to the Row, looking for a good place to set out his hat for a few more hours.

He still had to eat, after all.

:How much of this can you trust?: Yfandes asked.

:Well, I'm hardly going to be able to run Truth Spell on her,: he replied, staring up into the darkness and listening to old Petar snoring loud enough to shake the chimney down. *:Although—gods help me, it seems as if something was doing* that *for me. And you have to admit, this report of alternate petting and abuse certainly explains some of his reaction toward women. ''Mothers'' in particular.:*

:But it doesn't explain what happened that night.:

One of the two girls murmured in her sleep. Vanyel shivered, and pulled his blanket a little closer. The cold of the dirt floor was seeping through his thin straw pallet. *:There's more. I know there's more. I think she—or whatever it was that made her talk—is testing me, and I don't know why. Gods, and the questions I have—why allow only blood relations to serve the Remoerdis Family? And* *why does it feel as if the old lady is—Gifted? Or geased, bespelled. Or both, I don't know. And I don't dare test her to find out, with Vedric in the city:*

:Mm,: she agreed. *:Wise. What's he up to?*

:Being utterly charming,: Valdir replied. *:He's got the locals coming more and more over to his side. And he's agreeing with them on every point. It's hard to believe that this is the same man my sister called a viper.:*

:Interesting. And these Lineans are a hard-headed lot.:

:It would just about take an angel to change their minds about the Mavelans,: Vanyel told her. *:But Vedric seems to be doing just that.:*

Petar snorted, coughed, and turned over. There was silence for a moment, then he snorted again, and the snores did *not* resume.

:Take the chance to get to sleep while you can,: Yfandes advised dryly.

But sleep refused to come.

Tonight had been particularly bad. Not only had Bel made another try, but Valdir had fended off the attentions of someone else as well.

Even if he *hadn't* taken Bel's glare as warning that she meant what she'd said about not taking up with her customers, he'd have avoided this one. *Shaych,* yes—but in a way that made Valdir's skin crawl as much as Bel did. The man hadn't been physically repulsive, but there was something twisted about him, something unhealthy. Like a fine velvet glove over a taloned hand. The man had looked at him with a hunger that made him shiver with reaction even now. He had reminded Vanyel—not Valdir—of the mage that had called himself "Krebain."

I don't know what to think anymore. If I'm not shaych, then why can't I just do what Bel wants and get it over with? If I am, then why did that hunter revolt me? He turned onto his side, curling into a ball against the cold, the ache of his empty stomach, the misery his own uncertainty was causing.

*And today—gods. That sick little game I was playing on the serving girls. Leading them on—*knowing *I was leading them right down a dead end. Yes, I got information—but I was actually* enjoying *deluding them, hav-*

ing a little power over them. Gods, that was sick. And I would have gone right on *playing little sex-flirtation games if 'Fandes hadn't threatened to kick me into next week. I'm turning into something I don't much like.*

He curled up a little tighter. *I don't even know my own feelings any more.*

He tightened his lips in exasperation. *Look, Van, you're supposed to have been trained in logic. So* why *don't you try putting things into some kind of category, you goose? Maybe you don't know what you feel, but you certainly know what you* don't *feel. You've been agonizing over* that *enough lately! Then figure out what it is that everything you* don't *care for has in common.*

:It's about time,: came Yfandes' sardonic comment.

He was startled—and then angry. He very nearly made some kind of nasty retort back to her, but *she* was blocking, and he wasn't so angry that he'd try to breach her shields just to tell her off. For one thing, he wasn't sure he could—for another, the attempt *might* give him away to Vedric.

But he certainly wanted to. . . .

The next several days were some of the worst Valdir had ever spent. He played his fingers to the bone every night until the last customer left. He dodged Bel, not always successfully, by day. He took her beatings with teeth-gritting meekness, avoided her increasingly heavy-handed attempts to trap him, and did his best to minimize the damage she inflicted. He was cold at night, and starved by day; Bel's idea of "meals" being scarcely enough to keep a mouse alive. And his own unhappy thoughts kept him awake more often than not.

He went back to the former maid Reta's tiny house faithfully every two days, only to be turned away with nothing.

Then, finally, after close to a fortnight—an endless series of attempts to see the old woman and being turned away from her door—Reta finally agreed to speak with him again.

"I wasn't sure you'd be back." Reta held the door open for him, and he slipped past her into the tiny, painfully neat sitting room. She closed the door carefully, and sat down on her settle beside the hearth. Valdir took the only other seat, a stool. The old woman regarded him thoughtfully while he curbed his impatience, and hoped that *this* time some more information would be forthcoming.

"No, I wasn't certain you'd be back," she repeated.

"Why wouldn't I?" he asked, just as quietly, as he ignored the hollow feeling in his stomach. He'd been here long enough that the meager rations and short sleep were beginning to affect him, and while he'd recharged his mage-energies fully, his physical energies were becoming exhausted. He woke up five and six times a night, cramping with cold, and even with the supplementary food he was spending his pittance of earnings on, he was beginning to have spells of light-headedness. Most of his money was going to buy Yfandes grain, anyway. But Reta held the key, he was sure of it. If only he could persuade her to part with the information. Her—or whatever power had controlled her the first time he came to her door.

"This isn't a tale of high adventure," she pointed out dryly. "And it isn't a bedroom farce. It's not terribly interesting, it's not good song-fodder, and it's sad."

"Sad?" He raised an eyebrow. "Why sad?"

She examined the hands she held folded in her lap, as if they were of great interest. "That poor child Ylyna, she never really had a chance to grow up. Oh, she was grown in body, but—*They* kept her a child, a frightened child they could manipulate. I find that sad."

"They" meaning the Mavelans. "Why didn't you say something?" he asked, trying to understand what could have led her to stand by and watch, and not act.

She shrugged. "Who would have listened? I was Her Highness' personal maid, as I was Deveran's mother's. Deveran would have thought me either besotted or bewitched. He wasn't known for thinking much of women in the first place." She shook her head and stared at the ring on her finger. The peculiar, dull white stone seemed to brighten for a moment, and her voice and expression became abstracted, as it had the first time she'd spoken openly.

It's happening again! Valdir held his breath, all his

exhaustion, his personal concerns forgotten, hoping against hope. . . .

"No, Deveran had no faith in the good sense *or* the honesty of women. After all, his own mother had betrayed him by dying when he most needed her, or so his own father kept claiming. And Ylyna—*not* a virgin, possibly mad, and surely little better than a trollop—certainly didn't help matters."

Valdir could not stay silent; he protested such inexcusable, willful blindness. "But the way she treated Tashir—"

"Was likely the way *she'd* been treated." The old woman shook her head again, continuing to stare at the stone of her ring. "When you reach my age, you have generally seen a great deal. Adults who have been beaten as children beat their own children. And—other things. I sometimes wonder if *that* isn't what Holy Lerence meant when he said 'the sins of the fathers shall be taken up by the sons.' " Her eyes grew even more thoughtful—or entranced. She didn't seem to be paying any attention to him.

There was something stirring here. Again he felt some Power moving under the powers he could detect easily. *Gods! I don't dare try to probe for it.* The frustration maddened him. He could *feel* it, something deep, and powerful, it vibrated so that he felt it rather than "detected" it; the way he could sometimes "feel" the vibrations of a note too low to actually hear.

But it was *stronger* this time, much stronger, and it seemed to be stirring to *his* good, for the old chambermaid was saying things she hadn't more than hinted at before.

"What other things was she doing?" Valdir prompted in a whisper, hands clenched together so tightly they ached. This was it. This was what he was looking for. The secret no one knew. The key to it all.

She sounded as if she was talking to herself. "When Tashir grew older—and handsomer—she started looking at him differently. The gods know Deveran hadn't come to her bed for four years, and wouldn't allow any male servants near her, only women. She had never had *any* pleasure except in bed, I think. I wonder if that wasn't the only thing she thought she could do well.'' The old woman was gazing deeply into her stone and not at all at him now, and her voice was very low, so that he had to strain to hear it. She shifted just a little, and he caught the sharp smell of lavender from the folds of her dress. ''Tashir began looking more and more like his uncle, and he was *still* terrified of her. Of *her,* who never frightened anyone, and couldn't even command respect from her servants. It must have been too seductive to resist, that combination; fear, and the handsome young face and body. She set out to seduce her own son into her bed.''

Valdir froze. *No—that's—my gods—*

She continued on, still speaking in that same, dreamy voice, as if she was speaking only to herself. ''That frightened him even more, I think, once he realized what was going on. Poor child. I hardly believed it at first; I just thought the petting was getting a little—overwarm. She'd use any excuse to get her hands on him. Any excuse at all.''

Valdir licked his dry lips, but couldn't make his voice work.

Reta sighed. ''And Deveran either didn't know or didn't care; I tend to think the latter. He had what he wanted; three sons indisputably his, and likely to reach maturity. What happened to Tashir didn't matter. The *only* person who cared what was happening to him was the old arms-master, the one Deveran had retired. Karis. *He* had taken to teaching the boy, when he saw no one else would. He protected him as much as he could. Which wasn't much, but it was something. He gave the boy a place to hide— and a person to look up to who was stable, sane, and fond of him.''

''A good man?''

And possibly another way to get Tashir to open up—

''A very good man. A pity he was in the palace with the rest of them.''

Valdir wanted to curse, and restrained himself only by a strong effort of will.

''Finally it got to the point that Tashir *couldn't* keep her away—and that wizard-power of his intervened. He had a kind of fit; smashed half the bower before it was over. That was when Deveran decided.''

''Decided what?'' Valdir asked.

At that moment, the power faded abruptly. One breath it was there. Then it was gone. Her eyes finally came back to their normal sharp focus. ''What?'' she asked him, looking up at him suddenly.

Gods—the spell's broken. Oh, Lady of Light, help me persuade her. Would she finish the sentence? Could he convince her on his own? ''You were going to tell me what Deveran had decided to do about Tashir,'' he prompted. ''That night.''

''Oh.'' She shrugged, indifferently. ''That. I thought everyone knew about that.''

''*I* don't,'' he pointed out. ''And nobody wants to talk about it, much.''

''It's simple enough. Since Vedric was making such a big to-do over the boy, Deveran decided to let *him* deal with the problem. Deveran was going to send the boy to his Mavelan relatives—permanently. That was what he told Ylyna after they cleared the boy and the mess out of her bower. That he intended to tell the boy at dinner.'' She sighed. ''And I can only assume, given that Tashir was even more frightened of that den of madmen than he was of his mother, that this was exactly what happened, and what brought—everything—down.''

He hadn't realized how much time he'd spent in the little sitting room; when he took his leave of Reta, he was appalled. *One* candlemark to sundown.

Panic stole thought. He could only think of *one* thing. Home.

He *had* to get home, before it was too late. He didn't *dare* try to Mindtouch Savil from here; that would be as stupid, with Vedric so near, as riding through the gates in full Whites on Yfandes.

He ran across town, dodging through foot and beast traffic, trying to reach the east gate before they closed it for the night. Once closed—he wouldn't get out until morning. He didn't *dare* cast any kind of spell to get him by, no more than he dared Mindtouch Savil. Vedric would detect spellcasting even faster than the use of a Mind-Gift. And every moment he stayed here was another moment the same disaster that wiped out Tashir's family could move to harm *his*.

The sun was dropping inexorably toward the horizon; he had a pain in his side, and he was gasping for breath—and *still* he wasn't more than halfway to his goal. He stumbled against a market-stall; recovered; ran on. He realized with despair that he was *not* going to make it in time.

And candlemarks could count; could be fatal, given what he knew now.

It *was* only too possible that Tashir had done exactly what he'd been accused of; that he had been pushed too far by his father's ultimatum, and he had lost his hold temporarily on his Gift and his sanity. It was only too likely that he had unleashed power gone rogue and had destroyed his own home and everything and everyone in it.

Valdir stopped, unable to run any farther; clung to the corner of a building at a cross street, and watched the sun turn to blood, and sink below the horizon.

Taking with it his hope.

Valdir slipped into the Pig and Stick, keeping to the wall and the shadows as much as he could. He managed to get within touching distance of Renfry, and froze there, unmoving, in the shadows behind him.

He prayed that Renfry was about to finish a set, and that he had not just *begun* one. The tavern was hot, and he was sweating from his run. His side still hurt, and he wanted to cough so badly his chest ached with the effort of holding it back. Sweat ran down his back, and into his eyes. Odor of bread and stew and spilled ale made his stomach cramp up with hunger, and his eyes watered. The lamps flickered, and he gripped the wall behind him, as the room swam before his eyes.

Too long on too little. Oh, gods, keep me going!

Finally Renfry finished, and waved aside requests for more. "Not now, lads," he said genially. "Not until I wet my throat a bit."

He turned, and saw Valdir behind him. He started to say something—then took a second, closer look at him, and his eyes grew alarmed.

He picked up the gittern by the neck, and grabbed Valdir's elbow with his free hand. Without a single word, he propelled the unresisting Valdir before him through the door leading to the kitchen.

It was light enough in here, though twice as hot as the tavern common room, what with two fires and the brick bake-oven all roaring at once. A huge table dominated the center of the room; an enormously fat man in a floury, stained apron was pulling fresh loaves out of the oven with a long wooden paddle and putting them to cool on the table. There were two boys at each of the fireplaces, one turning a spit, one watching a kettle. A fifth boy was sitting on a stool right by the door, peeling roots.

Renfry pushed the boy peeling roots off his perch and shoved Valdir down onto it.

"What's wrong?" he said, "And don't tell me it's nothing. You look like somebody seeing a death sentence."

Valdir just nodded; he'd already concocted a story for Renfry, and one that fit in with what he'd already told the man. "I've—" He finally coughed, rackingly; swallowed. "I've got to get out of here. Now. Tonight."

Renfry looked at him narrowly. "Wouldn't be that little matter of a song, would it?"

Valdir just looked at him, pleadingly. "If Vedric finds out I'm here," he whispered truthfully, "he'll probably kill me. You didn't tell me it was *Vedric* here."

"*Vedric!*" Renfry exploded. "Great good gods, boy, you sure don't pick your enemies too carefully! Oh, *hell.*"

He folded his arms and gazed up at the ceiling, brows knitted together so that they came close to meeting. "Let's see. First off, we got to get your things away from Bel. Huh . . . got it!"

He slipped out into the taproom and returned within a few moments. "I just paid that little sneak brat of the cook's to pinch your things. If *he* can't nip 'em, nobody can. Now—how much coin you got?"

Valdir turned out his purse. There wasn't much. Renfry counted it carefully. "Tel!" he shouted into the chaos of the kitchen. "How much day-old bread and stuff can I get you to part with for twenty coppers? Be generous, the boy has to run for it."

The massive cook blundered over to their side of the big central worktable, peered at Valdir, and then at the tiny heap of coin. "Huh. Apples is cheap right now; got some with bad spots. All right fer the road, no good t' store. Bread, uh—got some I was gonna use fer stuffin'. Let ye have it all. Got some cheese w' mold all through. Mold won' hurt ye, just looks like hell an' tastes mighty sharp; people round about here don't care for sharp cheese. Skinny runt like you, hold ye least a fortnight."

Renfry gave Valdir a look brimming with satisfaction. "That'll get you across the Border, easy, and there's a Harvestfest going on over there right now. Boy with a voice like yours that can't get coin at a Harvestfest don't deserve t' call himself a minstrel."

"Hey, 'Fry!" An insolent urchin slid in under Renfry's elbow, Valdir's pack and blanket in one hand, his lute in the other. "These whatcha lookin' fer?"

Valdir snatched the lute out of the child's hand and held it to his chest, his eyes going moist. "Oh, gods—Renfry, I—"

I never dared hope for this much help from him. Never even prayed for it.

"*Don't* you cry on me!" Renfry growled, cuffing his ear. "Just getting my competition out of town, I told you. Tel, here—pack up the boy's food." He scraped everything but two small silver pieces off the table and poured them into the cook's hand. The handful of copper bits vanished into a pocket of the stained apron, and a hand rivaling Bel's for size and strength took the pack. "Now, listen careful, because I'm only going to tell you this once. You go down to the *west* gate. I know it's the wrong way, just circle around the city walls once you get outside. You ask for Asra. You got that?"

"Asra," Valdir repeated, nodding. "West gate."

"You tell him Renfry sent you, and you give him *one* silver. That's his standard bribe to let folks out after dark, and don't let him tell you different. Then when you get to the Border, you give the other to our lads. That'll get you past them. Valdemar folk don't give a hang about who crosses to their side, so long as you don't look like a fighter or a trader. Fighter they'd question, trader they'd tax. You got that?''

"One silver to Asra at the west gate, one to the Border Guards.''

"Good lad.'' Renfry nodded approvingly. "Now belt that blanket around you under your cloak; you're going to need it, it's cold out there. When you get 'round the walls, you take the east road as far as the *second* farm on the right tonight. You stop there. There's a haybarn right on the road and the old boy that owns it don't give a hang if people sleep there so long as they don't build fires. After that, you're on your own.''

Valdir was pulling his threadbare cloak on over the blanket when the cook returned with his pack bursting at the seams. He tucked the two tiny coins into his now-empty purse, slung pack over one shoulder and lute over the other, and turned to Renfry, trying to think of some way to thank him.

Renfry took one look at his eyes, and softened. "Damn. Wish you could have stayed a while,'' he said gruffly, and suddenly pulled Valdir into a quick, rough embrace. "Now get out of here, before Bel comes looking for you.''

Vanyel made the best meal he'd had in a fortnight of half a loaf, the cheese, and a couple of apples. Yfandes got the rest.

:Funny, how you seem to be able to find friends in the most unexpected places,: she mused. *:Sometimes I wonder. . . .:*

"Friends? What are you talking about?'' he asked her, cinching the blanket pad in place, and pulling himself up on her back. "Gods.'' He clung there for a moment, as another wave of disorientation washed over him.

:Never mind. Are you all right?:

"I'll be fine. Just low on resources, and worn out.'' Anxiety cramped his stomach a moment. He wouldn't

have stopped long enough to eat if he hadn't found his
legs giving out as he circled around the city to his meeting place with Yfandes. The shadows under the trees
seemed sinister. The wind in the near-naked branches
moaned as if in pain. He *had* to get back—

—*but the old man was one of those that died.* The
thought kept nagging at him. *He must have loved that old
man, given his reaction to Jervis. That wasn't feigned. I
can't believe that he would have killed the only person
he trusted, even in a fit of uncontrolled rage and fear.*

Never mind. The important thing was to take this
knowledge back, *now*—before it was too late. Before the
same thing could happen at Forst Reach. It still might
not have been Tashir who killed the Remoerdis Family,
but he dared not take that chance.

"All right, 'Fandes," he said aloud. "Let's get *out* of
here."

And she leaped out onto the moon-flooded road.

Eleven

If Vanyel had dared to Gate so close to Vedric Mavelan he *would* have. But he didn't; he didn't dare alert him to the fact that a mage powerful enough to Gate had been within the city. *If* the Mavelans were somehow behind the disaster after all, he would be a fool to alert his quarry. So he and Yfandes pounded into Forst Reach just after dawn—

To find everything as peaceful as when they'd left.

:I told you,: Yfandes said, in a maddeningly reasonable tone of mind-voice as she pulled into a tired walk. *:I told you if anything had gone wrong we'd have* felt *it, the way we felt the first surge. Didn't I tell you?:*

Visions of slaughter and mayhem melted, taking with them the fear that had strengthened and supported him. When they got to the stable, Vanyel just slid wearily off her back, vowing not to say a word.

Because if he did, he'd take her head off. He *hated* it when she said, "I told you so."

And he did not want to get into a fight with her, didn't even want to have words with her; she didn't deserve it. *Much*.

He hurt; he ached all over, and he was half numb with cold. His legs trembled a little as he walked beside her into the stable, his boots and her hooves echoing hollowly on the wooden floor. He managed to get her stall open, and he spent as much time as he could leaning against something while he groomed her. There was, thank the *gods,* hay and water already waiting.

"Get some rest," he told her, fatigue dulling his mind and slurring his words. "I'm going to do the same."

He didn't remember how he got to his room; all he

really remembered was leaving Medren's lute by the door, stripping his filthy rags off and dropping them on the floor as he staggered to his bed, and falling *into* the bed. Literally falling; his legs gave out at that point. He held onto consciousness just long enough to pull off the patched breeches and his boots, drag the blankets over himself and wrap them around his chilled, numb body; as soon as he stopped shivering, he was asleep, and oblivious to the world. At that point, Tashir *could* have replicated the massacre in Highjorune, and he'd have slept right through it.

He woke about mid-afternoon, still tired, but no worse than when he'd first arrived home. The filthy rags he'd worn were gone. Evidently one of the servants had come in and picked up after him, and it was a measure of his exhaustion that he not only hadn't woken, he hadn't even *heard* the intruder. He was not pleased with himself; carelessness like that could get him killed all too easily under other circumstances.

On the other hand, it means I'm obviously nowhere near as jumpy as I was, which is all to the good.

The first order of business was food and a bath, and stopping by the kitchen on the way to the bathhouse solved both at the same time.

But the *next* order of business—and one that made him wolf down the first decent meal he'd had in a fortnight practically untasted, and *while* he bathed—was a long talk with Jervis and Savil.

"The boy's staying so close to Jervis you'd think he'd been grafted there," Savil said. Vanyel followed her out to the salle as the late afternoon sunlight gilded everything with a mellowing glow. "It's been entirely quiet, *ke'chara*. Not so much as a murmur out of the boy, or a single plate gone skyward." She looked at him quizzically, with a touch of worry. "To see you practically *flying* back, and in this state—I wish you'd tell me what's going on."

Vanyel shook his head, and his hair fell annoyingly into his eyes again. He hadn't had a chance to get it cut;

it was a lot longer than he was used to wearing it, and he wasn't sure if he ought to find the time to do something about it or not. He raked it back with his fingers and suppressed his flash of annoyance at it. "I will, as soon as I have both you and Jervis together. I don't want to have to repeat myself, and I want to hear *both* of your opinions at the same time. It's—some of what I found out is terrifying, and *none* of it is pretty. And I *don't* know what to make of it."

Savil brooded on that. "I thought you were going to find answers over there."

"I did," he replied, deeply troubled. "But the answers I found only gave me more questions."

Jervis was alone in the workroom of the salle. *Which might be the first piece of good luck I've had in a while,* Vanyel thought with reluctance. Jervis' eyebrows went up when he saw the expression on Vanyel's face, but he didn't move from his chair; he only put down the vambrace he'd been repairing, and waited for them to settle themselves.

"You're back, hmm?" the armsmaster said quietly. "From the look of you, I don't know as I'm going to like what you're going to tell me."

Vanyel shut the door carefully behind Savil; he would have *preferred* to stand, but he was just too tired. He compromised by perching on a tall stool, and then looked from Jervis to his aunt and back again, at a real loss as to how to broach the whole subject.

"Did you find out who put fear in the boy?" Jervis prompted.

That's about as good a place to start as any. Vanyel took a deep breath. "Yes," he said, and began his tale.

Jervis and Savil heard him out in complete silence, hardly even breathing. Savil's face was expressionless; Jervis, though, looked ready to call *somebody* out. Vanyel, for starters.

"That's it," Vanyel finished, starting to slump with weariness, his shoulders aching with tension. "That's what I found out. And you have to admit, the answers I got certainly fit the symptoms."

"Dammit Van," Jervis said tightly, plainly holding his

temper in check, "I am bloody well tempted to call you a damned liar to your face!"

"Why?" Vanyel asked bluntly, too weary for diplomacy.

Jervis colored, and growled. "Because that's *nothing* like the things Tashir's been telling *me!* The way *he* tells it—"

"Wait a minute! Do you mean Tashir's been talking about his family to *you?*"

"He trusts me! Can't the boy trust somebody other than you?"

Vanyel told himself that Jervis was only reacting much the way *he* would if the boy were in *his* protection, and managed to cool his rising temper. "Why don't you begin at the beginning, and tell me what *you* heard?"

What emerged was nothing less than a fantasy, if what *Vanyel* had learned was true. In his long talks with Jervis (and it seemed that there had been several), Tashir had painted a perfect, idyllic family for himself, one in which the members were forced by circumstance and enemies to present a very different face to the outside world than the one they showed each other. His mother, for instance; Tashir depicted her as the long-suffering plaything of her Mavelan relatives. According to him, once she discovered Deveran's kindness, she took a stand firmly by the side of her wedded lord, but played the part of the discarded, unwanted spouse so as to give the Mavelans no reason to think she could be used against Lineas and its ruler.

And according to Tashir's tale, Deveran was not the bitter, half-impotent dancer on the line between Baires threat and Lineas politics. He was supposedly a stern but kindly patriarch of the Linean throne. Deveran, so Tashir had told Jervis, had only disinherited him under pressure from his people. No, there was never any question in Deveran's mind as to who Tashir's father was. No, there had never been a fight, never been anything other than a small misunderstanding that they had settled that very night.

Fiction, first to last.

"That doesn't even square with what the boy told me!"

Vanyel retorted, disgusted with the game the youngster seemed to be playing. "*He* told *me* that his father hated him—that knocking him to the ground that night was only out of the ordinary because Deveran hadn't knocked him about much in public before!"

"Hell!" Jervis replied, his face flushing. "The boy was half-crazed an' scared outa his wits."

"All the more reason that he should have told me the *truth*—he didn't have time to make up some tale!"

Jervis started to protest, and Vanyel raised his voice to interrupt him. "And the part about the fight *wasn't* just from Tashir, it was from Herald Lores!"

"A fathead," Savil put in reluctantly, "but an honest fathead."

Jervis lunged to his feet. "An' how much of this is 'cause you *want* that boy's tail?" he snarled, hands knotting into fists at his sides.

Vanyel went hot, then cold. "If *that's* what you think, I see no point in any further discussion. Think what you like—*do* what you like—but obstruct me, and I'll haul you off to Lissa in manacles."

Jervis froze.

"Before I am anything else, armsmaster, I am *Herald* Vanyel, and my first priority is to my king and land. If I judge this boy is a danger to either, I will give him into Randale's custody. *Not* mine, armsmaster. But I must, and *will* have answers, and I will not permit anyone to even attempt preventing me from finding those answers."

Vanyel rose stiffly from his stool, pivoted, and stalked towards the door.

He hadn't taken more than a few steps, when Jervis' strangled, half-smothered "wait" stopped him in his tracks.

"Why?" he asked, not turning.

"Because—I—we gotta figger *out* this thing." Jervis cleared his throat. "All of us."

Vanyel turned back, still angry, but suppressing it. "Very well. If we're going to figure this mess out, you'll have to take *my* word as being at least as good as the boy's."

Jervis plainly didn't like that, but only protested, "How in *hell* can we take two stories that're *that* different?"

"Look at the one that fits the symptoms," Vanyel's voice was grim, and his face felt tight. "He's afraid to let women between the ages of eighteen and forty even *touch* him—assume the story he told you is true—Ylyna alternately beating him and loving him, and *then* trying to seduce him—"

He wiped his forehead, and his hand came away wet with nervous sweat.

"Gods. Think about how Treesa treats *every* attractive male, including me. She comes on to every man like a flirt. It's only a *game* to her, but *think* how that must have looked to Tashir—the way he'd react. Given my version is true, you could predict he'd do *just what he did*—panic, and let his Gift act up and frighten her off—*just* as I was told he did with his mother. Think about how he *hides* from Withen! And think about the way he clings to *you,* Jervis! *Everything* makes sense."

Jervis faltered. "Well, yes, but—"

"And everything points straight at Tashir as the unconscious murderer," Vanyel continued, heartsick.

"Now that I *will* not believe!" Jervis shouted, surging to his feet. "That boy is no *kind* of a killer! Hell, he damn near castrated himself in practice yesterday, pulling a cut when Medren lost his helm!"

"Who *else* could it be?" Vanyel shouted back, overriding Jervis' protests by sheer volume. "He had the power, he was at the scene, and he *had the motive!* There's nobody, *nobody,* with any kind of a motive *except* Tashir!"

"*No!*" Jervis insisted, eyes going black with anger. "No, I *won't* accept that! Look how he kept from hurting anybody in Treesa's bower."

"But crazed with fear, wild with anger, can you speak for that?"

"Even crazed—how could he kill that Karis? He *loved* that old man, he must have, to trust me so much just because I look like him!"

Vanyel sat heavily back down onto the stool. "I don't know," he admitted in a low voice. "That's only *one* of the things that's been bothering me. In all of the cases of Gifts gone rogue that I've ever heard of, the rogue never hurts anyone but the ones directly in his way. *Everybody* was killed in this case, and that *doesn't* make sense. It *might* make sense if he panicked completely and thought he was killing witnesses, but he didn't have enough time to reason something like that out, not from all I learned. And from what I know of his personality—no. I can't see him killing in cold blood even to save himself.'' He rubbed his pounding temples with his fists. Fits of anger always gave him a headache. ''The first half of the story fits, but the second doesn't. I just can't reconcile the two.''

''There're other questions,'' Savil pointed out from her seat on the cot. Vanyel looked at her in surprise; he'd forgotten she was there. ''Lots of other questions. Some of them may tie in, others may not, but the fact is there's too many of them. Lord Vedric's behavior is certainly peculiar. It doesn't in the least match what I've heard of him. Either the man has reformed, or he's up to something. Then there's the puzzle of the Remoerdises, the Linean Royal Family. Why did Deveran insist that only those related to his family serve in the palace? Why is the place *built* on top of a damned mage-ode? Why are the Lineans so completely against mage-craft?''

Vanyel shook his head. ''You think those questions are crucial?''

''Don't you?'' She stood, and smoothed down the front of her tunic. ''You know damned well they are, or you wouldn't have brought them up. I tend to agree with Jervis; Tashir is no killer. I agree with you that *your* tale of how the boy was treated fits his behavior a lot better than the one he told Jervis. And there is *something* we're missing. Something important. *I* think we ought to all think about it.''

''What about that tale he's been feeding Jervis?'' Vanyel asked.

''I think whoever runs into him next ought to call him on it—no, let me amend that. Whichever of the two of *us*, Van. Jervis, I'm sorry, but if it comes to magic, you're defenseless. I'm pretty certain Van and I could contain the worst of anything he could do.''

"The boy wouldn't hurt anybody, and especially not me,'' he insisted stubbornly. "I know it, damn it, I just *know* it!''

"Forgive me, but I'd rather not take the chance,'' Savil said dryly. "I hate picking up my acquaintances in palm-sized pieces. We've eaten this particular bird down to bones; let's let things simmer for a bit, and let's do something about dinner.''

"Gods.'' Vanyel slid off the stool, held out his hands and watched them shake with a certain bemusement. "I *just ate,* and after this to-do, my stomach should be in knots. Instead, I could eat a cow.''

"Don't fill up,'' Savil cautioned him, as they left Jervis mulling over the unpleasant things he'd heard. "There's Harvestfest tonight.''

"What?'' He looked at her, bewildered. "Harvest— can't be—oh, gods—''

He counted up the passing days in his mind, and when he arrived at *today,* he could feel the blood draining out of his face. "Oh, gods. It's Sovvan. I lost track of time. . . .'' He stopped dead in the path, legs gone leaden, mind gone numb. Sovvan-night. Year's turning.

The night Tylendel had died.

Coming on top of all the rest of it—exhaustion, confusion, the verbal fight with Jervis—

It was too much. What little emotional balance he had left evaporated so quickly that he felt dizzy, as if he was dangling over a precipice.

His internal turmoil must have been mirrored clearly on his face. Savil moved closer to him, brows knitting in concern. "Van—*ke'chara*—let it go. You aren't helping yourself by brooding.'' She put her arm around his shoulders. "Go down to the barns with the others. I'm going to—''

He scarcely felt it. All he could see was—

—a crumpled, lifeless shape.

He clamped an iron control down over his face. "That's not something I can do,'' he replied stiffly. "I can't forget, *especially* not tonight. I won't ever forget. . . .''

"Then, for the gods' sake, for your *own* sake, find something to distract you—music, dancing—"

"No, Savil." He pulled away from her, and forced himself to walk steadily toward the keep. "You deal with grief your way, and leave me to deal with it in mine."

"But—"

He shook his head stubbornly, unwilling to say more, and not sure that he could. *Forget 'Lendel? How can I forget—how can I ever forget?*

Oh, 'Lendel—

There was only one place where he could escape the sounds of celebration; the stone porch on the north side of the keep. All other interests had vanished when he realized what night it was; now all he wanted was solitude.

The lingering warmth of this fall had fooled him; usually Sovvan-tide was marked by ice-edged rains and bitter winds.

Like the storm that night—

Usually he tried to find something useful to do—like stand guard-duty, or spell someone at courier, or even take the place of one of the Guardians watching the Web. Anything, so long as it was work, and didn't involve interacting with people, only serving them.

He'd completely forgotten that he'd be spending Sovvan here, in presumed idleness; leisure that would only give him the opportunity to remember how utterly alone he was.

It hadn't been this bad the first few years; in the first two, in fact, there had been moments when he thought he'd felt that treasured and familiar presence waiting, watching. But as the years passed—and it became clear that he was and would *always* be alone, Sovvan-night had become an occasion for profound depression unless he was *very* careful not to give in to it. *This* Sovvan-night bid fair to be an ordeal; he was too exhausted, and too shaken, to put up any kind of fight against himself.

He watched the sun die in glory; watched the stars come out, flowering against the velvet sky. He closed his eyes when the sparks of white began to waver in his vi-

sion, and struggled anyway in a losing battle against self-
pity and heartache. *I've wept enough; tears won't ease
this, they'll only make it worse. I wish I was being Valdir.
I wish I was back at Haven.*

He thought briefly of Yfandes, and rejected the notion
of going to her. She couldn't help him, much as he loved
her. Her presence would only serve as a reminder of how
much he had lost to gain her.

*I need something to keep me occupied. Savil was right
about that. Something that will take concentration.*

There was only one task he knew that could possibly
fill all his thoughts, take all his attention. *Magic. I'll
build some illusions, good, tight ones. I can use the practice. I* need *the practice.*

He perched on the edge of one of the stone benches,
the gritty granite warm from the sun it had absorbed this
afternoon, and concentrated on a point just in front of
him. *People, they're hardest. Starwind. He's vivid
enough.*

He closed his eyes, and *centered.*

It took very little to cast an illusion, just a wisp of
power, and he didn't even need to take it from his reserves. The ambient energy around him was enough. He
visualized a vibrant column of light growing in the air in
front of him, then began forming the shapeless energy
into an image, building it carefully from the feet up.
Green leather boots, silky green breeches, and sleeveless
tunic, all molding to a tall, slender, wiry body. Implicit
strength, not blatant. Waist-length silver hair, four braids
in the front, the rest falling free down his back, a cascade
of ice-threads. Golden skin. Then the face: pointed chin,
high cheekbones, silver-blue eyes with a wisdom and humor lurking in them that could not be denied, and a smile
just hovering at the edge of the thin lips.

He opened his eyes—and before him stood the *Tayledras* Healer-Adept Starwind k'Treva.

For one moment he had it; perfect in every detail.

Then the hair shortened and darkened to curly blond,
the face squared, and the eyes began warming and darkening to a soft and gentle brown.

His heart contracted, and he banished the illusion and

began another, quickly: Savil. This one started to go
wrong from the very beginning, and with a gasp of pain,
he wiped it out and started on a third. Not even a human
this time—one of the little lizards that served the *Tayledras,* the *hertasi.*

But the *hertasi* began growing taller, and developed
blond hair.

"Oh, *gods*—" He banished the third illusion, and buried his face in his hands, shaking in every limb and bat-
tling against grief.

This—this is the worst Sovvan I've ever had, he
thought, feeling sorrow tearing at his chest until it hurt
to breathe. *It's the worst since you died. Oh, 'Lendel,
ashke, I can't bear it, and I have no choice! I'm so tired,
so very tired—my balance is gone. And, to know it's going to go on like this, year after year, alone. . . .*

*I don't know how to cope anymore. I don't know how
anyone can be this lonely and still be sane. . . . I don't
even know how sure I am of myself. I thought you were
the only person I could ever love, but this business with
Shavri has me all turned 'round about. And Tashir—I
came so close to giving in to temptation with him. . . .*

All I am *certain of is that I need you as much as I ever
did. And I'd give anything to have you back.*

He bit his lip and tasted the sweet-salt of blood; took
his hands away from his face, and willed his eyes open.
Nightshadows of leafless trees moved ebony against char-
coal; the last frost had killed the insects, and the birds
had mostly flown south by now. There was no sign of
anything alive out there; just barren shadows dark as his
soul, as empty as his heart.

A wisp of glow drifted in the air in front of him, and
he gave in to his anguish, to the perverse need to probe
at his heartache.

*To hell with it—how can I hurt any more than I do
now? And everything I try turns to 'Lendel. Not Shavri—
which ought to have told me* who *I love more.*

Once again he closed his eyes and began to build a
new illusion, one formed with passionate care, and at a
level of detail only love could have discerned in the original. The way that one lock of gold-brown sunstreaked

hair used to fall—just touching the eyebrow. The depth of the clear, brown eyes, sometimes sable, sometimes golden, but so bottomless you could lose yourself in them. The square chin, so—high cheekbones, so—the generous mouth, so ready to smile or laugh, the strong pillar of the neck. Shoulders ready to take the weight of the world's troubles. Body of a fighter or a dancer; gentle hands of a healer—

It didn't take long, now that he was no longer fighting with himself.

Oh, Tylendel—

Vanyel looked up to see his handiwork, and sobbed, once, reaching out involuntarily to touch empty air.

The illusion was nothing less than heartbreakingly perfect. The Tylendel of the joyous days of their one summer together stood before him, so *alive* Vanyel fancied he could see him breathing, that in a moment he would speak.

And I could do that, too; I could make him breathe and talk to me. No, I couldn't bear that. It's hollow enough as it is. Oh, gods, why? 'Lendel—

Someone gasped behind him, and as he started and lost control of it, the illusion shattered, exploded outward into a hundred thousand glittering little bits that rained down and vanished, melting away before they touched the pale stone of the porch. Vanyel whipped around to see a dark and indistinct shape beside the black hole of the door.

"Who's there?" he snapped, hastily wiping his eyes with the back of his hand. "What do you want?"

"I—it's Tashir." The young man came toward him hesitantly. "Medren told me you were back. I wondered where you were. Where you've been."

Depression abruptly became anger at being disturbed, and the desire to hurt fountained in him. He wanted someone, *anyone,* any creature at all, to suffer inside as much as he did at this moment. He *knew* it was base; knew that Tashir would be an easy target, and that he *could* hurt him. He hated the desire even as he felt it, and it sickened him as much as he wanted it. He fought it down, but the anger remained, red and sullen. This young man, for whom Vanyel had been risking his life, had been undermining everything he'd built here. It wasn't just that Tashir had been lying; it was that what he had told Jervis had come close to destroying the fragile beginnings of friendship that had cost both of them so much pain and soul-searching to create, had set them at each other's throats like enemies, and had left them, once again, uneasy and grudging allies at best.

"I've been finding out the truth," he said softly. "While *you* seem to have been busy trying to hide it." The anger blossomed, and he briefly lost control over it, just long enough that he growled a single sentence.

"Why did you lie to Jervis?"

"I didn't!" Tashir's voice cracked as Vanyel rose and walked toward him, one hand flaring with mage-light. The blue light reflected off Tashir's face, revealing the youngster's surprise and growing fear. The young man's eyes widened, his expression froze, and he backed away from the Herald step by forced step. He didn't stop until his thighs hit the stone railing and Vanyel had him backed into a corner with nowhere to go.

"You did," Vanyel whispered. "All those stories you told him about your perfect, loving family—that's all they were, stories. Lies. I've been in Highjorune, Tashir. I spent the last fortnight there, talking to people. One of them was your mother's maid, Reta."

The branches of the bushes nearest Tashir began to thrash as if tossed by a wind, though not a breath of air stirred anywhere else. Vanyel didn't have to see them to know that the young man had unleashed his Gift in panic. He let it go for a moment, waiting to see how violent Tashir would become. Fallen leaves whirled up in a mad dance to engulf both of them, beating at Vanyel ineffectually. But with nothing more at hand to work with than leaves, the attack wasn't even a distraction. Vanyel savagely clamped down on the young man with a shield not even an Adept could have cracked, and the leaves drifted back down to the ground and the porch.

Tashir cowered against the stone railing, averting his eyes as the mage-light on Vanyel's hand flared. Perversely, the display of subservience only made him angrier. He fought down his temper and got himself back under control, managing at last to gaze down upon the youngster with his anger held in check.

"Well, Tashir?" Vanyel whispered tonelessly. "Are we ready to hear a little truth now?"

"A-about wh-what?" Tashir croaked.

Vanyel formed the light into a ball and sent it to hover just over his head with a flick of his wrist. He folded his arms, and compressed his lips, forcing his anger to cool a little more.

I'll invoke Truth Spell on him. Then at least I'll bloody well know when he's lying.

"I think," he said, finally, "that we can start with your father."

He called up the *vrondi,* and when it surrounded him with faint blue light, Tashir's pale face stood out with sharp-edged distinctness against the night-dark shadows behind him. Word by agonized word, he dragged a story out of Tashir that was virtually identical to the one that Reta had told him. Three times more, whenever Vanyel dealt with the subject of his mother, the boy unconsciously attempted to evoke his Gift; he failed to break the shield Vanyel still held on him each time. Vanyel noted with a smoldering, sullen calm that while Tashir *did* freeze physically when this happened, he was *quite* conscious, if not in conscious control of what he was doing.

Finally Vanyel decided to force the issue—to deliberately evoke the same state of mind the younger man must have been in on that fatal night.

"The night I found you," he said, "your father told you something, and you refused him, and he hit you. Do you remember what that was?"

Tashir shook his head, a breath away from hysterical breakdown. The blue aura of the Truth Spell continued to glow.

"He told you that he was going to send you to your Mavelan relatives to stay; that he was washing his hands of you."

It was hard to tell in the blue glows of mage-light and Truth Spell, but Tashir seemed to become paler. Vanyel shook his head regretfully, and deliberately turned his back on the youngster. "*I* don't know what to do about you," he said expressionlessly. "You've brought me nothing but trouble, and you're about to cause a major diplomatic incident between Valdemar and Lineas. You *could* even start a war. I'm sorry, Tashir, but your uncle Vedric is petitioning that you be put into his custody. King Randale is likely to order just that. Given the circumstances, I think it would be the wisest thing if I admitted where you are and my part in this mess and turned you over to Vedric in the morning."

He waited for an attack; he waited for the shield to break under the stress of Tashir's Gift at the kind of level of manifestation that was indicated by the slaughter at Highjorune.

Instead, he heard a peculiar little whimper, and felt the pressure within the shield go null.

Vanyel pivoted in surprise just in time to catch the youngster as he fell over in a dead faint.

It took him the better part of a candlemark to revive Tashir. It took longer to convince him that although it might be the *wisest* thing to do, it was *not* the course of action Vanyel intended to take. The youngster was totally terrified of being sent into Mavelan hands, yet even under the stress of this absolute terror, his Gift manifested at no higher level than before.

Eventually Tashir believed him when he told the youngster that he would continue to shelter him, to try to find out what had really happened.

And then, when the young man had settled a little, he began the questioning again.

With a cool and calculated assessment of the stress he was putting Tashir under, Vanyel brought him to the breaking point over and over, until he was *certain* that nothing was going to evoke the kill-storm.

Finally the boy was too exhausted to be pressed further. And Vanyel wasn't too far behind him—at least emotionally. "Why, Tashir?" he asked, looking for *any* clue as to the truth of that night. "Why *did* you make up that fantasy for Jervis?"

"Because—because I wanted him to *like* me!" the

young man blurted desperately. "How could he like me if my own father hated me? How could he like me if he knew what my mother wanted to—"

Vanyel interrupted, trying not to show the frustration he was feeling. "Tashir, *Karis* tried to protect you. Why did you think Jervis would be any different?"

"But Karis was *there,* he saw what was happening. If I told anybody else they'd think I was *lying,* Mother said so."

Tashir paled again, but Vanyel assumed it was only the stress of having to face that unnatural relationship squarely.

"Karis," he whispered, "was *there.*"

"Tashir, from what I've been told, *she* was the one who lied; why would you think she'd have told you the truth about—"

"V-Vanyel," the young man interrupted. "Karis—they never told me *who* besides—was Karis—one of—was he—"

Then Vanyel saw what Tashir had finally realized; saw the plea in Tashir's eyes to be told that Karis was still alive, and couldn't answer it. He looked away—which was answer enough.

The youngster crumpled, holding the stone balustrade for support, his entire body shaking with harsh, racking sobs. Vanyel remembered, as he banished the shield and uncast the Truth Spell, that one of the most telling pieces of evidence *against* the youngster—in the eyes of Herald Lores, at any rate—was Tashir's *lack* of emotion when he'd been told what had happened.

Lores should see him now, he thought grimly, putting his arm around Tashir's shoulders and letting him weep himself out with Vanyel supporting him. His own anger was quite gone, and he was recalling his desire to make Tashir hurt as much as *he* did with a sick, shamed feeling in the pit of his stomach. Then Tashir turned to cry on Vanyel's shoulder, and it was all Vanyel could do to keep from losing control again, this time for a very different reason.

Finally the youngster pulled away, and Vanyel let him go. He walked back to his former seat on the bench at the farther side of the porch and slumped there, his head in his hands, not really thinking, only aching.

Because Tashir was *so* like Tylendel.

Holding him while he wept had been like reliving the past. The dead past. . . .

Hesitant footsteps behind him, and a shy sniffle.

Vanyel wished with all his heart that the boy would go—find Jervis, go back to his room, or seek solace at the festivities, *anything* but stay here with that far-too-familiar face, providing a ready-made knife to the heart, and not even knowing that he was doing so.

"Vanyel?" came the halting whisper. "Vanyel, who was that man? The one that disappeared when I startled you? I thought it was me, at first, but he was different."

"It was just an illusion," Vanyel replied, rubbing his temples, staring at the dark blot of his own feet against the gray stone. "I was practicing."

The youngster hovered just beside him. "But who is it?" he persisted. "It wasn't me, and it wasn't Uncle Vedric. And why were you casting a seeming of him?"

"Tylendel," Vanyel replied shortly. "His name was Tylendel. He's dead. He—*was*—my lover."

And half of my soul and all of my heart.

Tashir started back at that, out of touching distance, projecting clear revulsion and fear so clearly that Vanyel felt it like a blow.

Vanyel's temper snapped.

"Dammit," he snarled, rounding on the youngster, "will you *not* act like I'm going to pounce on you and rape you? I *don't* make a habit of hitting attractive young men over the head and dragging them off to my bed, no matter *who* they look like!"

Tashir put out a hand as if to keep him away.

Vanyel could not longer control his temper or his words. *"You* came to *me* not all that long ago," he snarled, "and I'll thank you to remember that I didn't take advantage of the situation! So you've changed your mind about being shaych; fine, I have no quarrel with you or with that, that is *your* decision and yours alone to make. I have no intention of making you change your

mind. But kindly remember that I'm a human being, and
I lost somebody—"

He fought the words past the grief. "—lost somebody
I loved more than anyone else on earth. He was my lifebonded, and I will be *without* him for the rest of my life.
You're not the *only* one in the world who's alone! You're
not the only one who's suffered!"

He turned away abruptly, got up, and stalked stiffly to
the stone railing, staring out into the lattice of bare tree
branches and trying to keep from breaking down completely. Behind him he could hear Tashir shuffling his
feet, the sound betraying uncertainty.

*Go away, boy. Leave me alone. Leave me to mourn my
dead, my beloved, and go chase my niece. Just leave me.*

But the footsteps shuffled nearer, hesitated, then came
nearer still, until Tashir stood at his right elbow. Vanyel
stared out ahead of him, at the branches, and the stars
that seemed to be caught there.

"Was he a Herald?" The voice was timid.

"No. A trainee."

Stop driving knives in me. Go away.

"How long ago?"

"Twelve years, tonight."

*Twelve years forsaken. Twelve long, lonely years,
knowing I'll never be whole again.*

"What happened?" the youngster persisted, sounding
very young indeed.

"He killed himself."

There. Are you happy? Now will you go away?

"But—" No condemnation, just bewilderment. "—why?
How could he—when he had a Companion?"

*So you know that already, do you? How if we die, they
die? But you don't know everything, laddy-boy.*

"She repudiated him. That's why he did it. He—
couldn't bear—the—"

He couldn't finish.

Silence, a silence marked only by the occasional rustle
of leaves. Vanyel hung his head and wrestled with his
grief and hoped the youngster would take the hint and
finally go away.

Tashir moved a little closer. "I don't understand," he

said, humbly. "I can't imagine what could have happened. Please—"

Vanyel took a deep, shuddering breath. Obviously the boy wasn't going to leave until he had his curiosity satisfied.

So tell him, and get it over with.

He looked back up at the remote and uncaring stars. " 'Lendel was Savil's trainee when my father sent me to her because I wasn't the kind of man he thought I should be," he began, trying to recite the words as if they described someone else. "What I didn't know then was that he was afraid I was fey, and he was trying to keep me from being shaych. He kept me amazingly sheltered, really; I had no idea that—well, I suppose—anyway, I knew I was different, but I didn't know why." His chest ached when he took a breath. "I was disliked at home. The fosterlings, my brothers, they all figured me for Mother's darling. And I just couldn't seem to fit in with them. Granted, I didn't make much effort to *be* liked after a while, but—well."

It was all coming back with the impact of something that had happened only yesterday. "So Withen sent me off to Haven, where I was even more a stranger." He tried to laugh; it sounded like a croak. "I was put with Savil and her proteges, and Savil was supposed to 'make a man out of me'—turn me into something like Meke, I suppose. What Father didn't know was that her favorite protege 'Lendel was shaych—openly shaych. Exactly what he'd tried to keep me from. I was lonely and desperately unhappy, and 'Lendel was kind to me even when I was rotten to him. Then I found out certain things about *him* from other sources and suddenly a lot of inexplicable things about myself had answers."

I watched you and wanted more from you than friendship—for days, weeks. And at the same time—I was so afraid. Not like this young fool is afraid; I was afraid that once I broke my isolation, you'd hurt me like everyone else had. But you didn't, 'Lendel. At least not in the way I'd feared. And in the end, it wasn't you who hurt me; it was losing you—

"Things—happened. 'Lendel and I became lovers,

then lifebonded. I know that now, I didn't know that then; all I knew then was that I'd have done anything for him, committed any crime to avoid losing him.''

"You weren't a Herald?''

"No, not even a trainee.'' His eyes blurred and burned. Vanyel blinked, and tears splashed down onto the balustrade beside his hand. "Tylendel had a twin; his twin was murdered in a feud. Murdered by magic. No one seemed willing to do anything about it. 'Lendel and Staven had been mindlinked; losing Staven drove him more than a little mad. He decided to take matters into his own hands, and I helped him by stealing the proscribed books of magic. I couldn't believe—I was outraged that no one had done anything about Staven's murder. I didn't know what I should have done, and I didn't see anything wrong with going out for revenge—especially not when 'Lendel was hurting so much. We slipped away on Sovvan-night—''

Dark and cold it was, and wind blowing fit to tear the clothes from your body. But not so dark and cold as the place inside 'Lendel that only revenge would heal—I thought. I only wanted him satisfied so I could have the Tylendel I knew back again. I never thought further than that.

"—we Gated to where the other family was celebrating. Since we were lifebonded and I had Mage-*potential*, 'Lendel could use my energy to make the Gate and his own to call up his vengeance. Which he did. He called up a pack of *wyrsa* and turned them loose.''

He felt the young man beside him shudder, but he was too caught in his memories to pay much attention. He could still see it; the image was burned into his mind for all time.

'Lendel, his face twisted with grief and rage, his eyes no longer gentle, and holding a black gleam of madness. The cowering people, seeing no escape—and Evil made flesh in the form of the four wyrsa, unholy meldings of snake and ferret, with their dagger-teeth and their burning sulfur eyes and their insatiable hunger that he could feel beating against his mind even now. And then the

thunder of hooves behind him and the equine shriek of defiance and loss—

"Gala came through the Gate when the *wyrsa* had made only one kill. She challenged the whole pack—she repudiated 'Lendel."

Sweet blue eyes gone dead and empty, mind-voice reverberating coldly down the link that bound him and 'Lendel. I do not know you. You are not my Chosen. *Then the internal* snap *of something breaking, and the utter desolation where love had been—*

"She attacked the pack. They pulled her down and killed her."

Tylendel's eyes with all of hell in them. Tylendel's heart a churning storm of loss and agony. Tylendel's soul a shattered thing past all repairing. Tylendel's mind holding no sane thoughts at all—

"Savil and two other Heralds came through the Gate and destroyed the *wyrsa*—too late, oh, gods—'Lendel's heart, his mind, his *soul* were broken. He got away from them when we reached Haven. They backlashed the Gate energy through me by accident, and my collapse distracted them just long enough for him to break free of them. He couldn't bear it—the pain of losing Gala, then having her *die* before his eyes—so he threw himself—off the Belltower—"

I wish they'd let me die with you. I wish they hadn't saved me when I tried to kill myself. Oh, 'Lendel, Tylendel, it wasn't supposed to end that way—

He couldn't look at Tashir. Couldn't. Tears fell silently and splashed onto his hands. He gripped the railing until his knuckles ached. There was nothing inside him but the same throbbing emptiness that had been left twelve years ago.

Twelve years, 'Lendel. Twelve years, and it hurts more, not less. Twelve years, and all I really look forward to is the moment it's all over—

Tashir was very quiet; Vanyel couldn't even hear him breathing, and only the sense of *presence* still at his side told him that the young man was still there.

"I'm sorry," Tashir said awkwardly. "That's a stupid thing to say, but it's all I can think of. I wish it had never

happened. I wish I could bring him back for you, Herald
Vanyel. Karis always told me people *could* feel that way
about each other, could really *love* each other and not
just pretend to, but I never—I never knew anybody who
did. I'm sorry I made you unhappy. I apologize for reacting like I did. If I'd known what you just told me, I'd
have realized how stupid I was.''

''It's all right,'' Vanyel answered him huskily, after a
pause to get the lump out of his throat. ''You couldn't
know. Lifebonds don't happen very often. When they do,
well, it's like Companion-bond; when one partner dies,
the other dies with him, usually. The only thing that kept
me alive was that I bonded to Yfandes that night. It
doesn't hit me like this very often, it's just—Sovvan-night,
and I'm bloody damned tired, and you—gods, Tashir,
you could have been him. It hurts every time I see
you, because half the time I don't see *you,* I see *him.*''

The young man was silent again, but it was a silence
that implied he was going to speak. And he did.

''I'm probably saying things I shouldn't, but you said
it yourself, Vanyel. It's been *twelve years.* Don't you think
that's an awful long time to be holding onto a memory
so tightly that it strangles you?''

He stepped away a little, as Vanyel finally turned to
look at the dark shape of him in shock and astonishment.
''People need you, and you can't help them when you're
like this. Jervis told me that you said that's important.
And *you* aren't the only one in the world who's suffering,
either. You aren't the only one who's ever lost his love.''

He backed up a little, then broke and ran for the door,
leaving Vanyel standing stiffly beside the railing, trying
to collect his wits.

Have I been that selfish? he wondered. *Is it selfish to
grieve for someone like this?*

I don't know.

*But he's right. I'm not the only one in the world who's
lost someone they loved. He lost Karis; and Karis was
the only person he ever knew who loved* him. *I have Savil;
I have 'Fandes. I have—*

Friends.

Gods.

He blinked, as answers finally put themselves together in his mind. *I said it myself; it wasn't* Shavri *everything turned into, it was* 'Lendel. *I do love Shavri, but not like that. It's just that I've been so long without caring for anyone that deeply that I couldn't untangle what it meant. I want to protect her, care for her, but because she's a friend who needs me more than anyone has ever needed me* except *'Lendel. And because she cares for me. It was only 'Lendel who gave me love without asking for any-thing—*

—good gods. That's it, isn't it. That's where the stick-ing point is. Everybody wants *something from me, or seems to. Mother, first of all; Melenna, Randi—they all want me to* be *something for them. Only 'Lendel wanted me to be myself. Only 'Lendel gave without asking what he was going to get. And now Shavri. And Jisa, who just* loves, *like only a child can love, without any questions at all.*

But that's not *wrong,* either; *I can't blame the ones who need things from me. But that may be something of the difference between friends and lovers. Interesting. But how is it that I can go to bed with a friend—*

Ah. I can't *go to bed with someone who's* not *a friend. How could I have lost what I knew when I was fifteen? That was what I* knew *when Krebain tried to seduce me. Sex and love aren't the same thing. But love and friend-ship are so close that you can't have love without having friendship. I could have continued to love 'Lendel even without sex. That's what had me confused. We became friends and lovers and beloved all at the same instant. There was something about him I would always have liked, even if I'd never loved him.*

The stars weren't any brighter for having just found some of his answers, but they seemed that way. *Poor Tashir—he doesn't have anyone. I had a true* love. *Not too many people can say that.*

He contemplated that for a moment. *I've been thinking awfully hard about how I lost him. Maybe it would be better to remember how I had him.*

Once again he set himself to build the illusion that had

shattered with Tashir's gasp; just as carefully, just as lovingly.

But this time remembering the good times.

Once again Tylendel stood before him, frozen in a moment of gentle joy. He remembered that moment well.

You gave me a gift I never expected to have; you gave me my music back, beloved. You told me that it was more important to you to hear music played for itself than to hear it enhanced by the strongest of Bardic Gifts. He found himself smiling, a smile with tears on the edge of it, but smiling. *Then I sang you a love song. The first one I ever sang for you. It was the first time I'd ever sung one with my heart in it.*

Tylendel had given himself up completely to the music he'd woven for him. It had been a moment completely free of any shadows because 'Lendel had chased the only one that haunted him.

Beloved, you knew how much I needed that back, and you gave it to me with open hands.

Memory *could* be sweet—even if it held an edge of sorrow.

I won't ever forget you, ashke, *but I can choose how I remember you. And I promise I'll try to remember with love, not tears.*

He allowed the image to fade.

So it's time I started doing something about people who need me, hmm? Just like you told me. And the most urgent of those is Tashir.

He yawned suddenly, then laughed a little at himself. *And I'm not going to do anyone any good falling asleep on my feet. So best I seek my virtuously empty bed. Morning is going to come far too soon.*

He looked once more into the sky—or beyond it. Even he wasn't certain which.

Good night, ashke. *Wherever you are. Wind to thy wings—*

Twelve

News, sped by Herald, Mind- and Mage-Gifts, and Herald-guided messenger birds, moved quickly in Valdemar when the King and Circle chose. But when they didn't—

They had not chosen to speed either edicts *or* news in the matter of Tashir and the mysterious slaughter of the Linean Royal Family. *That* news moved with the same plodding slowness as it did outKingdom. And that gave Vanyel and the youngster a respite.

But it was a short respite only; Vanyel had known that from the beginning. Vanyel wasn't much surprised when a messenger arrived the day after Sovvan from Captain Lissa. He had a fair notion of just what the sealed message-tubes the courier carried contained.

And he wasn't at all surprised to be summoned to Lord Withen's study when the messenger had departed.

The door stood open; Vanyel tapped on the frame, then entered when his father looked up. Withen wore a troubled expression, the look of a man who is uneasy about things over which he had little or no control. He motioned to Vanyel to take a chair, but Van only shook his head, preferring to stand. If Withen meant to take him to task, let him do so with Vanyel in some kind of "formal" stance.

"This—" Withen settled back into his own chair and lifted a corner of one of the papers lying on his desk. "I had the messenger read it for me; I wasn't sure I wanted Radevel to know what was going on until I talked to you. It's a politely worded 'request' from Lissa for permission to move her company of the Guard to the Ashkevron personal estates. And an explanation of why she's been ordered to move.''

Vanyel nodded. Given what he had seen on his way home—the way the Linean side of the Border had been fortified in just under a fortnight—he had realized it would be only a matter of time before Liss got orders to move from the Border-section facing Baires to that facing Lineas. And the Ashkevron family land sat squarely on the only road suitable for troop movements.

Withen coughed uncomfortably. ''Van, son—the boy you brought here—he's *that* Tashir, isn't he? Tashir Remoerdis. The Linean.''

''He is,'' Vanyel replied levelly. ''And the fact that he was Chosen *after* the Remoerdis Family died is reason enough to presume him innocent.'' He straightened a little. ''Father, you *know* I wouldn't have brought anyone dangerous here, but he needed a sanctuary, and this was the only place I could think of where no one would look for him.''

Withen interrupted him with a wave of his hand. ''That's not what I'm worried about. That boy wouldn't hurt a fly, I'd swear to it myself. It's—what do I do if Liss or somebody else comes looking for *you?*''

''You could give us up,'' Vanyel sighed, his muscles going to knots. ''In fact, you should.''

''Like *hell* I will!'' Withen rumbled. ''You brought him here for sanctuary, and by the gods, he's going to get it!''

Vanyel relaxed and grinned; the expression startled his father. ''Father mine,'' he said warmly, ''you have just eased my last worry. I was *not* going to foist this walking diplomatic incident on you unwilling, but if *you* have no qualms about continuing to shelter him—''

Withen snorted. ''I'll pick up blade and defend him m'self, if I have to.''

''I *hope* you won't have to; I *hope* I'll be able to find out who really did this, and clear Tashir entirely. If you don't mind, I'll take that chair you offered.'' Withen nodded, and Vanyel lowered himself into its support gratefully. ''Randale's playing a very tricky game here; Liss' troop is mostly made up of men from Forst Reach and the holdings in fealty to us. He knows damned well that no matter what the 'official' word is, they'll protect me, with silence, if nothing else, unless *you*—or Liss—indicate differently. Randale trusts my judgment, and he's giving me time to get this sorted out.''

Withen nodded, one eyebrow raised in tribute to Randale's cleverness.

"Don't worry, Father, I'll have word and time to get us out of Forst Reach and into hiding in the forest long before anyone dangerous could actually arrive here.''

"That was all I was worried about, except—'' Withen tugged his short beard unhappily, ''—*is* there a chance the Lineans would make a Border-war out of this?''

Vanyel weighed all the factors in his mind, including Vedric's apparent unwillingness to force the issue. He ruminated a long time, for the most part ignoring his father's increasingly gloomy countenance, before he was able to make a tentative conclusion. He stood then, hoping he looked more confident than he felt. "I don't think so, but I pledge you, Father,'' he said steadily, holding Withen's eyes with his own, ''before it comes to that, I'll turn both of us over to them myself.''

And I hope to Havens I never have to make good on that pledge.

The reaction to the news contained in the missive was mixed. On the whole, Vanyel's younger brothers seemed to welcome the prospect of "a little excitement'' with cheerful bloodthirstiness. Mekeal alone of all of them seemed of two minds about the whole thing, first joining in the boasting and enthusiastic weaponry practices, then taking to pacing about the keep muttering about "line-of-sight'' and "defensibility'' with a worried frown creasing his forehead.

Withen made it very plain when the youngster's identity became generally known that he shared Jervis' conviction of Tashir's innocence, and Tashir reacted to his show of faith with disbelief at first. But when Withen himself assured him of his sanctuary, Tashir reacted with a pitiful gratitude that would have softened harder hearts than Withen's.

It was because of *this* that Withen actually got embroiled in a shouting match with Father Leren over Tashir and the question of his disposition, guilt, or innocence; the first time Withen had ever disagreed with the cleric to Vanyel's knowledge.

Tashir's Companion had finally come in to take up nervous residence with Yfandes. This was something of a relief to Vanyel, since Ghost had been frightening the whey out of most of the workers on the holding; they'd see only a flash of something white, usually by night, and then it would be gone, and the rumors of a "demon-horse" were spreading. Vanyel was trying to coax both the young man and the Companion into a calmer state of mind in which deeper bonding and Mindspeech between the two would be possible, but neither of them were at all willing to be calmed. Ghost, in fact, showed a marked tendency to panic if even the lower half of the outer door to Yfandes' stall was closed while he was in it. Vanyel was about ready to give it up as a hopeless task when Jervis came looking for him, a startling grin transforming his craggy face into a mask of unholy glee.

Relations between the two of them were improving again—slowly. Vanyel suspected Tashir may have had a hand in that, though whether or not that was on purpose he had no idea. But although they were speaking without daggers behind the words, Vanyel had *not* expected to see that kind of expression on the armsmaster's face—ever.

"Van," Jervis whispered, while Tashir communicated with Ghost in his own way, with brush and murmured words Vanyel couldn't catch. "If you're done here, there's somethin' you *have* to hear."

Vanyel shrugged, and vaulted over the stall railings. "Tashir," he called over his shoulder, "why don't you two work off some of that nerve in a good long ride? You're too edgy to trance and I don't blame you."

Tashir looked relieved; Ghost lowered his head in a clear gesture of agreement. The young Companion stood steadily for Tashir while his Chosen pulled himself up onto his back, then nosed the stall door open and trotted out into the paddock.

"All right," Vanyel said, turning back to Jervis. "What is all this about?"

"Just come with me," Jervis said gleefully, and led Vanyel out of the stable to stand just under one of the windows in the tiny temple.

"—possessed at the best; a red-handed murderer at the worst!" Father Leren was shouting, his voice muffled by all the intervening stone.

"That boy's no more a murderer than I am!" Withen shouted back. "You were dead wrong about Vanyel, and by the gods, you're even more wrong about this boy! Van asked me for sanctuary for him, *I* pledged it, and I'm *not* taking back my sworn word!"

"You're putting your soul in jeopardy, Lord Withen," the priest thundered, "The gods—"

"The gods my ass!" Withen roared, in full and magnificent outrage. "There isn't an evil hair on that poor boy's head! Who made *you* the spokesman for the gods? Last *I* was taught, if the gods want something done, they don't bother with a damned mouthpiece, they do it themselves—*or* they choose a vessel and make their power plain! I haven't seen *you* glowing with holy light, old man!"

Leren sputtered, incoherent, obviously taken aback by this revolt of his erstwhile supporter.

"And I'll tell you one thing more, *I* judge who's to be Forst Reach priest. I put you *in,* and I can throw you *out* just as easy! If you want to *stay* Forst Reach priest, you'll keep your mouth off Tashir—aye, and while we're at it, off Vanyel as well! When you've done as much for Valdemar as he has, you can call him pervert and catamite to your heart's content, but till you do, you keep a respectful tongue in that head of yours! He's *Herald* Vanyel, first-rank Herald-Mage of Valdemar and confidant of the King, and furthermore he's *my son* and you'd better *damned* well remember that fact!"

Leren tried to say something else, but Withen's roar drowned him out.

Vanyel signaled that they probably ought to move on; Jervis nodded as he stifled snickers with his hand, biting the edge of it to keep from laughing out loud as they slipped away. Vanyel was too surprised to laugh; it felt as if his eyebrows were about to make a permanent home in his hair.

It was certainly the *last* argument he'd ever expected to overhear.

The falling-out found Leren taking his meals with the hirelings instead of with the family, a circumstance that Vanyel *tried* not to rejoice in, but couldn't help enjoying. It certainly made mealtime easier for *him* to face. The quarrel also gave Jervis ascendancy, and as a result of *that,* Vanyel thought he *might* be detecting a certain softening of Withen's attitude toward his firstborn, although what with everything and everyone stirred up it was impossible to be sure.

That was the state of things when Captain Lissa Ashkevron rode in through the gates of Forst Reach at the head of her company.

"Lord Withen," said the solemn hatchet-faced woman in dress blues, bowing slightly over her horses's neck in the salute of equals. She waited his response with her helm tucked at a precise angle under her left arm, her bay's reins held at an equally precise angle in her right. The blue-dyed rooster feathers mounted in a socket at the top of the light dress helm fluttered across her arm in the light breeze. Her brown hair had been braided and coiled atop her head with the same military precision that characterized the rest of her equipage.

This was the first time Vanyel had seen his sister "on duty," or in any kind of official capacity. She was certainly a far different creature from the careless, untidy hoyden he remembered her being as a child, or even the wild rogue she could become off-duty.

"Captain Ashkevron." Withen returned her salute, visibly torn between worry and pride.

"Permission to bivouac the troops, sir."

"Granted." Pride won out, and Withen beamed. "The South Home Pasture's been vacated; it's all yours, Captain."

"Thank you, my lord," she replied formally. "Sergeant Grayse, front and center!"

A Guardsman with a brown, round face that seemed vaguely familiar to Vanyel marched crisply from the front rank to Lissa's right stirrup, and waited.

"South Home Pasture; lead the troops there and bivouac. I'll join you shortly."

The sergeant saluted and pivoted, heel and toe, and Vanyel realized why he seemed familiar; Grayse was one of the holding families, and this solid young man must be one of the sons. He barked out a series of orders as Lissa moved her horse off the road; turned again and stepped out with the rest of the troop following as promptly as if they hadn't just spent all day on their feet. Lissa stayed on her horse at semi-attention until the last of her troop was out of sight, then grinned and tossed Vanyel her helm. She dropped her horse's reins as she vaulted out of her saddle, ground-tethering him. As soon as her feet hit the ground she made straight for Withen.

Vanyel caught the tumbling helm as she flung her arms around her father's neck and kissed him soundly, and then he held it out of the way as she made it his turn for an enthusiastic embrace, an embrace which he returned one-handed.

"Well, Father," she said, after kissing Vanyel just as thoroughly. "What do you think of my youngsters?"

"Fine!" Withen glowed. "Damn fine! Gods, I hardly knew my little daughter, up there on her warhorse and in her uniform and all!"

"I've never seen you on duty either, Liss," Vanyel reminded her. "I think you look wonderful."

She hugged him again, then stood beside him with her arm around his waist. "I'm just sorry it has to be under alert-conditions," she said soberly. "I'm sorry, Father. The last thing I ever wanted to do was—"

"Don't worry about it," Withen interrupted. "Now, is there anybody you want to quarter at the keep?"

"My Healer; I want him to have an infirmary set up. I bivouac with the troops."

Withen looked a little disappointed, but Vanyel found himself grinning with approval. "Good!" he said. "I didn't think it was my place to say anything, but it seemed to me down at the Karsite Border that all the best officers stayed with their troopers.''

"So I'm told," Lissa replied. "Don't worry, Father, you'll see more of me than you think." She hugged Vanyel hard. "Come on, little brother, help me get this nag in a stall, hmm?"

He let her go and handed back her helm. She caught up the bay's reins and walked beside him to the stable.

"Lord Marshal doesn't like the way things are shaping up," she said in a quiet voice as soon as they got out of earshot. "Vedric has been making himself into the Linean patron saint, what with supporting their protests to Randale and all. I *wish* I knew what he was up to; this doesn't square with any of the intelligence I've had on him up until now. As for you, my impetuous little brother, I've got *official* orders that if I find Tashir I'm to take him in, but I've also got this—"

She reached into her belt-pouch and took out a much-creased note with Randale's private seal on it, and handed it to him. Vanyel noticed that it was addressed only to her, and opened it.

Captain Ashkevron, it read. *Show this to your brother— you know which one I mean. This is an order. It overrides any other orders you may receive until you hear differently under my hand and seal. You haven't seen either Vanyel or the boy Tashir Remoerdis. You won't see them until I tell you that you have. Randale.*

Vanyel handed it back to her with no other comment than a slightly raised eyebrow.

"He's covering for you, Van," she said worriedly, "but he can't do that for much longer. Have you got any idea of what you can do?"

"Not at the moment," he told her. "But I soon will."

His generous room seemed very crowded with both Savil and Jervis sprawled across the window seat and a chair, respectively.

"Ideas?" Vanyel asked, looking from Savil to Jervis and back again. "I've got one, but I want to hear yours first."

Savil wedged herself in the window seat, back flat against one wall, feet braced against the opposite wall, fingers laced together across her knees. "You said you went across the Border to get answers," she said, as if she was thinking out loud.

"And I found them—some of them," he agreed, eyes half-closed, staring at the patterns that firelight and shadows made on her Whites.

"But you also found more questions. I'm wondering if you just weren't there long enough. And I wonder if we *all* really ought to go back there. With two Adept-class mages it ought to be ridiculously simple to come up with illusion-disguises for four of us."

"Hide the boy in plain sight you mean?" Jervis was sitting backwards on one of the straight-back chairs, with his chin resting on his arms. He blinked sleepily while Savil spoke. Now he raised his head and looked alert. "I like that! Last place they're going to look for the boy is back where he came from!"

Vanyel nodded. "That was something of the same idea I had. We could further confuse the issue—go *across* the Border as, say, four Heralds making up a peace envoy to Vedric. Once outside Highjorune, we could switch to magic disguises and come into the city by pairs—Jervis and me, Tashir and Savil. One thing they won't be expecting, and that's Tashir with a woman. We meet up at an inn, say, on the better side of town. I could be a Bard this time, instead of a minstrel; you lot could be my entourage. Nose around, see what we can find out."

"Van, I think you and I need to actually get into the palace," Savil put in, staring up at the ceiling. "I think we ought to try and find out exactly what happened and what that attack was. If it was magic, that alone would rule Tashir out."

"Hmm." Moisture beaded the outside of his goblet. He ran his finger down the side, collecting the droplets, and traced little patterns on the table in front of him with a wet forefinger. "Do you think getting Tashir back into the palace might trigger his memory as well?"

"It might," Savil said, moving her gaze down until she caught his eyes. "It's worth a try."

"Then let's do it."

"I never thought I'd see *this* nag cowed!" Jervis chuckled, the rising sun at his back throwing their shadows far ahead of them on the dark-paved road. Three of the four shadows were as long-limbed and graceful as the Companions that threw them. The fourth crow-hopped from time to time as the raw-boned, ugly stud Jervis sat made his displeasure as obvious as he could.

Savil laughed. "He doesn't look too cowed to *me!*"

"Compared to what he was like before your two ladies chased him up and down the paddock all night, he's an angel!" Jervis chuckled, reaching out and hitting the stud between the ears with his fist when he bucked a little too hard. The gray stud squealed and laid his ears back; an answering squeal from Kellan and a showing of her formidable teeth settled him back down.

"I hate to think what Meke is going to do to me when he finds out what we've done," Vanyel murmured. He was still feeling guilty about "borrowing" the stud without a "by your leave."

"What else were we going to use?" Savil asked in a sweetly reasonable tone of voice, as Yfandes snorted. "That blasted stud of Meke's was the closest thing to white on the holding, besides being the only beast with the endurance to keep up with three Companions!" She chortled. "Come to that, he's a good match for Jervis as a Herald, provided you're seeing the real Jervis and not the glamour you put on him."

Jervis *did* make a very unlikely looking Herald. Tashir fit a set of Vanyel's cast-off Whites, left from when *he* was seventeen, fairly well. Vanyel and Savil *had* their uniforms, of course. But for Jervis it had been a case of hasty make-do. He wore one of his own shirts, and had squeezed himself into a pair of Vanyel's white breeches, but they'd had to sacrifice a sleeveless leather tunic of Savil's, opening the seams on both sides and punching holes, then lacing it onto him. He wore his own boots—brown—but they hoped no one would notice that.

''So long as we aren't dealing with anyone who can see through the glamour we'll be all right.''

''Are you sure any spy Vedric might have on the Border won't pick this up?'' Savil asked.

''Well, Heralds are *supposed* to feel a little of magic. A *full* illusion would radiate *far* too much, but an enhancement should pass without any trouble.''

''But won't Vedric pick up the illusion-disguises once we're in town?'' Jervis said suddenly. The stud took advantage of his distraction to try to buck him off.

Yfandes nipped the stud's flank, Kellan kicked him, and Jervis bashed him between the ears, all simultaneously. Vanyel choked down a laugh.

The stud shrilled his indignation, but settled again.

''He would, if the ambient magic in Highjorune wasn't going to mask *my* relatively weak spells. The illusion is *only* going to be on the Companions, to make them something else. Hardly a whisper on the wind.''

The stud tried to rid himself of the bit. ''You fixed his outside,'' Jervis said wistfully. ''If you could only do something about the *inside* of his ugly head. . . .''

Held to the pace of the stud, it took them three days to reach Highjorune. To pass the gates, Kellan and Ghost became donkeys led by an old peasant woman and her son. Vanyel became a Bard on a showy gold palfrey, and Jervis his man-at-arms and general servant. If attention was to be drawn, Vanyel wanted it drawn to *him*.

And indeed, he drew enough attention coming through the gates to more than distract the guards from the old woman and her offspring behind them. Vanyel and Yfandes pranced and preened, sidled and danced—and in general made a thoroughgoing nuisance of themselves. Jervis grunted, looked long-suffering, and earned the sympathy of the gate guards. The stud tried to take off someone's hand and got a fist in his teeth for his trouble.

No Row taverns for Vanyel, not this time. He lodged in the best inn in Highjorune, right across from the residency of the Master of the Weaver's Guild. *Not* so incidentally, that put the palace and all its mage-energies and shield-spells between him and the house where Lord

Vedric was staying. Hopefully, any disturbances the illusions were creating would be lost in the greater wash of the shields and the node beneath the shields.

"Somebody's tried to break the shields," Vanyel observed, staring fixedly out the window.

"You can tell that from here?" Jervis asked, surprised, looking up from sharpening his dagger.

"Uhm-hmm." Vanyel probed deeper, and let his eyes unfocus. "I can even tell what spells he used. And that it was a *he* and not a *her*. Nobody I recognize, but I'd bet it was Vedric."

"Couldn't you—I don't know—get a look at Vedric so you'd know for certain?"

Vanyel turned restlessly away from the window and shook his head. "No. Probing him to get his signature would tell him I was here. Having the palace between us wouldn't hide me long if he started looking for another mage. I don't like it, though. I wish I knew for certain. And I wish I knew why whoever it was tried to breach the shields. It can't be pure curiosity, not with spells that powerful being used. Oh, I can *guess* that it's Vedric, and that he wants to get in there to destroy some kind of evidence, but I'd much rather know for certain if my guess is wrong or right."

"Well, *I* wish Savil and the boy would get here," Jervis growled. "I don't like the notion of us bein' split up like this."

"I agree," Vanyel began, when a tap at the door interrupted him.

He whirled, but it was Jervis who answered it and with a grimace of relief let in Savil and Tashir.

"Where in *Havens* have you been?" he demanded. "You were s'pposed to be here long before sundown!"

"Detained," she replied, smugly. "And what I got was worth the delay! What would you two say to a motive for the Mavelans to destroy the entire Remoerdis Royal House?"

"What?" Jervis and Vanyel exclaimed simultaneously.

"We were playing peasants seeing the sights," Tashir said tiredly. "One of the sights is the Great Hall of

Justice. They keep important documents in there, under glass, so that anybody who can read can see them. I remembered one of them was the treaty between Baires and Lineas and told Savil, so that's why we went there."

"It took a fair amount of Tashir playing gawker to give me time to read it; by then it was dinnertime, and they shooed us all out." Savil threw herself down in a chair beside the table, picked up the knife Jervis had been sharpening, and examined it critically. "What it all comes down to is this: if one of the two Royal Houses dies out—and there are provisions about it being 'through misadventure, pestilence, or acts of the gods,' in other words, it can't be because of *proven* assassination by the other House—the surviving House gets the thrones of both. And that's all in ink and parchment under the signature and seal of Elspeth. Remember? Valdemar oversaw the treaty in the first place, and Valdemar is responsible for administering the provisions of it."

"If I ever knew that, I'd forgotten it," Tashir confessed into the silence.

"In other words, if Tashir is declared guilty of murder, the Linean throne gets handed over to the Mavelans—and Valdemar has to *enforce* this?" Vanyel said, incredulously.

"In a nutshell." Savil replied.

"Great good gods—"

"That ain't real likely to make Valdemar popular around here," Jervis observed. "Not that they're real popular after Van runnin' off with the boy. And if that ain't a pretty good reason for the Mavelans to kill off the Linean House and slap the blame on Tashir—who's Linean, even if he was disinherited—I don't know what would be."

"Nor I," Savil agreed grimly. "*Very* tidy little plot. Well, Van, you wanted a motive."

"I certainly got one." He returned to the window, and stared out of it. "And I have an *excellent* reason for Vedric making himself so popular with the Lineans." There was still some lingering sunset afterglow to make the sky a pearly light blue—and against it, the palace loomed ominously dark.

"Exactly. When everyone finally gets around to checking that treaty, Vedric will be the *only* Mavelan the Lineans will accept. And they *might* even do it with good grace, if he's done his job right."

"Savil," he said slowly, "I think our very first order of business is going to be—"

"The palace," she supplied.

"These seals were definitely tampered with," Vanyel observed. "A little more power behind the attacks and the shields might well have come down."

Yfandes paced up beside him and extended her nose to the door, closing her eyes. *:Blood-magic,:* she judged. *:Faint, but there. Most of the energy traces are ordinary sorcery, but whoever set the spells is used to using blood-magic, and that will taint everything he does.:*

"Which means it's not Heraldic—which we figured. And probably not a local. Working mage-craft around here would get you into trouble with your neighbors quickly, but working blood-magic would get you caught and hung." Vanyel licked his lips, and glanced around at the darkened courtyard. Acting on a hunch from Savil, they'd cleaned out their belongings from the inn and brought everything with them. Now he was glad they had. He raised his voice just a little. "Conference—" he called softly.

Four humans and three Companions made a huddle. Mekeal's stud was tethered as far away as possible. "Whoever tried to break the shields used something tainted with blood-magic," he said. "Yfandes smelled it out. Now *I* have a problem of defense here. Jervis, Tashir, every time we pass the threshold we're going to weaken those shields further. I think maybe we'd better change our plans because I don't think those shields are going to take much more weakening, and the only way for me to reinforce them will be from inside."

"That won't necessarily work either," Savil observed. "You'll just be patching. The weak spot will still be there."

"Exactly," Vanyel nodded. "It isn't going to be pleasant, but what I'd like to do is to just cross *once,* to keep the strain to a minimum.''

His immediate answer was a silence in which the sound of dead leaves skittering across the cobbles was enough to set his nerves jumping. "Set up in residence, until we figure out what happened, you mean?" Savil asked. He nodded. She pursed her lips, and gave a reluctant assent. "I'm inclined to agree. Blood-magic *will* break shields the way nothing else can, and I'd rather this place wasn't left open to tampering. But what about the Companions?"

"They leave," Vanyel said unhappily. Yfandes Sent a wordless burst of protest. "I'm sorry, but I can't think of any place that's safe for them inside the city walls. The west gate stays open at night; but it's guarded. If I put a no-see, no-hear spell on them, they'll make it out all right. And if Vedric detects it, it won't matter; the stir I'm going to make by opening the shield ought to keep him thoroughly occupied."

Jervis cleared his throat. '' 'Nother thing; we run into trouble, that way *they're* free t' run for help.''

Vanyel bit his lip thoughtfully. "Good point. 'Fandes, *I* don't like it either, but—"

:I see no other recourse,: she answered, pawing the cobbles and radiating unwillingness.

"And you'll have to look after that damned stud."

:May I kick him if he won't behave?: she asked, raising her head and ears hopefully.

Vanyel grinned to himself. Other than Jervis, Yfandes had suffered the most from the stud's behavior; the beast kept trying to induce her to mate. "As much as you have to. From here to Karse if necessary. Be my guest."

:Then this is not altogether an unpleasant prospect. Kellan, Leshya—: She waited for the humans to remove their packs from the saddles, then trotted to the tethered stud and freed him with her strong white teeth. With heads high and eyes fixed on Vanyel with acute interest, they waited for him to cast the spell.

Since the four of *them* already knew that the four mounts were there, the spell had very little effect on the onlookers. But Vanyel could See them surrounded with a distorting shimmer that meant the cloaking was in effect. Yfandes Mindsent him a wordless wave of love and concern, and with the stud's reins still in her teeth, turned toward the open gate to the courtyard. Then, with squeals and nips, the three Companions drove the stallion out of the gates and into the swiftly darkening streets.

Vanyel focused his inner eye on the place where he meant to set a portal in the fabric of the shields, then moved his hands in a complicated, mirror-imaged gesture. Through closed eyelids, he Saw the energy walls of the shields part just enough to let a tall man through.

"It's open." He looked with outer eyes again, and watched Jervis feel his way along the invisible—but patently tangible—shield-wall, until he came to the spot opposite Vanyel. Vanyel wasn't sure which was funnier, his expression when he couldn't force his way past the shields, or his expression when he found the "hole."

"I can't hold this too long," he warned; the other three snatched up their packs and his, and Medren's poor, battered, secondhand lute, and hurried up the stone stairs as far as the double door. They waited, white against the dark bulk of the door, while Vanyel slipped across the boundary and resealed the shields behind himself.

He took the stairs slowly, and regarded the purely physical barrier. "Tashir," he began.

The boy looked at him in startlement.

"Young friend, this is where you see how *useful* that Gift of yours is. *My* strong suit is *not* Fetching, and I've only seen this door once, remember." Vanyel folded his arms and raised an eyebrow at him. "I also distinctly recall that I barred the door behind Lores. *You* surely remember what the door and bar look like, and your Gift *is* Fetching. Let's see you raise that bar."

"But—" Tashir began to protest. Savil looked as if she might object as well, but Vanyel silenced her with a look.

"Do it, Tashir. You're better at this than I am."

The young man took a deep breath, closed his eyes, and took a wide-legged stance in what may have been an unconscious imitation of the one Vanyel had taken, and frowned.

Vanyel *had* been giving him what rudimentary instruction he could, when he could. It wasn't much. But as Vanyel had half suspected, away from the disapproval of his family and *into* an environment in which "magic" was actually encouraged, he'd begun practicing, probably in an attempt to get his rogue Gift under some kind of conscious control. All of them could clearly hear the grate of the bar in its sockets on the other side of the closed metal-sheathed door; Jervis clapped Tashir on the back, startling him, as the door creaked open a thumbs'-breadth.

Vanyel did the same, a bit more gently. Tashir grinned at both of them, teeth flashing whitely in the first of the moonlight. "Good work, young man," Vanyel congratulated him. "Now let's get ourselves under cover before somebody curious comes by."

Savil was already pushing the door open; the rest of them followed her into the absolute darkness of the entry hall. She waited until Vanyel had closed the door and rebarred it before fashioning a mage-light and sending it upward to dance and flare above her head.

"Gods!" she hissed, shocked at the extent of the wreckage in the next room.

Jervis moved past her to stand at the top of the stairs, shaking his head. "I've seen wars and looters that weren't *this* thorough. What'n hell did that?"

Vanyel glanced over at Tashir, who had lost his expression of triumph and had become very pale. His eyes were shadowed; his expression haunted. Vanyel put his hand lightly on the youngster's shoulder in encouragement, and felt him tremble.

Savil joined Jervis, oblivious to Tashir's distress, walking very slowly. "I can tell you what *didn't*," she said, unexpectedly. "Tashir."

The youngster jerked in startlement.

"You're sure?" Vanyel asked softly, feeling a tense core inside him go limp with relief. He really *hadn't* believed it was the boy, but still. . . .

"Positive. You get under the glare of the node-energy, and this place is dusted all over with magic." She closed her eyes, and reached out her hand as if to touch something. "There's a very old spell tied to the node that's rooted somewhere just ahead of us. But there's a second spell overlaid on the walls themselves, and *that's* what caused this mess. Van, let me handle that one; it's a trap-spell, and I'd rather you didn't trigger it.''

"I'll second that. You're much better with set-spells than I am. Tashir, Jervis, did you understand that?''

Jervis nodded.

Tashir looked both frightened and hopeful. "She said that there was a magic spell on the palace that—did all this? But why does that eliminate me?''

"Because you haven't even Mage-*potential*. Your Gift isn't *magic*, as we use the term. Real magic leaves traces of itself behind, like the dust a moth's wings leave on your hands when you catch it. You *couldn't* have done something that would leave those traces; you're not capable of it; for you, manipulating mage-energies would be like trying to carry water in a bucket with no bottom.''

"And that's good enough evidence for Valdemar,'' Jervis put in. "Trouble is, I'd bet it ain't good enough evidence for Lineas.''

Tashir's face fell. "That's only too true,'' he said, crestfallen.

"So our job is to *find* good enough evidence for Lineas.'' Vanyel took on unconscious authority. "First off, let's clean out one of the smaller chambers and set up living quarters. Then we'll get some sleep; we'll be better off working by daylight.''

Savil dropped out of her half-trance and rejoined them. "I agree. I don't want to tackle anything that tricky without a full night's sleep. Tashir, this was your home; what would be the best place for us to set up where we aren't likely to be seen or disturbed?'' She shivered in a sudden chilly draft. "*And* where we can build a fire; I don't fancy freezing to death in my sleep, and there's a winter bite to the air at night.''

Tashir looked about; although he had lost some of his apprehension, there was still fear and great unhappiness in him that Vanyel could Sense without effort. *Small wonder. Everyone he ever knew died here.*

"The kitchen, I think,'' Tashir replied. "And there

wouldn't have been anybody back there when—'' He shuddered, and not from the cold.

"Another thing to consider,'' Vanyel said gravely. "We're all likely to come on some very grisly relics, and of us all, Tashir is the least used to such things. Tashir, *don't* go off alone. Stay with one of us; Jervis, by preference. If at any time this gets too much for you, just go straight back to the kitchen until you get yourself settled again. I *do* want you to try and remember what happened that night. I *don't* want a repetition of what you did in Mother's bower. It's not that I think you'll hurt anybody because I know you won't.'' He managed a little smile of encouragement. "It's that you'll be *noisy,* lad. There's not supposed to be anybody here. I'm sure Vedric has figured it out, but he might not dare act on his knowledge just yet. We want to keep him from having reasons. We don't need someone sending for your Uncle Vedric to lay the ghosts, now, do we?''

Tashir paled, and Vanyel was immediately sorry he'd mentioned either ghosts or Vedric. The youngster shook his head wordlessly.

"All right, then let's get to the first stage.'' He shouldered his pack; the others did the same. "Tashir, it's up to you. Find us that kitchen.''

Thirteen

None of them slept particularly well. The first light of dawn saw three of the four lying open-eyed and tense on their sleeping mats; held prisoner by cold, nebulous fears, and waiting for someone *else* to make a sound that indicated rising. Vanyel was actually the last to claw his way out of uneasy half-dreams, which wasn't surprising, considering how exhausted he was. *He* felt the wakefulness around him after a confused moment or two and made a mage-light without thinking. Three gasps of startlement answered the first flare of the light; three pairs of eyes reflected blue flickers back at him.

"If you were all awake," he said, still sleep-mazed and confused, "why didn't you just get up?"

He told Jervis later that—on reflection—he was surprised no one killed him for that question.

There were still usable supplies in the kitchen; dried, salted, or otherwise preserved, and the kitchen had its own pump and well, which solved the problem of where they were going to get water. Trying to ignore the nagging thought that they were robbing the dead, Vanyel helped Jervis cobble together a tolerable meal of bacon, tea, and biscuits.

They sat on folded blankets beside the hearth to eat it; the windowless kitchen was dark, and it somehow *echoed* more than it should. Even Jervis was affected by the somber atmosphere, casting surreptitious glances over his shoulder at the shadows behind him.

"I think we're going to have to divide our attentions," Vanyel said quietly, as they sipped their tea from an assortment of whatever containers had come to hand. "Does anyone object to my taking charge?" He waited, but no one said anything. "Fine. Savil, I'd like you to look into the trap-spell; find out what it does, or did, if you can. *And* how it was set here in the first place. Jervis, Tashir, I'd like you two to start going over the palace, room by room. Jervis, you've been in and out of highborn homes for a good part of your life; you know what *belongs* and what doesn't. I want you to look for anything that seems odd or out of place. Tashir, you're to try and trigger your memory of that night. While you're both at it, we need candles down here, and a bit more in the way of blankets and bedding would be nice."

"And you'll be—?" Jervis raised a thick, grizzled eyebrow. His tone was not accusatory, just inquiring. Once again he and Vanyel had achieved a delicately balanced friendship. It was beginning to grow into something closer and less tentative, something more like a reliable partnership.

A partnership built on respect, and concern for the boy. That Tashir had confessed his fictions hadn't hurt.

"I'll be doing exactly the same, but from the bottom up; I want you two to work from the top down." Vanyel grimaced. "I don't think things are going to be very pretty in the cellars, and, to be brutal, I'm the one of us most recently off a battle-line. I *don't* want Tashir to have to deal with the kind of things I may find down below. I *did* learn that your father wasn't holding any prisoners, Tashir, but I doubt the searchers spent much time in the cellars looking for victims."

Tashir blanched, and took a large, audible gulp of tea.

"Eventually there's one more thing I'll be doing—I've got a hunch that the magic-node beneath the palace plays a major part in the *why* of all this; I want to find out just what the connection is, if I can. There has to be some kind of a connection; I cannot believe that *Tayledras* Adepts just *left* a powerful node like that undrained and unattended. That kind of carelessness goes counter to everything I know about them. *Even if they were forced out,* they'd have come back to release the mage-lines and drain the node—if not the original clan, then the descendants, or allied clan. I think that old spell Savil mentioned is very likely to have something to do with that."

Tasks assigned, they parted. Vanyel had taken the cellars for another reason; he and Savil were the only ones capable of producing their own light without needing to resort to candles or lanterns. They *had* no such physical lights, and there obviously were no windows in the cellars.

He had cause to be grateful for a strong stomach before the morning was over. He'd been right about searchers not checking below. And Lores had not exaggerated the violence of the massacre in the least. Even this old, the shredded remains were appalling. But he had seen remains as bad, or worse, over the past year. And he began to discover a pattern: where there had been no people present, the damage to *things* was minimal, or nonexistent. The more people, the greater the damage.

He did find candles, and the wine cellar. The former he took up the stairs and left at the kitchen landing; the latter he sealed. Half the casks had been split and all the bottles shattered. And as for what remained intact—he rather doubted anyone would ever want to drink from casks that had been stained and spattered with—

Well, it was better not to dwell on it.

They could drink what they found in the kitchen, or water.

From the look of things, four of the servants had been drinking and dicing down there when the disaster had struck. At least, he *thought* it was four. There were four overturned mugs beside the dice and pile of coins, but he couldn't find more than six hands before he gave up searching.

And the hands were the only parts still recognizably human.

It was odd though; four of those six hands had worn rings exactly like the one the maid Reta had worn; dull silver with strange, dead-white stones. *Reta's* ring had plainly been something other than ornament, but although he Mindtouched one of the rings cautiously, Van could find nothing out of the ordinary about it.

And yet he had seen a ring identical to these acting on his behalf. They *could* be just the badge of the household, yet in magic-fearing Highjorune, why would the ruler's own household wear something spell-touched?

Vanyel wondered; it all tied in, somewhere, somehow. He had to find the key.

But answers were not forthcoming; not yet.

He lost track of time down there, and certainly under these circumstances his stomach was not likely to remind him. It felt like being on the Border again; every muscle tensed and waiting for something to leap on him from behind. And no Yfandes to guard his back. He'd never been so conscious of being completely alone before; he might easily have been the only living being in the entire palace. And it was far too easy for his overactive imagination to people the shadows beyond his mage-light with pathetic or vengeful spirits.

When he finally completed his inspection of the cellars and their occasionally grisly contents, it was with profound relief that he climbed the kitchen stairs to emerge, blinking, into brilliant light.

That was the first welcome surprise in a long while. Someone had taken it upon himself to remove the bundles of candles. That same someone had stuck them on every available surface all over the kitchen, and lit them. Light transformed the look of the place from that of a gloomy cave to a normal island of commonplace, a bright and cheerful haven of sanity. It was a profligate use of candles, but there were hundreds of candles. Vanyel stepped into the kitchen with a feeling of having left a little hell behind him.

Tashir and Jervis were by the hearth, sorting through several large bundles.

"Where's Savil?" Vanyel asked. He squinted into the light. "What time is it?"

Tashir jumped, and stared at Vanyel with a momentary expression of panic, as if he did not recognize him immediately. Jervis continued with his sorting, unperturbed. "She's tryin' to track down *where* that trap was set up," the armsmaster replied. "And it's early evening. Give us a hand here, eh? We come up with some likely stuff out of closets and chests; if you get it sorted out an' made up as beds, I'll see to dinner."

Jervis was as good as his word; by the time Savil drifted in, still a little unfocused, he had another fair meal put together.

The blankets, comforters, and sheets that Tashir and Vanyel had made into tolerably comfortable beds smelled strongly of sendle and lavender; proof enough that they'd been laid away in storage. Vanyel judged by Tashir's silence and white lips that the two had probably come across the same appalling signs and stains of slaughter that he had, though probably not the actual remains. The party that had searched the palace had most likely dealt with the actual bodies. Which was all to the good; if Tashir had seen what Vanyel had been dealing with, the boy might well have snapped. Vanyel gave Jervis high marks for unexpected sensitivity; in the state of nerves the young man was in now, one bloodstained sheet come upon in a bundle of bedding he was expected to *use* would likely send him into hysterics. Safer, far, to have searched out the linen closets and taken things sealed away for winter use.

And it was also probable that the pattern below had been continued above; rooms that had been occupied at the time of the massacre might not *have* anything usable in them anymore.

Savil wandered over to the fire and sat down absently on the bed nearest her pack. "Any luck?" he asked her. She shook off her vagueness and finally looked *at* him instead of *through* him.

"Yes and no. I think I've got the site narrowed to the second floor, and I think I know *how* it was set. Someone brought in a catalyst, then using that catalyst, enlarged and strengthened the spell's compass over a long period of time. With no shields on this place, it would have been apprentice work once the initial spell had been set." She accepted a plate from Jervis without looking at it. "It's nasty stuff, *ke'chara*. Makes my skin crawl. Hard to force myself to probe it, now that I know it's there. Like some kind of web with something incredibly evil at the heart— and I'm over on the edge of it, trying to see into the heart without waking what's there. And there's something very, very odd about it. It reeks of blood-magic, as you might well expect, but there's 'blood' involved in it in a *much* subtler way.''

"Eat," Vanyel advised, guessing that she hadn't paused for food or drink since this morning. "Jervis, did you and Tashir find anything?"

The armsmaster chewed and swallowed before answering. "Maybe. If you're done below, I'd like your word on it. It's a room, first floor, smack square in the center of this building. Not much bigger nor a closet, an' has just one thing in it; a floor-t'-ceiling pillar; same stone as the outside. Might just be a kinda kingpost for the palace, it's bigger around than I can reach, but I never seen anything like it. You said look for odd, well, that's odd.''

"Tashir?"

The young man froze in mid-bite, and stared at him like a cornered rabbit.

Vanyel felt an uncomfortable sympathy for him. His own Empathy told him Tashir was dancing on a hair-thin thread of nerve at the moment. There was no doubt in Vanyel's mind that he *was* trying to jar his memories loose. There was also no doubt in his mind that the youngster was, literally, going through hell. But there was no help for it; if the mystery was to be solved and Tashir cleared of guilt, it was likely to take all four of them to do it.

"Tashir, what do you know about this room Jervis found?" he prompted.

Tashir swallowed and licked his lips. "Nothing," he replied faintly. "They wouldn't ever let me in there. Everybody else got taken in at least once, but not Mother, and not me.''

"Tashir, that's *something*," Vanyel chided gently. "You said 'everybody'; do you mean that literally? Servants, too?''

The young man nodded so hard he started to tip his plate off his knee. Jervis caught it before it spilled. Tashir hardly noticed, he was so intent on Vanyel. "Servants, too, Vanyel. Everybody.''

"That's more than odd; that's smacking of a mystery.'' He brooded for a moment, staring at the crackling flames in the hearth. He was greatly tempted to seek the place out now, this instant.

But then he thought of the empty rooms filled with wreckage and the long, haunted halls he'd have to traverse to get there. He hesitated, and shivered. Strong stomach, battle-trained or not, there was a limit.

I don't think so. I'm not up to it. Besides, I'd rather not chance a light being seen from outside. It'll be there in the morning.

"D-d-d-do you want to go there tonight?" Tashir stuttered, patently not relishing the thought at all.

"No, Tashir, not tonight," he replied, half-smiling as a rush of relief brought a little more color to the youngster's cheeks. "Not tonight," he repeated, echoing his own thought. "We've all had enough for one day. It's been there all this time; it'll be there in the morning."

Jervis broke the silence that followed. "Van, I was noticin' something. Rooms where there wasn't any folks, hardly anything's smashed. Maybe a curtain torn, chair broken, that kind of thing. Rooms where there *was* people, they're wrecked. The more people, the worse."

"It's the same down below," Vanyel told him, as Jervis continued demolishing his dinner thoughtfully. "Savil, does that kind of pattern suggest anything to you?"

She scowled with concentration. "Yes, but I can't think what. Damn!"

Vanyel followed a stray thought. "Tashir, when they broke in and found the mess, where were you?"

"Th-the Great Hall," he faltered. "I just sort of woke up and I was there."

"And the worst wreckage was in the Great Hall?" Vanyel turned to Jervis for confirmation.

"Near as I can tell from what I've seen so far."

As he tried to trigger his own memory, he had a momentary flash of that dream he'd had, of being surrounded by a whirlwind of devilish creatures. He realized with a start that made him sit up straight that *that* dream actually had an echo in *his* recent experience. The fire flared on the hearth, and with it, memory.

He'd been playing bait, at the beginning of the Karsite

campaign, sitting all alone in an old keep just behind the Border.

The keep was supposed to be held by nothing more formidable than an old man and a handful of retainers. Certainly the Guard was days away at the best forced march pace, though that shouldn't have mattered. Because no one was supposed to know that the keep was held so weakly. And no one was supposed to know that it guarded a very strategic supply route.

But someone did know; someone had been leaking information to the Karsites. Poorly-guarded keeps of strategic importance behind the Valdemar lines were being decimated, the occupants slaughtered, leaving holes the strategists didn't learn about until it was too late. Or worse—when the strategists checked on their supposed holdings, they found keeps somehow occupied by hostile forces.

Vanyel read the signs of magic, and had known only magic could counter these attacks. So Vanyel had ridden Yfandes to exhaustion to reach this one, a likely target. He'd cleared out the old man and his following, and waited.

And the attack had come, in the form of a gretshke-Swarm; demi-demonic creatures (mostly head, teeth, and appetite) that, taken individually, were inconsequential. An ordinary fighter could deal with one—or two; and they certainly were not immune to cold iron. But a Swarm—that was another matter. The Swarm contained hundreds, if not thousands, of the creatures. You could kill them by the dozens, and still they would overwhelm you, like encountering an avalanche of starving rats.

A mage didn't control a Swarm; he just unleashed it. When the food was gone, or when they were sated, they would return to their own plane if they were given an exit. So a mage using them would customarily lure a Swarm to the Portal to their plane that he had opened within his target area and cast a shield about the target to keep the Swarm from escaping. He would wait an appropriate length of time—usually no more than a candle-mark; the Swarm was fast—and open the Portal again to pull whatever of the Swarm remained back to their own *plane. He would take the shield down then, and an oc-cupying force could move in.*

All this required someone on the level of Adept; which made it likely that the mage in question was one of the three Adepts the Karsites had hired when they began this. One of the three had threatened, then launched the brutal incineration of an entire town; the town had been saved, but in stopping him Mardic and Donni had called the flames on themselves in a desperate attempt to confine them.

It had worked. It had been a brave, unselfish—and ul-timately fatal—ploy. The best that could be said was that their pain had been mercifully short.

Vanyel had been determined that before he was pulled off the lines, he would have that particular mage's life. By preference, given the other things they'd done, he would have all three, but he wanted that one.

The only problem was, the mages themselves refused con-frontation; striking time and time again where he wasn't.

By the time of this ambush he'd had enough. He had begun hunting them with the patience and stealth that would eventually earn him the name "Shadowstalker" when he tracked down the second Adept.

But that was in the future; at that moment, the first step on his self-appointed road of revenge, he had been wait-ing in the darkened keep, fueling the delicate illusion that made it appear to that unknown enemy that only the old man and his dozen retainers and fighters were within those walls, and all were asleep.

He felt the shields go up; he felt the portal open.

The Swarm descended on the Hall of the keep, where he waited for them beside the firepit in the center. And he threw up his own shield, abandoning the illusion, and watched as the Swarm ravened outside it, tearing the scant furnishings of the Hall to shreds in frustration, un-able to reach the meat so tantalizingly out of reach.

While he smiled grimly and set up a second shield be-tween the Swarm and the portal. When the mage opened the Portal again, then established a probe to check on the results of his work, Vanyel would seize on the probe be-

fore he could withdraw it, and use it to send him an unexpected surprise.

It was the image of the Swarm shredding cushions, furnishings, and tapestries that interested him now; an image he sent swiftly to Savil, who seized on it with an exclamation. Jervis raised his eyebrow.

"We think we may have an explanation for all the destruction," Vanyel explained absently, as he and Savil conferred in Mindspeech. "It's complicated, and there's a lot of 'ifs' and 'buts.' It may take us a while to unravel them, but the explanation fits the current evidence."

Jervis just shook his head. "If that's magery, then it's too much for me, Van," he said, yawning. "I'll leave that to you. I'll just show you that room and let *you* deal with it, eh?"

"I'll do that," Vanyel replied, then turned his mind to looking for the traces that would tell him *what* kind of things had torn the hall to shreds—because that would tell him a great deal about *how strong* the enemy was— and importantly, might even give a clue as to *who*.

But in the end, he and Savil sought their beds without any answers but one. *How strong* was *very*. Adept at least.

Because the traces that would have distinguished what the trap-spell had unleashed had been skillfully wiped away. All that remained was the heavily camouflaged spell itself (which only an Adept could have detected under the camouflage) and the bare traces of *magic* that had alerted them in the first place.

Jervis and Tashir were already asleep when they gave up.

"Sleep?" he asked Savil, hoping she'd answer in the affirmative.

"We might as well. We aren't going to get anything more tonight." She stretched once, and began burrowing into her blankets, practically radiating exhaustion. Vanyel realized then what kind of strain she was under—all this complicated, involved sorcery, *and* maintaining her position as the Web's Eastern Guardian. He resolved to take more of the burden from her as soon as he could. This was not fair to her, nor was it good for her.

I wonder if there's a way to tie all the Heralds into the

Web, as power-source at least. That would take fully half the burden off the Guardians.

"Want me to put out the candles?" he asked, glancing around at the burning tapers still bedecking corners of the kitchen.

She opened one eye thoughtfully. "No. Just leave them, if you would. It isn't as if we need to hoard them, and I don't think I want to go to sleep in darkness for a while."

Vanyel thought it over a moment, and nodded. "You know what, teacher-mine?" he said softly. "Neither do I."

She chuckled wearily, and closed her eyes again. "Absurd, isn't it? Here we are, two of the ranking Herald-Mages in Valdemar—afraid of the dark."

He wrapped himself up in his own blankets. "If you promise not to tell anyone, I won't either."

A light snore was his only answer, and he fell asleep with the comforting glow of the candles all about them.

The tiny room vibrated with power.

It was a round room; stone-walled and wooden-floored-and-ceilinged. The walls were pale sandstone, the rest pale birch. The pillar of stone clearly reached higher than the ceiling and lower than the floor. And the room, with barely enough space to walk around the dark pillar was, very clearly, set up with permanent shields, like those in the communal magic Work Room at the Palace in Haven. Small wonder neither he nor Savil had detected this artifact before. Vanyel set a cautious hand to the pillar of charcoal-gray, highly polished stone, as Tashir and Jervis watched him curiously. It was warm, not cool, and felt curiously alive.

And very familiar.

This was a *Tayledras* heart-stone. The Vale of k'Treva had such a stone, a place where the physical, material valley itself merged and melded with the energy-node and intersection of power-flows "below" it. Such a stone was the physical manifestation of the energies fueling the *Tayledras* magics, and this physical manifestation was peculiarly vulnerable to tampering. So the heart-stones were guarded jealously—and *always* deactivated when *Tayledras* left a place.

This one *should not* be here, except, perhaps, as a dead relic of former inhabitants. It should not be alive, and more, responding to his touch, physical and magical, upon it.

"This—" he faltered, and pulled his hand away with a wrench. "Jervis, you were right. This is *not* something I would expect here. I'm going to have to Mindtouch it."

"Anything we can do to help?" the armsmaster asked quietly.

"To tell you the truth, I'd rather you took Tashir out to the Great Hall to see if you can help him remember," Vanyel said, trying to keep the fascination of the heart-stone from recapturing him. "There isn't much you can help me with, and you two *being* here would be a little distracting. But if you'd poke your nose in here from time to time—"

"Anything I should watch for?"

"Well," Vanyel replied wryly, "if I'm turning blue, that's probably a sign something's wrong. Other than that, trust your own judgment."

Jervis' answering laugh was gruff, and sounded a little like churning gravel, but it proved that of the four of them, he was the one least affected by their macabre surroundings. "All right, let me take the boy out, and we'll see if we can make some progress."

"Thanks." *And thank you, Jervis, that we can trust each other now. I don't think I could be doing this otherwise.* Without waiting to see them go, Vanyel turned back to the stone pillar, and placed both palms and his forehead against it—

And it took him into itself.

For a very long time he was conscious only of the incredible, seething maelstrom of the energy-node itself. It was like plunging into the heart of the sun, and yet remaining curiously unscathed and untouched. It was different from tapping into the node; there he was outside, separate from the energy he sought to control, and he was dealing with a single, thin stream of force. Now he was a part of the force, with no intent—or chance—to control it. But control was not what he wanted; he wanted only observation, and answers.

But to have an answer, one must first ask a question. He framed it in his mind, carefully inserting all the nuances into it he could.

In words, it would have been a simple, "Who left this here?" In thought it was infinitely more complex than that; asking "who" specifically, and "who" as a class.

The heart-stone was not an intelligence, but it *remembered*. And every question that was balanced by an answer would call that answer out of the stone. Vanyel got a very clear picture of *Tayledras* Adepts; several of them, all of them radiating great power, including one with the peculiar blue-green aura of the rare Healer-Adept. That particular Adept was much clearer, and lingered longer in the mind, and the implication was that it was this Healer-Adept that was responsible for having left both stone and node still in their active state.

If Vanyel could have started with surprise, he would have. Although they could, and on occasion *did*, act as ordinary Healers, *Tayledras* Healer-Adepts concerned themselves with Healing, not people, but environments. At restoring the balance nature had intended. At Healing the hurts that either magic or the hand of man had dealt there. That a Healer-Adept would have deemed it necessary to *leave* this potentially disastrously-dangerous energy source in lands soon to be settled by ordinary humans—that seemed to indicate that there was a terrible need that overrode all other considerations.

"Why?" he asked, urgently.

And felt himself being drawn down—deeper—below the bedrock, and into the roots of the earth itself. And he realized with a shock that the pillar was that deeply rooted, too.

There was tension here, a tension that increased as he went deeper, a vast pressure to either side of him that squeezed him until he could scarcely breathe. And still the force that had seized him to answer his question drew him deeper, and deeper still, to a point where the rock began to warm about him.

Then he saw it. Running from north to south, invisible

from above, yet carrying implied within it such peril that his blood ran cold, was a crack in the last layer of rock itself. A fault; a place of slippage, following the river bottom.

That was natural enough; what was *not* natural was the hole punched through the fault down to the molten core of the planet, something probably left from the Mage Wars. *That* was what the heart-stone was planted above.

And all of Highjorune was built directly on that fault. More, it extended the width of Lineas and out into the unsettled lands. If it slipped—

And it was only a matter of time before it slipped and caused a catastrophe that would destroy the city in fire and earthquake—and much of the surrounding country beside. Vanyel could not imagine why it hadn't happened *before* this—until he *Saw* where the energy of the node was going.

It was feeding into a complicated spell so convoluted and involved he could *never* have set it himself. It could only be the handiwork of that *Tayledras* Healer-Adept— and it looked to be the masterwork of an entire lifetime as a mage and an Adept. It was holding the wound closed, and keeping the fault from slipping.

More, it would, given time enough, *Heal* the wound and the fault, redistributing the strain elsewhere, until this was no longer an area of instability. But it would take time, hundreds of years or more, and any great siphoning away of the node-energy would deprive the spell of needed power. And if *that* occurred—depending on the amount of energy stolen from its proper usage, there would come anything from a minor tremor to the major, devastating disaster the Adept had been trying to prevent.

The force that had him let him go, and he drifted back to the "surface" more than a little dazed.

But he still had one more question. What was the connection between Tashir's family and this artifact at the heart of their palace?

That answer came immediately, and almost as words.

They were the Guardians.

And with that came a rush of knowledge that rocked him physically away from the stone. He opened his eyes to find himself pressed back against the wall, staring at the pillar of dark, volcanic basalt, with his mind seething with information.

He staggered out of the tiny room, carefully closing the door behind him, and made his unsteady way into the kitchen, bypassing the Great Hall entirely. He wanted to lie down, very badly. This was not the first time he'd queried a heart-stone, but it was the first time one had responded with such a flood of facts and memories. The heart-stones *he'd* merged with had been slow, old, and so peaceful that the answer you wanted might take *candlemarks* to drift within grasping. By contrast, this one practically flung responses at you before you finished the question.

He made the kitchen easily enough, and spent some time sticking up new candles and lighting them before wobbling back to his bed and falling facedown into the blankets.

He must have slept, because the next thing he knew, the others were clattering about the kitchen, there was a smell of frying bacon, and his stomach was declaring war on his backbone.

He rolled over on his back, stiffly, painfully, and Savil immediately knelt at his side and peered into his eyes. "You were in shock-sleep," she said. "We couldn't wake you. I hope to hell you got something worth it."

He took a deep breath, and discovered that his ribcage was sore, that all his muscles ached. He must have held them tensed for hours. He nodded. "Answers," he said—croaked, rather. "I got answers. I got *answers.* Savil, that's a heart-stone in there. And it's awake!"

Her mouth had dropped open the moment he'd said the words "heart-stone." She shut it again with a snap. "Eat first, and get something to drink. *Then* tell us."

He sat up slowly, more than ever grateful for all the soft comforters to cushion his aching body from the stone floor of the kitchen. There was a fire in the hearth, and the other three seemed warm, but he was cold—cold.

Jervis shoved a plate into his hand, Tashir a cup of tea into the other. Savil and Jervis then pretended to deal with the remnants of their dinners. Tashir made no such pretense, hovering at Vanyel's side and watching every mouthful he took with impatience.

It was a little embarrassing, but Vanyel could not find it in his heart to blame him.

When he put down the empty plate, the other two gave up all pretensions and hovered around him.

"I'll try to make this short," he said, feeling a little awkward with all their attention so fixed on him. "This palace is situated on top of a place where several lines of magical energy meet and collect—we call that a 'node.' Nodes—the very powerful ones, that is—frequently *aren't* natural. They can be created artificially by a particular group of Adepts called the *Tayledras*—the 'Hawkbrothers.' " At Jervis' and Tashir's look of blank nonrecognition, he added, "They live in the Pelagirs. Most people have never heard of them. Fewer still will ever see them. Savil and I are among the few."

Savil nodded. "They're very secretive, and for a good reason. They do—almost as naturally as breathing—something damned few other mages are even capable of *imagining*. They manipulate the energy fields of the world around us."

Vanyel interrupted her gently. "They do two things, really; they drain magic left from the old wars away from lands that ordinary people are moving into, and they use that magic both to Heal those lands and to create sanctuaries for magical creatures that are displaced by the folk moving in. When they settle in a place, they generally create a node under it to use. When they *leave* that place they *always*—or so *I* always thought—deactivate and drain the node, and reroute the power-lines running to it."

"That's what Starwind always told me," Savil agreed, shifting her position so that she rested her chin on her knees.

"Well, they didn't this time," Vanyel replied. "The node is *still* fully active, and the heart-stone that is the physical link to it is still alive. That's what that pillar is, Tashir, the heart-stone. And that brings me to *why*."

He licked his lips and closed his eyes for just a moment, to center himself. "Some time when people first

moved into this area, Tashir, one of the *Tayledras* remained behind, and selected your remote forefather to be
the hereditary guardian of the heart-stone. He charged
him to keep it safe, and to see that *no one* in Lineas ever
dabbled in magic. That charge has been passed down to
everyone with the blood of the Remocrdis Family—
because that blood carries Mage-potential with it, and because that very wise ancestor of yours saw no reason to
limit the guardianship to a favored few. The more guardians, he thought, the safer—and I think he was right.
After all, this has gone on for generations without *any*
inkling of the power here leaking outside of Lineas.
That's the meaning of those rings everyone—except you
and your mother—wore. They link the wearer to the heart-
stone and the guardianship, and the spell that binds
wearer to ring and to the guardianship allows the stone
to act upon *the wearer* to keep them safe, and to safe-
guard itself. I actually saw that last in action—your mother's maid Reta was moved by the heart-stone to tell me
some of what I needed to know. It was quite uncanny;
she acted for all the world as if someone had put a second-
stage Truth Spell on her. Back to the subject. *You* didn't
get one, and weren't sealed to the stone, because your
father didn't believe you were of his blood. To settle *that*
question, the stone says otherwise. The stone recognized
you as being of the blood the moment you entered the
room. You *are* the true-born son of Deveran Remoerdis
of Lineas. And if your father had ever conquered his own
doubts and suspicions, and allowed you into the room,
even as an infant, he would have known that, too.''

Tashir hung his head, and Vanyel could see his shoulders shaking. He laid his hand on top of one of the
youngster's, and Jervis put his arm around the young
man's shoulders for a moment.

''Now—the reason *why* the node was left active; there's
an instability underneath Lineas; *right* underneath Highjorune. The node is literally holding it together. If it were
to be disturbed, *especially* if it were to be drained, as a
careless or ignorant mage might manage, Highjorune
would certainly be destroyed by a terrible earthquake,
and quite probably all of Lineas, a good section of Baires,

and even some of Valdemar. *That* is why the people of
Lineas have been trained to shun and discourage mages.
That is what your people have held in trust for centu-
ries—and I think that the power of the node is also why
the Mavelans want Lineas. Unfortunately, I suspect they
see only the powerful node, and have made no effort at
discovering why it is there.''

''I doubt they'd care,'' Savil said dryly.

''I wish I knew differently.'' He put down his mug,
and rested his forehead on his own knees. ''Gods,'' he
said, his voice muffled. ''Well, we have part of the puzzle.''

He felt a hand on his shoulder; Savil's. ''Tired,
ke'chara?'' she asked.

''Not *tired,* precisely,'' he replied, raising his head
and smiling into her eyes. ''Just a little—divided. You
know what querying a heart-stone is like; you become
part of it. It's *hard* being a rock; they have such a strange
sense of time—and priorities.'' He shook off his feeling
of disorientation and patted her hand. ''No matter, now
that I've got that solved, I can help you with that trap-
spell. If you can get me safely inside it, I *think* I can
unravel the components enough to tell what triggers it
and what it acts on.''

''We're getting somewhere, too,'' Jervis put in diffidently. Tashir raised his head and sniffed, once, then
scrubbed the tears from his cheeks with the back of his
hand and nodded. ''You want to tell 'em, Tashir, or you
want me?''

''I can,'' he said, though his voice quavered a little.
''I remember *why* those things couldn't get me the way
they got the others. I was—pushing them away with my
head. I remember doing that; I remember them trying to
get at me, and I remember just shoving—like this—''

He screwed up his face with effort, and Vanyel found
himself being pushed across the floor, away from the boy,
bedding and all. When he reached out his hand, he encountered what was almost a surface, as if the air itself
had solidified.

Tashir dropped the effort with a gasp. ''It hurts to do
that,'' he said, ''but it hurt less when I was scared.''

Vanyel nodded. "And the reason that the others held their attackers off for a little while—which was why the rooms with people in them were torn apart—was because of the rings. The stone told me that there's some limited protections spelled into the rings by the ceremony of binding. Unfortunately those protections were mainly meant to be used against someone trying to probe a guardian's mind, not against someone trying to kill him."

"One more day should see us with all the answers," Savil observed.

"Let's just hope they aren't answers we don't want to hear," Jervis replied grimly.

Sensitized by the heart-stone to what magically *should* and *should not* be associated with the palace itself, Vanyel took the lead the next morning, making a check of every room in the palace. Once they found the trap-spell catalyst, they would have a much better chance of unraveling the roots of the spell itself.

There was nothing on the first floor, and nothing in the private quarters, not even Ylyna's. But when they reached the guest rooms—

The taste of evil was in the air of the primary suite so thick that Vanyel could hardly believe that Savil didn't sense it, too. This was a set of five rooms reserved for the most important of visitors, the suite that the Mavelan representatives had undoubtedly occupied during the signing of the treaty and the wedding. The effluvium of *wrong* was strongest in the reception chamber, a room of linen-paneled walls hung with weaponry and the heads of many dead animals, and furnished with a variety of impractical and uncomfortable unpadded wooden chairs, and one large desk. He traced it, growing more and more nauseated by the moment, to of all things, an ornamental dagger hung in plain sight on the wall above the hearth.

He didn't touch it—he couldn't bear to—but he didn't need to. It had been there for years; perhaps as long as eighteen or twenty. The spell had been given plenty of time to permeate through the physical fabric of the palace like a slow poison in the veins of an unsuspecting victim.

"That's it?" Savil said incredulously. "I must have passed this room a dozen times."

Vanyel shrugged, and found himself a marginally comfortable chair. They were likely to be here a long while, once Savil got started. "Did you test that dagger, or were you looking for something hidden?" he asked.

"Something hidden," she admitted ruefully, walking slowly and reaching for—but *not* touching—the dagger. Her eyes unfocused. "That's it," she replied after a moment.

"All right. I'll link to you, and you slip me inside the spell," Vanyel told her, bracing himself in the chair. "Get out as soon as you can; you've been draining yourself quite enough as it is."

"Not as much as you, *ke'chara*," she retorted, her lips thinning, as she took a seat on the floor at his feet, and laid her hands over his wrists.

"But *I'm* not a Web-Guardian," he pointed out with ruthless logic. "Come on; let's get this over with."

He closed his eyes and evoked a light trance-state; *centered*, then *reached* for a deeper level of Savil than he touched in Mindspeech.

Like hand taking hand, he linked with her; followed her blindly through a twisting, torturous maze of fire and shadow and confusing shapes in which the slightest misstep would mean things he preferred not to think about. Savil knew what she was doing; if *she* couldn't weave her way through this thing, no one outside of k'Treva could.

:Brace yourself, love. I'm going to toss you in.:

He "made" himself as compact and small a "bundle" as he could—and felt himself hurled—

He crawled on hands and knees into consciousness. He opened burning eyes, his stomach in knots; his head pounding, and wanting a bath more than he'd ever wanted anything in his life. He felt filthy inside as well as out.

Savil was still kneeling beside him, holding both of his cold hands in hers, staring intently into his eyes. "You're back," she said.

"I'm back," he replied, swallowing bile. "You won't like it."

"I don't like it now." She released his hands, and he rubbed his eyes with his knuckles.

"Remember what you said, about 'blood' being involved very subtly in this? It is; and given what I found out about the guardianship of the heart-stone it's sickeningly logical. When this spell is triggered *on* someone, it not only goes for them—but for *everyone* sharing blood-relationship with that person that is also a mage or carries the potential. *Everyone,* right down to babes in the womb."

Savil's face grayed a little. "So whoever did this—"

"I've got that, too. Last person to trigger it was *dear* Uncle Vedric Mavelan. Last person targeted was Tashir. So much for all his protests about wanting to help the lad."

"Tashir?" Her voice rose at least half an octave. "But then—that means that Vedric *knew* the boy wasn't his!"

Vanyel grimaced, and tried to sit up straighter. "Exactly. He knew it all along, and made *no* attempt to clear either his sister, or the youngster. Now, I have a few guesses as to why there seem to be inconsistencies. The biggest is why the maid Reta I spoke to survived. My *guess* is that Vedric shielded the palace to avoid blood in the streets and the question of why Tashir would murder people he didn't even know existed. If he hadn't, it's pretty likely that people would have looked elsewhere for a perpetrator, rather than to Tashir. And that shield would explain why the Mavelans weren't attacked, since they were related to Tashir through Ylyna."

"And why Ylyna was killed with everyone else; she must have been carrying Mage-potential," Savil mused aloud.

"The thing is—this is a trap that resets itself. Until we destroy the maker, anyone that knows how can set it against anyone else."

He sat bolt upright, as the shields on the palace buckled and weakened under a furious attack.

"Did you—" Savil exclaimed, blanching. "—gods, of course you felt that; they're your shields. There's somebody out there trying to get in!"

"*Will* get in," Vanyel corrected grimly, launching

himself out of the chair. "It's Vedric. He knows we're in here. He's probably figured out that we know what happened—or soon will. He can't afford to let us escape."

The shields shrieked in his mind as another attack battered at them. Vanyel started down the hall at a run, followed by his Aunt.

:Yfandes!: he called, snaking the Mindtouch around Vedric, hoping the mage would be too preoccupied with his attack to sense it.

:Here—:

Grateful that thought took less time to send than words, he told her all they'd learned. *:Time to run for it, love. Have Kellan stay with the stud, you and Ghost head over the Border at top speed. Vedric's on to us. If we lose this—:*

:I will see that the Kingdom knows,: she replied grimly. *:I will see you avenged. Then I will come to you.:*

She cut him off before he could protest, and there was no more time to spare for protests.

"We have," he cast over his shoulder at Savil, "maybe a candlemark or two to figure out what we're going to do."

Fourteen

They skidded into the Great Hall, feet slipping on the debris, startling Jervis and Tashir considerably as they came to a halt beside them. Savil held her side and panted a little.

"What—" Jervis began.

"Vedric's out there," Vanyel interrupted him. "He's trying to break through the shields. I expect he knows we're in here; I expect he figures we've learned the truth of what happened. *He's* the one that triggered the trap-spell; he used Tashir for the target, and the damned thing's set to take *anyone* of the bloodline of the target with Mage-potential."

Tashir had been sitting on a cleared space on the floor. He stood, slowly, his expression frozen, his face drained. *"I remember,"* he said, his voice tight and strained, *"I remember now."* He turned away from them, and pointed a shaking hand at the door that led to the second-floor stairs. "I was running down those stairs. I was going to run away. I told Father that—I told him that I'd rather dig ditches than go to Baires. He laughed at me, he said he doubted I had the spine—and I hit him. I didn't mean to, but it just happened. I was afraid he'd do something horrible and I ran. I ran through here and out the door, and—and—*I couldn't get out!* It was like hitting a wall! I didn't even think, I just turned around and started running for the stable door, and when I got *here*—" He pointed at his feet. "I—it—happened. Like, I don't know, like a whirlwind, only there were all these teeth and eyes, and pretty soon it was filling the whole room and tearing everybody and everything around into *shreds*—"

His voice spiraled up into hysteria, and Jervis shook his shoulders.

"Tashir, come on, lad, we've got troubles *now,* don't you fall apart on me."

The young man shivered like a trapped rabbit, but he nodded, and there was still some sense in his eyes.

"I repeat; Vedric's out there." Vanyel shuddered as he felt his shields buckle a little more. "He'll be in *here* soon. I sent the Companions out of here; Kellan's minding the stud, she and Ghost and Yfandes are going for home. One way or another, the truth is going to get out, but there's only one way out now for us. Savil, I'll hold him, while you build a Gate and get Jervis and Tashir out of here."

She nodded, face gray and grim. "Where?"

"Haven, by choice; no one is going to extract him from Randale's hands once he hears the whole story." He was only giving half his attention to the conversation; the other half was busy weaving reinforcements to his disintegrating shields.

"But—" she protested.

"Dammit, Savil, just *do* it; *I* can't. Gating that far would probably kill me!"

"Vanyel," she interrupted urgently, "what happens when he triggers the trap on *you?*"

He felt himself pale, felt his spellcasting falter. "Oh, gods—let me think—*you* should be all right if I can just hold him off long enough for you to alert somebody to protect you. Medren is Bard-Gifted with no Mage-potential, he should be safe enough. My sibs—no potential. Father!"

"Is safe," she told him. "How do you think I got half these white hairs? I spent a week in the nodes weaving protections for him when I first met Starwind. When I realized how powerful an Adept I was, I also realized that very few enemies were going to be able to come at me directly, so they *might* choose to come at me through my brother. I made *sure* there was no chance of that while I had the energy and leisure. Is there *anybody* else?"

"No," he said. But his mind was screaming the real

truth at her even as his lips formed the lie. *:Savil! Jisa—oh, gods, the children—:*

:What?:

He grabbed her shoulders so tightly it surely must have hurt enough to leave bruises as his fingertips dug into the flesh. *:I have three children. Brightstar and his twin are in k'Treva, under their own shields, Starwind's and Moondance's, so they're safe enough, but Jisa—*

:Jisa? How? Why?:

His thoughts were not particularly ordered or coherent, but he did his best to get the sense across to her. *:Savil, don't ask; she's mine by blood, Randale and Shavri wanted it, that's all you need to know. She's not under shield.:* He wanted to *pound* the fear he felt for them into Savil. *:And Shavri's at risk through Jisa. I don't know if Shavri's got the potential or not. You have to get back there—gods—I never meant anyone else to know, but there's no choice—Jays. Trust Jays. Tell him the truth; I think he'll understand. No one else. Gods, if Randale was only a mage—go, Savil!:* The battering at his shields grew fiercer. *:Just go! I can't hold him much longer!:*

He released her shoulders, and Savil turned without another word and faced one of the open doorways. She held up her hands, and Vanyel felt the slight disorientation that always accompanied the moment when someone invoked Gate-energy around him. He left the little group of three and sprinted across the wreckage-strewn hall and up the staircase to face the door and try to keep Vedric in check long enough for them to escape.

He fought silently, fighting as he had never fought before, fighting not only for himself, but for his friends—and for his land, for without Shavri, Randale would fall to pieces. The last of his shield reinforcements cracked and fell away just as he felt the wave of dizziness that signaled the opening of the Gate itself. And the outer door exploded open, breaking two of its hinges and shattering every window in that wall, just as he felt a wash of pain—

Pain that signaled the Gate being traversed, and then going down again.

That pain nearly did him in; he was barely able to get

his own personal shield up in time to deflect the light-
nings Vedric called down on him.

"Hold him, boy!" came an urgent voice behind him.
"He *knows* we know—he doesn't dare let us live!"

"*Jervis!*" Vanyel tapped recklessly into the node, and
flung fire into Vedric's face. He didn't dare look around,
but he spat a stream of heartfelt curses in four languages
at the armsmaster. "*Damn* you," he screamed, deflect-
ing a paralysis-dagger and countering with an ice-storm.
"Get under cover! What in the *hell* do you think you're
doing?"

"What Savil told me," came the unperturbed voice
from behind and to his right, as Vanyel tried to shatter
Vedric's shields with hammering blows of pure force.
Vedric turned them, though not easily; Vanyel could spare
no more attention to the armsmaster. To deal with Vedric
would take every scrap of concentration.

They were equals, or so close as made no difference.
Vanyel had the node to draw on, but Vedric was being
fed from somewhere outside himself, too. The entryway
shook; the glass of the windows that had been shattered
in the first exchange rose up and flew at him. He pulver-
ized the flying shards of death with a single blow. Now
flakes of stone and plaster rained down on them, and the
paving beneath their feet cracked.

Then Vedric smiled—and triggered the trap-spell.

Hastily Vanyel extended his shield to cover Jervis. A
whirlwind Swarm of creatures—as Tashir had described,
seeming mostly teeth and eyes—circled them, screaming their outrage at not being able to reach them. They
weren't the *gretshke* beings he'd encountered—they were
at once less *hungry* and more evil. The Swarm he knew
attacked to feed, these things attacked only to rend and
tear, to maim and destroy, for the pleasure of destruction
and the pain it caused.

Shrieking in frustration, the Swarm spiraled up and
away, passing through the ceiling unhindered—and were
gone.

Vedric smiled again. "Well, Herald Vanyel—I presume that is who you are—aren't you going to try to rush
off to the rescue of your family, your kindred?"

Vanyel just laughed at him.

That was *not* the response Vedric had expected, and it shook him. But what shook him even more was the backlash a moment later as his Swarm attempted to find victims, and were thwarted again—and again—and again—

Failed spells recoiled on their caster; that was one of the first lessons Starwind had taught him. And a spell this powerful, if backlashed, *should* have knocked Vedric to his knees.

But it didn't.

It seemed as if the Mavelan mage-lord took the backlash, and siphoned it off somewhere.

That was when Vanyel realized exactly where Vedric was getting his unprecedented power. The entire Mavelan family had united (for once) and was feeding this, their chosen representative, with all their combined powers.

Vanyel could hammer at him until dark with no effect.

He deflected another lightning-strike, and thought frantically. Even if he defeated Vedric, that *wouldn't* take care of the rest of the family unless he could somehow get at *them* through the linkage to the mage-lord.

Then he knew *how* to manage that.

Raw node-power.

Only *Tayledras*-trained or an Adept with the dearly-bought control he and Savil shared could handle it. He remembered how, when he had defeated the changeling-mage Krebain, he had nearly killed himself by flooding it through his system. Only one thing had saved him; the fact that Moondance, a k'Treva Healer-Adept, had gotten to him within heartbeats after he'd blasted himself. If he poured *that* through Vedric and into the meld before they realized what he was doing, there would be no saving of any of them. Without being prepared to handle that kind of power, they would be destroyed.

But to do that, he would have to drain the node to a level where he might trigger a quake. And he would have to *touch* Vedric.

He had been very carefully avoiding looking at the mage-lord. Now he looked across the space intervening between them and saw—

Tylendel. As Tylendel would have looked *now,* had he survived into full manhood.

He froze.

The momentary pause in the parry-riposte of the mage-duel broke Vedric's rhythm and concentration. He looked up and stared at Vanyel as if wondering what the other was up to.

That broke the grip of heartache holding him, for *nothing* could have been less like the Tylendel Vanyel had loved than the creature that looked at him out of the mask of Tylendel's face. There was craft there, and guile—and a terrible cruelty. The kind of cruelty that would see nothing wrong with setting an innocent boy up to be abused and neglected most of his life. A heartlessness that had finally served the helpless boy up as a sacrifice, as the expendable tool that gave Vedric power, and never once felt a twinge of guilt or regret.

A strengthening surge of anger galvanized him, and he reengaged with every resource he had, fighting his way through lightning, fire, force-walls, everything Vedric could throw into his path. He could see the puzzlement in Vedric's eyes as he won each step across the room, paying for each fingerlength in pain when Vedric's weaponry penetrated his shielding and scored on him, but taking those fingerlength gains despite the pain. He forgot Jervis, forgot Tashir, forgot everything but the fight to win to within arm's-reach of the mage-lord.

Multicolored curtains of power danced in front of him barring his way. They scorched him as he parted them.

Two steps to go.

One.

He reached out and seized Vedric's arms, and at that moment the mage seemed to figure out what his goal was. Panic spasmed across his face.

But it was a realization that came too late.

Vanyel opened himself up to the node *completely,* and let the power use him as a channel, as he had when he melded with the heart-stone. It poured through him meeting no resistance—

And into the meld that was the Mavelan family.

Vedric's spine arced; his mouth opened, but no sound emerged. For one moment he glowed like a young sun—
—Vanyel's mind rocked under a multivoiced scream of agony that seemed to go on and on and forever—

Then it was gone, and so was Vedric. There was nothing left but a pile of white ash at Vanyel's feet and two handfuls of ash that he dropped onto the pile.

Vanyel stared at the ash, dully—and when the entryway swayed, he thought for a moment that it was his own fatigue that made him stumble and lose his footing.

But as Jervis scrambled toward him to grab his arms and shake him, he understood. The node—he'd drained enough power so that the fault had gone unstable.

The building rocked again, as Jervis continued to shake him. "Come *on,* you damned fool!" he shouted, right into Vanyel's face. "Those damned shields that Vedric set up t' keep us from gettin' away are still there! Gate us outa here before the building comes down on our heads!"

He wrenched himself out of Jervis' hands and faced the ruined outer door, holding up his hands and beginning the Gate-spell, while around him the room bucked and heaved like a boat in a storm.

The pain was incredible.

Letting the node-force use him had left him raw; it was only knowing that Jervis would perish with him that kept him going. He could see the court beyond the door—or rather, what the quake was leaving of it. The palace was disintegrating around them, and nothing living was going to stay that way for long here.

Finally the Gate was complete; the courtyard winked out with a wrench that felt as if someone had torn Vanyel's guts out, and in its place was the corridor just outside the Ashkevron family chapel.

Vanyel's knees gave out and he collapsed. He had just enough energy to wince a little as half the wall collapsed between him and the Gate.

There was nothing but pain now; and he lacked even the strength to weep.

Jervis was shaking him; he tried to push the man's hands away, but it was like a babe trying to push away

the hand of an adult. "Go," he panted, too spent even
to moan. "Can't—hold it—stable."

There's nothing left. I overestimated again—

He could feel the Gate pulsing with the beating of his
own heart. In a moment it would collapse.

"Go—now," he tried to urge the armsmaster. He was
so tired; he'd give anything to be able to rest, beyond the
pain.

Shadow-Lover—

Death had long since lost any fear for him. He had
been courted by the Shadow-Lover for so long that His
embrace would be welcome, if only it would bring him
peace. There was nothing left—not even his will.

But Jervis had enough will for two.

"I'm not goin' without you!" the old man growled, as
the palace walls cried in a hundred agonized voices
around them. "You remember what you said about giving
up? Dammit, Van, don't do it now! *There's nobody to
pick up your load if you give up on me!*"

The words reached through the haze of pain and weakness as nothing else could have. He struggled to his feet,
Jervis supporting him, as the palace bucked around them.
Jervis started for the open Gate, more than half dragging
him over the rubble, and finally draped his arm across
his own shoulders and *carried* him through the Gate itself.

He'd thought there could be no worse pain than passing
that Gate.

He discovered a heartbeat later that he was wrong.

There was a flash of light on metal as Jervis' boots
clattered onto the stone of the corridor floor. It was training, a training that refused to admit to having no strength,
that made him squirm sideways in Jervis' grip.

But it wasn't quite enough. There was a rush of dark
cloth toward them, and the hard impact of something
driving into his stomach and jerking upward—

"*Leren!*" Jervis roared. "What in—"

And pain that blacked out everything else sent him
bonelessly to the floor as Jervis let go of him.

Somewhere—in some other world beyond the pain—
there was a sound of scuffling. All *he* knew was the pain

he agony that was the center of him, as he lay on his side and clutched his stomach, something hot and wet trickling between his fingers.

Heal—I have to Heal myself— He *had* just enough Healing-Gift to save himself. He *reached,* feebly. *—no strength—*

:Chosen!: Yfandes' mind-voice, faint and far-off—and a brief, unsteady surge of energy from *her* to *him,* all unlooked-for; energy that could Heal him.

But something else brushed his mind, a sense of dark and evil wings.

It was *with* Leren. A dark force that ruled Leren, and it was poised to strike at the armsmaster.

He had a choice; save himself—or save Jervis.

Which was not a choice at all.

No!

Vanyel took that borrowed strength and hurled it at the unprotected, unsuspecting darkness like a spear of light.

It penetrated.

But it did not kill. The darkness fled, wounded, but not conquered, as Vanyel began fading into a darkness of his own.

Gods—Leren—controlled.

Jervis' voice. "Bastard got distracted. Got him with a chair," the man said, from that other world. "He won't be going anywhere for a while. Boy—boy, did he mark you?"

It was becoming very hard to breathe; his frantic gasps after air just made the pain worse, and didn't seem to be bringing anything into his lungs.

Someone rolled him onto his back and he cried out.

"Lady's tits!" Jervis swore. "Bloody bastard!"

Vanyel opened his eyes, but he couldn't see anything but a tiny spot of brightness in a sea of black. The blackness called him—

Jervis slapped his face lightly, and the blackness receded for a moment. "*Don't* leave on me, boy," he said urgently, supporting Vanyel in his lap. "Stay with me!"

Vanyel did his best to obey, as Jervis bellowed somewhere over his head for a Healer, but he was cold, and getting colder, and there didn't seem to be any room for anything but agony.

He tried to open his eyes again, when he heard frantically running feet. There was a strange Herald in Whites on his left, and a swirl of green robes as a Healer dropped down beside him on his right.

"Gods!" he heard the latter swear, in an audible panic. There were hands pulling his away, and a wash of weakening that followed a gush of something, warmth that poured out of him, and over the hands that replaced his. "I—oh, gods, we're losing him!"

"Like hell!"

"I—"

Everything—voices, vision, even the pain—began to fade. Everything except the stranger kneeling at his left side. Though his face remained oddly shadowed, there was a soft, argent glow about him, like starlight, that brightened with each passing moment.

:Take my hand, Herald Vanyel.:

Vanyel blinked, struggled against his fading sight, tried to hold to consciousness.

:My hand.: The strange Herald held his right hand out to Vanyel, and there was entreaty in that mind-voice *:Will you not take it?:*

The urgency in the request pulled at him; this was important. Important that he fight past the pain to obey the stranger. Moved by some deep conviction that he didn't understand, he found a tiny crumb of strength; just enough to move the fingers of his left hand and place them, sticky and warm with his own blood, into the stranger's outstretched palm. The stranger's hand closed over his, and his lips curved in a smile of triumph.

He was standing. The pain was gone.

So was the wound. The strange Herald still held his hand, but about them was—nothing. Only a kind of peaceful, tranquil gray emptiness.

The stranger's face was still shadowed—except for the eyes, a blazing glory of sapphires and light, a light never seen in Vanyel's world.

Not in the mortal world that Vanyel knew. *Not* the natural world.

Therefore this was not the natural world—and this was no mere Herald.

Vanyel released the stranger's hand and sank slowly to one knee, unable to look away from those incandescent eyes. Then the stranger smiled, and the smile was as brilliant and overpowering as the gaze. That smile was no sight for mortal eyes, and Vanyel managed to drop his gaze before he was lost to it. He bowed his head over his knee in profound obeisance to the Power that had chosen to wear the guise of a human, and a Herald.

"Lord," he whispered, unable to muster enough coherent thought to say anything more.

"Vanyel, no," replied a voice of amber, silk, and steel.

He felt hands, gentle hands on his shoulders, hands that drew him up to his feet. He dared a glance at the Power's face, and was caught again, a moth in sapphirine flame.

"No, Vanyel," He said, shaking His head, denying Vanyel's assumption. "Not 'Lord.' Only a messenger, a servant. You mustn't kneel to me."

The longer he looked into those eyes, the easier it became. "I'm—dead," he said steadily, feeling nothing at the words except a soul-deep relief that it was finally over, that he could rest.

But the Other shook His head again. "No. Not yet, Vanyel." He hesitated a moment, and His eyes were shadowed with pity. "Vanyel, because of what you are, what you have become, and that you stand at the crossroads of many possibilities, it is given to you to choose."

"Choose?" he said, honestly bewildered. "Choose now?"

"Life," replied the Power, His eyes dimmed, as if with unshed tears, "Life, or—" He touched His hand to His own heart. "—or myself."

Then he understood what stood with him in this timeless nothingness, what gazed at him with eyes of sorrow; beautiful, perfect, and serene.

The Shadow-Lover.

"Ask me what you will," Death said, eyes radiant,

and voice soft with compassion. "You must choose ir full knowledge of *what* your choice will mean."

"What do I go to," Vanyel asked, marveling at his own steadiness, as he ached for the peace those eyes promised him, "if I choose to live?"

"Pain," Death replied, bowing His own head so tha Vanyel could no longer see those eyes. "Loss. You wil see good friends die, one by one, until you are alone You will find yourself growing apart from others, day by day, until there seems to be nothing but loneliness and your duties. You will receive hurts and will not die o them, though you may long to. And the end—will be only more pain."

"And—the alternative."

"For you—peace. And an end to pain and loneliness and grieving."

Vanyel felt all the burdens of his existence heavy upor him; felt taxed beyond his strength. But he had not missec that subtle phrasing, and he asked a further question though he knew in his heart that he would hate the an swer.

"And what of those I leave behind?"

Death looked up again, and held his gaze with those brilliant, depthless eyes—and was it his imagination, o did a sad, proud smile touch those sculptured lips for a moment?

"They will come to me," Death said quietly. "And sooner, and in greater numbers, than if you choose to live. The Valdemar you knew will be no more; her people will struggle to maintain their freedom in a shrunker land, bereft of allies and hemmed about by enemies. You are not the only hope, Vanyel, but you are Valdemar' best hope."

Vanyel closed his eyes in a spasm of despair, strugglin to maintain his composure. He was so tired—so ver tired. So tired of pain, of loneliness, of a life that seeme harder to endure each day. But what he had told Jervi was no less than the truth. He could no more leave hi duties unfulfilled than he could repudiate Yfandes. Es pecially not now—not *knowing*, by the word of a Powe that would not tell him false, that there was no one else to do what he could do.

But he was so tired.

"What is magic's promise, Vanyel?" asked the vibrant voice. "You thought you knew the answer once. Is it still the answer you would give now?"

He rose out of his own soul-deep weariness, and realized that—no, the promise of magic's power—*to a Herald*—was *not* what he had thought at seventeen. And *that* was the difference between what *he* was, and what those of Vedric and Krebain's ilk were.

"It isn't a promise made to me," he replied, slowly opening his eyes and meeting Death's unblinking, steadfast gaze. "It's a promise made to those who depend on me, on my strength; it's a promise I haven't fulfilled, not yet, not completely." He closed his eyes again, and bowed his head, feeling tears of weariness slipping from beneath his lashes and not wanting the Other to see them and his weakness. "It's a promise that gives me no choice. I—have to go back. No matter how—tired—I am—"

There was a whisper of sound, and a feather-light touch on his jaw. He opened his eyes, and Death's hand lifted his chin so that his gaze again met those beautiful eyes. There were tears in Death's eyes, tears that matched his own, and a tender, sorrowful smile on Death's lips.

"I have never been so grieved—and so glad—to lose," he said, and touched his lips to Vanyel's. Their tears mingled on his lips as Vanyel closed his eyes; he tasted on the kiss, his own salt, bitter tears—and Death's sweet—

Strong arms closed about him, supporting him, holding him against a comforting shoulder, as Death held him with all the sensitivity of the lover that He could be.

Vanyel yielded to the greater strength, and crumpled in his arms, his shoulders shaking with silent sobs. Gentle hands caressed his hair, and gentle words came to his ears.

"Not yet, beloved," Death murmured, breath moving against his ear, lightly stirring his hair. "There is no time here, while I will it so. You need not take up your burden until you feel ready to meet your life again."

So he wept out his weariness, his longing for respite. He wept, and then he rested on Death's shoulder.

"Vanyel, is it only duty that calls you back?"

"No." He found another tiny crumb of strength and slowly straightened in the Power's arms. "No—it's more than that. Moondance said it a long time ago. I lost my own hearth-fire, but that's no reason why I can't warm myself at the hearths of my friends, not when they've offered that warmth." He blinked, and realized that he was smiling. "Not so many friends," he said, half to himself, "But all of them—*good* friends."

"Worth returning for, Vanyel?"

"Yes," he replied simply.

Death actually laughed softly. "So long to learn what Moondance meant?"

"Sometimes I'm a bit dense." He wiped his eyes with the back of his hand. "For some reason I never had any trouble figuring out what death was all about; but life—that's taken me until now."

The Power held him for a moment longer, then let him go. He met the compassionate, luminous blue eyes for one final time, and saw them flare with a strange mixture of pride, grief, and joy. "Vanyel," Death whispered "One thing more—there is one who would make his farewell to you."

Vanyel *felt* someone behind him, a lesser presence than the Shadow-lover, and turned.

"Hello, Vanyel," said Jaysen, holding out his hand. "Or—I guess it's good-bye."

"Jays?" Vanyel took the hand, momentarily stunned. "Oh, Jays, no—I didn't—"

"No, *you* didn't. Don't go all guilty on me." Jaysen actually smiled, ruefully. "It was my own stupid fault for being so distracted by the fact that you went and fathered our little pet that I gave those things of Vedric's a chance to get at me."

Tears burned his eyes. "But—"

"*Stop* that. I *knew* you'd take it that way, that's why asked—Her—Lady Death—to let me see you. *It's not your fault.* Now *listen* to me, neither of us have much more time."

"The Web—you're the Northern Guardian—"

"Exactly. You'll have to take my place. More than that, remember what you were thinking earlier? About making *all* the Heralds the power source? *Do* that, Van. Figure out how." Jaysen squeezed his hand urgently. "It's important. Figure out how to change the Web-spell so that it doesn't *need* Guardians anymore, just the Heralds themselves. You're the only one of us that can do that. I'm *charging* you with that, Van."

He nodded, and met Jaysen's eyes evenly. "I promise."

"I—" Jaysen's eyes softened for a moment. "There's something else She told me I could tell you. Maybe it'll help. She said you won't be alone."

He released Vanyel's hand, and stepped backward, already beginning to fade.

"She promised, Van. And I promise."

Then he was falling, falling—

For a confused moment after he opened his eyes, he thought that the slumped form in Whites in the chair beside his bed was the Messenger—

But his hiss of pain as he tried to move woke the other, and he saw that it was a mortal and a friend, after all.

"Tran?" he whispered. "Tantras? What are you—"

Tantras' face was lined with exhaustion, and his eyes were red with weeping.

"Van, I have to tell you—"

"We lost Jays," he whispered, remembering, feeling the emptiness.

Oh, gods— He was not aware that he was weeping until a sob shook him and made him gasp with pain.

Tantras just handed him a square of linen, and, moving to sit gingerly on the side of the bed, held him until exhaustion left him no more tears to weep.

"We thought you ought to hear it from a friend," Tantras told him, helping him to lie back. "I should have known you already knew."

"How?" Vanyel whispered. "He didn't tell me how."

"He couldn't keep the Swarm off—so he and his Companion—you know better than me how that works."

"Final strike," Vanyel answered numbly. "Take your last target with you. Oh, *gods*—if I'd just been there."

"What good would you have done?" Tantras chided. "No one can be two places at once, Van. Not even you. Lady Bright, we came within a hair of losing *you,* and that's something I'd rather not think about. Lissa's Healer *still* doesn't know how he pulled it off. He swears he had divine help at the last moment."

Vanyel just stared at him, finding it hard to imagine a world without Jaysen in it.

A gentle tap broke the silence between them, and a maid hurried in, face blank—

Hiding fear.

"Milord Herald-Mage?" she faltered, holding a pitcher.

Not "Vanyel," or even "milord Van," he thought, with a catch in his throat. *Now I terrify even the ones who grew up with me around. I'm a stranger even to my own.*

"Yes, Sondri?" he said, as gently as he could.

"I brought ye summat t' drink."

"Thank you."

She left the pitcher and glass beside the bed, and hurried out.

Fear. Vanyel felt another wrench inside. And there was only one way to deal with the pain of it.

Tantras had enough Empathy to feel something of his withdrawal. "Van—" He touched Vanyel's shoulder. "Van, what are you doing?"

Van looked at him bleakly. "You saw her," he whispered. "It's just like you told me. I frighten people. And now even more than before. I wiped out the *entire* Mavelan family, or at least all of the ones in the meld. I had *divine aid* in being Healed, or at least that's what they're telling each other out there. I frightened them before, now I terrify them. It *hurts,* Tran. It *hurts* to feel that fear."

"So you're withdrawing behind walls again." Tantras shook his head. "Van, that's not the answer."

"What is?"

Tantras only shook his head dumbly.

"At least my walls give me a little peace. And I won't

wall my friends out, I promise." He tried to smile, at least a little.

"But you won't look for new friends either. *Or* love. Van, you're making a serious mistake."

"It's mine to make."

"I can't stay," Tantras said, after a long silence. "I have to courier messages back. I only waited to tell you."

Vanyel nodded, grief too profound to be purged with one spate of weeping rising to block his words. "Duty; we all have it. That's what kept me, Tran, that, and finally figuring out what I'm doing here. And that's what Jays died for—duty, and protecting the ones we all love." He stared at a spot on the opposite wall while his eyes burned and blurred. "Thanks for waiting to tell me."

Tantras eased off the bed, and squeezed his hand. "Rest. When there's more to tell, we'll get the word to you."

"Thank you," he murmured, closing his eyes. He heard soft footsteps crossing the floor; heard the door open and close. Then knew nothing more for a very long time.

The Healer had done his best, but the wound Father Leren's knife had left was only half healed, and still very sore. Vanyel had just discovered that getting from his bed to the chair beside his table was a sweating and pain-filled ordeal. The Healer had sternly warned him about the consequences of tearing open half-healed tissues, and Vanyel was inclined to take him very seriously, given the way he was hurting. He didn't want to make a bigger mess of his midsection than it already was. As it was, he'd have an L-shaped scar for the rest of his life. Gut wounds were definitely not on his list of favored ways to earn a little rest.

Getting dressed had been an ordeal, too, but the Healer had said he could have visitors, and he *wasn't* going to see them bundled in bed like an invalid.

He eased himself down into the chair with a hiss as someone knocked on the door to his room. "Come," he called, wiping the sweat from his forehead with the back of his hand.

It was not anyone he had expected. It was Melenna.

A much subdued, sobered Melenna.

"I came to see if you were really all right," she said, shyly, "and to ask Herald Vanyel for a favor, and some advice."

Herald Vanyel. Not Van. And the fear is in her, too.

"Please, Melenna, sit down. I can't imagine why you'd want my advice, but—"

She remained standing. "Vanyel," she said softly. "You—and me. There's no hope, is there?"

He looked up, and the honest longing in her eyes made his heart go out to her, the anger and frustration of the past few weeks evaporating. The gods knew, he knew *exactly* how it felt to long for something you'd never have—or never have again. "I'm sorry, Melenna, but I won't lie to you. It was hopeless from the start. A woman can never be anything more than my friend. I *do* value you as a friend, and the mother of my very young friend Medren, but I can't offer you any more than that."

She bent her head, and quickly wiped her eyes, all coquettishness gone. "I—you know how I feel. Couldn't you—pretend? It would make Lady Treesa and Lord Withen awfully happy. And I wouldn't mind, really I wouldn't."

He looked away from those sad, sad eyes. The offer was terribly tempting. But ultimately, a lie. "I know it would make them happy, but I'm a Herald, Melenna. I can't *tell* lies—how could I live one? And you *would* care, eventually. It would make you very unhappy. There are other men—*shay'a'chern*—who've talked with me, who tried just what you're suggesting. In the end, instead of two people who were only moderately happy most of the time, there were two people who were desperately unhappy all the time. The wife was jealous of his lovers, and his lovers were jealous of her, and it went downhill from there." He shook his head. "No, my friend, it won't work. I'm sorry."

She wiped another tear away. "I'm sorry, too," she said. "But to tell you the truth, I'm mostly sorry for myself, and a little bit for Treesa." She sighed. "Can

—ask you a favor? And you can say no. It's about Med-ren."

"If it's about Medren, the answer is probably 'yes,' " he said. "Your son is a delight to any musician, and a charmer all by himself."

"Would you—sort of be his guardian until he's settled? He's never been away from home at all. I know he isn't shy, but that's the problem. He seems a lot older than he really is, and that's my fault, I guess. He could get in with a faster crowd than he can handle."

He stared at her, astounded. "You'd trust *me*—?"

She returned his astonished stare levelly. "I'm not very clever, sometimes," she replied, "but I listen, I listen a lot. You're very honorable, and in all the stories about you and—others, there's only been *men*. Not boys. Be-sides, Medren told me how he offered to pay for lessons, and how you turned him down. Yes, I trust you. I'll al-ways trust you. I've loved you, Vanyel . . . for a very long time."

Greatly moved, Vanyel took her hand and kissed the back of it gently. "Then I will be very honored to see Medren settled properly," he replied. "And I can only pray that I will always be worthy of your trust."

She got up before he could say another word, and headed for the door—

Only to be run over by the rush of people crowding in, as the door slammed open.

"Now *look,* you peabrain—" Savil was shouting, as Vanyel's head began to spin.

"Look *yourself,*" Withen shouted back, shaking his finger at her. "The damned Lineans won't accept any-thing *but* the boy!"

"But he's a *Herald,*" Lores wailed over the din.

Vanyel's head began to spin, and he clutched the edge of his table. Rescue came from an unexpected source.

"Shut UP!" Jervis roared, in a tone of voice that hear-ened back to the parade ground.

Silence descended so suddenly that Vanyel's ears rang.

"Would someone mind explaining what all this is about?" he whispered into it.

* * *

"Let me see if I have all this straight," he said, after everyone had said his or her piece—except Melenna, who'd found herself trapped by the influx of people and hadn't had the courage to push past them to escape. "Tashir now holds both thrones according to the treaty. Now that he's been acquitted, the Lineans are willing to accept him, and the Bairens are willing to take about anybody so long as it isn't a Mavelan. The problems with this are: first, he's a Herald, which means he has to be trained, and would normally mean he'd abdicate lands and titles; second, he doesn't *want* to be a King; third, he's very young, which would be a temptation to others to come and attack, and would drag Valdemar into defending his kingdom for him."

"Something like that," Withen admitted, as the others nodded.

"Why me?" he demanded. "Why am *I* suddenly the arbitrator?"

Savil flourished a piece of parchment. "Because according to this little piece of paper I have, under Randale's *official* seal, you understand the problems, so you're appointed full and final authority."

:*I'll get you for this, Savil.*:

:*You can try.*:

He massaged his temples, and wished for wine. "All right, let's take this slowly. First of all, we've waived the rules for Heralds before when they were the only heirs. It isn't done often, but I think it's called for in this case. Lores, your Gift is Fetching, right?"

Startled, the Herald nodded.

"Fine, I hereby appoint you Tashir's mentor, to stay with him and teach him until you feel he's ready for Whites. You can serve double duty that way; mentor and envoy. Now—Tashir, would you be willing to take the ruling seat if we arranged for you to make the two lands a vassal-state? That means you are holding the lands of Randale, and it would make them part of Valdemar."

Tashir considered that for a moment, his face sober. "D-does it have to be—do I have to be a King? I don't want to be a King. It's pretty stupid, anyway, to be a King of something you can ride across in a few days."

"Provided you can get your people to agree, I can't see what difference it makes."

"Then I'll be a Baron," Tashir replied, sitting up very straight. "Lord-Baron of the March of Lineas-Baires. If there aren't any straight-line heirs, it all goes back to Valdemar."

Vanyel sighed his relief. If Tashir hadn't been willing to take the damned power seat—civil wars were *not* what Valdemar needed on the Border.

"Now, when there's a ruler as young as you, he usually has a Council of older people to advise him—"

"There isn't one," Tashir interrupted. "Father had one, but they all died."

"True. Have you any objections to my appointing you one?"

Tashir shook his head, and Vanyel plowed on before anyone could stop him. "First Councilor and Chamberlain, Herald Lores. Second Councilor and Seneschal, Kaster Ashkevron. He's Meke's right hand, Father, *and* he's Meke's accountant. Any objections so far?"

Withen snapped his mouth shut on whatever he was going to say, and shook his head.

"Right. Third Councilor, have somebody sent over from your local temple—pick a scholar. Fourth Councilor, the current Chief Elder of Highjorune. Fifth Councilor—huh. You'll need a Marshal, a good military advisor, I would think. Jervis."

"Huh?" Jervis responded, "I what?"

"He'll be very good," Vanyel continued before he could object, "and Radevel is *certainly* capable of taking over here as armsmaster. And since you're a bachelor, you'll need a Castelaine—otherwise you're never going to have cooked meals or clean shirts." He went blank for a moment—until his eyes fell on Melenna.

" 'Lenna?"

She jumped.

"Think you'd be able to keep Tashir in roasts, herbs, and clean linen?"

"Me?" she squeaked. "Me? Castelaine?"

"Of course, there's a catch." Vanyel was beginning to enjoy this. "You'll have to be ennobled, but Randi *did*

give me full powers.'' He saw with a hidden smile tha
Tashir was beginning to look happier. Melenna had stood
up for him once already and she was the mother of his
good friend Medren—two points already in her favor, a
least in his eyes.

''But—but I—but I don't know a thing about—''

''B—beanshucks,'' Withen rumbled, changing his ep
ithet in mid-syllable. ''You've been doing Castelaine duty
here for years. Treesa'll have vapors, of course.''

Savil interrupted him. ''Let her have vapors. If she
doesn't want to mind Forst Reach, let Meke's lady dea
with it. I know young Roshya. She's a bright little thing
and I know she's been properly trained. That's one o
your worst problems here, Withen—too many trained
hands and not enough jobs for them.''

Melenna turned anxious eyes toward Vanyel. ''Herald
Vanyel? Do you think that I—could—''

''I think you'll do just fine. Now—does that solve al
the problems?''

Because I'm about to run out of brilliant ideas, energy
and the ability to hold off pain.

''I think so,'' Savil replied. ''I think we can start of
by collecting Kaster and showing Tashir something o
what he'll be dealing with.''

''You won't need me, will you?'' Jervis asked sud
denly.

''Probably not—at least not for a while.''

''Then I need a word or two with young Van here
Could you send to fetch me when you need me?''

Savil raised one eyebrow, but nodded.

The mob left, and Vanyel sagged as Jervis put a pitche
down on the table before him.

''Gods. That was a *hell* of a way to spend my first da
out of bed.'' He cast a wistful glance at the pitcher. ''
don't suppose that's wine, is it?'' The Healer, used t
fighters, who would use the infirmary as a good place t
hold an impromptu party, had forbidden him wine. H
was getting *very* tired of cider.

Besides, the drugs the Healer had given him were to
strong. He wasn't taking them except to sleep, and th
pain-dulling effects of alcohol would have been welcome

"Well—cider," Jervis said slyly, "and help." He reached inside his jerkin and held up a little bottle of apple brandy. "Couldn't get wine past that snoop, but I could this. Figured you could use it. Little bird told me you probably weren't taking those pills."

He poured a generous dollop of brandy into each mug before adding the cider; Vanyel accepted his gratefully. "What little bird?"

"One name of Lissa. I've been playin' her eyes an' ears over here."

"She could be right," he admitted. "She knows I hate to be muddle-headed these days."

Jervis grimaced. "*Anybody* been on front-lines hates be muddle-headed. Wish them Healers'd figure that out."

"Have you heard anything out of Highjorune? Like 'bout the palace, and the heart-stone?"

"Buried, and gonna leave it that way. Seemed safest. Van, you *really* think I should do this?"

"Why? Don't you?"

Jervis chewed his lip. "I dunno," he said after a moment. "Tashir trusts me. I'm getting too old to try and beat sense into more young heads than one at any one time. What do you think of the notion? Too damned foolish to believe?"

"I think you'd make a good Marshal," Vanyel replied honestly. "You've certainly proved that you aren't too old to change."

Jervis snorted. "You say that after I nearly ruined your life for you?"

"But you saved it," Vanyel pointed out. "If you hadn't been there, I would either have let the palace bury me, or I'd have gone down under Leren's knife. I'd have been dead before anyone found me. I think we're even."

"Huh." They drank in silence for a moment. The pain of Vanyel's wound seemed a bit eased.

"About Leren—you heard anything yet?"

Vanyel shook his head. "I was hoping you'd get around to him. I have some information for *you,* since you're relaying to Liss. Leren *was* mage-controlled."

Jervis swore under his breath. "So he *was* tryin' t' take us both out a-purpose. If he hadn't gotten distracted—"

"Exactly—and I'm the one that distracted him for you there was—I felt something about him, but it got away from me."

Jervis shook his head. "Damn. We found out he wa planted on us by the Mavelans. And *now* the priests o Astera are sending 'finders' into every damn temple alon the Border here, to see how many more there are lik him. Seems the Mavelans *bought* themselves a temple school. The High Prelate is not what you'd call pleased But I guess Leren's even twistier than we thought?"

Vanyel nodded. "I told Savil this morning and she re layed it to Haven, but Liss might as well get it from you He may have been serving the Mavelans, but he was serving somebody else, too. And I don't know who or what It was no power I recognized."

"And you won't ever find it from him. Liss couldn get it out of him, and whoever it was killed him befor she could turn him over to Heralds."

Vanyel swore creatively and descriptively in *Tayledras* "Savil didn't tell me *that*."

Jervis grimaced. "She didn't know. Liss' sergean found him dead in his cell just this mornin', guts tor out, and nobody next or nigh him since they'd brough him dinner. But Savil an' Lores an' Tashir showed u right after that, an' *that* kinda got lost in tryin' t' figge out what to' do 'bout Tashir."

"Magic."

"Seems so."

Vanyel pondered for a moment. "Did you ever fin out why he tried to kill me?"

"Oh, aye. That was easy enough. Leren knew wha was goin' on here; that Mavelan bastard was keepin' hi briefed. That much Liss got outa him afore he got hi insides tore out. Vedric figured you were getting too clos to the truth about the boy. When he breached the shield he *didn't* know we'd unraveled everything. *He* had it fi ured that his spell was too good to unravel. What *h* meant to do was send you Gating home, and the boy wit you. Leren was supposed to knife you both. They figure

ou'd use the same place to Gate into as last time, so
.eren was waiting once Vedric contacted him. What they
idn't figure on was Savil and me bein' there, nor you
nd Savil splitting up, and they didn't figure on *me* bein'
/ith you an' not the boy.''

"I'm glad you were,'' Vanyel said, softly. "If it hadn't
een for you throwing my own words back in my face—
'ell, I wouldn't be here.''

"Is that a thing to thank me for?'' Jervis asked unex-
ectedly. "How much you going to take before you
rack?''

"As much,'' Vanyel replied deliberately, "as I have
.''

Jervis pondered that a moment. "Van—are we friends
ow?''

Vanyel closed his eyes. "We're friends. And I think I
now what your next question is going to be. You want
> know why I'm sending you away with Tashir.''

"Somethin' like.''

"I'm trying to scatter my targets. I had a lot of time
> think, the past couple of days. I figured out something.
nemies might not be able to get *me,* but they can get at
e through the people I care tor. Some of them—they're
:etty well protected. But ordinary people, like you,
ledren—'' He shook his head. "So I'm trying to send
>u all away—*far* away from me. The farther away you
'e, the safer you are. Either you'll be too distant to get
, or it will look as if I don't care. Either way, *you'll* be
l right.''

"And you'll be alone.''

"That's better than knowing you took a mage-bolt be-
:use someone wanted to rock *me,*'' he retorted, and
vallowed the contents of the mug at a gulp.

Silence, then Jervis reached out and refilled his mug.
anyel found himself getting a little light-headed. "Let
e ask about something inconsequential; how's Medren?
; he going to forgive me for wrecking his old lute?''

"Lute?'' Jervis chortled. "He'd have forgiven you for
recking Forst Reach so long as you came back safe.
inny thing; remember you said Medren'd be safe from
e Swarm because he was Bardic-Gifted and not Mage?

You was almost right. Seems like the instant the Swarm
tried t' find a target here, ev'ry one of his lute string
snapped. How's that for strange?''

Vanyel shook his head. *Too close. Too damned close
I was right.*

''Anyway, he's safe at Bardic; word came back from
Bard called Breda that 'if there's any more at home like
him, they're staging a raid.' ''

''So he's doing well?''

''Better than well. I think that's the reason Melenna
decided to take that Castelaine position. I think she's
startin' to look at being something other than 'Somebody's lady' or 'Somebody's momma.' I think maybe she
wants to take a shot at being Somebody, herself.''

''Good,'' Vanyel said, and meant it.

''You know,'' Jervis raised one eyebrow, ''your father
still don't half believe but what you were after Tashir's
tail the whole time. Aye, and Medren, too.''

Vanyel snorted.

''In fact,'' Jervis continued, ''to hear *him* in his cups
you've had half the boys in Valdemar.''

Vanyel put his mug down. ''If that's a question,'' he
replied acidly, ''you can tell him from me that it's been
so damned long that both you and those damned sheep
in Long Meadow are starting to look good!''

Jervis gave him a long, thoughtful look, and Vanyel
wondered if he'd said too much, too freely. He tried to
ready an apology—when Jervis gave him a long, slow
grin.

''Stick to the sheep,'' the armsmaster advised impu-
dently. ''They don't snore.''